BOOKS BY P. J. PARRISH

South of Hell*
A Thousand Bones*
An Unquiet Grave
A Killing Rain
Island of Bones
Thicker Than Water
Paint It Black
Dead of Winter
Dark of the Moon

*Published by POCKET BOOKS

"A really fine writer."

—John Sandford

"Wonderfully tense and atmospheric . . . keeps the reader guessing until the end."

—*Miami Herald*

"A good, fast read, satisfying plot, and characters you'll want to meet again."

—*San Antonio Express-News* (TX)

"Edge-of-the-seat suspense."

—Michael Connelly

"Parrish is an author to read, collect, and root for."

—James W. Hall

"Opens like a hurricane and blows you away through the final page . . . A major league thriller that is hard to stop reading."

—Robert B. Parker

"A masterpiece of shock and surprise . . . from the startling opening to the stunning finale."

—Ed Gorman, *Mystery Scene*

"A superb, highly atmospheric, thought-provoking thriller. . . . Tense, exciting scenes."

—*Lansing State Journal* (MI)

SOUTH

OF

HELL

P. J. PARRISH

POCKET STAR

New York   London   Toronto   Sydney

Pocket Star Books
A Division of Simon & Schuster, Inc.
1230 Avenue of the Americas
New York, NY 10020

This book is a work of fiction. Names, characters, places, and incidents either are products of the author's imagination or are used fictitiously. Any resemblance to actual events or locales or persons living or dead is entirely coincidental.

Copyright © 2008 by PJ Parrish

All rights reserved, including the right to reproduce this book or portions thereof in any form whatsoever. For information address Pocket Books Subsidiary Rights Department, 1230 Avenue of the Americas, New York, NY 10020

First Pocket Star Books paperback edition August 2008

POCKET STAR BOOKS and colophon are registered trademarks of Simon & Schuster, Inc.

For information about special discounts for bulk purchases, please contact Simon & Schuster Special Sales at 1-800-456-6798 or business@simonandschuster.com.

Cover design by Jae Song

Manufactured in the United States of America

10 9 8 7 6 5 4 3 2 1

ISBN-13: 978-1-4165-2588-2
ISBN-10:   1-4165-2588-2

To my sister, Kelly,
a very wise old soul

SOUTH
OF
HELL

Chapter One

It was just south of Hell. But if you missed the road leading in, you ended up down in Bliss. And then there was nothing to do but go back to Hell and start over again.

That's what the kid pumping gas at the Texaco had told her, at least. Since she had not been here for such a very long time, she had to trust him, because she had no memory of the place anymore.

A rain was threatening. She had been watching the gray clouds gather over the cornfields for the past half-hour.

"You sure you know where you're going, little lady?"

She looked over at the driver of the truck. He was an old man, with tufts of gray hair sprouting from his head and ears.

Back at the Texaco, she had watched all the big trucks racing past on the highway, too afraid to stop one of them for a ride. When the old man had pulled in, she had gotten into his truck only because the truck was small and he seemed so old and harmless. Still, she clutched the backpack tighter as she felt his eyes on her.

"Yes," she said. "Lethe Creek Road. It should be right up here somewhere."

The old man's red-rimmed eyes stayed with her for a moment, then he looked back at the road. She didn't look at him, because she didn't want to talk to him. She just wanted to get where she needed to go.

The backpack was heavy on her lap, and she shifted her thighs under its weight. It had been hard lugging it all this way, but she had no idea when she set out what she was going to need, or for how long, so she had put everything in it she could carry: cans of tuna fish and stewed tomatoes, tins of sardines, a half-empty box of Hershey's cocoa, and a carton of Premium saltines. Anything she could find in the house that would last. She had even thought to take an empty plastic milk carton to hold water. At the last minute, she had gone down into the cellar and taken the last four jars of plum preserves.

No one would know they were gone. No one would know she was gone.

"This the road?"

She glanced at the old man, then looked out the window. The fields were empty, still covered with their blankets of winter straw. She nodded, and they drove on.

A dull roll of thunder came from the gray sky over the fields.

"Looks like we got more rain coming," the old man said.

She closed her eyes. A different sound in her ears, a different storm in her head, a flashing memory of green curtains twisting in the wind.

Run! Run! Run!

Bursting through the green curtain. Feeling the corn stalks tearing at her bare legs. Kneeling in dirt, hands over her ears so she wouldn't hear.

The image made her go cold. It was new. It had never been there before. Or that voice, either. Others, yes, but not this one.

She felt a jolt as the truck left the blacktop for gravel, and she opened her eyes.

"Huh, look at that. I didn't even know there was a house down this road."

She didn't look at the old man. Her eyes were on the old house. It had always been so small in her memory because she had never really believed it existed. But now here it was, growing larger and larger and larger.

The truck stopped in front of a fence. She didn't move. She couldn't stop looking at the house.

"This it?"

She didn't hear the old man.

"Little lady? You sure this is the place you're looking for?"

She found her voice. "Yes." But she didn't take her eyes off the house, because she was sure if she did, it would slip away, just like it always did as she awoke from her fevered sleep. It was a while before the ticking of the truck's old engine drew her back. The house hadn't vanished.

She gathered the backpack to her chest and looked over at the old man. "Thank you for the ride," she said.

His mouth was a hard slash, but his eyes were gentle. "You shouldn't be takin' rides from strangers. Not right for a young girl to be hitchin'."

She nodded.

"Looks deserted. You got kin here?"

"Yes, sir."

He looked toward the house with doubt but then reached across her and opened the door. She jumped out, hoisting the backpack up onto one shoulder. The old man gave her a final look, thrust the truck in reverse, and was gone.

She looked around. The farm's other buildings registered in her consciousness—three small gray plank ones almost hidden in the tall weeds and, beyond, the barn, a looming hulk against the dark sky. She looked back at the old farmhouse.

It had always been there in her head, like a blurry picture, but now the details were coming into focus: red brick, green roof, long slits of windows. Everything angles, crags, points, and hard lines, like there was not a corner of comfort to be found anywhere inside.

It started to rain. It was so quiet the *pop-pop-pop* of the drops falling on the oak leaves overhead was the only sound she could hear. Even the voices were quiet, like they were all holding their breath, waiting.

She climbed the locked fence and walked to the porch. There was a padlock on the front door. It hadn't been visible from the truck. The old man would never have left her here if had he seen it.

You got kin here?

Yes, sir.

She had lied to him. There was no one here. Anybody could see that plain as day. Maybe she had always known it was going to be like this. But that was why she was here now, because she had to make sure.

Her heart was starting to pound, and she felt a choking feeling rising in her throat, that feeling she got sometimes that she couldn't catch her breath. She took a few deep, careful breaths to calm it, but something told her that this time it wasn't going to work. She was sweating, too, even in the cold rain.

She forced herself to start moving again. Walking slowly, the backpack heavy on her shoulder, she went around the east side of the house.

Another porch, this one crumbling and decrepit, with a rusting icebox shoved into a corner. There was a door but it was boarded over.

No way in—and she had to get in.

She was behind the house now, picking her way carefully through the waist-high weeds. Just more windows, too high for her to reach, some with boards nailed over them. By the time she made a full circle back to the side porch, her heart was racing, and her head hurt so much she had to close her eyes for a moment.

That's when it came. A flash of a new image—a blue wooden door. She opened her eyes. But where was it?

She returned to the back of the house, her eyes raking the thicket of weeds. The blue door was here, she knew it was.

No, wait, no. *Two* blue doors. But *where?*

She pushed her way through the brambles. Her hands began to bleed as she pulled at the thick wet growth. She drew back, gasping.

Cellar doors. Old wood boards cracked and bleached, the blue gone almost to gray.

She set the backpack in the weeds, grabbed one of the handles, and pulled. It opened with a groan and fell back against the weeds with a thud.

She stared down into the dark. Then, without another thought, she grabbed the backpack and went down.

Five steps down. She knew that!

And although there was no light in this place, she knew she had to go to the right. Because that was where the other stairs were, the ones that led up into the house.

Awful smells of dank stone and wet earth and the skittering whispers of animals, but she didn't stop to think about it, just moved slowly but surely through the darkness until her outstretched hand found the wood rail.

Ten steps up. She knew that, too.

At the top, she pushed the door open and stepped through.

Gray light, like a shroud, around her. Dim shapes floated at the edges of her vision—just furniture and boxes—and a wash of smells, dust and paper and something sickly sweet but so faint she almost thought she imagined it.

She dropped the backpack to the floor and moved slowly down a narrow hallway. It led to a small room with faded green wallpaper peeling away in damp layers. The next room was like the first but with yellow flowered paper, most of it in piles on the scuffed wood floor. A third room had light fixtures dangling bare wires and more moldering walls shedding their paper skins.

She stood in the center of the third room, a cold draft swirling around her. It felt like the house itself was moving around her and she was inside it, inside its heart, inside the heart of a dying animal.

Voices.

Where were they coming from? They had always been inside her head before, but now . . .

Outside her head now. Like they were just a step away in the next room. She went to the front of the house.

Another small room, this one with blue-patterned wallpaper and yellowed lace curtains. The voices were loud here, louder than the usual whisper. And they were—

She turned.

There, in the far corner, she saw it, a small upright piano, dark wood under a gray coat of dust, the top heaped with long, thin boxes.

The voices, so loud here, the same ones that came to

her when she slept. She had never been able to make out what they were saying. But now . . .

She stared at the piano.

Suddenly, she could hear them perfectly. The voices were singing!

Catch Don set a seal
Oh do you know so sweet
You and me, Pearl, no matter hurt.
New rips in two in stormy. Sue lures while
You pray on guard all day trembling a while.

The sting of tears in her eyes. The voices were real. She hadn't been crazy, she hadn't made them up. Those voices that always came to her in her dreams. They were real, and they were singing real words. The words made no sense, but she didn't care. The words were real, and so was this place, and so was she.

You and me, Pearl, no matter hurt.

She shut her eyes tight. The voices were getting louder.

You and me, Pearl, no matter hurt
You and me Pearl no matter hurt
youandmepearlnomatterhurt
hurt hurt hurt
hurt hurt hurt!

Suddenly, a loud bang. It felt like the floor was moving beneath her feet, like the walls were moving inward. She bolted from the room.

Another bang. Just thunder, just thunder. But it propelled her forward.

She was back in the kitchen. Rain was beating on the small window over the old sink. Or was the beating sound in her head? She couldn't tell anymore, because something bad was happening. Something was rising up inside her, worse than anything she had felt before, something bad beyond her heart when it beat too fast and beyond her skin when it grew slick with sweat and beyond her head when the voices shouted.

This place, this room. Something bad here.

A boom of thunder. She clapped her hands over her ears and shut her eyes.

But she could still see it, see it playing on the curtain of her lids. Red. So much red. A thick flow of red everywhere.

Run! Run! Run, Amy! Run! Hide!

She opened her eyes.

The cupboard. There, in the corner, near the sink.

She dropped to her knees, her fingers grasping the rusted handle. The door opened, and she crawled inside. She pulled the door closed and pressed into the dark corner. Tried to make herself small, smaller, smallest until she disappeared.

She started to cry.

Then. Then . . .

A whisper. That one soft voice that sometimes found her in her dreams, rising out of the screeches of the others, coming to her in this dark place now, soft around her like a blanket.

You and me, no matter how hurt
You and me you and me

The other voices faded away. The banging stopped. It was quiet. The invisible blanket was still there, holding her.

You got kin here?

She hugged her knees and rocked herself in the dark.

"Yes," she whispered. "Yes, yes, yes."

Chapter Two

They had been down this road before. They had been down it so many times that even with the night as dark as it was, even without the blue wash of a moon above or the yellow glow from a house nearby to help light their way, they knew where they were going.

Still, Louis had the feeling something was different this time.

"You okay?" he asked.

The tall man walking by his side didn't answer.

"Mel?"

"Yeah." A clearing of his throat, like the crunching of the gravel under their shoes. "Yeah . . . yeah. I'm fine."

Louis didn't look over at his friend, didn't have to. He knew Mel Landeta was lying. Something had been bothering him all night. Louis sensed it from the moment they sat down to eat at Timmy's Nook. The talk over grouper sandwiches and beer had been of the usual stuff: the Miami Heat's seven-game skid, cop gossip from O'Sullivan's, and how Louis had spent the last week sitting outside a Fort Myers motel so some guy could prove his wife was cheating on him.

When the small talk and beers had run out, Mel had

gone mute. And now, as they walked the dark stretch of road back to Louis's cottage, his quiet hung heavy in the cool April air.

"Mel, what's on your mind?" Louis asked finally.

A long pause. "Lizards," he said.

"What?"

"You heard me, lizards."

"Mel, if you don't want to talk—"

"I'm serious. I was thinking about the lizard I saw out on your porch. It had no tail."

"The cat probably got it," Louis said.

Mel was quiet for a moment. "Lizards can grow their tails back. Do you know that?"

Louis shook his head slowly, knowing Mel couldn't see it.

"Lizards, sponges, starfish, even worms. They can all regrow their body parts," Mel said.

They walked on, slowly.

"And newts," Mel said. "You poke out a newt's eye, and you know what happens? He grows a new eye. So that's what I have been thinking about. How come a fucking newt can grow a new eye and fucking scientists can't figure out why a fucking human being can't?"

A car rounded the bend ahead of them, and Louis blinked in the glare of the headlights. They waited on the sandy shoulder until it passed.

"How about one more beer before I drive you back?" Louis said.

"I guess one more won't kill me," Mel said.

When they got to the low dune that fronted the cottage, Louis put a hand on Mel's arm and guided him across the dark yard. Mel stood on the screened-in

porch until Louis flicked a light on in the living room.

"You live like a pig, Kincaid," Mel said.

"I just cleaned this morning," Louis said, going to the refrigerator.

"Dirty socks and cat poop. Get some air freshener."

Louis brought two Heinekens back. Mel took one and folded his long body down onto the sofa. Louis flopped into the chair opposite, watching Mel. He hadn't seen him in a couple of weeks. Still, theirs was an old-marriage kind of friendship, where long pauses in conversation were left unfilled and long times apart needed no rebuilt bridges. It was the kind of friendship where one man knew when to walk a wide berth around the other. But this, Louis sensed, was not one of those times.

"Your eyes bothering you?" Louis asked.

Mel was holding the beer bottle against his forehead. "I already gave up driving. Maybe I'll give up walking next."

Louis took a long pull from the beer. The silence lengthened. Finally, Louis picked up the remote and flicked on the TV but kept the volume off. *Miami Vice* was on. Louis watched Sonny steer a speeding Cigarette boat down the Intracoastal, the boat's fishtail wake sparkling against the pastel blur of hotels. Louis noticed Mel was staring at the TV, but he knew his friend couldn't make out any of the details. Mel had been battling retinitis pigmentosa for almost ten years now, and he saw life as if through a plastic shower curtain. That was how Mel once described it—when he talked about it, which wasn't often.

"Do you ever think about past lives?" Mel said.

Louis looked over at him. "What do you mean?"

"What your life might have been like if you had done things differently."

Louis took a drink of beer. "No."

"I've been thinking about it a lot lately," Mel went on. "Thinking about my life before I hit that kid."

Mel had told him the story. How when his failing eyesight first set in, Mel had refused to acknowledge it, refused to tell his chief that he no longer had any business being behind the wheel of a police cruiser. Then one night in Miami, a couple of years ago, Mel broadsided a car he hadn't seen coming. The seventeen-year-old kid driving the car spent a year in physical therapy. Mel had been forced to resign quietly but had talked his way into a detective's job on the smaller Fort Myers PD—until he finally turned in his badge on his own. He'd been living on disability ever since, sometimes helping Louis with his PI cases.

"I think we live many lives inside this one," Mel said. "Lives that begin and end in an instant, like the eight seconds it took me to hit that kid. Or the minute or so it takes to tell someone you don't love them anymore."

Louis looked down at the beer bottle, wiping the condensation with his thumb and wishing Mel would shut up. He was dangerously close to wandering into something he and Louis had never talked about: Mel's long-ago relationship with Joe, Louis's girlfriend.

"Fuck, I'm sorry," Mel said. "I'm done ruminating. But I'm not done drinking. Get me another, would you?"

Louis went to the kitchen, grabbing another beer for himself, too, figuring Mel was about fifteen minutes away from falling asleep on the sofa, saving Louis the long drive back over the causeway to Fort Myers.

On the way back to the living room, he noticed the red message light was blinking on his answering machine. He was tempted to let it go until morning,

but it might be a new job offer. Or a message from Joe.

He hadn't talked to her in a week. It had been three months since she moved to northern Michigan to take the job as undersheriff of Leelanau County. He missed her. Missed the sound of her voice, the feel of her skin against his, the smell of Jean Naté in his sheets.

He hit the button.

But the voice that came from the machine was male. Deep, with a flat southern Michigan timbre.

"Hello . . . uh . . . this message is for Louis Kincaid. The PI? You probably won't remember me, but my name is Jake Shockey, and I'm a homicide investigator with the Ann Arbor PD."

Louis set the beers down and turned up the machine's volume.

"You were the responding officer on a missing persons case back in 1980," the voice went on. "It's still unsolved, but a few new leads have surfaced, and when I was reviewing your report, a couple of things jumped out at me I'd like to ask you about. You know, the kinds of things we don't always think were important at the time. So—"

The tape cut off. Louis immediately hit the button for the next message. For a few seconds, there was only the shuffling of papers and the impatient slam of drawers. Then Shockey's voice again.

"Damn machines," he said. "Anyway, this is Shockey again. What I was saying was, I would appreciate it if you'd consider coming up to Ann Arbor to help me light a new fire under this case. We're willing to cough up the airfare and lodging. So, if you could spare the time off from whatever it is you do down there as a PI, let me know. Call me when you get in. Thanks."

Shockey left his home number and clicked off.

Louis waited, hoping for a message from Joe, but there was nothing else. He walked back to the living room and handed Mel his beer, then dropped back into the chair.

"He sounds like a real charmer," Mel said.

"Can't say. I don't remember him."

"You remember the case?"

"Not a clue."

They were quiet. Louis's eyes went to the muted television again. Now Sonny had some dirtbag in a pink shirt smashed up against a turquoise wall.

"So, you going?" Mel asked.

When Louis didn't answer, Mel let out a low burp and went on. "Sounds like a pretty good deal to me. Little paid vacation back to A Squared. Stroll around the campus, drink some beer, breathe in the sweet air of youth, relive those moments of reckless adventures and lustful indiscretions. I would give anything to feel twenty again. Wouldn't you?"

"It was only nine years ago."

"Right. But tell me it doesn't feel like another life now," Mel said.

Louis stood up and walked to the screen door, looking out. It was too dark to see the water, but he could hear the familiar heartbeat of the Gulf in the crashing of the waves, feel its breath in the tangy, salty breeze.

Six months, a year ago . . . maybe it wouldn't have felt like another life. But it did now. He felt as if that young man back in Ann Arbor had faded away or even died. And this new man in his place? Far from perfect and riddled with spaces that still needed filling. Yet . . . this man, this newer him, this man was comfortable in his skin, had made a home for himself on this island. When had that changed? And what had caused it? The nearness

of the people he had allowed into his life? Margaret and Sam Dodie, Mel. And Ben, of course, because maybe it took the love of a young boy to help make you grow up.

And Joe . . .

She was the one who had really saved him.

Louis heard a grunt and turned. Mel had stretched out on the sofa. He was asleep.

Louis took the beer from Mel's hand and set it on the table. An old throw lay nearby, and Louis laid it across Mel's legs, knowing he would want it in a few hours when the cooler breezes snuck into the old cottage.

He looked back to the answering machine. Something Shockey had said suddenly registered. *Homicide* detective. What was a homicide detective doing investigating an old routine missing persons case?

He replayed Shockey's message, but there was no other information. He paused, then dialed Joe's home number. For the third time in two days, the answering machine picked up. He listened to the crisp words in her low voice and waited for the beep.

"It's me again," he said. "I'm coming north."

Chapter Three

The air smelled of freshly turned earth. Was it just the wind bringing in the odor of a nearby farm? But Louis didn't remember there being any fields this close to the city.

That's what Ann Arbor was now, still a college town,

the one he remembered from his four years here. But since he had left, it seemed to have taken on the rigor of a bigger place, with traffic and noise encroaching on the quiet sanctity of the University of Michigan campus.

Louis left the rental car in a lot, thinking a walk to the police station would do him some good after the long trip. Two hours sitting on the ground at the Tampa airport before they finally got in the air. Another lost hour at Detroit Metro while a Northwest clerk tried to find his missing suitcase. It had turned up in San Antonio, and the clerk promised it would be delivered to his hotel that night.

The one sweater he had packed—hell, the one sweater he had kept since moving to Florida—was in the suitcase. And now, as he headed down South University, he zipped his windbreaker to his chin against the chill, thinking maybe he should have driven after all.

A bell tolled. He couldn't see it, but he knew it was the Burton Tower. He counted three bells. Shit, on top of everything else, he was going to be late. He spotted a phone and dialed the police station.

"Don't bust your hump," Shockey said. "Where are you now?"

"By the Law Quad," Louis said.

"You know Krazy Jim's?"

"The burger place?"

"Yeah. Meet me there."

Louis stepped out of the phone booth into a cold drizzle. He hurried across the street and through the stone archway leading into the cloistered confines of the old Law Quad.

He didn't stop. Neither did the memories.

The cold marble floor of the dining hall where he usually ate alone. The cell-like feel of his dorm room. The

sound of his roommate's drunken snores that drove him to the quiet solitude of the Law Library's reading room. There, under the fifty-foot vaulted ceiling, there, under the soft glow of the brass lamps, there, under the stained-glass weight of tradition, time seemed to stand still. There, in that vast Gothic cathedral of a place, the ache of loneliness was somehow lessened.

As he neared the western arch, his eyes went up to the old leaded windows of the Lawyers Club. It was where the law students lived. It was where he had so desperately wanted to be.

Once. Another lifetime ago.

He emerged onto State Street, heading west. On Division, he spotted the red awning of Krazy Jim's Blimpy Burgers. The windows were fogged over, blurring the sign that boasted "Cheaper Than Food." Inside, a vapor of grease and smoke enveloped him.

Louis spotted a man in a gray raincoat at the front corner table. He was red-faced and beefy, with the kind of hard, darting eyes that could never belong to a college professor. The man stood up as Louis approached.

"Kincaid?"

"Yeah. You Shockey?"

"That I am." When Shockey held out his hand, Louis caught the glint of his gold detective's badge and a holstered automatic beneath the raincoat. Shockey's handshake was hard, his hands rough. Not the hands of a detective who spent long hours at a desk.

"So," Shockey said, "you remember me now that you're looking at me?"

Louis took in the pockmarked but roughly handsome face with its coffee-colored eyes and chopped dark hair.

"No, I don't. Sorry."

"I remember you," Shockey said. "I was there the first day you showed up in uniform. We all wanted to get a look at the poster boy."

"What?"

"You know, the new cop of the 1980s. Someone who was—"

"Black?" Louis said.

Shockey stared at him, then broke into a crooked-tooth smile. "No, man," he said. "Someone with a friggin' college degree."

Louis let the words just hang there until Shockey cleared his throat. "You hungry?"

The smell of frying onions made Louis's stomach churn with hunger. "Yeah, I could use a bite," he said.

"Let's get in line, then," Shockey said.

Shockey went to the counter and got a plastic tray. Louis followed suit.

"You know," Shockey said, "when I looked you up, I was expecting to see attorney-at-law after your name. Kinda surprised to find out you weren't nothing but a lousy peeper living in a cottage and working insurance crap."

Louis dug a Coke out of the cooler and slid his tray behind Shockey's.

"I heard you got kicked out of Michigan a few years back for screwing up some big case the state guys were working on," Shockey said.

Louis stayed quiet.

"But I guess that just proves what I been saying all along," Shockey continued. "Police work is all about instinct and guts. Either you got them or you don't, and you can't get them from a diploma."

They had moved up to the griddle, where a big black woman in a white apron and a red head scarf was making hamburgers in a fog of steam.

"Gimme a quint egg on onion roll, Irma," Shockey said.

The woman grabbed five golf balls of meat, slapped them onto the grill, and smashed them with her spatula. She cracked an egg next to the meat. Then she looked up at Louis.

"Cheeseburger with fries," Louis said.

The woman pointed the spatula at him. "You need to order the fries first! And the cheese last!"

"What?"

"You heard me."

Shockey held up a hand. "He's a virgin, Irma."

The woman glared at Louis. "Don't care if he's a eunuch. Rules is rules."

Shockey turned to Louis. "What do you want?"

Louis was silent.

"Damn it, what do you want?" Shockey said in a fierce whisper.

"Cheeseburger," Louis said, staring at the woman with the spatula.

Shockey turned to the woman. "Double on kaiser, Irma."

She scowled at Louis, slapped two balls onto the grill, and smashed them down.

"I wanted a cheeseburger," Louis said to Shockey.

"Forget it."

Shockey slid his tray toward the register, pulling out his wallet.

"What about my fries?" Louis asked.

"Forget them, too."

A kid in a hairnet deposited two paper-wrapped lumps on their trays, and Shockey paid. They wove through the bodies to the table by the front window. Shockey slid into the wood bench, keeping his eyes on the window and the door. Louis had no choice but to balance his ass on the small wooden swivel chair. His eyes took in the grease-stained walls and battered old tables.

"Why do you come here?" Louis said.

Shockey nodded toward the greasy paper lump. "Try it."

With a shake of his head, Louis unwrapped the paper and took a bite of the burger. It was delicious. Even without the cheese.

Shockey was still working on his five-patty monster with a fried egg by the time Louis finished his. He was trying to decide whether he wanted to square off again with the griddle woman but decided he would wait to eat dinner later with Joe.

He got a glance at his watch. If he got out of there in the next half-hour, he could still make Echo Bay by ten.

Shockey saw him. "You got somewhere to go?"

"No," Louis said, wiping his hands with a paper napkin. "So, why don't you tell me why I'm here?"

Shockey set his burger down and grabbed a napkin. "Like I told you on the phone," he said, "it's about a missing persons case. A twenty-four-year-old woman by the name of Jean Brandt was reported missing by her husband December 4, 1980. A BOLO was put out on her '71 Ford Falcon, which disappeared with her, according to the husband. A week later, when you were on patrol, you spotted the car parked at the Amtrak station down on Depot Street."

Louis tried to bring the memory back, and it came

slowly. It had been an icy night crammed with nuisance calls and fender-benders. He had a habit of rifling through the BOLOs and alerts, hoping to break the boredom of the shift. The old red Falcon was parked in the last space at the train station, pillowed with snow, one of the tires flat. He didn't remember much else except the license plate. It was hanging, as if someone had tried to take it off but had given up after stripping the screw.

But one memory was clear. The plate had not been from Washtenaw County. It had been from Livingston County, north of Ann Arbor. Which meant that the missing woman's disappearance would have been Livingston County's jurisdiction, regardless of where her car was found. So the only way Shockey would be involved now was if her body had turned up in Ann Arbor.

"Where'd you find her?" Louis asked.

Shockey cleared his throat. "What?"

"The body. You guys found it, right?"

"No," Shockey said.

"What about these new leads? Do you have a witness or something besides the car that connects her to Ann Arbor?"

Shockey pushed his tray away. "Not exactly."

"So, why are you pursuing a cold case that doesn't even belong to you?"

Shockey took a moment to grab another napkin and wipe his face. "I'm kind of in charge of the cold cases. This is one that always stuck in my craw. I met the husband, Owen Brandt, when he tried to pick up the Falcon. He was a real scumbag, and he said then he thought his wife had run off on him. My gut always told me he

killed her and left the car here to make us think she left the state."

Louis glanced at his watch.

"I'll ask you again. You got somewhere to go, peeper?" Shockey said.

Louis looked across the table at Shockey. He was about forty but looked older. And in that moment, everything about the man seemed to crystallize. He was a dinosaur, assigned to brush the dust off a few cold cases while the young cops—the ones with diplomas—were pushing their way up in the ranks. Shockey was hearing their footsteps and was probably fighting like hell to hang on to his gold badge. Solving the case of a missing wayward wife in quiet little Ann Arbor just might help him do that. At least, for a few more years.

Louis knew, too, why Shockey had wanted to meet here instead of at the police station. He didn't want the other cops to know he had to call on a PI to help him do his job.

"Look," Louis said, "all I did was spot the vehicle. I sent my report to Livingston. The car was towed, and I was done. What the hell could I offer the case now?"

"You searched the car, right?"

"Of course I did. It was procedure."

"You search it good?"

"Yeah, I searched it good."

"You sure about that, peeper?"

What was this? He didn't need this shit. First, he couldn't get a cheeseburger, and now this old wash-up was on his case. But even as his body was tensing to get up and move forward, get on the road so he could see Joe, his brain was moving backward.

Back to that night at the train station, standing out in the bone-chilling sleet, chipping at the ice on the door handles so he could look inside the car. The car was unlocked, and he found nothing inside but cigarette butts and an old Arby's bag. The trunk latch was broken, held closed by a rusted coat hanger. Cold, wet, and miserable, he had run his flashlight over the mess of tools and old newspapers, slammed the trunk shut, and retreated to his squad car to call it in.

He met Shockey's eyes across the table. The question was still there.

"I didn't miss anything," Louis said.

"I still got the car," Shockey said. He had the barest grin on his face. It pissed Louis off.

"How about if we go take another look?" Shockey said.

The impound lot was in a neighborhood of trailer parks and storage rental barns out by the airport. Shockey pulled the sedan up to the gates of the razor-wired chain-link fence, got out and hustled to the gates.

Louis watched through the slow sweep of the wipers as Shockey unlocked the heavy padlocks and swung the gate open. Louis was staring at the big yellow sign that shouted BEWARE ATTACK DOGS as Shockey slid back into the driver's seat.

"What about the dogs?" Louis asked.

"There's no friggin' dogs," Shockey said, putting the car into gear.

Once inside the lot, Shockey parked the sedan at the side of a large metal hangar of a building. Louis got out into the cold drizzle.

A low whining noise drew his eyes up, but he couldn't see anything in the rapidly fading light. The whine grew into an ear-splitting scream as a smudge of lights emerged from the clouds. Louis almost ducked as the jet streaked overhead and was gone.

"This way," Shockey said.

They walked behind the building, down a row of cars, which seemed to grow older and dirtier the farther they went. They passed some motorcycles, a few boats on trailers, and an old tractor. Then came rows of old refrigerators, bicycles, and a stack of doors. The farther they went into the yard, the rustier and more random the piles of debris became. It was like some old cemetery where the fresh graves still had someone to tend them while the old ones had long been abandoned.

Louis stopped and lifted a plastic-encased tag hanging from a rusty bicycle. Written on it was a case number, a scribbled name, and the year: 1968.

"How long you guys keep this stuff?" Louis asked.

"Forever," Shockey said, walking on. "A few years back, we had a guy who was awarded a new trial after twenty years in the pen. Lucky us, we still had the evidence, and he was convicted again."

Louis followed Shockey around the corner of the building. The red Falcon was parked nose-in against the fence. A weather-worn tarp covered the front end, but the wind had blown it up to expose the trunk. Shockey sighed in disgust as he brushed mud and dead leaves from a back window. Then he looked back at Louis.

"This is it," Shockey said.

Louis stepped closer and peered in the side window. The interior was clouded with gray shadows, but there

was enough light to see. The ashtray was still stuffed with butts, and the Arby's bag was still in the backseat.

"Have you had anything examined yet?" Louis asked. "Dusted the car for prints?"

"Not yet," Shockey said. "This sat here for nine years. I told you, I just recently reopened the case."

"Okay," Louis said. "What was it I was supposed to have missed?"

The trunk was still secured only by the rusty coat hanger. Shockey unwound the wire and lifted the trunk. Louis peered inside. At first, he saw the same tools and old newspapers he had seen nine years ago, but then his eye caught something else. Tucked under a crumpled *Detroit Free Press,* the strap of a bra.

He picked up a screwdriver and used it to lift the newspaper. The bra was once white, but the fabric was dull and yellow now, the lace across the left cup rotting away. The right cup was smeared with a brown liquid.

Blood.

Louis looked at Shockey. His first impulse was to deny the existence of the bra back in 1980, but the truth was, he couldn't be absolutely sure. In the dark and in a hurry to wrap up a report on an abandoned vehicle, it was possible he missed it.

"So, what's the problem?" Louis asked. "This is evidence of a crime. Why haven't you bagged it and turned it over to the lab?"

"This is why," Shockey said. He reached into his raincoat for a piece of paper and handed it to Louis.

It was a report—*his* 1980 report on locating the Falcon. And it was not a copy. It was the original. Louis scanned it quickly.

Upon a routine search of the vehicle and the trunk, I arranged a tow. Tow truck responded at 12:45 a.m. Notification made to AAPD detectives and to Livingston County 12/11/80 that vehicle wanted in their BOLO had been located at 325 Depot Street, Ann Arbor, Mich. Neither Owen Brandt, owner of the vehicle, nor ATL subject, Jean Brandt, was on scene.

Louis handed the report back to Shockey. "I still don't understand what the problem is. This report is accurate and doesn't change your finding the bra."

"I don't think that's how a defense attorney is going to see it," Shockey said.

"What are you talking about?"

"Look at it this way," Shockey said. "The wife disappears in December 1980. Her car is found a week later, and a cop searches it and puts in writing that there was nothing in the car to indicate a crime. Nine years later, a bloody bra turns up in the trunk."

"Stuff like that happens."

"It could happen if there hadn't been a search of the trunk in 1980," Shockey said. "Aren't you smart enough to see how a defense attorney will play this?"

"Why don't you tell me?"

"Okay, you're up on the stand," Shockey said. "Officer Kincaid, you put in your report you searched the trunk. Inside were some tools and old newspapers. Did you move the newspapers, officer? Of course I did. Did you have a flashlight, Officer? Of course I did. Then how come you didn't see the bra, Officer? Could it be you didn't see it because it was planted later by the police?"

Louis looked back at the trunk. He understood what Shockey was saying. He'd faced enough defense lawyers to know how things could get twisted, but he wasn't sure that's what this was about. The trunk wasn't that cluttered. There was a screwdriver, a wrench, and a crowbar. An old can of oil and some newspapers. Even in the sleet, he would have sifted through it. It was procedure, and back then, he never broke procedure. No way did he miss this bra.

"Look, peeper," Shockey said, "I'm just telling you that it won't work for a judge or a jury the way it is now. I need you to change your report."

"You want me to say I never looked in the trunk?"

Shockey reached into his pants and withdrew a second sheet of paper. "I got a blank form here," he said. "Just like the ones we used in 1980. I want you to rewrite everything and leave out the fact that you searched the car. Say it was frozen shut or something."

Louis took a step back so he could get a better look at Shockey's face.

"You're one stupid sonofabitch," he said.

"Let's not get personal—"

"Not only are you asking me to commit a crime, but there are other copies of my report out there," Louis went on. "How could you expect to get away with something like this?"

"The only other copy was in the missing persons file on Jean Brandt. And it no longer exists."

"You destroyed it?"

Shockey was quiet, his hand still extended to Louis, the blank paper growing limp in the rain. In the gray light, the lines and whiskers on Shockey's face looked

etched in dried clay, and his eyes were swimming with a sick kind of desperate hope.

Another plane whined overhead.

"You planted the bra, didn't you?" Louis said.

"I'm telling you, it's Jean Brandt's bra, and it's our only hope of getting a warrant to search the farm," Shockey said. "Owen Brandt is a monster. He killed her, and she's buried out there on that farm. I know it."

"I don't care," Louis said. "I won't falsify a report for an over-the-hill dick who has no other way to hang on to his job than to lie his way into a courtroom with phony evidence."

Louis walked away from Shockey. In the distance, he could make out the mist-fuzzed lights of the runway at Detroit Metro. The heavy air was suddenly cold. He dreaded the drive back to the city with this jerk.

"I'll pay you!" Shockey hollered.

Louis spun to face him. "Pay me?"

Shockey came to him. "Look," he said, "if you had any guts or brains at all, you'd still be wearing a badge. I know all about you. You barely get work as a PI, and your real job is a part-time security gig watching rich people get a tan."

"Shut up."

"You got three hundred smackers in the bank, a car that's damn near older than you are, and your net income for last year wasn't enough to feed the fishies down where you live. Tell me you couldn't use ten grand."

Louis wanted to slug him. "Take me back to Ann Arbor—now," he said. "And if you say one more word about any of this on the way, I'll report you to your chief. You got that?"

Louis walked away. When he got to the gate, he looked back. Shockey had returned to the Falcon. The wind had picked up, and he was fighting to secure the tarp back over the trunk, searching for a way to fasten it down.

The blank report was lying in the mud.

Chapter Four

The College Inn was a motel hard by the I-94 spine that connected Ann Arbor with Detroit. His room had the disinfectant, moldy-carpet smell of a place that had hosted one too many beer parties.

Louis stayed in the room just long enough to put in a call to the Echo Bay Sheriff's Department. The dispatcher told him Undersheriff Frye was tied up all evening at a mayor's banquet. Louis left a message and then a second one on Joe's home phone to call him when she got in. Then he headed down to the bar.

The place was packed with bodies, noise, and smoke. Louis was wondering why a dingy bar in a rundown motel was so packed when he spotted the TV in the corner of the room.

Basketball.

Then his eyes began to pick up all the maize-and-blue ball caps and sweatshirts.

Worse, Michigan basketball.

"Turn up the fuckin' sound, Fred!" someone bellowed.

Worse yet, the NCAA championship, Michigan versus Seton Hall.

Louis elbowed his way to the bar. It took ten minutes to get the attention of the sweating bartender.

"You serve any food here?" Louis yelled over the din of drunks and the pregame cackling of the sportscasters.

"Free tacos 'til ten," the man said, pointing to a buffet table.

"Bring me a Heineken," Louis said.

"Don't got."

Louis sighed. "Stroh's."

A few long pulls from the beer did a little to wash the bad taste Shockey had left. Louis ordered a second beer, and his gnawing stomach finally propelled him to the buffet, where he filled a paper plate with three soggy tacos. There was an empty stool by the waitress station, and Louis pushed in front of a beefy kid in a GO BLUE sweatshirt to claim it.

"Hey, man!" the kid sputtered, puffing out his chest.

"Get lost," Louis said.

The kid backed off with a scowl. Louis sat hunched over, wolfing down the tacos, his eyes on the TV but not really watching.

He was thinking about the woman with the spatula back at Krazy Jim's and the look on her face when he screwed up his order, like she knew he didn't belong there.

How did she know?

In his four years as a student here, he had never once set foot in Krazy Jim's, had never gone to any of the student hangouts. No fried eggs at Angelo's after pulling an all-nighter, no sangria at Dominick's with a Sigma Kappa beauty, no winter-refuge pizza at the Cottage Inn, no postgame brews at the Brown Jug.

He had never felt comfortable in those places. The

only place he could remember going to more than once was the old Fleetwood Diner. There he could sit in silence with his books, watching the bums and cops just coming off shift as he sipped dark chocolate milk made to order with Hershey's syrup. No one bothered him there. He never felt out of place there.

Another lifetime ago.

"You want another?"

Louis looked at his watch. It was after ten. He shook his head, set his empty Stroh's in the trough, and headed back up to his room.

The red button on the phone wasn't blinking. He knew Joe was busy lately. The Leelanau sheriff, Mike Villella, was retiring, and Joe was the automatic candidate for the position in the election six months from now. She was trying hard to impress the locals, and in a town like Echo Bay, putting in an appearance at the pancake dinner meant as much as keeping the poachers in line.

Still, why the hell hadn't she called when she knew he was only four hours away?

Louis kicked off his shoes, grabbed the remote, and lay down on the bed. He flipped on the TV. It went right to the NCAA tournament, like the satellite was programmed to pick up anything remotely to do with UM sports.

His eyes slid to the phone. He muted the game, picked up the receiver, and dialed. Mel Landeta picked up on the second ring.

"I figured you'd be at O'Sullivan's," Louis said.

"Raining like hell down here tonight," Mel said. "Hold on a sec."

The phone clattered. In the background, Solomon

Burke's "A Change Is Gonna Come" fell to a whisper. Mel picked the receiver up again.

"How's Michigan?" he asked.

"A waste of time."

"What does the cop need you for?"

"It's an old missing persons case," Louis said. "A woman disappeared nine years ago, but her car was found abandoned. I was the responding. The detective who worked the case is trying to reopen it."

"I hear an 'and' coming."

"He planted a bloody bra in the trunk, and now he wants me to change my report."

Louis could hear the click of a lighter as Mel fired up a cigarette. "What about copies of the original?"

"Only one. He says he destroyed it."

Mel was quiet.

"He's a burnout who's hearing footsteps," Louis said. "He thinks reopening an old case is going to drown out the sound."

Mel still didn't say anything.

"What?" Louis said.

"Nothing," Mel said.

"Don't give me that shit."

"What you just said is something only a young man can say."

Louis was quiet. On the silent TV screen, Glen Rice hit a jumper. Screaming and stomping thundered from the room next door.

"Maybe there's something more," Mel said.

"Like what?"

"Tell me more about the woman."

"Her name was Jean. Married to some guy named Owen

Brandt. They lived on a farm somewhere west of here." He paused. "The husband reported her missing but later admitted he thought she had just run off with someone."

"You remember what she looked like?"

Louis hesitated while his brain retrieved a memory. "Not really."

"Pretty?"

Louis couldn't bring the face into focus. "What's your point?"

"Cherchez la femme."

"Help me out here a little, Mel."

"Il y a une femme dans toute les affaires; aussitôt qu'on me fait un rapport, je dis, 'Cherchez la femme.' "

"More help than that."

"Roughly translated, 'There's a woman behind every case; as soon as they bring me a report, I say, 'Look for the woman.' You ever think this Shockey guy might have known this woman? And maybe that's why he's so hung up on the case?"

Louis was still trying to see Jean Brandt's photo in the missing persons file. A shard fell into place: an old snapshot gone faded orange and too blurry to make out anything but dark hair.

"Are you going to help him or not?"

"The guy tried to bribe me, Mel. I'm just going to walk away."

He could hear Mel lighting another cigarette. "You going up to see Joe before you come home?"

"Yeah, if I can ever get a hold of her."

"She busy again?"

Louis was quiet. He had never talked to Mel about the strain fifteen hundred miles was putting on his and

Joe's relationship, but Mel's radar picked up on things.

"Well," Mel said, "I'm beat and need to get some sleep. Tell Joe I said hello when you talk to her."

Louis said goodbye and hung up. For a few minutes, he just sat on the edge of the bed and stared at the phone, the cheers and rumblings from adjoining rooms a dull roar in the back of his mind.

There's a woman behind every case.

Maybe Mel was right. Maybe Shockey had been in love with Jean Brandt, and maybe it was the memory of her and what he didn't or couldn't do for her nine years ago that drove his desperation now.

Louis supposed guilt over letting her disappearance go unresolved was a better motivator than trying to hang on to a job, but he still wasn't sure it was enough to keep him here to help Shockey. What could he do that the Ann Arbor PD or Livingston County Sheriff's Office couldn't?

The phone rang.

Louis grabbed it. "Joe?"

"Hey, you got the keg over there?"

"Wrong room, buddy," Louis said.

He hung up and lay down on the bed, staring at the yellowed ceiling tiles.

Nine years. Shockey had been missing her for nine years. Nine years that must have felt like a lifetime for him.

Louis pulled himself to a sitting position and dug Shockey's home phone number from his pocket. The paper was damp, the blurred numbers hard to read. The phone rang eight or nine times, and Louis was about to give up when Shockey's voice cut through the line.

"Yeah?"

"Detective, this is Kincaid. One question. Were you involved with Jean Brandt?"

There was silence on the other end of the line. Then a long exhalation. "Yeah, I was in love with her."

Louis shut his eyes. "Okay, Detective. I'll give you one more day to convince me this is worth my time. But I don't want to hear any more crap about falsifying reports. You got that?"

"Yeah."

Louis rubbed his brow, nagged by the feeling that he was going to regret this.

"So, what do we do?" Shockey asked. "Where do we start?"

"I want to see this farm. Where is it?"

"It's about a half-hour west of Ann Arbor, just south of Hell."

Chapter Five

Louis turned up the collar of his jacket against the rain and stepped closer to the gate of the Brandt farm. A rusty metal sign nailed to a wood post kept him from venturing farther: TRESPASSERS WILL BE SHOT.

He had never spent any time on a farm. He'd been raised in the village of Plymouth, Michigan, for the most part, growing up with all the standard city-issued conveniences. His only experience with farm life had been from movies. Or as seen through the windows of the family Ford during boring Sunday jaunts to the Irish Hills or the long drives up north for the annual vacation.

He remembered thinking at ten years old that farms must be pretty neat places to live. Picking apples right

from the tree or jumping from the upper window of a barn into a pile of hay or riding a horse any time you wanted.

Louis stared through the mist at the Brandt farmhouse.

But this place held no such warmth.

It was a crumbling, two-story, red brick house with a steep-pitched, green-shingled roof. The covered wood porch was missing its front steps, railing slats, and most of its gingerbread. The smaller side porch was filled with wet boxes, piles of yellowed newspapers bound with twine, and a small rusted refrigerator—what Louis remembered someone from his childhood calling an icebox. The tall windows, some boarded up, some still shrouded with tattered lace curtains, looked back at him like blank eyes through the overgrown bushes.

Beyond the house, Louis could see three wooden outbuildings, once painted red but now faded to gray, the sides listing, the roofs sunken. In the weeds, four rusted machines lay in a circle around a huge hulking thing with arms and giant gears, like a family of petrified prehistoric monsters.

There was junk everywhere—pitchforks, coils of barbed wire, wagon wheels, pocked metal drums, a faded green tractor with JOHN DEERE spelled out in rust. And dominating it all, a crumbling cathedral of a barn, its massive doors padlocked.

Louis surveyed the farm. It was hard to believe anyone had lived here just nine years ago. The place had the feel of a land destroyed by war or abandoned to plague.

He heard the door of the car close and turned to see Shockey making his way across the gravel road. He was working his long arms into his dingy raincoat.

Shockey stopped at the gate and stared at the house.

He hadn't said much on the way out here, and Louis had not pushed it, sensing that whatever else there was to this story was not something Shockey talked easily about.

But now that they were here, only a few yards from where Jean Brandt had lived, and maybe died, it was time.

"Did it look like this when you knew her?" Louis asked.

Shockey stuffed his hands into his pockets. Again, he seemed to steel up, and Louis gave him a few seconds to get a grip on his thoughts and memories.

"I drove by here a couple of times right after she disappeared," Shockey said. "It looked a little better than this but not much."

"Tough way of life," Louis said.

"It wasn't the farming that wore her down," Shockey said. "She grew up on a farm not that far from here. It was Owen Brandt who made it rough."

"How'd you meet her?" Louis asked.

"She used to come to the farmer's market in Ann Arbor and sell potatoes and cukes and things," Shockey said. "I loved the vine-ripened tomatoes, and I'd browse the market on Sunday mornings and pick up the fresh stuff I couldn't get from Kroger's."

"She came to the market alone?"

"Yeah." Shockey nodded. "That's why I noticed her. She was a little thing and used to unload all those baskets by herself, set up her table herself, and load back up again at dark. After watching her a few times, I offered to help."

"When was this?"

"June 1980."

"How long after that first meeting did you start an affair?"

Shockey's jaw ground in thought and maybe a lit-

tle embarrassment. Again, Louis let him have his time.

"A month," Shockey said finally. "But it was hard to be together. Brandt kept a tight leash on her and expected her home exactly three hours after sundown. If she was late, she got beat."

"So how'd you make time?"

"About an hour before dark, if she hadn't sold all her stuff, I'd buy it, and then we'd do a quick load-up and head for the motel."

Louis glanced around. The rain had thinned to a fine spray, blurring the land for miles, leaving everything obscured in fog. He wanted to suggest that they sit in the car to finish this conversation, but Shockey seemed more unguarded, as if he felt he was giving Jean Brandt more respect by telling her story out here in this godforsaken place.

"What about when summer ended?" Louis asked. "She wouldn't have come to market then. Did the affair continue into winter?"

"She could only get away a few times after October," Shockey said. "She told Owen she had female problems and had to see a specialist in Ann Arbor. Bastard never questioned that, didn't want to hear anything about her problems, so he let her go."

"You said you met at motels," Louis said. "Why not go to your place?"

Shockey sighed. "I was married. I had a kid."

"So that's why you didn't come forward when she disappeared," Louis said. "You didn't want your wife to find out."

Shockey sniffed and pushed his wet hair off his forehead. He was staring at the house again. "That, and I didn't want to lose my job," he said. "We had—hell, we still have it, but no one pays much attention to it now—we had a morals clause in our job description. I would've been fired."

"Not to mention you might have been considered a suspect in her disappearance."

"Yup."

"Why now?" Louis asked. "Why open this after nine years?"

"Brandt's been in prison in Ohio for the last seven years. He beat up a woman and threw her out of a car," Shockey said. "He was paroled a week ago."

Louis was looking at the farmhouse.

"He almost killed that woman. I know he killed Jean," Shockey said. "And I am not going to just stand by and let him kill again."

"You've let this get personal," Louis said. "I don't need to tell you that's not right."

"I'm older than you," Shockey said. "And the older you get, the heavier the shit becomes, the shit you didn't take care of when you were younger. You live under it, thinking it will go away by itself. But it doesn't."

Louis was quiet.

"And no matter how much good you do later, it never makes things right."

"Did you plant the bra in the trunk of the Falcon?" Louis asked.

"Yeah."

"Who did it belong to?"

"My ex-wife."

"Whose blood was on it?"

"Mine. I got the idea almost a year ago," Shockey said. "I knew Jean and I had the same blood type, and I cut myself and bled on it and then left it in my backyard for months trying to make it look old."

"And the ten grand and my expenses to come here. Where was that money going to come from?"

"My retirement fund."

"You're a real piece of work, Detective."

Shockey faced him, his eyes as empty as the farm-house's windows. "I'm not sorry," he said. "I'd do it again if I thought I could get away with it."

Louis shook his head. This case was about as cold as they came. Not one shred of evidence or a viable lead.

"Kincaid," Shockey said, "Owen Brandt abandoned this place like a month after Jean went missing. But he never hired anyone to work this farm for him, and he never put it up for sale. Why do you think that is?"

"You think Brandt buried her out here?" Louis asked.

"I know he did."

"How big is this place?" Louis asked.

"Sixty acres."

Louis took a long look around. There was nothing but a cold, lonely grayness as far as he could see and he thought about the possibility that Jean Brandt's bones were buried out there somewhere, forgotten by everyone but Shockey.

"Are you going to help me?" Shockey asked.

Louis met Shockey's eyes. But his mind was churning backward a few years. Kneeling in the sand in Florida, digging a hole with his hands to bury a piece of evidence, the only thing he could do to bring justice to a dead girl. He did understand. He understood something else, too: what it was like to love a woman so much you'd do al-most anything for her.

"I'll help you, Detective," Louis said. "But it will be my way. Are we clear?"

"Yeah," Shockey said. "We're clear."

Chapter Six

The soft knocking came through to his ears like the *tap-tap-tap* of a hammer. The sound lay tangled in a dream he was having about fixing the air conditioner in his cottage during a hurricane. The dream was a strange kind of paranormal slide show with a parade of characters he hadn't seen in years. Some jock buddy from high school, an old bearded professor, and a girl who had laughed when he asked for a date.

He opened his eyes with the sense that those same people were there in the motel room with him, but there was no one. Just darkness and a glow of neon against the curtains.

The knock came again.

Had to be some drunk kid looking for a leftover keg. Louis shoved back the blanket, flipped on the bedside lamp, and stumbled to the door. The fluorescent light in the hall blinded him.

"Look, I told you guys—"

Then she came into focus.

Pale face with chiseled cheekbones, thin lips the color of peaches, and a mane of brown hair, not pulled back in her usual ponytail but down around the collar of her rain-beaded black leather jacket. She had a .45 automatic clipped onto her belt.

"Joe."

She glanced down at his boxer shorts, then raised a brow, amused at his shock to find her at his door at five A.M. Then she put a hand behind his neck to pull him to her for a hard kiss. The kind that had been building during the four-hour drive down from Echo Bay.

He broke away first. "What are you doing here?" he asked.

"Mel called me and told me you were going to stick around here and help this Detective Shockey, so I asked Mike for a few days off and came on down."

"Mel called you?" He blinked, not yet fully awake.

"Aren't you glad to see me?" she asked.

"Of course I am. Come here."

He pulled her to him this time and shut the door. In a clumsy dance of turns and wet kisses, he walked her backward to the bed. She dropped her purse and the envelope she was carrying, and they fell onto the bed.

Her arms circled his neck, and for the next few seconds, they wrapped themselves in each other. She worked his boxers off, but he was having a harder time with her leather jacket and the stubborn snap on her snug jeans.

"Wait, wait," she said, breathless. "I'll do it."

Joe stood up, unclipped the gun, and began to undress. Louis reached down to pick up her purse and the envelope to set them aside. He noticed the writing on the front of the envelope: BRANDT/JEAN AND OWEN.

He looked at Joe. Her back was to him as she peeled off her blouse. "What is this?" he asked.

She glanced over her shoulder. "Oh, just some research I did for you."

He unclasped the envelope and pulled out the papers. The top sheet was a copy of the missing persons bulletin Ann Arbor PD had sent out nine years ago. Under that were a few newspaper clippings from various southeastern Michigan newspapers that covered the story, then a six-sheet compilation of Owen Brandt's criminal record.

"How did you even know Brandt's name?" he asked.

"Mel told me," she said. "I just thought I'd do you a favor and pull some background."

"You didn't have to do this, Joe," he said. "Shockey's trying to keep things low-key."

"I was just trying to save you time," she said. "I know how hard it is to get the information when you don't have a badge."

He looked up at her quickly.

She was standing there in just her bra and panties, all sharp angles, long, lean muscle, and silken hair. The image should have been enough to wash away all thought *and* the sting of her last comment, but it wasn't. He turned away slowly and found himself looking at the missing persons bulletin.

It was a standard photocopy, the same thing you'd see hanging in police stations anywhere in the state.

> NAME: Jean Lynne Brandt
> DATE OF BIRTH: June 6, 1956
> HEIGHT: 5'3"
> WEIGHT: 102
> HAIR: Brown
> EYES: Brown
> DISTINGUISHING MARKS: None
> LAST SEEN WEARING: Blue dress, brown coat.
> JEWELRY: Gold wedding band
> MISSING SINCE: 12–4–80

There was a blurry picture in the upper right corner. Jean Brandt stared back at him, a heart-shaped face and dark eyes that had a defeated glaze to them. Her hair was covered in a scarf, a few wisps of dark hair framing her forehead.

A solid gray sky filled the small space around her, and

even though Louis couldn't see any buildings, he had the sense that the photo had been taken at the farm.

It was a bad picture to attach to a police bulletin, taken from a distance, unfocused, and sloppily cropped too close to the right side of her head. It probably had been cropped to remove Owen before they copied the bulletins. But Louis was sure the cops hadn't done the cutting. Maybe Owen had.

And he knew Shockey was right. Owen didn't give a damn about Jean, alive or dead.

Suddenly, the light went out, and the bed jiggled. Joe's arms came around him from behind, folding over his chest and beginning an eager caress.

"Come on," she whispered in his ear. "I just wanted to help. Don't be mad."

Her hands slipped down the front of his body, and she started chewing at his shoulder with catlike nibbles. He finally closed his eyes and tossed the folder, turning to take her into his arms.

Chapter Seven

They were standing at the side of the gravel road. The light rain that had started around six that morning was still coming down.

"So you're just going to leave me here?"

Louis turned to look back at Joe.

"You know you can't come," he said.

She pursed her lips. "I'll wait in the car," she said.

He heard the thud of the car door as he walked away but didn't look back. At the padlocked gate he stopped at the TRESPASSERS WILL BE SHOT sign. He thrust the flashlight into a back pocket and scaled the fence, landing in the wet grass on the other side.

He paused to glance back at Joe's Bronco. He could see her watching him, and he knew she was pissed. As a cop, she couldn't set foot on this property without a warrant. She knew that. Just as she knew that as a PI, he wasn't subject to the same strict legal restraints.

He trudged through the high, wet weeds, a small nubby pit in his gut relishing the fact—for once—that she had a badge and he didn't. Even as his head was telling him what a macho asshole he was for thinking that, even as his dick was telling him how much he had loved being inside her last night, even as his heart was telling him how much he loved her.

He climbed the three steps onto the sagging wood porch and looked back one more time to the car. Hell, she was just trying to help. He would make it up to her tonight with dinner and a good bottle of wine.

There was another padlock on the front door. This one was new. Something else new—a bright orange FORECLOSURE sign—was pasted to the glass of the front door. Louis didn't remember seeing it the first time he had been here with Shockey, and even out by the gate, the bright orange would have been noticeable.

Louis looked around for options. Some of the windows were boarded up, but a few were still exposed, the rippled old glass filmed with years of dirt.

He walked around the corner of the house, looking out over the land. The sheer size of the rolling land

and the overgrown trees and weeds shielded the house from any neighbors. He couldn't remember even seeing another house on the drive down the lonely and rutted Lethe Creek Road.

There was no sound except the caw of a crow. He spotted the huge black bird perched on the wheel of a rusting tractor. It was hunched down in its oily wet feathers, staring at him.

He jumped up onto the side porch. Three weathered planks were nailed over the door. He grabbed the edge of the top plank with both hands and pulled. With a loud crack, the board came off. A heavy fluttering sound. He turned. The bird was gone.

It took five minutes to work the other two boards off. He peered into the dusty window of the door. It looked like a kitchen beyond.

No lock on this door. He tried the knob, and it turned easily—too easily—but the door didn't budge. He pressed a shoulder against it and gave a hard shove. The door creaked open.

He looked back at the road. The Bronco wasn't visible from where he was. With a final glance around the grounds, he went into the house.

The smell. Not what a house should be but weirdly familiar. Then it hit him what it reminded him of: the basement of one of his foster homes in Detroit. Closed and fusty, with the powdery smell of old decaying newspapers.

He closed the door behind him and took in the small room. It was a kitchen, though most of what anyone normally would identify with a kitchen was gone. No appliances, just dusty outlines on the scuffed blue linoleum.

Dark scarred wood paneling halfway up the walls, then faded yellow paper spotted with black mold. One wall of built-in cupboards in the same dark wood, the doors flung open to empty shelves. A dripping sound drew his eyes to a sink under the room's single small window. The water had left a vivid streak of dark red rust in the grimy white sink.

He moved to the next room, stepping carefully over the piles of trash on the dull wood-plank floor.

An archway led to what he assumed had once been a dining room. It was filled with stacks of cardboard boxes. He could make out a round oak table in the middle with several slatted chairs. The table was heaped with more boxes. Each was sealed with packing tape and imprinted with the same letters: HANSEN BROS. AUCTIONS AND ES-TATE SALES.

He started down a narrow hallway, clicking on the flashlight against the gloom. The beam picked up old pictures and carved frames propped against the blue-papered walls. More Hansen cartons. A broken ladderback chair.

The place was a warren of small rooms, each with a different wallpaper and different linoleum. Faded stripes, pastoral scenes, and flowers on the walls. Checkerboards, geometrics, and ugly patterns on the chipped and peeling floors.

He had come to the front of the house. Two large windows, draped with yellowed lace panels, let in the gloomy light. He clicked the flashlight off. The room—he guessed it was called a parlor at one time—was empty except for a dust-covered upright piano shoved in the corner. The top of the piano was stacked three feet high with long, thin boxes. He took one down, and the box

crumpled in his fingers. It held a player piano roll, the paper as fragile as papyrus.

He set the roll back on the piano and left the parlor.

The flashlight led him back to the hallway. He shined the beam into two small closets. Empty. At the staircase, he paused, his fingers on the railing. It had been a beautiful thing once, this mahogany staircase, its posts intricately carved and beaded, its newel topped by a crown. It was the only thing in the whole house that still whispered of the grandeur this home must have had a century ago.

Dusting his hands, he started up. The stairs groaned under his weight. The rooms grew smaller, dingier, and more barren. He poked the flashlight into each of the three doors. More peeling wallpaper and wet, cracked ceilings. No furniture, no boxes. No signs of life.

He pushed open the last door. He thought it was just another closet, but then the flashlight beam picked up the dull white of a filthy claw-foot bathtub. No sink, no toilet. Nothing else in the room except a string hanging from an empty socket in the ceiling.

He closed the door. A tendril of cold air curled around his neck. He turned in a slow circle, looking for its source, and saw the small window at the end of the hall. The rippled old glass had a hole in it with a web of cracks, as if someone had thrown a rock through it.

He went to the window and looked down. There was a gray wood outhouse in the backyard. He let out a long, slow breath. That explained why there was no toilet in the bathroom.

Why had he come here? Even as he asked himself the question, he knew the answer. It was the way he had always worked. Going back to the homes of victims had always

helped him. It never gave him anything tangible, anything he could even articulate. Just a vague feeling, like his senses were vibrating on a sharper frequency, like the life that had once pulsed in these places could reveal secrets.

He stared at the outhouse. This place, this time-warped, forgotten place. There was definitely a feeling here, an almost palpable feeling of despair, but it was laid over a brittle hardness that he couldn't quite bring into focus. Something had tried to thrive here in spite of everything.

Jean Brandt's face was in his head then. How could a woman like that survive in this soulless place? Maybe Shockey was wrong. Maybe she had just run off, just like her husband said.

Who could blame her?

He went downstairs. Back in the kitchen, he paused for one last look around. He spotted an axe leaning up against a cabinet and went to it. Its wood handle was scarred, its blade caked with dark red. He ran a finger over its dull edge.

There was no point in letting his imagination go crazy. Shockey had that cornered. He looked at the streak on his finger. Just some rust.

Outside, he stopped to make sure the door was pulled tight. He used a rusted hammer he found on the porch to pound the boards back into place. When he was satisfied that the door looked secure, he went out into the yard.

For a moment, he just stood there, surveying the outlying buildings. There were four that he could see, three shedlike structures and the looming gray-plank barn.

He walked a wide circle around the rusted hulk of a huge machine trapped in briars and went to the first build-

ing. A peer into the broken windows revealed what looked like a tool shed. The second building appeared to be a garage of sorts for machinery. The entrance was blocked by shoulder-high weeds and a pocked green tractor. The third small building held only sodden sacks of feed.

He remembered the outhouse and trudged through the weeds to it. The door was gone. He could see inside, see the piles of curled magazines stacked in the dark corner, see the dirty, crumpled papers on the bleached plank floor, see the warped board covering the seat.

He drew in a breath and then used the end of the flashlight to flip the board away. For a moment, he couldn't move, couldn't bring himself to act on what he was thinking. Then he stepped inside, clicked on the flashlight, and trained the beam down into the hole.

Dark brown sludge. Tips of old paper.

The smell finally made him fall back. He ran a hand over his face.

What did you expect to see, Kincaid? Fucking bones?

It was raining again. He lifted his chin upward and let it fall on his face. He looked back over the land.

The barn was the only thing left. He made his way toward it through the high weeds. It was a massive structure, two stories from what he could see, and built into a sloping hill with a gentle incline leading up to the huge main doors. He wondered again what he expected to find. A fragment of a dress or collar buried in the hay? Jean Brandt's bones on clear display in a horse stall?

He went up the incline to the entrance. A heavy new chain and padlock secured the doors. He backtracked and went down, walking a circle around the barn. Deep in the weeds, he spied two missing boards toward the

ground. A sharp pull on one yielded a hole large enough to wedge through, and he was inside.

He drew up short. He was on a ground floor of hard-packed dirt. The smell was sweet-sour with moldering, wet hay. The spare light streamed through the gaps in the boards of the high roof. The soaring space was quiet, like the world outside had fallen away. He had never been in a barn before. All of it made him suddenly feel like he had stumbled into an old, decrepit church.

The details began to register. Beams draped with age-hardened leather harnesses. Metal skeletons of machines whose functions he could only guess at. Bales of sodden hay spilling innards onto the wood floor. Dust motes dancing in the gray beams of light.

Louis felt a coldness touch his spine.

Something was wrong in this place. Worse than the house.

He continued his exploration, poking the flashlight into grain bins and stalls, shining the light into every crevice and cranny. There was an old wooden ladder leading up to a loft but neither the ladder nor the board above looked strong enough to support his weight.

Finally, he wiggled back out through the hole. The rain was coming down hard. Sticking the flashlight into his waistband, he hurried back to the front of the property. He could see the Bronco still waiting on the road. Joe had the engine running against the cold.

He was almost back to the house when something caught his eye. It was just a hint of red hidden in the weeds, but it was the red of old paint, not rust. It was almost covered by the garbage surrounding it, old coils of barbed wire, tin cans, and dead leaves. But Louis could

see two small wheels and white lettering of some kind. He bent down and pushed aside the weeds.

It was a small wagon. The white letters on the side of it said RED RIDER.

He pulled it out of the weeds. And the other letters on the rear of the wagon, hand-painted but still clear, jumped out at him:

AMY.

Chapter Eight

They stopped in Hell to call Shockey. Louis was furious and wanted to meet him as soon he and Joe got back to Ann Arbor. Someone at the Ann Arbor station told Louis that Shockey was working a murder scene south of the city and wouldn't be back until dark.

A child. A child had been in that house.

How could Shockey not tell him that? And where was she now? Dead and buried, along with her mother? Or were they both safe somewhere, running not only from Owen Brandt but from Shockey, too? Maybe Shockey's love for Jean was closer to obsession, and maybe Jean had fled from both men.

"Louis," Joe said, "slow down, you're coming into town."

Louis eased off the gas pedal and swung the Bronco up the State Street exit ramp.

"You don't know for sure a girl was there at the same time Jean was there," Joe said. "Any kid could have had that wagon there at any time."

"There was a name—Amy. And that wagon looked like it had been there a long time."

"But you don't know if she's a daughter or a niece or maybe just a kid who lived nearby."

"Nearby? You saw that place, Joe. The nearest house was a mile away, at least."

Joe was quiet for a moment. "It could mean nothing," she said finally.

"It means something."

"You said you didn't see any children's things in the house."

"Everything was boxed up," Louis reminded her. "And I couldn't unseal them, or they would know someone had been inside. I'm bending some rules here, Joe. You know that."

She fell silent again, staring out at the road. Louis glanced at her. She had the same kind of look on her face now as when he had left her standing outside the gate back at the farm.

He steered the Bronco through the traffic, everything growing close and congested as they neared the city.

"Louis, there's a cop behind us," Joe said. "He's been there since we crossed the river."

Louis glanced at the rearview mirror. It was a white Ann Arbor PD cruiser, and it was definitely following them. In the slow sweep of the cruiser's wipers, Louis couldn't see the cop's face. What did he want? It had been stop-and-go traffic since leaving the freeway, and he knew he hadn't been speeding or run any stop signs.

The blue lights came on, and the siren yelped.

"Shit."

Louis looked for somewhere to pull in, but the one-way streets and parked cars made it a tough task. He fi-

nally found a spot in front of a small store with a rack of books outside under its awning.

As he turned off the engine, his gut knotted. Here he was in this liberal hamlet of academia, but he still couldn't shake the bizarre thought that he was being pulled over because he was a black man with a white woman in his car.

Louis put the Bronco into park and reached for his wallet, his eyes flicking to the mirror.

The cop got out of the car. Louis let out a breath. He was black.

Other things registered as the cop came closer. He was a hulking guy, with a weightlifter's chest beneath the dark blue windbreaker. A body that complemented his don't-fuck-with-me walk.

Louis rolled down the window, and the officer peered into the Bronco. The rain dripped from the brim of his plastic-covered garrison hat onto Louis's arm, but the guy didn't apologize or move back. His brown eyes went first to Joe, assessed her as being no threat, and dismissed her. He looked to Louis with a standard no-nonsense cop stare.

Louis held out his license and Florida PI identification card.

The officer took them, gave them a cursory glance, then stepped back. "Get out of the car, please."

Louis blew out a sigh and shoved open the door. The cop had an inch on him and probably thirty pounds, all of it muscle. His name tag read: SGT. ERIC CHANNING.

"Turn around and put your hands on the car," Channing said.

"What'd I do?" Louis asked.

"Officer," Joe called, "I'm the undersheriff for Lee-lanau County. May I ask what this—"

"I know who you are," Channing said, "and no, ma'am,

you may not ask anything. Turn around, Mr. Kincaid."

Louis faced the car and put his hands on the hood. Channing gently kicked his feet apart and began frisking him. The rain was cold on the back of Louis's neck as it dripped inside the collar of his sweatshirt.

Louis bristled under the pat of the mittlike hands. He kept his focus on the weird white artwork in the bookstore's window. A hunched old woman with the words AUNT AGATHA over her head and underneath, in big letters, MYSTERIES. It seemed strangely fitting.

"You're licensed to carry a concealed weapon," Channing said. "A Glock, if I remember right. Where is it?"

Louis wondered how Channing knew that, but he didn't ask. "It's in the glovebox."

Channing told him to stay where he was and walked to the passenger side of the Bronco to get the Glock. Louis watched him, not understanding exactly what was happening. Channing knew Joe was a cop and had a weapon. He knew Louis had a permit for one, too. Yet he had not been concerned about either as he walked up to the Bronco. Which meant Channing felt he was never in any danger because he knew exactly whom he had pulled over.

"I could confiscate this until you leave the state," Channing said as he came around the rear of the truck with the holstered Glock.

"You could," Louis said. "But most law-enforcement officers are pretty decent about it. And I'm up here on police business. I'm working with Detective Shockey."

"I know that."

"And I'm a former cop."

"I know that, too."

"Then why are you out here busting my balls over nothing?"

"Is that what she is to you?" Channing asked. "Nothing?"

Louis glanced at Joe. What the hell kind of remark was that? This asshole didn't know a damn thing about Joe.

"What are you talking about?" Louis asked.

"February 1980."

"What?"

Channing shook his head in disgust. "You don't even remember her name."

"Who?"

"Kyla. Kyla Marie Brown. Ring a bell?"

The memory swept in like a punch. He'd thought about Kyla on and off for ten years, but it was never as powerful as it was right now. Maybe it was being back here in this city. Or maybe it was looking into the eyes of this stranger and knowing he knew.

Louis glanced across the street, searching for a response and trying to figure out just who Channing was, how he knew about Kyla, and why the hell he cared. Channing offered the answer.

"She's my wife now," he said.

Louis cleared his throat. "Look, if you're here to tell me to stay away from her, don't worry. I have no intention of seeing her," he said.

Channing just stared at him. The man hadn't moved a muscle. Louis looked at his holster in Channing's hand. The leather was getting soaked.

"What do you want from me?" Louis asked.

"I just wanted to look a real asshole in the eye," Channing said.

"What?"

"You heard me."

Louis held the man's eyes. He didn't know what the hell was going on, so he wasn't going to say anything. But he wasn't going to look away, either. He slowly held out his hand. Channing made no move to give him back the holster and the IDs.

"Are we done here?" Louis asked.

"I'll be watching you," Channing said. "I'll be watching you real close. Do you understand what I'm telling you?"

There was nothing he could say without elevating this to an argument or worse, so he nodded slowly.

Channing held out the Glock and Louis's ID cards. Louis accepted them and watched Channing swagger back to his cruiser and drive away.

Louis tucked his wallet back in his jeans, but it took him a moment to find the will to get into the Bronco. When he did, he just sat there, hands on the wheel.

"Who's Kyla Marie Brown?" Joe asked.

He picked the first place that he thought might be quiet and without students, a bar tucked into a red brick building on West Liberty called Old Town Tavern.

The place was almost empty, the Tiffany-style lamps casting the dark wood in shadows and the sound of the TV over the bar echoing off the tin ceiling. Louis steered Joe to a wood booth in the back. They both automatically started for the side facing the door. She looked up at him, and he let her slide in. He sat down across from her. The waitress came over, and Louis ordered a Heineken. He was surprised when Joe said she wanted only a glass of water. Joe waited until the girl had brought the beer and water, then trained her gray eyes on Louis.

"All right," she said, "so who is Kyla Brown?"

"You remember last December when you told me about your rookie year in Michigan?"

Joe nodded.

"And I told you then that I had something to tell you, too," he said. "Something that had been on my mind for a while."

"I remember," she said. "But you never brought it up again."

He took a drink of his beer to buy some time, then set the bottle down. "Kyla Brown was a girl I knew in college here," he said.

Joe picked up the water and look a long drink. When she set the glass down, her fingers found the napkin beneath, and she began curling its edge. He recognized the gesture as something she did when she was preparing herself for something that might be unpleasant. As a cop, she was never unsure of herself, but he could see a small glimmer of womanly concern in her eyes now.

"I wasn't in love with her," he said. "I was twenty, getting ready to start my senior year, and I had big plans for law school. Kyla was just . . ."

He stopped, realizing how shitty this was sounding.

"Just an easy lay?" Joe asked.

Louis looked up quickly. There was no judgment in her voice. It was just the way Joe talked, but still it stung.

"Not really," he said. "I liked her, but I didn't love her. I didn't want to get involved with anyone then. I tried to let her down easy, but she kept calling. By January, it had gotten pretty bad. Finally, I stopped answering the phone."

He paused again, a new memory slipping in. It wasn't real important, but hell, he might as well tell her all of it.

"I was already seeing someone else."

Joe sat back in the booth, her eyes fixed on his. "I think I will have a glass of wine."

Louis left the table and walked to the bar. He kept his back to Joe as he waited, staring absently at the line of booze on the shelf but seeing faces in his head. Old faces came easily to him most of the time. Kyla's was no different.

Skin the color of almonds. Hair always carefully arranged in a straightened sweep around her full, smooth cheeks. Eyelashes so long he could feel the brush of them against his face when he kissed her. Full lips, always glossy with cherry-red lipstick, something called Scarlet Fever. On anyone else, it would have looked cheap. On her, it was nothing but class.

The bartender set down a glass of red wine, and Louis took it back to the table. Joe had taken off her leather jacket and was sitting at an angle, her feet propped up on an empty chair. Fingers still working the napkin.

"House red okay?" he asked, setting the glass in front of her.

She nodded and took a drink before looking back at him. "So, if she didn't matter to you then, why does she matter to you now?" she asked.

Louis let out a long, slow breath. "Somewhere around the end of February, she came up to my dorm room. It was sleeting hard that night, and she was soaked. And she was so mad she was shaking. She was screaming at me for not answering her calls. Guys were coming out of their rooms and watching all this, and I couldn't calm her down."

Louis looked up, making sure he had Joe's eyes before he went on. "She told me she was pregnant," he said.

Joe didn't move, holding his stare for what seemed

liked minutes, her eyes shifting with questions and possibilities.

Louis took a long swallow of his beer and set the bottle down slowly. It would have been easy to look away from Joe now, but he didn't.

"The first thing I thought was, 'I don't want to fuck up my life.' " He hesitated. "The first thing out of my mouth was, 'Get rid of it.'"

Joe pushed her glass aside, took her feet from the chair, and leaned back, drawing into the farthest corner of the booth. But her eyes never wavered from his face, and he still wasn't sure what he was seeing there. He finally had to look away. Down at the green glass of the beer bottle. He focused on the little red star in the center of the beer label until it went blurry.

"She slapped me," he said. "Then she started hitting me in the chest, so hysterical she could barely stay on her feet. Finally, she just stopped and looked at me and said, 'Fine, I'll just get rid of it.' "

"What did you say?" Joe asked.

"I said, 'Go ahead.' "

Joe lowered her eyes. His found the exit sign over her bowed head and stayed there. The bar was quiet, not a sound, not even the clink of glasses. He wanted to look back at Joe, but he couldn't. He was afraid if he did, something would different. Something would be gone.

Then Joe touched his hand, and he looked at her. "You're a different man now," she said. Her fingers laced themselves through his. "Which is probably a good thing. I could never fall in love with that other guy."

Louis found a wry smile. "Yeah, well, that other guy gets worse," he said. "A few days later, I borrowed a cou-

ple hundred dollars from my roommate and sent it to her to pay for the abortion."

"You ever think much about why you reacted the way you did?"

Louis sat back, withdrawing his hand. "Fear," he said. "Fear of being trapped, fear of being nothing."

"Do you think you should go talk to her?" Joe asked.

"And say what?"

"Sometimes 'I'm sorry' is enough."

Louis shook his head.

"Her husband must have had an eye on you since you got here," Joe said. "That tells me she told him about you. Women don't tell their men about other men in their past unless it was bad. You can apologize. Whether she accepts it or not is up to her."

Louis was turning his empty bottle in circles on the scarred table.

"I have another thought to throw out at you," Joe said.

"What?"

"Why do you think Channing even bothered to stop us and tell us who he was?"

"He didn't want me anywhere near Kyla."

"She hates you. You're no threat to his marriage."

"What are you getting at?" Louis asked.

"Maybe it's not Kyla he wants you to stay away from."

He knew exactly what Joe was suggesting, and the thought settled over his skin with an eerie tingle. Still, it took him a second to reshape it into any kind of real possibility.

"What if she didn't have the abortion, Louis?" Joe asked.

But the question was in his head before Joe had even

said it. And with it came the realization that the question had always been there inside him.

Chapter Nine

Some people spend the present doing nothing but revisiting the past. Louis thought his foster parents were often like that, always talking about past Christmases or trips up north. His friend Dodie was like that, too. Beer bottle in hand and a setting Florida sun behind him, his favorite opening to a conversation was, "When I was young . . ."

Louis had never seen the point. Good or bad, whatever it was, it was over. Why keep reliving something you couldn't change? Or get back?

He wasn't sure he felt that way anymore. Maybe it was because now he was making memories worth remembering. It had been different before. He had been different before. Before he had started spending time with twelve-year-old Ben Outlaw, who was teaching him the fine art of how much glue to put on a model spaceship. And before Joe, who was teaching him just how little glue it took to hold two people together.

He blew out a breath and stared at the house.

It was a two-story frame house on Catherine Street, painted a pale blue, with old-fashioned white shutters. A thicket of dormant rose bushes buffered the small porch. The blooms were probably beautiful in the summer. Colorful, like her.

He had found the address in a phone book. Not under Eric Channing, which was to be expected. He didn't know any cop who listed a phone or address. Then he looked under Kyla and K. Channing but found nothing there, either. It was only when he was closing the book and feeling a guilty pang of relief that he decided to try once more and look under Brown.

There had been two K. Browns listed, one out near Ypsi and one here in Ann Arbor. He figured the Ann Arbor cops still had to live in the city, so this was where he had come first.

His heart was kicking up, and he looked around, trying to relax, hoping to spot something that would tell him if this was her home.

There was a newspaper lying on the narrow walk and a pair of rain boots sitting on the top step. Next to them was a cardboard box with HALO HATS stamped on the side in big black letters and a UPS invoice taped on top. There was no mailbox on the curb and no car in the drive.

And no toys anywhere.

He walked to the porch and drew a breath as he lifted his hand to rap on the screen door. Before he could, the door swung open.

Kyla.

She wore a cream-colored suit with eyelets around the collar. The eye shadow and red lipstick were there but tempered with age and sophistication, the red more burgundy, the silver more charcoal. She had stopped straightening her hair, and it formed a short black cap of soft curls around her round face.

Her eyes fired with contempt. "Go away," she said.

"Please," Louis said. "I just want five minutes."

She started to close the door, but to his surprise, she paused. "That's all I wanted from you ten years ago," she said.

"I know."

She dropped her hand from the door and waited, again surprising him with her decision to stand there and hear him out. He had no idea where to begin, so he started with the simplest of thoughts.

"I'm sorry, Kyla."

She said nothing. Nothing from her but that stare.

"I was a selfish sonofabitch," he said. "I said some terrible things. You deserved better from me."

Still nothing but that steely stare.

"I was stupid," he said. "All I could see was my future going down the drain, and I panicked."

Her eyes dipped to his jeans and sneakers. "That law degree you wanted so much," she said. "Did you ever get it?"

"No."

"What *did* you become?"

The fact that she didn't know told him Channing hadn't shared his traffic stop with her or any of the background information he had gathered. Made sense. It had been Channing's intent to bully Louis into keeping his distance.

"I became a cop when I got out of school," he said. "Now I'm a private investigator."

Her expression went from surprise when he said "cop" to scorn at "private investigator." She ran a red-manicured finger through her hair, her anger waning to annoyance.

"Why are you here?" she asked. "Are you in some kind of twelve-step program and on the part where you're supposed to say you're sorry?"

"No," he said. "I'm in town on business, and . . . it's hard being back here without remembering. I know there's nothing I can do to change a thing, but I wanted to tell you that I know how much I hurt you."

"You expect my forgiveness?" she asked.

"No, I don't expect a thing," he said. "I just needed to say it."

Kyla looked away, blinking back a glimmer of tears. Her hatred for him was still radiating off her in waves, but there was something else going on inside her, too. Something that was softening everything else.

"You've said what you needed to," she said. "And I've given you more time than you gave me. Now, please go away, and don't come back."

She started to close the door again. He put a hand to the screen.

"Kyla, wait, please," he said. "I need to ask you something else."

"What?" she asked.

"Did you have the abortion?"

Without so much as a blink, she answered him. "Yes."

The door closed.

Joe let the curtain fall and turned to face the dingy room. The clock on the nightstand told her it was only nine-thirty, but it felt later.

Where the hell was he?

He had dropped her off at the motel and sped off in the Bronco. He had asked her first, asked her if she minded. She had said no, she didn't. But she did. As much as she knew he needed to go see Kyla, as sure as she was of his love, she had felt something shift. Maybe it was his eyes

when he had looked at her over the table in the bar earlier. Maybe it was his voice when he said he was going to see Kyla. Whatever it was, it told her that things were never going to be the same between them again.

She kicked off her shoes, went to the bed, and sat down, cross-legged, her back against the flimsy wood headboard. She picked up the remote, clicked the TV on, and then clicked it off again. Her eyes went to the small plastic coffee maker on the dresser and then to the empty spot below where a mini-bar should have been.

Damn, she wanted a drink. But she didn't want to chance going out and missing his call.

Why the hell hadn't he called? He had been gone four hours.

She switched on the TV again, punching the button and half watching the images flip by. A cop harassing a gang member on *Knightwatch*. Dan Rather looking dour on *48 Hours*.

She stopped clicking. Clair Huxtable in a turquoise power suit and perfect hair, sitting in her pretty living room with her button-cute daughter Rudy in the crook of her arm.

Joe watched the show until a commercial jarred her back to the motel room. She sat there, the remote in her lap, staring blankly at the TV.

She was pretty. Had to be.

She was younger. Younger than he was, probably.

She was black. No matter what he said, it had to matter.

And a child . . .

Maybe they had a child together.

Joe shut her eyes.

Where the hell was he?

The phone rang. She pounced on it. "Louis?"

"Hello, Joe."

It wasn't him; the voice was too deep. It took a moment for it to register. She turned off the TV. "Mel?"

"I wasn't going to give you a third guess. It would have been insulting."

She smiled. "I'm sorry, I was just waiting for Louis to call. He's been out all night."

"On the case?"

"No. It's a personal thing he had to take care of."

"An old college friend?"

"You could say that."

Mel was quiet for a long time. "He went and saw Kyla, didn't he?"

"You know about her?"

"Yeah."

Joe let out a big sigh.

"What was that for?" Mel asked.

"He told you about her, but somehow he just couldn't quite bring himself to tell me until today."

"He's like that. You know that."

She was quiet.

"Why are you worried about this, Joe?"

"I didn't say I was."

"I know you too well. Don't lie to me."

She shifted the receiver to her other ear and leaned her head back against the headboard. Mel did know her, maybe better than anyone—except her mother. Mel had been there for her right from the start. The day she walked into the Miami Police Department wearing the new uniform, he had been the only man to say welcome. They had started seeing each other two years later, on the quiet be-

cause he was a detective and she was just a patrolman. She had been only twenty-five. He was ten years older. She was in love with him. But three years in, he broke it off. She could still remember the night—sitting in the dark of his car in the lighthouse park on the tip of Key Biscayne. Him telling her he was slowly going blind.

I'm not going to let you be stuck taking care of an old asshole like me, Joe.

Neither of them had ever mentioned marriage, but he had somehow sensed she was expecting it. She was so angry at him. It took her years to see that it was for her own good. He knew that the only thing she really loved was her work.

Four years later, she made detective. They were put on a case together. He was at the end of his career. She was just getting to the best part. They became partners, and she helped him keep his blindness a secret as long as he could. Even after Mel moved to Fort Myers, they stayed in touch. They had a history together, after all.

Joe heard the click of a lighter as Mel fired up a cigarette.

"It was a long time ago, Joe. He doesn't love her," Mel said.

"It's not her I'm worried about," she said.

"The man loves you, Joe."

She shut her eyes. "I'm worried about what will happen to us if there is a child. Because I know Louis well enough to know that this will change him. And I don't know if I want him to change."

A pause on the other end of the line. Joe could almost see Mel sitting in the dark of his apartment. "Have you told him this?" he asked.

"No."

"You should."

She was quiet.

"Well, maybe you're worrying for nothing," he said. "Maybe there's no kid."

"Yeah, maybe," she said softly. She pushed her hair back from her face. "I have to go, Mel," she said.

Another pause. "You're trying to get rid of me."

"No, no, I just don't want to talk right now."

"Okay. I'll back off. But you know where to find me when you do."

"Yeah, I do."

"Night, Joe."

"Mel?"

"Yeah?"

"Thanks."

"What are friends for?"

She hung up and sat back in the bed, staring at the TV. *Perfect Strangers* was on now. She hit the off button, tossed the remote aside, and swung her legs off the bed. Shrugging out of her clothes, she went into the bathroom to take a shower.

She was just wrapping a towel around her wet hair when she heard the door. She hurried out to the bedroom and drew up short.

Louis was standing there. No, not standing. Wavering.

His eyes took a long time to find her, and when they finally did, they were glazed. She could smell the alcohol from six feet away.

"Where were you?" she asked.

"Stopped for a drink." He moved away, peeling off his jacket and throwing it to a chair. It missed and fell to the floor. He ignored it.

"You could have called," she said.

He didn't answer. He dropped onto the edge of the bed and started tugging at his shoes.

"Did you see Kyla?" she asked. It was a struggle to say her name and to keep her voice even.

Louis didn't look up. He dropped one sneaker to the floor and started working on the other.

"Louis, talk to me," Joe said.

The other shoe fell with a thud. He sat there, his back to her, hands on his knees, face down.

"Louis—"

"Joe, just leave me alone, okay?" he said quietly.

She started toward him. "No, I won't leave you alone. Did you see Kyla? Did you ask her—"

His face swung up to her. "There's no baby, okay?"

She stopped cold, the harshness of his voice like a slap.

He brought up a shaky hand. "I just want to go to sleep," he said softly. He turned away, his fingers clumsily working on the buttons of his shirt.

She went into the bathroom. She looked at herself in the mirror. Her face was burning, but she was as white as the tile walls, almost as if she were fading into them. Snatching her crumpled jeans and shirt from the floor, she yanked on her clothes. She ran a quick comb through her wet hair and went back into the bedroom.

"I'm going down to get something to—"

Louis was sprawled on the bed, clothes still on, eyes closed.

She grabbed her purse and left.

Chapter Ten

The woman behind the glass arched her brow in annoyance. She wore a blue Ann Arbor PD uniform, but her name tag said she was an administrative assistant.

"I'm sorry, Mr. Kincaid, Detective Shockey did not leave us your name," she said. "And you are not on the approved visitors list. I can't let you back into the squad room without authorization."

"Then call him," Louis said. "Tell him I want to see him now."

He felt Joe's hand on his arm, tugging him away from the window. He resisted, then followed her. The stale alcohol was still trickling through his veins, creating a swell of nausea, and he put a hand on the wall to steady himself. He could hear Joe calmly talking to the woman behind the glass.

"I'm Undersheriff Frye from Leelanau County. It's important we talk to Detective Shockey. I'm sure he'll see us."

He heard the woman pick up a phone and say there was an undersheriff from up north and an agitated man waiting for Detective Shockey in the lobby.

Louis took a drink from the water fountain and walked to the glass doors to look outside. The sunlight was making his eyes water. The floor felt like it was moving.

"You okay?" Joe asked.

"I'm fine," he said. "It's not the first time I've been hungover."

"It's a first for me," she said. "I've got to call Mike."

He watched her walk away to the pay phone nearby. He had awoken this morning still wearing his clothes.

His shoes were in the corner, and he guessed Joe had been the one who had removed them. He sure as hell had no memory of it. Or much of anything from last night. Joe had been quiet all morning, and he knew she was pissed. He knew this wasn't the time to try to mend anything, though. He could barely think right now.

He heard heavy footsteps and turned. Shockey was coming toward him like an unblocked linebacker. He grabbed Louis's arm and pushed him out through the front doors. Louis was standing on the walk before he could make his mind work enough to react.

He jerked away from Shockey. "Don't you ever grab me again."

"I asked you not to come here."

"And I asked you to tell me everything you knew about Jean Brandt," Louis said. "Why didn't you tell me Jean had a kid?"

Shockey blinked. "What?"

"A kid," Louis said. "There's a toy wagon out at the farm. It has AMY painted on the side. Who is Amy?"

"I don't know."

"Stop lying to me, you sorry piece—"

Louis stopped himself, seeing two uniformed patrolmen approaching. He pulled in a breath, and he and Shockey both waited until the cops disappeared into the station.

"Jean never mentioned a kid," Shockey said. "I'm telling you the truth. We talked about everything, but I swear, no kid."

"Then how do you explain the wagon?" Louis asked.

"Hell, I don't know," Shockey said. "Probably belongs to some neighbor kid."

"There's not a house for miles around that place, you know that."

"Then maybe someone else lived there for a short time after Brandt left."

"Brandt never sold it."

Shockey was quiet.

"There was pink wallpaper in one of the bedrooms," Louis said.

"My ex-wife put pink wallpaper in *our* bedroom," Shockey said. "That doesn't mean anything."

"I *know* there was a kid there," Louis said.

"Then what happened to her?" Shockey asked.

"What do you think?" Louis asked.

Shockey froze for a second, then moved away, raking his hair. He seemed genuinely stunned. Louis wanted to believe he was, but the man had been playing on the edge of the truth since this began.

Shockey turned back to him. His face was slack, but Louis could almost see the gears in his brain working, like he was trying hard to remember something.

"Okay, okay," Shockey said. "Maybe Jean had a kid, I don't know. But I swear to God, she never said anything."

"We need to find out for sure," Louis said.

Shockey didn't seem to hear him. He was still stunned by what Louis had told him.

"Shockey," Louis said, "where do you want to start?"

Shockey scratched his forehead. "Well, without an age or birth date, there's no point in checking state records," he said. "You should start with the schools out there."

Louis let out a stale breath, his head throbbing. "They won't tell me anything," he said. "Their records are confidential."

Louis heard the door behind him open and saw Shockey look beyond him. Shockey thrust out his hand as Joe came up to them.

"Detective Jake Shockey," he said, introducing himself. "You must be the undersheriff."

"Joe Frye, Leelanau County," Joe said with a smile.

Shockey tipped his head toward Louis. "You with the peeper on a personal visit or working the case with him?"

"Mostly the first, a little of the second."

Shockey gave Joe a quick, appraising look, then turned back to Louis. "Folks in those towns out there will talk to a sheriff."

He nodded to Joe. "Just let her flash her badge."

The school in Hell was a three-story, red brick building. To the right was a playground, to the left a football field. There were a bunch of screaming kids on the swings and a squad of teenage boys running sprints on the field. The two contrasting stretches of grass were testament to the school's service to students from kindergarten to high school.

"Got your badge out?" Louis asked.

Joe glanced at him and led the way into the school's dim lobby. At the door stenciled with the word OFFICE, Louis held the door open so Joe could go in first.

A woman with winged glasses and a thick cardigan sweater rose from a desk to greet them. While Joe introduced herself, Louis looked around. Beyond the windows, he could see the football field's scoreboard, one of those old hang-the-numbers kinds, with a cut-out of a roaring lion mounted on top.

The secretary's voice drew him back to her.

"Amy Brandt?" the woman said. "Can't say I've ever

heard the name. Do you know what grade she would have been in?"

"Old enough to have a wagon and young enough to still want to play with it," Joe said.

They waited while the woman rifled through a file cabinet. "I'm sorry," she said. "I have no Amy Brandt."

Louis had the thought that maybe Amy might be a middle name or a nickname. "Do you have *any* Brandts?" he asked.

The woman reached back into the drawer and pulled out two folders. "I have a Geneva and an Owen."

"May we see Owen's?" Louis asked.

The secretary came back to the counter and started to hand the file to Joe. Louis intercepted it and flipped it open. He had no idea what could be in there that could be of any use, but he wanted to look.

The first paper was a history of Owen Brandt's time in school. He started kindergarten in 1953, missed a year in 1962, and finally dropped out in the tenth grade.

Louis sifted through the rest. Report cards, heavy with D's and F's, teachers' notes, class schedules, and a list of family contacts.

"Geneva was his older sister," he said to Joe.

Joe was flipping through Geneva's file. "I know. Nothing important in her file. Mediocre grades, lots of absences. Looks like she left school at sixteen."

Louis found a form titled "Disciplinary History." It was filled with the handwriting of teachers, starting in grade school: fighting, insubordination, fighting, truancy.

"Look at these," Louis said, sliding the paper to Joe.

Age ten. Owen hit Mary Jane Wilson in her face with his fist. Suspended three days. Age fourteen. Owen tore

Betsy Miller's blouse. Sheriff Potts called. Suspended three weeks.

"I have a feeling that was more than a torn blouse," Joe said.

Louis nodded. He closed the file and handed it back to the secretary. Joe thanked her, and they left the school. As they walked across the parking lot, Louis fell a few paces behind. Joe turned to look back at him when she reached the Bronco.

"Something wrong?" she asked.

"Sorry about that remark about you having your badge ready," he said.

"No problem."

"It was just the hangover talking."

"Forget it," Joe said. "Where do you want to go now?"

"I want to talk to some people in town," he said. "Just because the kid never made it to school doesn't mean she didn't exist."

He counted seven buildings in Hell. On one side of County Road D32 stood a general store, a Marathon gas station, the Brimstone Café, and a souvenir shop called the Devil's Lair. On the other side of the blacktop road was the Tree Top Tavern, a real estate office that doubled as a doughnut shop, and a second souvenir store called Lucifer's. Halloween costumes, mostly devils, hung in the window. Near the door sat a barrel of plastic pitchforks.

"These people are scary," Joe said as she climbed out of the Bronco.

Louis closed his door and looked around, a small memory kicking in: passing through this place on one of his foster father Phillip's long Sunday drives. He'd been

about eleven and wanted to stop and get a devil mask. His foster mother, Frances, was a little sharp as she told him she wouldn't hear of it. It had taken him years to figure out that it had nothing to do with him but everything to do with the crucifix that hung over her bed.

Louis pulled the picture of Owen Brandt from his pocket, and they went inside the Devil's Lair.

The old place was packed to its wood rafters. Shelves of T-shirts and sweatshirts emblazoned with I'VE BEEN TO HELL AND BACK. Racks of Halloween costumes. Counters heaped with red coffee mugs, plastic skulls, bobble-head devils, and hats printed with flames.

The middle-aged guy behind the register was bagging up some shirts for a woman. Louis waited until she was gone, then introduced himself.

The man seemed impressed by the fact that there was a real private investigator in his store. "My name's Harry," he said. "What can I help you with?"

Louis showed him Brandt's photo. "Do you know this man?"

"Yeah," Harry said. "That's Owen Brandt."

"You know much about him?" Louis asked.

"Haven't seen him for years," Harry said. "He used to come into town once in a while. Buy some gas or groceries. Big, friendly guy."

Louis held out the picture of Jean Brandt. He had cut off the missing persons part of the bulletin, leaving only her face.

"You ever see him with this woman?" Louis asked.

Harry peered at the photo and started to shake his head, but a memory hit him. "Oh, yeah, I did," he said. "One time, maybe 1977 or so. We were all sitting over at

the Brimstone having coffee, and Owen pulled up. He came inside, but she stayed in the truck. I could see her pretty good because we were in the window booth."

"Was she alone in the truck?" Louis asked.

"Far as I could tell," Harry said. "I remember thinking how strange it was for Owen to leave her out there in the cold while he came in and ate himself a nice hot breakfast."

Louis picked up the two pictures.

"In fact," Harry went on, "I remember that same winter, Fred from over at the gas station drove down to deliver Owen some firewood. Normally, Owen chopped his own or came and picked it up, but his truck was broke or something."

"What happened?" Louis asked.

"Fred said he started to help Owen unload the wood," Harry said. "But Owen told him never mind, and he got the woman from inside the house to come help him. It was freezing cold, and Fred said Owen made that woman make all these trips back and forth carrying logs that weighed more than she did."

"Did you ever see a child with Owen Brandt?" Louis asked.

Harry's brow rose in surprise. "A child? No."

"This Fred fellow from the gas station, did he mention seeing a child?"

Harry shook his head. "He would've, too, because later that night at the bar, we all talked about how crappy it was to make that woman work like that."

"Thank you," Louis said.

He went back through the store, but Joe was gone. He stepped outside to see her coming out of the café, carrying

two Styrofoam cups. She met him at the rear end of the Bronco and gave him one.

"You find out anything over there?" he asked.

"Just that people here liked Owen Brandt, as far as they knew him," she said. "No one ever saw a child with him."

"I want to try the places across the street," Louis said.

Joe let out a small, frustrated sigh. He knew she thought this was a waste of time, but he didn't say anything as he started across the road.

No one in the bar or the other gift shop knew Owen well enough to offer an opinion, nor had anyone ever seen him with a child. He had better luck at the real estate office. The woman behind the desk stood up quickly when Louis showed him the picture.

"Yes," she said. "I know him. He called me once about selling that farm of his."

"When?" Louis asked.

She opened a file cabinet behind her and came out with a thin folder. The single piece of paper in it looked like an appraisal.

"It was November 3, 1980," she said. "He heard about the big food-processing companies that were trying to buy out the small farmers and he wanted me to come down and take a look and figure out how much he could get if he decided to sell."

"Did you go to the farm?" Louis asked.

"Yes," she said. "I remember we stood outside, and, well, just between me and you, the place was kind of decrepit. It was like just out in the middle of nowhere at the end of this dead-end road. I knew the big companies didn't care about the buildings, and I could have used the

commission. But I still remember wanting to get away from that place as fast as I could."

"While you were there did you see a child? Or any evidence that a child lived there?" Louis asked.

"No," she said. "But he wouldn't let me inside."

"Did you see a woman out there?" Louis asked.

"No."

"So Brandt seemed interested in selling?"

"Very much so," she said. "But about a month later, right after Christmas, I called him back and he said he had changed his mind. Said something about not wanting to sell something that had been in his family for generations."

Louis thanked her and left.

Joe was sitting in the driver's seat when he got back to the Bronco, leafing through some of the papers she had brought with her from Echo Bay.

"Find anything?" she asked.

"Just that Owen Brandt was looking to sell that farm in November, 1980, but a month later, after Jean disappeared, he suddenly changed his mind."

Joe set the folder aside and started the engine. She did a U-turn in the parking lot, pulled up to the road, and stopped.

"We go left to get back to Ann Arbor, right?" she asked.

"We're not going to Ann Arbor," he said. "We're going back to the farm."

"Why?"

"I want to look through those storage boxes," he said. "Kids need stuff. It couldn't all just disappear."

Joe shoved the Bronco into park and turned to face him. "Louis," she said, "it's bad enough you entered the

house illegally once. Ripping open sealed boxes without a warrant is another thing altogether. You could jeopardize Shockey's case in court."

"I won't be looking for evidence of a murder, just some indication that a kid lived there. No one ever needs to know."

"And if you just happen to *find* evidence of a murder?" she asked. "What happens then?"

"Then I put it back, reseal it, and we find another way to expose it later."

"You're asking me to stand by and watch you break the law," she said.

He held her eyes for a moment. "You can always go home."

She turned away from him, hands resting on the wheel. Then, with a hard jerk of the gearshift, she put the Bronco into drive and headed south out of Hell.

Chapter Eleven

Just like Crazy Verna . . .

That was the first thing that came into Owen Brandt's head as he stood in the doorway of the bedroom in a house on Locust Street in Hudson, Michigan.

The dead woman lay in her bed. Her skin was gray, her eyes sunken, her ragged black hair thin, giving her face the look of one of the those cheap rubber Halloween witch masks they sold at that souvenir place back in Hell.

He was glad her eyes were closed, at least. Death never bothered him, but he really didn't want to look into his sister's eyes when she was starting to rot.

Geneva . . . poor old Gen.

He hadn't seen her in nine years. What a reunion.

They had never been close. Even though it was just her and him in the house most of the time. Even though she had tried to keep Pa from beating on him, even snuck him some food those times Pa had locked him in the barn. And after Ma died . . .

Died, shit. Ma had always been strange, but after that winter, when she ran all the way to Lethe Creek and tried to drown herself, things got really weird. "Crazy Verna," the folks in Hell called her after that, and Pa had to keep her locked up in the attic until that day she finally did off herself.

Gen tried to take Ma's place for a while. But the first chance she got, what did she do? She ran off at sixteen with that truck driver guy she met at the Texaco and never looked back. Left him there alone on that farm with that old bastard.

"Fuck you, too, Gen," Brandt muttered.

He wiped his nose. The stench was getting to him, and he didn't want to stay long in case smells like this got into his clothes. He didn't have too many shirts and only one pair of jeans, and he didn't want them all stunk up by some rotted corpse.

He nodded a goodbye to his sister and went back through the house, looking for her purse. He found an old leather thing sitting on a table in the living room. Nothing in it but an empty wallet and some pennies. He tossed it aside and looked around.

The sofa was stained with what smelled like urine and had towels draped over the back. He moved to the kitchen, remembering that Geneva used to keep money in coffee cans. The room was cleaner than he expected, all the dishes washed and stacked neatly in the sink. On the shelf above the stove was a Maxwell House coffee can. He opened it. There was fifteen cents in the bottom.

He set it back and scanned the room.

Where was the girl?

Not that it mattered. She was old enough now to be out on her own. Hell, after Pa died, he went out on his own, making his own money, spending most of his time on the street, and hustling cash. A girl could do even better if she knew how.

Brandt rifled through the kitchen drawers, gave the other rooms a quick search, and left the house. The green Gremlin was sitting in the driveway, puffing thick clouds of exhaust into the icy morning air. Brandt slid into the passenger seat.

"Did she give you any money?"

He glanced at the woman behind the wheel. Margi wasn't so bad in the dark, but she looked like hell in the daylight.

"She's dead," Brandt said. "Let's go."

"But where we gonna get money?" Margi asked. "I only have twenty bucks. Where we gonna go on twenty bucks?"

"We can go to Hell," Brandt said.

"Come on, Owen," she said. "Where are we going for real? I'm tired. Where are we going to stay tonight?"

"I try to make a joke, and you're too fucking dumb to even get it," Brandt said. "Drive. Go back to the freeway, and head north."

"I'm tired of driving. I've been doing all the driving ever since we left Ohio. How come you can't drive?"

"'Cause I ain't got no fucking license, and I'm on parole," Brandt said. "Now drive."

Margi set her lips and slapped the gearshift into park. "You promised me a nice hotel."

Brandt backhanded her, catching her hard in the mouth. She covered her face, a small trickle of blood on her fingers.

"You bastard," she whispered.

"Drive, or I'll smack you again."

Brandt looked out his window, fighting the urge just to toss the bitch from the car and leave her on the curb. But he had to remember—he was free but not completely free. Parolees weren't ever completely free. He couldn't break any laws, like driving this shit car. He couldn't drink, and he couldn't go see any of his prison buds. And he couldn't throw a woman from a car. Not again.

Plus Margi had something else that was going to keep her around for a while longer. A workers comp settlement from when she slid on some corn syrup and broke her leg at the Spangler Candy Factory down in Ohio. Seventeen thousand dollars, compliments of the Dum Dum Suckers folks. Damn lawyer didn't know when they'd get it, though.

"Look," he said, making his voice sound a little nicer. "Just shut your mouth and drive, okay?"

"Where we going?"

Brandt sighed. "I told you, we're going to Hell. It's a real place. I got property up there. A real farm. We'll stay there for a while."

"A farm?" Margi asked. "I never been to a farm. Do you have animals there, like cows?"

"The only cow that will be there is you, Margi," Brandt said. "Now drive."

Chapter Twelve

Louis left Joe at the gate again. As he walked toward the side door of the house, he looked back at her. He had been telling himself all morning that his sour mood was just the hangover and that tomorrow, when he felt better, things would be back to normal.

But in the fifteen miles of stiff silence as they drove to the Brandt farm, he had come to a different conclusion. It wasn't just the constant pounding in his head. It was something he could not have imagined feeling a few days ago.

He didn't want Joe here with him.

He jumped the fence and went up onto the side porch. The boards he had pounded back across the door on his first visit were still in place. So was the rusty hammer he had set on the railing. As he reached for it, his ears picked up a small tinkling sound.

He turned quickly, scanning the yard for something that could have made the noise—a hook banging softly against a metal structure, a dangling chain, or maybe even old wind chimes. Nothing.

The sound came again.

A piano. From *inside* the house.

He quickly but quietly pried the nails from the wood and tried to ease open the door. The screech of the door against the linoleum floor sounded loud in the still, cold air.

The tinkle of the piano stopped.

Louis hurried through the kitchen and down the hall to the parlor. The room was latticed with sunlight coming through the old lace curtains, but nothing seemed disturbed. Except the piano stool. It was pushed back slightly from the piano, the wood seat wiped clean of dust.

"Hello?" he called.

For a second, he heard only the echo of his own voice. Then he caught the sound of footsteps, soft and quick across the planked floor, moving toward the back of the house.

He followed the sound, opening doors to empty rooms and small closets. He paused at the base of the stairs to the second floor, holding his breath and trying to pick up a creak of wood or a door closing.

"Hello!" he hollered. "Hello!"

He heard a furious rattling above his head, like someone desperately trying to open a locked door. He darted up the stairs, drawn by instinct to a small rear bedroom that overlooked the barn and the fields. Before he reached the doorway, the rattling of the doorknob stopped, replaced by fast footfalls that seemed to drift without direction through the house.

"Please stop running!" Louis called. "I won't hurt you."

From below came the scrape of a door. He hurried down the stairs, out of breath by the time he reached the kitchen. The outside door was wide open, the room icy with cold air.

Damn it.

He went to the porch and looked first toward the Bronco. Joe was standing against the passenger door, arms crossed. If someone had run in that direction, she

would have seen the person and already been in pursuit.

Louis spun toward the backyard, his hope waning as he scanned the other buildings. Nothing. He went back inside the house and stood in the center of the kitchen, his head tripping with questions beyond *who* had been in here. Whoever it was knew this place. Knew it well enough to move stealthily and quickly through the maze of rooms.

Some neighbor kid who liked exploring? Or some bum using the abandoned place as a refuge? No. Neither would stop to play a piano.

Had the intruder been a woman? Had it been Jean?

He started back out to the porch, thinking he could at least search the buildings. But there was something strange right here, in this kitchen. He turned a circle, stopping as he came to face the west wall. The first time he had been here, all the cupboards had been thrown open. Now, the door of the middle lower cupboard was closed.

He moved closer.

The exterior was slatted wood, painted a dull, dark brown. A few of the narrow boards in the front were missing, giving it the look of a makeshift wooden crate.

He bent and listened for a noise from inside. When he heard nothing, he braced himself for the possibility that someone might bolt at him, then jerked the door open.

A child was huddled inside.

No, not a child. A young girl.

Thin arms clutching her knees, tangled brown hair the same color as the cupboard doors. And her brown eyes beneath the shaggy bangs—terrified, almost feral.

"She's dead," the girl whispered.

• • •

Joe wandered along the edge of the road, kicking at rocks to vent her irritation. At Louis, for coming back so drunk last night he couldn't talk and then this morning because he wouldn't talk. And at herself for taking it from him.

You could always go home.

Why hadn't she?

"Joe!"

She turned at the sound of his voice. He was leaning out the side door of the house, waving at her.

"Joe!" he hollered. "Come in here!"

She walked to the fence and stopped. He knew she couldn't come onto the property.

"I need your help!" he called again. "Please."

He suddenly looked back inside the house and disappeared. Joe gave him a few seconds to come back to the porch. When he didn't, she stuck a boot toe in the fence and climbed over. Halfway across the yellowed grass, a bad feeling in her gut, she broke into a trot.

Louis was standing in the center of the kitchen when she walked in. The kitchen registered only as a brown blur, the moldy smell pricking her nose.

"What is it?" she asked.

Louis pointed to the bottom row of cupboards. An open door blocked her view, and she stepped around it to look inside. A young girl stared back at her.

"Oh, my God," Joe said softly. "Who is she?"

"I don't know," Louis said. "She won't say anything except 'She's dead.'"

"Who's dead?"

"I don't know. That's all she said."

Joe dropped to her knees. The girl's brown eyes sharpened with an unexpected alertness—assessing Joe and her ability to hurt her.

"Who are you?" Joe asked.

The girl took a slow peek up at Louis, then her gaze came back to Joe, studying her as if she were trying to make a connection that kept getting interrupted.

"My name is Joe. Tell me yours."

The girl's eyes brightened. "That's my name, too," she whispered. "Amy Jo Brandt."

Joe looked quickly at Louis, then back at the girl.

"Will you come out of the cupboard for me?" Joe asked.

Amy looked again at Louis and gave an almost indiscernible shake of her head. Joe motioned to Louis to back away. He did, taking a position against the far wall.

Joe extended a hand, and Amy took it, allowing herself to be drawn from the cupboard. When she rose to her feet, she pulled away from Joe, pressing herself against the cupboard, a small hand raised to keep Joe from touching her. Her dirty fingers were trembling.

Joe took a long look at her.

Amy was small, barely reaching Joe's chest. A T-shirt, faded blue and a size too small, pulled tight across her small, budding breasts. She wore ragged jeans on narrow hips. Her face was smudged with dirt, her hair a long tangle.

"Who are your parents, Amy?" Joe asked.

"My mother's name is Jean," Amy said. "My father . . ." She dropped her head, and her face disappeared behind her hair.

"Is your father's name Owen?" Louis asked.

Amy's eyes shot up to Louis, and she took a step back.

"Joe," he said, "you'd better ask the questions. She doesn't seem to want to talk to me."

Joe went closer to Amy. The girl didn't shrink away,

but she was watching Joe's every move, her wariness not easing until she was sure Joe was coming no closer.

This was a familiar scene, Joe thought. For most of the years she had worn a police uniform, this had been her territory: quieting the crying child, taking the statement from the rape victim, or comforting the woman whose boyfriend had knocked out her front teeth. At one time, she had resented it, this assumption by the men that she had some magic connection by virtue of her sex. But the feeling had lessened when she made detective at Miami Dade Police Department as her understanding had grown that her empathy was her greatest tool.

"Is Owen your father, Amy?" Joe asked.

Amy hesitated, then nodded.

Joe wasn't sure where to go next. "How old are you?" she asked.

Amy looked up at Louis, as if this question were too personal to answer in front of a man.

"It's okay," Joe said. "He won't hurt you."

"I'm thirteen."

Amy shivered and glanced down to the cupboard, wanting something from there but afraid to reach for it. Joe bent down and grabbed a jacket, also taking note of the other items inside. A small, filthy blanket, a blue backpack with a cartoon animal on it, and a plastic milk bottle filled with water.

Amy's jacket resembled something an older woman would wear, clean but ripped in the sleeve. Joe checked it for any weapons or ID but didn't find either. She draped it over Amy's shoulders. Amy chose to slip her arms into the sleeves and held it closed over her chest.

"Where do you live, Amy?" Joe asked.

"I live here now," Amy said. "I have kin here."

Suddenly, Amy pushed away from the wall and rushed to the closed door that led to the hall. The knob was loose, and she couldn't get it to turn.

"Amy," Joe said. "Stop."

"I need to hide."

Joe grabbed her gently by the shoulders. Amy spun around and smacked Joe in the face. Then she froze, hands in the air, eyes clouded with confusion.

"I'm sorry, I'm sorry," Amy said. "Please don't put me in the hole. Please."

Joe rubbed her cheek, her mind already conjuring up images of what "the hole" could be. "It's okay, Amy," she said. "No one is going to hurt you."

"Joe, she said someone was dead," Louis said. "Ask her about that."

Joe looked over her shoulder at Louis. "We don't know what this girl has been through, Louis," she said in a low voice. "We don't even know where she came from. She might have run away—"

"I didn't run away," Amy whispered, slumping against the door. "I came home. I'm so tired. Can I sleep now?"

Louis took a step forward. Amy either heard the creak of the floorboard or sensed his movement, and her eyes snapped up, wary and wide.

Joe motioned Louis back again.

"You have to ask her," Louis said.

Joe turned back to the girl. "Amy, you said that some-one was dead. Do you remember that?"

Amy's eyes jumped around the kitchen. "I don't want to be here. Something bad happened here." Her eyes came back to Joe. "Can we go to the parlor?"

"Why the parlor?" Joe asked.

"I'm supposed to wait. I think I'm supposed to wait there. Can we go to the parlor, please?"

Joe nodded. Amy seemed to know exactly where she was going, walking a direct but unsteady path down the hall.

There was only one place to sit—the piano stool. Joe thought Amy would take that seat as hers, but she didn't. She sat down on the floor near the front window, back against the wall, knees up. Here, away from the kitchen, at least she seemed calmer. Joe stood by the piano. Louis stayed back by the door.

"Can you tell me now, Amy?" Joe asked. "Who is dead?"

"Aunt Geneva."

"Do you know how she died?" Joe asked gently.

"No," Amy whispered. "She got sick. She was sick for a long time. I had to cook noodles and wash her with the blue cloth. She only liked the blue cloth, not the yellow ones. She smelled bad sometimes."

"So you lived with Aunt Geneva," Joe said.

Amy nodded.

"How old were you when she got sick?"

"I don't know."

"Think. How big were you?"

"I had to use a step stool to do the dishes."

Joe let out a soft sigh. "Do you remember where Aunt Geneva lived?"

"One-seven-three-oh-four Locust. Like the bug. One-seven-three-oh-four Locust in Hudson, Michigan. From the school, take Bagley Avenue to Elm Street, go three more blocks, and turn right on Locust. Last house on the left."

Joe glanced at Louis. He had a notebook out and was

writing things down. At least they had an address now. But Joe wasn't sure where to go next with her questions. She looked around the parlor. Amy had said she had to wait in here. For what? Or for whom?

Joe crouched down so she was even with Amy. "Why do you have to wait here, Amy?"

"I'm waiting for Momma," Amy said. She put her head down on her knees.

Joe looked up at Louis. He had stopped writing, and she knew what he was thinking: Was it possible Jean Brandt was still alive? Had she told her daughter to meet her here?

Joe touched Amy's arm. The girl's eyes came up. The wariness was gone. She just looked exhausted now.

"Did your mother tell you she was coming here?"

Amy nodded. "She said she'd be here in the morning."

"When did you last see her?"

"The other night."

"*Where* did you see her?" Joe asked.

"In my dream."

Joe sighed. "Have you seen your mother when you're awake?"

"No, but sometimes I can hear her."

Joe looked up at Louis again and gave a subtle shake of her head.

"Ask her about her father, Joe," Louis said.

"I don't think we should right now," Joe said evenly.

"He hurt Momma," Amy said suddenly. "He hurt her bad."

Joe's eyes shot back to Amy.

"I'm so tired," Amy whispered. "It's over now."

She closed her eyes, as if she were succumbing to a powerful drug. Seconds later, she went limp. Joe caught

her as she tipped over and lowered her gently to the floor. Joe checked her pulse. It was strong. But they still had to get her to a doctor and have her checked out.

Joe rose and went to Louis. "You stay here with her," she said. "I'll drive down the road and call the Livingston County sheriff."

"I think we need to keep her with us," Louis said.

"What?"

"She could be a witness, Joe. She could have seen Jean's murder."

"Do you hear yourself?" she asked. "You're a thirty-year-old man who wants to keep a runaway teenager with you against her will. That's kidnapping."

Her words seemed to register some reality with him. He dropped his head for a moment, then rubbed his brow. "Joe, you know what foster care is like," he said. "And she may not even get that far. She'll probably end up in a state hospital."

"Louis, we have no choice. By law, I have to turn her in."

"Then let's take her back to Ann Arbor," he said. "She's Jean's daughter, and Shockey will make sure she gets the best home available. And legally, she'll be in police custody."

"No," Joe said. "She belongs to Livingston County. And that's where I'm taking her."

Louis stared at her. He had no real authority here, and Joe knew that. She also knew how much that was bothering him. If he did actually try to take Amy somewhere other than the Livingston County sheriff, Joe could—and probably would—do whatever she needed to do to stop him. Even if it meant putting him under arrest.

"Will you carry her to the car, please?" Joe asked.

Louis walked to Amy and knelt to pick her up. It was an awkward lift, but Amy seemed to be in a comalike sleep, and she didn't wake up.

"The front door's padlocked," Louis said. "We'll have to go back out through the kitchen."

Joe followed him to the kitchen, holding open the door as Louis angled Amy through the frame. Joe tried to work the door closed, but it was caught on the buckled linoleum, and she finally just left it.

As she rounded the corner of the house, she saw Louis had stopped. He was staring at a car parked in the road behind her Bronco. A rusty green Gremlin. Two people inside. Ohio license plates.

The passenger door opened, and a man stepped out, looking at them over the roof of the car.

It was Owen Brandt.

Chapter Thirteen

Louis stayed where he was, on the grass, cradling Amy in his arms.

Owen Brandt walked toward the gate, keys in hand. He was a stocky man, buffed by six years of lifting weights in the prison gym. His face was the color of a raw steak, the cheeks scored by deep lines down the sides of his mouth. Small spikes of black hair stood on end around his head.

He unlocked the gate and pushed it open, his dark

eyes never leaving Louis and Joe. Stepping inside the gate, he faced them, jingling the keys like a pissed-off jail guard.

"Who the hell are you?" he asked.

Louis and Joe came forward together. Brandt assumed a blockade position between the gate and the road behind him. He wore a dirty denim jacket and baggy jeans, and Louis could not tell if he had a weapon on his belt.

"I asked who the hell you people are," Brandt said again.

Joe held up her badge, only long enough to let Brandt see that it was gold but not long enough for him to read the county name. But Brandt had seen too many cops and had been in prison too long not to notice the sleight of hand.

"Let me see that again," Brandt said. His lips curled when Joe held it up. "Where the fuck is Leelanau County? That even a real badge?"

"It's real," Joe said. "And it's good throughout the state. Now step aside and let us by."

Brandt didn't move, his gaze narrowing in on Amy, first with curiosity, then with shock as recognition set in.

"That my girl you got there?" he demanded.

"Step aside," Joe said.

"Now wait a minute," Brandt said. "That's my girl, and you don't have no right to take her anywhere."

"She's a runaway in need of care," Joe said.

"She ain't no runaway if she's home, and that's her home," Brandt said, gesturing to the house. "Now put her down."

The thud of a door closing drew Louis's attention be-

hind Brandt. A woman had climbed from the Gremlin. She was short, her bleached blond hair a pile of frizz atop her thin face. She wore an oversized black leather jacket over licorice-stick leggings. As she wobbled across the road on spiked black heels, Louis could hear the clatter of her plastic bracelets.

Joe's gun suddenly came level, held out in front of her in one hand. With her other hand, she motioned for the woman to halt.

"Stay where you are," she called. And to Brandt, "Now, you, put your hands on the gate and spread your feet."

Brandt stared at her with hatred.

"Now!"

Brandt stepped reluctantly to the gate and assumed the position of a man who had been frisked a hundred times. Louis shifted the sleeping Amy to get a better hold and continued toward Joe's Bronco, praying the girl would not wake up now and see her father.

When he got to the truck, Amy started to slip, and he adjusted her again, trying to balance her while he opened the door. The blond woman was suddenly next to him, the air thick with a sweet perfume.

"I'll get that for you," she said, opening the door.

Brandt's voice shredded the air. "You stupid bitch!" he shouted. "Don't you help them do nothing. Get your ass back to the car!"

The woman's face shot up, and she stared at Brandt for a moment, then turned away, head down.

Louis set Amy in the backseat of the Bronco and buckled her in, then reached to the console for his Glock. When he got back to Joe, she had finished her pat-down of Brandt. She had holstered her gun and had nothing

else in her hands, which meant she had found no weapons on Brandt. Too bad. It would have been a parole violation, and they could have locked him up.

Joe walked away to talk to the blond woman. Louis stayed with Brandt, his Glock at his side. But Brandt didn't seem interested in him. He was watching Joe.

"This ain't right, what you're doing here," Brandt said. "You can't be inside my house without a warrant. That's the law."

"Shut up," Louis said.

Brandt ignored him. "And it don't matter where you take her, because I'll just go and get her back," he said. "And they'll give her to me, too, because I'm her father, and people out this way understand that. Fathers have rights. That's the law, too."

Joe finished talking to the woman and motioned for Louis to join her in the Bronco. She took the driver's seat and had the engine running by the time he climbed in. He waited until they were a mile down the road, making sure the Gremlin had not followed them, before he put his gun back into the console.

Amy was still sound asleep.

He looked to Joe. Her profile was sharply defined by the harsh sun. Eyes unblinking, lips drawn, jaw tight. Adrenaline from a potentially dangerous confrontation or something else?

"You okay, Joe?" he asked.

"I can't stomach the thought of that man having Amy in that house and being alone with her."

Louis was quiet. He knew she was thinking the same thing he was—that if they took her to Livingston County authorities now, Brandt would have her within hours.

"But damn it, Louis, what you want me to do could cost me my reputation—and the election next fall," Joe said. "And it's not only disrespectful to Livingston County, it's against every procedure I've ever been taught. I just can't take people wherever I want to."

"Joe, I don't want you to do anything but help her," Louis said. "How you choose to do that is totally up to you."

Joe slowed for a stop sign at a T intersection. There were no signs, but he knew that north led them to the city of Howell, the county seat for Livingston. South would take them to I-94, the freeway that went to Ann Arbor.

"Help me out here, Louis," she said. "How can we explain to this local sheriff why we took Amy to Ann Arbor?"

"We could tell them she's a key witness in a homicide," he offered. "And that we're taking her into protective custody. With Brandt back in town, they'll believe that."

"Amy was only four when Jean disappeared," Joe said. "We have no reason to think she witnessed anything."

"We can hope."

"Hope . . ." Joe whispered.

She sat for a moment longer, then hit her right blinker and turned south.

Joe dropped Louis at the Ann Arbor police station so he could tell Shockey about Amy and make arrangements with the police in Hudson to do a welfare check on Geneva Brandt.

Then she swung by the College Inn, left Louis a note, grabbed her overnight bag, and checked herself and Amy into the only hotel in the city that had two-room suites and an on-site bar, the Ann Arbor Hilton.

Amy was groggy but managed the walk down the long hotel hall without asking where she was going. Joe unlocked the door and, with a gentle push, guided her inside. Amy wandered to the middle of the living room and turned a slow circle as she looked around.

Joe unzipped her bag, dug out a hair brush and the oversized Cleveland Browns T-shirt she used as her nightgown. Then she went into the bathroom, soaped up a warm washcloth, and snatched a towel. When she returned to the living room, Amy was gone. Joe spun to the door. The chain was still on.

She found Amy in the bedroom, perched nervously on the edge of the bed. Joe sat down next to her and carefully pulled her hair back to wash her face.

Good Lord.

One washcloth was not going to be enough. The girl was filthy, dirt caked behind her ears and in her hair. And now Joe noticed a smell, too.

"Amy, will you take a shower?"

Amy turned to her, confused.

Joe sighed and pulled her to her feet. Amy trailed along behind her without protest. She stood limply in the bathroom while Joe turned on the water, her eyes brightening with a glint of interest at the rise of steam. But she made no move to undress herself.

Joe started with the dirty blue T-shirt, easing it up Amy's body. Amy let her take it off, her arms going up and flopping down like a rag doll. She wore no bra.

Joe unsnapped the blue jeans and pulled them down Amy's skinny legs. Amy surprised her by balancing herself on Joe's shoulder as she stepped out of them. Her panties were blue and too small, the elastic biting into the skin.

As Joe reached for them, she looked up at Amy's face.

She wasn't sure why, but she half expected the girl to tense at this point. Most abused girls would have started fighting her long before this. But Amy was simply watching her, that same empty expression on her face.

Joe lowered the panties. There was a small spot of blood in the crotch.

"It came again," Amy said. "I'm sorry."

Joe stood up, relieved that the blood was not the result of a recent assault and grateful that Amy had finally spoken.

"It?" Joe asked. "You mean your period?"

"Just *it*."

Joe set the panties in the sink and went back to her overnight bag. She found a tampon and returned to the bathroom. Amy's sad brown eyes registered no understanding at the sight of it.

"Do you know what this is?" Joe asked.

"No."

Joe sighed. "Okay, never mind. We'll make do for a while 'til I can get to the store. Why don't you get in the shower?"

Amy looked to the bath but didn't move. Joe pulled the curtain back and took Amy's hand, urging her firmly into the tub. It took Amy only seconds to appreciate the warm rush of water. With the deepest sigh Joe had ever heard, Amy closed her eyes and turned into the spray, like a child in the rain.

Joe watched her, waiting for her to pick up the soap or reach for the washcloth. But it was clear that Amy wanted nothing more than to feel the water, so Joe took on the task of washing her. Amy didn't seem to mind

being touched, but she also didn't respond to anything. Joe had to tell her the simplest things—turn around, lift your arm, rinse your hair.

It was just as difficult to dry her. Joe finally gave up and returned to the living room to rummage through Amy's backpack, hoping to find clean underwear.

The top of the bag was cluttered with sardine cans, saltine crackers, and uncooked popcorn. Under that, Joe found a pair of jeans, the denim elaborately marked with colorful swirls, circles, and glued glitter. She dug deeper and found one pair of clean panties.

Joe started to restuff the bag, but her eye caught something in the bottom. It was an old cardboard kaleidoscope, like something you'd find in a bin at some long-forgotten dime store. Joe set it aside. She noticed a book at the bottom of the bag and pulled it out.

It was *A Tree Grows in Brooklyn*. Joe knew the story. It was about a young girl named Francie who struggled to survive in a home without love and a place without hope.

"That's my book," Amy said from the doorway. "Please don't take it away."

Joe turned to her. Amy had put on the clean Browns T-shirt Joe had left in the bathroom. It hung like a sheet on her body, the shoulders wet from her dripping hair.

"Have you read this book?" Joe asked.

"Many times."

"What is it about?"

"Finding things where there isn't anything to find. Can I have my book?"

"In a minute," Joe said. She held out the panties. "Go put these on, and use a dry washcloth for . . . the it. Okay?"

"I understand," Amy said.

Amy left and returned a minute later, hand out again

for her book. Joe gave it to her. Amy started to put it into the backpack but paused. She rummaged through the backpack and then looked up at Joe.

"Where's Toby?"

"Who?"

"Toby," Amy said. "Did you take him?"

"I didn't take anything out of there, I promise," Joe said. "What—who—is Toby, Amy?"

"He's my rabbit," Amy whispered. "He's missing an ear. I must have lost him."

She looked inconsolable. But then she slowly repacked the backpack, zipped it up, and stowed it under the coffee table. When she drew herself to her feet, she looked around again, as if she was just realizing she was in a hotel room.

"Where am I?" Amy asked.

"Ann Arbor."

Amy's eyes sparked with something Joe had not seen until this moment—life.

"Go Blue," Amy said.

Joe blinked in surprise. "Where have you heard that before?"

"Mr. Bustin had a Go Blue room at his house," Amy said. "He went to school here. He missed this place very much."

Amy walked to the window, holding back the heavy drape so she could look out. Joe knew there was nothing to see but an alleyway Dumpster with a glimpse of a gas station at the corner.

"I thought Ann Arbor must be a beautiful place for Mr. Bustin to miss it so much, but it isn't," Amy said. "It looks just like Hudson."

"Is Hudson far from here?" Joe asked.

"It's way down by Ohio, I think," Amy said. She had been still looking out the window and turned suddenly toward Joe, her expression clouded. "Aunt Geneva died in her sleep. She shouldn't be there alone. Can someone go help her?"

"Someone is already on their way."

"Good," Amy said. "I didn't know what to do with her, but I didn't think she'd mind if I left. But I think I'm selfish now."

"Why?"

"Because I don't miss her," Amy said. "I only feel free. Is that selfish?"

Joe watched her, fascinated by the way Amy's strange young mind seemed to work and the way she was changing—no, maturing—right before her eyes. She was starting to like this girl.

"Amy, how did you get from Hudson to the farm?"

"I went out to the highway and waited until someone came along. I was in—" She was counting on her fingers. "I was in three big trucks, two cars, and a small truck."

Joe shook her head slowly. "How did you know where to go?"

"Aunt Geneva talked about the farm all the time." Again, Amy's face clouded. "I don't remember much about it. I guess I was pretty little when I went to live with Aunt Geneva."

Joe wondered how Amy had come to live with Geneva. Had Owen just dumped the girl on his sister after Jean disappeared? "Amy, do you remember anything about how you came to live with your aunt?"

Amy hesitated, then looked back out the window. "I was just little," she whispered. "I remember Poppa woke

me up and took me down to the car. He said we were going for a ride. It was very cold, and I was scared, because Momma wasn't going with us. We drove for a long time. When I woke up, I was in a big bed by myself."

"Amy, come sit down," Joe said gently, patting the sofa.

Amy let the drape fall and slowly came to the sofa, perching on its edge. Her eyes were locked on Joe, expectant, as if she was waiting for more questions.

"Why did you leave Hudson to go back to the farm?" Joe asked.

"I don't know," Amy said. "I just knew I had to go. Aunt Geneva told me I should never go back there. She told me bad things happened there a long time ago and that it was an evil place. But I had to go back anyway."

"What exactly did your aunt tell you?" Joe asked.

"She told me lots of stories," Amy said. "But I can't remember them."

"Do you remember the things you told me at the farm?"

"I was alone at the farm. I've never talked to you before."

Joe was quiet. She was beginning to suspect Amy had some sort of blackout at the farm, maybe a weird kind of seizure that had triggered her childlike state and a temporary amnesia. A medical condition like that might explain her need for deep sleep and her nonsensical jabber.

"Can I eat now?" Amy asked.

"Of course you can." Joe started for the phone. "How about I order—"

Amy knelt and dragged her backpack from under the coffee table. Joe watched as Amy unzipped it and pulled out a can of sardines, setting it on the table.

"Amy, wouldn't you rather have a pizza?" Joe asked.

"I can only eat what is on the list," Amy said. She began carefully to roll back the tin's top.

Joe set the phone down, went to the kitchenette, and brought back a plate and a fork. She set it in front of Amy on the coffee table. Joe watched as Amy sat cross-legged on the floor, picking the sardines from the can with her fingers, ignoring the plate and the fork. When she went to wipe her oily hands on her shirt, Joe caught her wrist and handed her a towel.

Amy used the tip, then tucked the towel into her collar, like a bib. She didn't look up, and she didn't make a sound for five minutes. Then she wiped her fingers again, dabbed at her mouth, and carefully rolled the tin top on the can flat. Still without a word, she picked up the plate and the can and walked to the sink.

The unused plate went back into the cupboard, and Amy reached down to the lower cupboard to throw away the can. Her fingers paused an inch from the knob. She was frozen.

"Just put the can in the sink, Amy."

"There'll be ants if I leave it."

"No, there won't. Put the can in the sink."

Amy closed her eyes. "I'm very tired."

Joe went to her and took the can. Amy's eyes were glazing over. Set off by memories of the cupboard back at the farm?

"Why don't you go into the bedroom and sleep now?" Joe said.

"Will you stay here with me?"

"Yes."

Amy walked to the bedroom, her step a little un-

steady. Joe followed, stopping at the door to watch her. Amy went to the closet and pulled a spare blanket from the top shelf.

Joe thought she simply wanted to sleep on top of the flowered spread, but Amy set the blanket on the floor in the corner, then knelt to arrange it in an almost perfect square. When she seemed satisfied, she curled up on it, pulling the extra over her shoulders.

"Amy, why are you sleeping on the floor?"

"So I can hear you if you call to me in the night. Would you please turn out the light? I'm not afraid of the dark."

Joe flipped the switch, but she didn't move away from the door. The shadows grew deep, the only light a faint glow from the living room behind her. She could not take her eyes off the small girl huddled on the floor. And she could not stop the images her mind was churning up of things that may have happened at the farmhouse or on Locust Street.

Then she heard something.

She thought it was the chirp of a bird but it was too soft, too childlike.

Joe stepped closer to Amy.

The sound was coming from the folds of the blanket. Amy was singing.

"Catch Don . . . set a seal . . . oh do you know so sweet, you and me, Pearl, no matter hurt . . . New rips in two in stormy . . ."

Amy's voice trailed off as she fell asleep.

Chapter Fourteen

Joe was napping on the sofa when she heard the rattle of the hotel-room door. It was followed by a soft knocking, and she rose, glancing at the clock. Almost midnight. Through the peephole, she saw Shockey's pitted face.

She opened the door for Shockey, and Louis followed, carrying a cardboard box, which he set on the coffee table.

"You got my note," Joe said.

"Yeah," Louis said. He glanced around the room. "This is a big improvement. Expensive?"

"We'll split the cost," Joe said with a small smile.

"Where's Amy?" Louis asked.

"Asleep," Joe said, nodding toward the door she had left ajar.

Louis took off his jacket and moved immediately to the pizza box sitting on the table. Joe went to the small fridge to get him a beer.

"You want one, Detective?" she asked.

Shockey shook his head.

Joe grabbed a Heineken for Louis and poured herself a glass of wine. "So, is there really an Aunt Geneva?" she asked.

Louis was eating, and Shockey answered. "Yeah," he said. "Right where the girl said she'd be. Looks like she died of some kind of cancer. But they're doing an autopsy anyway. From what Louis told me about this girl, she sounds a little loony, and we need to make sure the girl didn't murder the old bag."

"You should have seen this place, Joe," Louis said. "This old house out in the sticks, and the inside was like no one had cleaned it in years. No wonder the poor kid—"

Joe held up a hand, looked toward the open door of the bedroom, and went to close the door before she turned back to Shockey and Louis. "I think Amy is a lot closer to normal than we first thought," she said.

"What do you mean?" Louis asked.

"When she woke up here, she was very sensible," Joe said. "Except for being shy and maybe a little emotionally stunted, she carried on a normal conversation."

Louis picked up a second slice of pizza. "She say anything more about Brandt?"

Joe shook her head. "Nothing important. She didn't remember us being at the farmhouse or that she had even spoken to me before."

Shockey scratched his chin. "That doesn't sound normal to me," he said.

"I know it sounds strange," Joe said, "but what if she has some medical condition that causes her to have waking blackouts?"

"Easy enough to check out," Shockey said. "I've worked with a lot of doctors in town. I'll find her one."

"Yeah," Louis said, "but not tonight. It's late. Let her sleep."

Shockey glanced at Louis. Joe suspected the topic of what to do with Amy had been discussed already.

"Look, Louis," Shockey said, "it was everything I could do to stop my lieutenant from calling Family Services this afternoon. He agreed to wait until I got a chance to evaluate the girl myself. But we have to call them. You know we do."

"It's midnight," Louis said.

"They get calls at midnight all the time. It's their job."

Louis tossed the slice of pizza back into the box, walked to the bedroom door, and opened it. Joe could tell by the subtle stiffening of his shoulders that he was looking at Amy curled up on the floor.

"Is there any way they would give us temporary custody of her?" Louis asked as he quietly closed the door.

"Us?" Joe asked.

Louis looked to her. "Yes."

"Louis, I have a job to go back to," she said. "I'm supposed to be there tomorrow. I can't stay here to babysit this girl because you can't stand the idea of her going into the system."

"But what about Brandt?" Louis asked. "Eventually, they'll have to notify him, and he'll get custody. What then?"

"Me staying here a few more days won't stop that," Joe said. "That's a fight for family court. And as much as neither of us likes it, it's a fight you'll probably lose."

"I know a pretty good children's rights lawyer," Shockey offered. "I could ask him if—"

"Forget it," Louis said, shaking his head and moving away.

Joe went to the desk to get the list she had made earlier. Someone needed to make a run to the store, and maybe this was a good time to send Louis out and let him get some air.

"Amy needs some things," she said, holding out the paper. "There's a convenience store open down the road. Would you mind getting these things?"

Louis looked up at Joe. "I don't mean to be rude, Joe, but we've just spent five hours on the road."

"Well, I can't go," Joe said. "If she wakes up, she'll be terrified to find two strange men here. Please."

Shockey held out a hand. "Give it to me. I'll go."

Joe gave him the list, and he scanned it. His eyes came up with a question. "Ah, number four here," he said, his cheeks reddening. "What color is the box? I only know those things by the color."

Joe hid her smile. The man couldn't even say the word Kotex. "It's pink, if I remember right."

Shockey nodded and left.

Louis didn't look as if he had even heard the conversation. He was picking pepperoni off the pizza. Joe turned to look inside the box Louis had brought from Aunt Geneva's.

There were some clothes, but they were all in terrible shape, a print blouse missing most of its buttons, a pink sweater with holes, some faded T-shirts, two pairs of threadbare slacks, a dirty parka that looked like it belonged to a girl half Amy's age. There was a cheap plastic bead bracelet, a tangle of ribbons, and three books.

"Is this all you found?" Joe asked, picking through the meager offerings.

"Those were the only clothes that looked good enough to bring back," Louis said.

"Did you find a toy rabbit?" Joe asked. "With one ear?"

Louis shook his head. "No toys. Just those books."

Joe picked up the three books. *Gone with the Wind, Little Women,* and a children's book called *The Hundred Dresses.* She took *Little Women* with her to the sofa. The room was quiet as Louis ate his cold pizza and Joe skimmed the book. She had never read *Little Women* before and was surprised to find out that one of the sisters in the book was named Amy, another Jo. It was a curious

coincidence that Amy would have both names. Joe wondered if Amy's mother, Jean, had selected the combina-
tion intentionally.

"Why did you bring the books back?" Joe asked.

"I don't know. Just a feeling that they might mean
something to her and she'd want to have them."

He picked up the copy of *Gone with the Wind*. "I
tried to read this one once. Just couldn't seem to get into
it for some strange reason," he said, tossing it back onto
the table with a wry smile.

"Did you read a lot when you were a kid?" Joe asked.

Louis nodded. "Especially when I was being bounced
around between homes."

Joe kept her head down. "What was your favorite
story?"

"Things like *Treasure Island. Gulliver's Travels*," he said.
"I stole books from the library. And I bet that's stolen, too."

Joe looked inside the back of the book. It was from
the Hudson Public Library, taken out in 1986.

She picked up *The Hundred Dresses*. The copy on the
back said it was about a little girl who was so poor she
wore the same tattered blue dress to school every day,
and when she was teased, she told the other girls that she
had a hundred other beautiful dresses at home.

She felt Louis's eyes on her and looked up.

"I'm sorry, Joe," he said. "I've been a bastard for two
days."

"Apology accepted," she said softly, tossing the book
aside.

He sighed and pushed off the sofa to take his empty
bottle to the kitchen.

A cry drifted from the bedroom. Louis looked quickly
at Joe. "What was that?"

She hurried to the bedroom. In the darkness, she dropped to her knees next to Amy. She was writhing in the tangles of her blanket. Her breathing was labored, and she was whimpering.

"Amy. Wake up," Joe said.

"Stop, stop . . . stop. Don't—"

"Amy!" Joe said sharply.

Amy's eyes opened. Wide but unfocused. She was instantly still. When she finally recognized Joe, she scrambled to a sitting position, her chest heaving as she struggled to pull in a breath.

"Amy, what's the matter?"

The girl was pale from the effort of trying to breathe. The wheezing made an awful sound. "I can't . . ."

Joe's eyes shot up to Louis at the door. "She can't breathe!"

"It sounds like an asthma attack, Joe," Louis said. "Ben gets them. Try to get her to calm down."

"Amy," Joe said, putting her arm around her. "Try to slow down."

"I saw it. I saw it." Amy gasped.

"Saw what, Amy?"

"The ropes. The ropes on the hook in the barn. There was screaming. So much screaming."

"Slow down," Joe said. "Just try to breathe."

"The ropes . . . oh . . . they hurt. They hurt so much."

Amy's eyes filled with tears, as if she could feel the pain herself. "And he was digging . . . digging a hole in the dirt. It was dark. So dark and so cold."

Amy was making no sense, and Joe didn't know if she was in a state similar to the one she had experienced at the farmhouse or simply reliving a nightmare. She had to be sure.

"Louis, turn the light on."

The room brightened.

Amy blinked and looked immediately to Louis. "You have to go! You have to go now. Run!"

Louis put up his hands. "Okay. I'm going."

He left the bedroom. Amy watched him, staring at the door even after he disappeared. Joe touched her cheek to bring her back.

"Amy," Joe said. "Where are you?"

"I'm in Ann Arbor," she said, wheezing. Her breathing seemed to be less labored.

Amy shut her eyes, her thin chest rising and falling as she concentrated on trying to breathe. The girl must have had attacks before, Joe thought, because she seemed to be calming herself down now.

Joe waited, her arm around Amy. The girl's skin was pale and clammy. But at least her breathing had returned to near normal.

"Are you okay now?" Joe asked.

Amy nodded, her eyes closed.

"You had a bad dream," Joe said.

Amy's eyes shot open. "It wasn't a dream. I saw it. I saw the barn and the ropes and the hook. I saw the hole in the ground."

Joe hesitated. The last thing she wanted to do was make the girl remember things that might trigger another asthma attack or worse. But this could be an opening to a crucial memory about her mother's death.

"Amy," Joe said gently, "is someone buried out there at the farm?"

Amy nodded.

"Who was buried?"

"I don't know."

"But there's a grave out there?" Joe asked.

"Yes."

"Could you show us?"

Amy looked to the door again. "Is he gone? It's important that he's gone now."

"Yes. Amy, talk to me. Can you show us where the grave is?"

Amy pushed back her hair, her gaze moving around the room as if she was suddenly unsure what had happened. Her eyelids drooped, filming over with the need for sleep. She was leaving again, and Joe wished she could reach into that complicated little brain and bring her back.

"Okay, Amy, lie down."

Amy nodded and adjusted herself, but she didn't stretch out on the blanket. She curled forward, tucked her knees up, and laid her head on Joe's knee.

Joe sat still, not sure what to do or how much affection to show this girl. She knew she wouldn't be here long enough to walk Amy through the tough days and months to come, and she didn't want Amy to become too attached.

But even as she thought about that, her hand went to Amy's hair, and she found herself gently brushing a few strands back so she could see Amy's face.

"Now what?" Louis asked.

Shockey had returned from the store and was standing at the bedroom door watching Amy sleep. They had briefed him on what Amy had said.

"I don't know what happens now," Shockey said. "I'd like to think we have a witness to Jean's murder, but this

is a pretty weird situation. We'd have to convince a judge that what she told you wasn't a nightmare but a real memory."

"What happens to her if we do?" Louis asked.

"We take her into protective custody as a material witness," Shockey said. "Something like that would at least give a judge a good reason not to return her to Brandt."

"We don't have enough information," Joe said. "I don't think any judge will believe she saw Brandt kill her mother based on what she said. Not to mention that she was only four when it happened, and she's not very stable now."

Louis rose and walked a small, slow circle around the room. "What about a psychiatrist?" he asked. "Someone who can draw more of the memory from her."

"That's a good idea," Shockey said.

"Hypnosis?" Joe asked. "Eyewitness testimony elicited under hypnosis is not admissible. You both know that."

"Yeah, but maybe we'd get a lead out of it that we could verify ourselves," Shockey said. "She told you someone's buried out there. Maybe she can take us to Jean's body. And we sure as hell can use that."

Joe chewed her lip, her eyes on the closed bedroom door.

"Do you know someone, Shockey?" Louis asked.

"Yeah, yeah, I do," Shockey said. "She's retired now but used to specialize in kid psychiatry. We used her in court a lot. Her name's Mary Sher. I'll call her first thing in the morning."

Joe's eyes went from Shockey to Louis, a slow burn of irritation building inside her. It was probably a good idea to have Amy assessed for mental competency. But these two seemed more concerned with the case than with the

girl's fragility. And there was no way Amy was going to let two men take her anywhere without going into hysterics.

Joe pushed away from the sofa and walked to the phone. Neither Shockey nor Louis paid her any attention as she called Mike Villella. When she hung up, she turned back to them.

"Okay, I'm staying until Friday," she said. "I'll take Amy to the doctor—alone."

Chapter Fifteen

There was a bright red whirligig bird stuck on a stick in the lawn. Its wooden wings spun in the wind. Amy was watching it intently.

Finally, she turned to Joe and gave a small smile. "There are a lot of wah-wahs in the yard," she said.

Joe had been looking at all the lawn ornaments— gnomes in the barren flower beds, a blue gazing ball on a stone pedestal, a pair of plastic fairies, and a flock of pink plastic flamingos—and at first she didn't think she heard Amy right.

"Wah-wahs?" she asked.

Amy nodded. "That's what Aunt Geneva called them, the things people put in their yards. She said they were stupid, but I like them. They make a house look happy, like it has toys to play with."

Joe let it go. "Come on, Amy, let's go in."

She led the girl up onto the porch, which was strung with a dozen wind chimes. Amy waited patiently while

Joe rang the bell, her gaze traveling over the chimes dancing to a discordant symphony of tinkles and clicks. Joe hadn't told Amy where they were going or why. And when they had pulled up in front of Mary Sher's bungalow, Joe was glad to see there was no sign announcing it as a doctor's office. There had been no repeat of Amy's strange behavior since last night, and Joe was hoping this visit wouldn't bring on another.

Joe rang the bell again.

A shrink . . .

Her own experience with psychiatrists was limited to the one trip mandated by a state police captain after the ambush that had left two of her fellow Echo Bay officers dead. She hated sitting in that office with that doctor's eyes locked on her, like he knew secrets about her that he would never tell. It made her feel . . . invaded and exposed. And she didn't want Amy to feel that way any more than she already did.

The door opened. A small woman of about sixty, with a pink face surrounded by a corona of red curly hair, smiled up at her.

"Hello, you must be Joe Frye," she said, extending a hand. "I'm Mary Sher."

Joe shook the woman's small, warm hand. She felt Amy hovering behind and stepped aside.

"And you're Amy," Dr. Sher said.

Amy just stared at the woman, then nodded, her face disappearing behind the curtain of her hair.

"Please come in. It's nice and warm inside."

Dr. Sher led them through French doors and into a living room of old plush furniture, dark paneling, and bookshelves. A red brick fireplace took up one end of the

room, and an old baby grand piano dominated the other, its top draped with a fringed shawl. Every inch of wall space was given over to paintings, French ballet prints, Victorian plates, African masks; every surface was filled with knickknacks, books, doilies, figurines, and even a tarnished Russian samovar. And lamps—there had to be at least ten in the room—everything from a glowing faux Tiffany to a two-foot-tall hula girl topped with a gaudy fifties-era flowered shade.

Dr. Sher saw Amy staring at the hula-girl lamp and went over and touched a switch. The light came on, and a second later, the figurine's plaster hips began to sway.

Amy let out a gasp of delight.

Dr. Sher looked at Joe. "My late husband and I found that in the Paris flea market." She gestured to a sinuous red velvet Victorian settee. "Please, make yourself at home."

Joe took a seat and looked to Amy, who now seemed to be examining the spines of the books. Dr. Sher touched Joe's hand. "Let her be for a moment so we can talk."

Dr. Sher pulled a carved chair closer. "Jake said you found Amy at her old home," Dr. Sher said, keeping her voice low.

"Yes," Joe said. "She seemed to have a need to get there, but she can't really tell me why. She said something about waiting for her mother—"

"Jake said her mother was dead," Dr. Sher interrupted.

Joe nodded. "Yes, and when we found Amy, she said she was waiting for her."

Joe went on to fill the doctor in on all that had happened with Amy so far, including the fact that other than one bad asthma attack and almost comalike sleep, she

seemed otherwise healthy. Mary Sher listened intently, nodding, hands clasped in her lap.

"What is it you need from me exactly, Sheriff Frye?" Dr. Sher asked.

"Call me Joe, please." Joe glanced at Amy, but she was still lost in the bookshelves. "We need you to evaluate her level of emotional and mental stability. We'll need this for the courts."

Dr. Sher nodded. "Jake said her mother might have been murdered by her husband," she whispered.

Joe let out a small sigh. "We don't know that for sure. And Amy's memories are too vague. I'm not even sure they are real."

"Do you think she was abused?" Dr. Sher asked.

"She said once her father hurt her." Joe hesitated. "She seems to be afraid of men."

But even as Joe said that, she had a new thought. Amy didn't seem to be afraid of Jake Shockey. This morning, when Shockey had come to the hotel to check up on her, Amy had been calm. She had even shaken Shockey's hand when Joe introduced him.

But Amy still didn't seem to want to be around Louis. Every time he was near, Amy's eyes would grow wary. It struck Joe suddenly: Was Amy responding to Louis this way because he was black? The school in Hell . . . that playground was filled with only white kids. Any school Amy went to in Hudson was probably the same, and she had left school early to take care of her aunt. Before that, she had been isolated on the Brandt farm. Was it possible the girl had never seen a black man before?

She heard the *plink* of the piano and looked over at Amy.

She was running her fingers lightly over the old ivory keys.

"Amy? Could you come over here, dear?" Dr. Sher said.

Joe looked back at Dr. Sher. "You want to start now?"

Dr. Sher gave her a gentle smile. "No reason to delay. Why don't you take a seat over by the piano, Joe?"

Amy came forward. Joe rose, and Dr. Sher motioned for Amy to sit down on the settee. Joe retreated to the piano bench.

"I like your piano," Amy said.

"Can you play the piano?" Dr. Sher asked.

Amy nodded, smiling. "With my feet."

"Your feet?"

Amy began pumping her feet up and down.

"There is a player piano in the farmhouse," Joe said from her corner.

"Ah," Dr. Sher said.

"My legs were too little to reach, but I saw Momma do it," Amy said.

Dr. Sher leaned forward. "Do you remember much about living on the farm, Amy?

Amy's feet stopped moving. "Sometimes."

"Only sometimes?"

"My memory isn't very good," Amy said softly. "I can't always tell the real stuff from the dream stuff." Her eyes seemed to be searching the doctor's face. "Do you know what I mean?"

Dr. Sher nodded. "Yes, I do."

"And sometimes . . ." Amy's voice drifted off.

"Go on, dear."

"Sometimes I wonder if I am crazy."

She had been speaking so quietly Joe had to lean forward.

"Are you a doctor?" Amy asked suddenly.

Dr. Sher glanced at Joe, then looked at Amy. "Yes, I am."

"Can you help me get better?" Amy asked.

"I think so," Dr. Sher said.

Amy sat back in the settee with a sigh. For a second, Joe wondered if she were going into one of her sleep episodes. But Amy just seemed to be deep in thought.

"Can we talk about the dream you had last night?" Dr. Sher asked. "The one about the barn?"

Amy looked up. Then she nodded slowly.

"Did that feel more like a dream or a real memory?" Dr. Sher asked.

"It was the first time I had that one," Amy said. She suddenly sat up straighter, again searching the doctor's face. "But I don't think it was a dream. I think it was real, and I want to remember it better."

"It might be hard. You were probably very young."

"I want to remember," Amy said, her voice growing agitated. "I *need* to remember so I can help her."

Joe was waiting for Dr. Sher to say "Your mother," but the doctor was quiet, studying Amy. Maybe confronting the memory of her mother's murder was too much to put the girl through right now. Joe was about to suggest that they bring the session to an end when Dr. Sher rose, came over to Joe, and bent low.

"Jake told me that Amy trusts you," the doctor said quietly.

Joe nodded.

"I might be able to access her memories under hypnosis," Dr. Sher said. "How do you feel about that?"

Joe was impressed with how Dr. Sher had handled things so far. "I'm okay with it, if Amy is," she said.

Dr. Sher nodded and went back to sit down next to Amy.

She reached over and took her hand. Amy didn't resist, didn't even jump at the contact.

"Would you like me to help you remember things better?" Dr. Sher asked.

Amy nodded quickly.

"Do you know what hypnosis is?"

Amy shook her head.

"It's like going to sleep but being awake enough to tell me what you are dreaming about."

Amy looked to Joe and then back at the doctor. "Okay," she said softly.

"I won't hurt you."

"I know," Amy said.

It took only minutes for Dr. Sher to hypnotize Amy. Joe had thought there would be swinging pendulums and hokey words, but the doctor had used only her voice to coax Amy into a sleep state. Joe had read that certain people were more susceptible to hypnosis than others. And she knew that doctors themselves didn't even agree on its validity. For every doctor who claimed it was a true altered state of consciousness, there was another to discount it as just heightened focus.

Watching Amy now, lying on the red settee, Joe wasn't sure what to believe. At least, the girl looked peaceful.

"Amy?"

"Yes?"

"I'd like you to go back to when you were little. Can you remember that?"

"Yes."

Joe could see the deep and even rise of Amy's chest through the thin fabric of her T-shirt.

"Where are you?" Dr. Sher asked.

"Farm . . . in my room. It's pink."

Joe remembered Louis describing a bedroom with pink wallpaper.

"Can you see anything else?"

"A kitten. I have a kitten."

Suddenly, Amy gave out a small cry.

"What is it, Amy?" Dr. Sher asked.

"He killed it."

"Killed what?"

"My kitten. I found it in the barn, and I wanted to keep it, but when I brought it into the house, he . . . he . . ."

"It's all right, dear. It's all right."

For a moment, there was no sound in the room except Amy's breathing. Gradually, it returned to normal.

"Can you tell me about the barn?" Dr. Sher asked gently.

"The barn," Amy whispered.

"Can you go into the barn?" Dr. Sher asked. "Can you go there and tell me what you see there?"

The girl's brows knitted slightly.

"Are you in the barn, Amy?" Dr. Sher prodded.

"I don't want to go in the barn."

Joe sat back and stifled a sigh.

"That's all right," Dr. Sher said. She glanced over at Joe and gave a subtle shake of her head.

"Ohhhh . . ."

Joe's eyes shot to Amy. She had her hands over her face and was moaning.

Dr. Sher leaned closer. "Amy, what is it?"

"No, don't . . . no, don't . . ." Amy said.

Joe rose from her seat.

"Amy?"

"Momma! Momma! Oh, no . . . don't hurt Momma! Stop! Stop!"

"Amy, it's all right."

"No! No! I don't wanna go! I don't wanna go in the hole!"

Joe came forward quickly. "Get her out of this," she said.

Dr. Sher looked up. "She needs to go through this."

Joe turned away.

"Where is he putting you, Amy? What's the hole?"

"Outside, outside . . . it smells so bad . . . dark. And if I cry again, he'll throw me down the hole. I have to be quiet until Momma comes to let me out. Be quiet . . ."

And suddenly, Amy fell quiet. Joe looked back. She had brought up her knees and was lying on her side, curled into a ball. Dr. Sher had her hand on Amy's forehead. She looked up at Joe with questions in her pale blue eyes.

"Doctor?" Joe said quietly.

Dr. Sher turned.

"Can you ask her about the barn again?"

Dr. Sher turned back to Amy. "Amy? Amy, can you hear me?"

"Yes."

"I need to you go into the barn. Can you go in there?"

Joe had moved closer, and she watched Amy's face. Her eyelids were fluttering, like she was trying hard to see something.

"What do you see in the barn, Amy?" Dr. Sher asked.

"Horse. Brown horse."

"Anything else?"

"Cow . . . just a cow."

Amy fell quiet. Joe was watching her face for any sign of distress, but there was nothing.

Then a soft sound. Amy was humming. Joe came up to stand behind Dr. Sher's chair.

Amy was hugging herself and singing. She was singing the same nonsensical song that she had sung last night before falling asleep.

Amy sang the song over and over, until her voice finally tapered off into soft, even breathing.

Dr. Sher sat riveted, a stunned look on her face. She switched off the small tape recorder she had set on the table by Amy's head. Finally, she leaned forward and took Amy's hand.

"Amy, I want you to wake up now," she said evenly. "We're going to count back from ten together, and when we get to one, you'll wake up, okay?"

"Yes."

At one, Amy opened her eyes. She looked first at Dr. Sher and then at Joe. She smiled shyly.

"Did I do okay?" she asked.

Dr. Sher smiled back. "Yes, dear."

"I sang the song," Amy said.

"Yes, you did."

"But this time, I sang the whole thing. I never did that before. I can remember it now."

Her smile widened. She swung her legs to floor and sat up, suddenly very alert. She focused on Joe.

"I'm hungry. Can we get a pizza?"

That morning, back at the hotel, Joe finally had persuaded Amy to try a slice of the leftover pizza, telling her that while it may not have been on Aunt Geneva's list of

edible foods, it was on Joe's. Amy had readily agreed to try it, willing to move on. Seeing how well Amy looked now, Joe wondered if she might be ready to move on in other ways as well. Maybe Dr. Sher was right. Maybe there was no way through this for Amy except by facing the ugliness head-on.

"Yes, we'll stop and get a pizza," Joe said.

Amy's face lit up with a smile.

Joe turned to Dr. Sher. "I'm sorry I tried to stop you. I should have trusted you. It's just that I don't know what I am seeing here."

Dr. Sher was watching Amy put on her jacket. "I really think I need to see her again. You can't expect much from just one visit."

Joe nodded.

"That song she was singing," Dr. Sher began.

"She's done it before. It seems to calm her."

"But you don't know what it means to her?"

Joe shook her head. "I've asked her. She doesn't remember it when she's awake."

"Apparently, she was able to retrieve it during the hypnosis. The song must be a good memory, something she goes to when the bad memories get to be too much."

"The song's nonsense, though," Joe said.

Dr. Sher was watching Amy and looked back at Joe. "What?"

"The words. They don't make any sense."

Dr. Sher's eyes locked on Joe's. "They make perfect sense. She's singing in French."

Chapter Sixteen

There was an advantage to working as a cop in a college town for almost fifteen years, Louis decided. Shockey not only knew the best doctors, but he knew lawyers and judges, too. One in particular, an arthritic old judge named Herman Fells. Fells, whose own daughter had been murdered twenty years ago, agreed to fit them in on his family court calendar between two other pending cases. Shockey had been forced to allow an agent from Family Services to attend the hearing, but because of his contacts, he had managed again to get someone sympathetic to keeping Amy out of the system.

Louis glanced at his watch. They had been inside the courtroom for more than an hour now—Joe, Shockey, and Amy. At first, he had been miffed that Joe had asked him to stay out in the hallway. Amy would be more relaxed—and lucid—if Louis was not in the small courtroom, Joe had told him. Louis hadn't asked Joe why she thought Amy didn't seem to mind Shockey being close.

It bothered him—but not enough to get in the way of things.

He looked at the doors. Shit, what was taking so long?

Maybe they didn't have enough information. Dr. Sher had suggested that Amy get a routine exam to rule out any physical problems, and Amy had passed. And Dr. Sher's own written assessment declared Amy competent to tell the judge how she felt about her father, Owen Brandt, and why she didn't want to be with him. That had to be enough to get her into a custody hearing.

The other things—her memories or dreams, the strange blackouts—those were like defense mechanisms, Dr. Sher had said, the brain's way of blocking out pain until it was ready to handle it.

He could understand that. He might not understand Amy, but he sure could understand the shield the brain brought down over some things. It had been only recently, on his last trip up to Michigan, that some of his own memories—the bad ones—had shoved forward. Like the time he had locked himself in a closet to avoid a belt whipping from one of his foster fathers.

But at least he knew that memory was real. Some of this stuff with Amy, like the smelly hole, the ropes, the dead kitten, he wasn't so sure about. He supposed they could be based in reality, maybe filtered though an overactive imagination.

But Amy being able to sing in French—something she couldn't do when she was awake—was one thing he didn't understand.

He reached into his jeans pocket and pulled out the paper Joe had given him last night. Dr. Sher, who had lived in Paris and spoke fluent French, had written out some of the words she had heard Amy singing. The English words he and Joe had heard had been only their own ears hearing the phonetic version. But Dr. Sher, listening to the tape over and over, had come up with a transcription of what she believed Amy was singing:

Caches dans cet asile ou Dieu nous a conduits
unis par le malheur durant les longues nuits
nous reposons tous deux endormis sous leurs voiles
nous prions aux regards des tremblantes etoiles

His own college French wasn't good enough to read it, so he called Dr. Sher that morning for a translation and had written it beneath the French:

Hidden in this sanctuary where God has led us,
united by suffering through the long nights
we rest together, rocked to sleep beneath their
cover we pray beneath the gazes of the trembling
stars.

He stared at the words, shaking his head. There was a logical explanation behind it. There had to be.

Joe had been the one to bring up the idea that Amy might have a split personality. But Dr. Sher had discounted it as too rare. And even if it were true, it still meant Amy had to have learned French somewhere.

That morning, Louis had made a phone call to the Hudson police and asked one of the cops to take a more thorough look inside Geneva's home. The cop had called back a while later and told Louis he had no found no foreign-language books, no keepsakes from places afar, and no brochures, photos, or magazines that suggested that Amy had ever ventured far from home. The cop also said there wasn't even a television in the home. And school records confirmed that Amy had stopped attending in the third grade.

As for the neighbor, Mr. Bustin, the one Amy remembered for his Go Blue room, the cop found out that Amy had visited him only a few times, that he did not speak French or any other foreign language, and that he had nothing in his home that Amy could have picked up.

A soft tapping drew his attention down the hall. A family was huddled at the end, a black woman and five

children. One of the kids, a girl who looked about six, was banging on the wall with a broken Barbie doll.

Louis folded the paper and put it back into his pocket.

He had almost bought Amy a doll that morning. Joe had sent him to Kmart to pick up things Amy would need for her court appearance. He had walked around the store for a long time before he actually started putting things in the cart.

His only experience shopping for kids was with Ben Outlaw. That was easy. Boys were quick, picking out T-shirts usually based on the cartoon graphic on the front. If things didn't fit perfectly, Ben never cared. He'd just roll up the sleeves or cut off the cuffs.

But Joe's list for Amy had been very specific.

Plain, *not* hip-hugger, blue jeans, size two. T-shirts with a minimum of a half-sleeve and no printing on the front, size small. A parka with a hood. Plain white underpants, no bikinis, size three. A pair of sneakers, size five. A plain white training bra, size 32A, no padding.

The bra had almost done him in. He finally found a clerk who helped him with that one.

Before he left the store, he had decided that he wanted to get Amy something personal, something Joe hadn't put on the list. After ten minutes of walking around among the toys, he gave up and headed toward the checkout. As he passed the jewelry counter, he saw a display of cheap necklaces. He settled on a small heart-shaped locket on a silver chain.

He hadn't shown it to Joe or Amy at the hotel room, because he wanted to give it to Amy in private. He hoped it would help him make a connection that Amy hadn't yet allowed him to make.

The courtroom doors opened with a soft bang. Louis rose quickly as Shockey came toward him.

"What happened?" Louis asked.

"The kid was great," Shockey said. "Judge Fells said he believed her stories about Brandt's abuse, but he didn't completely buy the fact that she may have seen Brandt murder her mother. He wasn't willing to dismiss it totally, either. He wants Dr. Sher to dig deeper."

"How long did he give us?"

"Ten days," Shockey said. "In the meantime, Family Services will notify Brandt that he has a hearing coming up. Brandt will have to get a lawyer and fight to get her back. He still might be able to do that if we don't come up with something to prove him unfit."

"Where does Amy stay until then?" Louis asked. "If Brandt even suspects she's remembering things, she'll need to be protected."

"Fells knew that," Shockey said. "Amy understood it, too. Fells told her she had two choices. She could stay in the juvenile jail, or he could order a cruiser to sit outside her new foster home twenty-four hours a day."

"What did Amy choose?"

Shockey smiled. "It was the damndest thing I ever saw," he said. "The kid stood up and said, 'How come I can't stay with Miss Frye? She can protect me. She has a gun.' So the judge turned to Joe and said, 'What about that, Sheriff Frye?'"

"What'd Joe say?"

Shockey laughed softly. "You should've seen her face, but I could tell she couldn't say no to that girl. Joe said she'd stay until the next court date. Now all I gotta do is get the department to pick up the hotel tab, and we're all set, at least for ten days."

The doors opened again. Joe and Amy came out. Amy was talking to her, excited about something, but he could tell Joe wasn't listening. Her mind was three hundred miles away, in Echo Bay.

"Look, guys," Joe said. "I have got to call Mike. I don't know how I'm going to explain this. Amy, would you stay here with Detective Shockey for me? For five minutes?"

"Are you coming back?" Amy asked.

"Yes," Joe said. "You'll be fine with Detective Shockey. Okay?"

"Okay."

Joe hurried off to find a pay phone. Amy pushed her hair from her eyes and wandered to the bench to sit down. There was a woman sitting farther down the hall, nursing a baby. The woman's breast and the baby's face were covered with a cloth diaper, but still Amy watched them, fascinated.

Shockey looked at his watch. "I gotta go. I have a meeting with my lieutenant at eleven. I have to bring him up to date on this stuff."

Louis looked at Amy. "Go ahead. We'll be fine."

"You sure?"

"Yeah."

Shockey went over to Amy and explained to her that he had to go, then gestured to Louis. She gave him a small nod and watched him until he disappeared out the glass doors. Then she glanced around, probably looking for Joe. When she didn't see her, her eyes came to Louis.

He walked to her slowly. She watched him, but to his surprise, she didn't look as if she was going to run. He sat down next to her and reached into his jacket pocket. Her eyes followed his every move, showing nothing but wariness until he withdrew the locket and held it out to her.

"I'd like to give you this," he said.

Amy stared at it. "That belongs to her," she said.

"No," Louis said. "It's for you."

Amy picked it from his palm and opened it. "There's nothing in it," she said.

"You can put anything inside you want."

Amy closed the locket and looked up. Her expression was no longer one of fear but of curiosity. She was staring at him so intensely that Louis had trouble sitting still.

Behind him, he heard the familiar *clip* of Joe's boots on the tile floor. Amy hid the locket quickly in her back pocket.

"Where's Jake?" Joe asked.

"Went to report in."

Joe's eyes went from Louis to Amy. "You guys ready?" she asked.

Amy rose and walked to Joe. She wanted to take Joe's hand, but Joe pulled gently away from her and started to the door. Louis rose to follow but stopped partway across the lobby, catching sight of an Ann Arbor uniform. Then he saw the face and the bald brown head of Sergeant Eric Channing.

Channing came forward. "You got a minute, Kincaid?" he asked.

Joe heard Channing's voice, and she and Amy paused at the door and looked back. Louis waved them on.

"You guys go ahead," he said. "I'll catch up."

Channing waited for them to leave. He drew a hand from his pocket and gestured to the bench. "Have a seat."

"I'll stand, thank you."

"Sit down. Please."

Louis dropped to the bench. Channing glanced to the doors, then down the hall, and finally took a place

next to Louis. Louis braced himself, not wanting another confrontation. But if this was going to be another warning, Channing was approaching it far differently from the first time. His expression was not that of a combatant but of a man who needed something.

"I told you I'd be watching you, and I have," Channing said.

"Look—"

"Be quiet," Channing said. "Let me have my say here. That girl you were talking to just now, is she the one I've been hearing about around the station? The strange one you and Shockey found at that farmhouse?"

"Yeah."

"Word is you've fought like hell to keep her out of the system and convinced your girlfriend to take care of her."

"What's that have to do with you?"

"Just answer the question," Channing said. "That true?"

"Yeah, so what?"

"I was standing over there, watching you a few minutes ago with her," Channing said. "You surprise me, Kincaid. You handled that pretty good."

"What do you want from me, Channing?"

"Five more minutes."

Louis shook his head and leaned on his knees. There was a trio of lawyers coming toward them, and Channing waited until they had passed before he spoke.

"I have something to show you," Channing said.

Channing reached into his back pocket and withdrew a worn brown wallet. He opened it and flipped through the plastic sleeves. When he found the photograph he wanted, he held the wallet open to Louis. Louis took it and looked down at the picture.

Her hair was a puff of cascading ringlets, light brown

with streaks of gold, as if the sun had lightened them. Her small face was the color of caramels. Her lips were pink and full like Kyla's. Her eyes were gray and somber—like his own.

"Her name is Lily," Channing said. "She's eight years old, and she's yours."

Louis stared at the picture, everything numb but the hard pounding of his heart.

"Kyla lied to you, but she was only trying to protect Lily," Channing said. "Don't hate her for that."

Louis finally pulled his gaze up and looked at Channing. "What changed her mind?" he asked.

"Kyla didn't change her mind," Channing said. "If she had her way, you would've left here and never known. It was my decision to come here and tell you. When I leave, I'm going to go home and tell her what I've done."

Louis looked back at the photograph. It was a long time before he was able to bring his gaze back up to Channing. "Why?"

"Why what?"

"Why would you jeopardize your marriage to tell me this?"

Channing let out a breath. "About a year ago, Lily started asking questions about her real father. Kyla and I gave her the standard stuff about how some parents aren't grown up enough to be parents, and eventually, mostly because she could see how much it bothered her mother, she stopped asking."

Louis was staring at the photograph again.

"But I know she hasn't stopped wondering," Channing said. "Kids who don't know their fathers never stop wondering. And things like that leave a hole in a little girl's

heart. And I love Lily enough to admit it's a hole I can't fill."

Channing rose and held out his hand for the wallet. Louis stood up and looked down again at the photograph of Lily, reluctant to let her go.

"Can I see her?" Louis asked.

"I figured you'd ask that," Channing said. "I would've been real disappointed in you if you hadn't."

"But I don't want to make a mess of it," Louis said. "And I don't want to make things harder on you and Kyla."

"I appreciate that," Channing said. "But I'll handle Kyla. You just . . ."

His voice broke, and he cleared his throat.

"You just sit tight and let me find the right time and place. I'll get back to you, okay?"

Louis gave Channing the wallet. It took him a moment to find his voice, another moment to find any words.

"Thank you, Sergeant," he said.

Chapter Seventeen

They had driven less than a mile when Louis asked Joe to pull over. He needed a quiet, empty space for this conversation. When he saw the Law Quad, with its open courtyard, he decided it was as close to a park as he would get.

Joe didn't ask why they were stopping. She didn't question him when he led Amy to another bench about fifteen feet away and asked her to sit there and read her book. And Joe didn't say a word as he sat down next to

her and let almost a full minute pass before he pulled his eyes from the stained-glass windows of the Law Library and met hers.

"I have a daughter," Louis said. "Her name is Lily."

Joe stared at him, not in shock at the news but in a tenuous kind of control.

"Channing seemed to feel that no matter what Kyla thought, it would be better for Lily if she knew about me."

"Kyla doesn't know he told you?" Joe asked.

"No."

"Don't you think that's rather unfair of you two?"

Louis hadn't thought about that, and Joe was probably right. But whatever had compelled Channing to tell Louis, it did not change what needed to happen now.

"How do you feel about this, Louis?" Joe asked.

"I'm . . ."

He paused.

"I don't know," he said. "I only know that when I looked at her picture, I wanted to know her. And I was glad she exists."

"Why? Does it ease your guilt?"

He heard something in Joe's voice that gave an edge to the question.

"No," he said. "It doesn't ease anything. Like I said, I just want . . ."

"Her forgiveness?"

He didn't like that question, either. "Joe, I'm trying to share something with you here," he said. "I don't need you to heap more shit on me over this."

Joe turned away, her shoulders stiff, her sharp profile even sharper with the tight set of her lips. He looked be-

yond her to Amy. She was examining the locket, opening it and closing it.

"Why do I have to know exactly how I feel about this right now?" he asked.

"Because you're about to turn a little girl's life—and her mother's—upside down," Joe said. "You can't walk into that not knowing if you have what it takes to see it through."

"I understand that once I walk in, I can't walk back out. I know that."

Joe met his eyes. "You walked out once."

"I was twenty and scared to death."

"And you're not scared now?" Joe asked.

He pushed off the bench and stepped away from her. Then he stopped, knowing he was doing the one thing he just said he wouldn't do, walking away when it got tough. And this was only a conversation with the woman he loved. If he couldn't answer her questions, how was he going to answer Lily's?

He turned to face Joe. "Of course I'm scared."

Joe's expression softened.

"But now that Channing has opened the door, for me not even to acknowledge her existence would be worse for her than if she met me and hated me."

Joe nodded.

He had never told her much about his own father, Jordan Kincaid, just the fact that the man had left long before Louis had a notion of what a father was. Maybe this would somehow help her understood why he had never talked about him. But still, as Louis watched Joe now, she seemed to be struggling to summon the emotional support she knew was expected.

"I wasn't trying to give you a hard time," she said softly. "I only wanted to offer an objective perspective. There are a lot of emotions at stake here, and sometimes we can't see through our own."

"I know."

She looked over to Amy. "We'd better get going," she said. "We're going to be late to meet Shockey."

Louis nodded and walked to Amy. She had the locket in her lap, pushing something into the heart-shaped space. He thought for a moment that maybe she had found a small picture somewhere or ripped one from a magazine. But it wasn't a photo she was placing in the locket; it was strands of what looked like her own hair.

She closed the locket quickly as he neared. "Is it time to go see Detective Shockey?" she asked.

"Yes. Are you ready?"

Amy stood up, hid the locket in her back pocket, and followed him and Joe back to the Bronco.

They met Shockey in a downtown café. All of the tables inside were full, and they were forced to sit outside under an umbrella that did little to protect them from the cool breeze and the cloudy skies.

Louis turned up the collar of his jacket and watched Amy. She wore a hooded UM sweatshirt. The hood was down, and her cheeks were pink, but she didn't seem cold. She seemed to like being outside, interested in the bustle of students and traffic around her, and he found himself again wondering how isolated her life must have been in Hudson with only a sick aunt for company.

Joe ordered Cokes for herself and Amy. Shockey ordered a beer, and Louis asked for a club soda.

"This is the deal," Shockey said, leaning over the table. "My boss says we can't get any judge to sign a search warrant for the barn based on Amy's dream."

"We knew that," Joe said.

"So I called the Livingston County tax assessor this morning," Shockey said. "Brandt's farm is in tax foreclosure. It'll go up for auction in less than two months."

"So?" Joe asked. "Until it does, it still belongs to him."

"Yeah, but it helps," Shockey said. "My boss thinks between that and the fact that Brandt hasn't lived there for nine years, we can make a good case to search the farm on the premise that Brandt abandoned it and forfeited his rights to consent."

"Abandonment takes ten years in this state," Joe said.

"But we've also got the fact that Amy was living there, and that makes her a legal resident. She can give us permission."

They all looked at Amy. She was listening intently.

"Amy's consent might hold up to cover the day we found her there," Joe said. "She was the only occupant at the time, and we had no reason to believe Brandt was even in the state. But now that he threw us off the property, her consent for a new search means nothing."

"Brandt's the one who said it's her home, too, Joe," Louis said.

"Even if they had been living there together for the last ten years, she's a minor," Joe said. "She can't give consent over the adult owner's objection."

"Yeah, but all that would be fought out months from now by the lawyers," Shockey said. "Right now, Brandt wouldn't know what his rights were or what the abandonment laws say."

"Do they have pizza here?" Amy asked.

"No," Joe said. "Here, look at the menu. Pick something else."

Amy took the oversized laminated menu and stared at it. Louis watched her. He knew she could read, and there were plenty of pictures, but still she seemed upset.

"So," Joe said, "you're going to lie to Brandt and do an illegal search and hope his lawyer isn't smart enough to figure it out six months down the road?"

"The place won't even belong to him six months down the road," Shockey said.

"Then why not wait until it goes up for auction and then ask the new owners for permission to search it?" Joe asked.

"And what if Brandt somehow pays the taxes?" Shockey asked. "And even if he doesn't, what happens to Amy? If we don't find something to put Brandt back in jail, he'll get custody of her."

"Miss Joe . . ." Amy said.

"No judge is going to give this girl back to an abusive ex-con who can't even support her," Joe said.

"Don't be so sure," Louis said.

"Miss Joe . . ." Amy said.

"Besides," Joe said to Shockey, "what makes you think she's even strong enough to take you back out there and show you where she thinks . . ." Joe glanced at Amy and lowered her voice. "Do you have any idea what that could do to her?"

"She doesn't actually have to go with us," Shockey said. "She can tell us where to look."

"She'll have to go through another session with Dr. Sher for that," Joe said. "That's not easy for her, and she might

never remember any more than she already has. Then what are you going to do? Dig up the whole barn floor?"

"Yeah, maybe we will."

"You're forgetting one thing," Joe said. "You and Judge Fells just appointed me Amy's guardian for ten days. Whether she is allowed to undergo more hypnosis or visit that farm is totally up to me. And I won't give my permission."

Louis and Shockey stared at Joe.

"Miss Joe . . ."

Joe finally heard Amy and looked to her. "What is it, Amy?"

"I don't see any of the things on my list on here," she said.

"This is a new list," she said. "The whole menu is a list. Okay?"

"Okay."

Joe sat back and crossed her arms. She was staring at something across the street. Amy lowered her menu. The soft brown eyes moved from Joe to Louis to Shockey and back to Joe. Louis watched her. Like all kids, she didn't need to understand the argument to feel the tension.

And he knew Joe was right. At this moment, Amy was a happy young girl, nothing like she had appeared in the cupboard at the farm. He couldn't ask her to go back there, not in person and not in her dreams.

Amy caught his eye. "I know you're fighting over my mother," she said. "You think she's dead, and you think that's what my dream was about."

"Amy, we're sorry—" Joe started.

"Don't be sorry," Amy said. "I know in my heart my mother's dead, or she would have come back for me. But I'm not afraid to go look for her."

"Amy, remembering what happened could be very painful for you," Joe said.

"But it's more painful for her," Amy said. "I think she's been waiting a long time for me to come."

Amy looked to Shockey. "And for you, too."

Shockey blinked rapidly. His ruddy face had gone gray. He held Amy's eyes for a moment longer, then rose quickly and disappeared into the restaurant.

Amy watched him, then looked down at her menu. "Tell him I'm sorry," she said. "I do that sometimes."

"Do what?" Joe asked.

"Get inside other people's heads," she said. "I shouldn't do that. It's not polite."

Joe looked at Louis. He wasn't sure what to say or if he even wanted to acknowledge what he knew Joe was thinking.

"So, if Dr. Sher says it's okay," Amy asked, "can we go back to the farm and see if I can remember more?"

Joe closed her eyes.

"I can do this, Miss Joe."

Joe blew out a slow breath, opened her eyes, and gave Amy a nod. "I'll ask Dr. Sher. If she says it's okay, we'll go back."

Chapter Eighteen

The ride from Ann Arbor to the farm took place in near silence. Louis was driving, with Shockey in the passenger seat. Joe and Dr. Sher were sitting in the back

with Amy between them. In deference to Amy, they had all agreed beforehand not to discuss the case.

Joe had been concerned about Amy ever since the day before in the café. Although Amy had insisted she wanted to go back to the farm, she had turned quiet afterward, her somber mood lasting well into the evening. Joe had sat at her bedside until two, waiting for the return of nightmares. But Amy had fallen into an immediate and deep sleep.

"I haven't been out this way in years," Dr. Sher said quietly. "I can't get over how much things have changed."

Joe glanced at the doctor, who was looking out over the empty fields.

"So many big trucks on this road now. And there used to be more farmhouses," Dr. Sher said. "Where have they gone?"

"The farms have been bought out by corporations," Joe said.

"How sad," Dr. Sher whispered.

Neither Shockey nor Louis seemed to hear. They were both off in their own worlds. Joe knew Louis was thinking about Lily. But Shockey? He had left the café with the barest grunt of a goodbye and had been oddly withdrawn today.

Joe felt the press of Amy's leg. "How are you doing?" Joe asked.

"I'm fine," Amy said. She, like the doctor, had been watching the fields stream by.

"You know you don't have to do this," Joe said. She caught Louis looking at her in the rearview mirror.

"I know," Amy said.

Amy took Joe's hand and held it the rest of the way.

A hard rain during the night had left the gravel road leading up to the Brandt farm a rutted mess. The house itself looked even more forlorn than Joe remembered. She watched Amy carefully as they pulled up to the gate. Amy had scooted forward and was staring at the house through the windshield.

The slam of the Bronco's doors as they got out split the quiet. Owen Brandt had left the gate unlocked. At least that made one part of this thing easy, Joe thought.

Dr. Sher was the last one to get out of the Bronco. "Oh, my," she whispered as she got her first good look at the house. Her eyes went to Amy, who had moved ahead to stand next to Shockey at the gate. Amy turned to look back at Joe, as if asking what she should do.

Shockey took the lead. "Remember, this is technically not a search."

Joe was tempted to ask him what the hell it was, then. But she kept her mouth shut. Now was not the time or place. At least there was no sign of Owen Brandt. The Gremlin wasn't here, and it didn't look as if he had been around. Except for one thing: the padlock was gone from the front door of the house. If they could get this over with and get out of here, maybe they could slide this whole thing by a judge—if they even found anything worth taking to court.

"Are we ready?" Shockey asked.

As if she knew she had to be the one to make this whole thing right, Amy stepped through the gate and started across the weeds toward the barn.

Joe and Dr. Sher fell into step behind her. As they neared the big double wooden doors of the barn, Louis came up behind Joe.

"The lock's gone," he said. "There was one on the doors the first time I was here."

"Then how'd you get in?" Joe asked. Then she quickly added, "Never mind."

Everyone waited while Shockey used both hands to slide the door open. The giant door moved with a screech. The odor of damp hay and manure floated out to them. Joe had the fleeting thought that it wasn't an altogether bad smell. Still, her stomach was in a knot.

What were they all expecting?

Shockey was staring hard at Amy, hoping that something here would trigger a memory that he could use to avenge the death of a woman he had once loved.

Louis's eyes were on Amy, too. But Joe had the feeling that he was seeing that picture of Lily instead.

Dr. Sher watched Amy with gentleness, but there was also a spark of intense and almost distant curiosity, like she was watching a grand experiment unfold.

Joe herself wasn't sure what she expected—or hoped for—out of any of this. Maybe only that no one got hurt.

Amy was standing nearest the open door, peering into the gloom. She swiveled her head to give them all one last look, then stepped inside.

Joe followed.

Up . . .

She couldn't help it. That's where she looked first. Up, up, up . . . into the rafters and the slanting light of the barn. She had been in a barn once before, on a field trip to a pumpkin farm when she was in fourth grade. But never had she been in a place like this before.

Space. Huge, soaring space. That was all she could think about. And that odd sweet-sour smell of old hay

and what she could only think of as the ghosts of the animals that had once lived here.

She shivered. The place was cold and swirling with the wind leaking through the old wood planks. She looked to Amy. She was just standing there, wrapped in her pale pink parka. She looked relaxed but alert, and Joe had the weird thought that she looked like her old dog Chips when he was listening to something no one else could hear.

"Amy?"

Joe turned at the sound of Dr. Sher's voice. The doctor had moved closer to Amy. Louis and Shockey were still standing just inside the door, watching.

Amy ignored Dr. Sher and moved deeper into the barn. She walked slowly, examining the stalls, the rusted skeletons of the old machines, the hay bales that had long ago shed their true shapes.

They all waited.

Suddenly, Amy stopped. "Horses," she whispered. She closed her eyes and tilted her head up. "I hear the horses."

Joe exchanged a glance with Dr. Sher. The horses had been a benign memory Amy had retrieved under hypnosis.

There was a long silence.

"The horses are screaming," Amy said. "They know something is wrong."

More silence. Amy still hadn't opened her eyes.

"They're here," Amy said.

Joe moved closer. They? She felt Dr. Sher at her side.

"Who is 'they,' Amy?" the doctor said.

"The men. They're here. And they want . . ." Amy's breathing quickened. "I have to hide, I have to hide. They can't find me, they can't find me."

Joe started toward them, but Dr. Sher waved her to stand back a little. Dr. Sher took Amy's hand.

"Can you remember what happened here, Amy?" Dr. Sher asked.

Amy nodded. Her breathing was becoming more labored.

"Can you tell me?"

A hesitation and a nod.

"It's all right, dear, I am here with you," Dr. Sher said. "Tell me what you see."

"Corn," Amy whispered. "I'm in the corn, and it's so cold. I see clouds over the horses' noses. The horses are scared, and the man in the carriage is whipping them. I see . . . they are looking for me. The men . . . looking for me."

Shockey had come up to Joe's side. "Men? Did she say men?"

Dr. Sher silenced him with her hand.

"I can't . . ." Amy's face screwed up. Joe hoped it was from concentration, but it looked like pain.

"Oh . . ."

"Amy? What is it?"

Joe watched as Amy clasped her hands together, holding them in front of her face. "No, don't, don't, don't."

"Dr. Sher," Joe whispered.

"She's all right," Dr. Sher said. "What's happening, Amy? Where are you now?"

"Here," she said. Her breathing had turned to short gasps. "It's cold in here. I have no clothes. He took my clothes . . ."

Joe shut her eyes. What the hell had Brandt done to this child?

Suddenly, Amy began to groan. "Oh . . . hurt . . . hurt . . . hurt. So much hurt!" Her hands were still clasped in front of her face. She raised them higher now, as if warding off a blow.

Her body jerked once, twice. Amy dropped to her knees, then to the dirt. She began to cough and gag.

Joe jumped forward, looking up at Dr. Sher. "She's having an asthma attack. Stop this now."

"Too late," Amy whispered.

She had suddenly gone very still. She lay there in the dirt, curled on her side.

Joe knelt and gathered Amy into her arms. Amy's eyes fluttered open. She looked first at Joe and then at Dr. Sher, who seemed frozen in place by what she had just seen. Finally, she knelt next to Joe.

"How do you feel, Amy?" Dr. Sher asked.

"Tired," Amy said.

"Do you remember what just happened to you?"

Amy nodded.

Joe looked at Dr. Sher. The woman didn't seem to know what to ask Amy—or what to do next. Louis came forward, and Joe knew he had to ask the question that was on everyone's mind. In her nightmare back at the hotel, Amy had seen someone hung from a hook in the barn—and someone digging a hole here.

Joe's eyes swept over the barn's dirt floor and came back to Louis.

"Amy," he said gently, "where did he dig the hole?"

Amy slowly broke away from Joe and rose. She walked five feet into the center of the barn and pointed.

"There," said softly.

• • •

The scrape of shovels. The grunts of the men as they dug. The soft cooing of doves in the rafters overhead. It all came to Joe now in a blur of sound as she sat with Amy on a hay bale in a stall tucked in a far corner of the barn. Dr. Sher sat on a milking stool nearby, head down, lost in thought.

Amy was sipping from a plastic cup. Dr. Sher had given her some tea from a thermos. They couldn't see Louis and Shockey digging from where they were. Joe hadn't wanted Amy to be in the barn if a body was unearthed and had tried to take her out to the Bronco to wait. But Amy had insisted on staying.

The sound of the shovels stopped suddenly.

Joe rose and went to the entrance of the stall.

About twenty feet away, Louis and Shockey stood motionless. Their heads were turned toward the open barn door.

Good God. It was Owen Brandt.

Joe's hand went instinctively to the .45 automatic clipped at her belt. She felt someone at her side and looked down to see Amy. She was staring at Brandt.

"Dr. Sher," Joe said. "Please keep Amy back here."

"What is it?"

"Just keep her back here."

Brandt had come further into the barn, his eyes shifting between Louis and Shockey and settling finally on Joe as she approached.

"What the fuck are you doing in my barn?" he said.

A jangling sound drew Joe's eyes to the door. A woman had come in, the blonde who was with Brandt the day they had taken Amy out of the farmhouse. Margi Ames. She was standing there, mouth agape, cradling a six-pack of beer to her leather jacket.

Brandt saw the hole. His eyes shot to the shovel in Shockey's hand. "What the fuck is going on here?" he demanded.

Shockey took a step toward Brandt, the shovel held like a weapon across his chest. He was breathing hard from the digging, his face red. His eyes were riveted on Brandt, and Joe realized this was the first time Shockey had seen the man since Jean disappeared.

"I asked what you're doing here!" Brandt repeated.

"Looking for Jean," Shockey said.

Brandt stared at him for a second, then laughed. "The bitch ain't here."

Joe was ready to jump in, but Louis was there, stepping in front of Shockey before he could move. Shockey's eyes blazed as he stared down Brandt.

But Brandt . . . he was looking somewhere else suddenly.

Joe turned to see Amy standing behind her.

"What's she doing here?" Brandt said, pointing at Amy.

"She's no concern of yours," Louis said.

"She's my daughter!" Brandt said. He started toward Amy, but before he could take two steps, Louis had his arm twisted behind him in a lock. Brandt squirmed and grunted.

"You take one more step, and I'll break your arm," Louis hissed in Brandt's ear.

Joe could feel Amy retreating, but she didn't want to take her eyes off Brandt. She sensed Dr. Sher move forward and pull Amy back into the shadows.

"Let me go," Brandt said to Louis. "I ain't gonna hurt the girl."

Slowly, Louis loosened his grip. Brandt bucked loose and backpedaled, rubbing his arm. "You got no right to keep me away from her," he said.

Joe pulled the court papers out of her jacket and held them out. "I'm her temporary guardian," she said.

Brandt snatched it from her hand, scanned it quickly, and looked up at Joe. "This don't mean shit. I'll get a lawyer."

"You do that," Joe said. Her eyes settled behind Brandt to the blond woman in the leather jacket. "You're going to need one when we bust you for parole violation."

Brandt laughed. "For what?"

Joe pointed to the beer the blond woman held. "That."

Brandt spun, saw the beer, and hesitated only a second. He reared back and smacked the woman in the right temple.

"You stupid bitch!"

The blonde yelped and crashed back into the barn door. Shockey was a blur, shovel swinging as he advanced on Brandt.

Joe was quick, but Louis was quicker. But Shockey got the flat blade of the shovel planted in Brandt's stomach before Louis could grab it and yank it away.

Brandt gasped and spun away, doubling over and holding his gut. Louis backed Shockey up against the wood door, pinning him.

"Jake! Enough!" Louis said.

"I'm going to kill him!" Shockey yelled. "I'm going to kill the fucker!"

"Enough!"

Shockey was bigger than Louis, and Joe thought for

a moment that she was going to have to help Louis keep
him back. But Shockey stopped struggling. He stared at
Brandt with cold hatred in his eyes.

Brandt was still doubled over, coughing and holding
on to the wall. The blond woman was lying in the hay,
whimpering and massaging her head.

And Amy?

Joe glanced back. She was standing quiet and rigid,
Dr. Sher's arm around her shoulder, staring not at Brandt
but at Shockey.

Suddenly, Shockey pushed Louis's arm away. He staggered forward, grabbed the shovel from the ground, and
walked slowly back to the hole.

He began to dig, his face red and dripping with sweat.
He stabbed at the ground in furious thrusts.

"Jake," Joe said.

The shovels of dirt kept flying.

"Jake, slow down," Joe said. "You'll destroy—"

A *clunk*, like metal hitting wood. Shockey stopped
and slowly turned the shovel head. A cascade of dirt—
and a skull tumbled out.

Joe heard a gasp behind her but couldn't take her eyes
off the skull. She didn't turn but said softly, "Dr. Sher,
take Amy out to the car."

Dr. Sher, shielding Amy to her side, moved quickly
around Joe and toward the door. No one watched them
go. Everyone was staring at the ocher-colored skull lying
in the dark dirt.

A sharp *clang*. Shockey had dropped the shovel. His
face had gone white.

"Jesus Christ . . ."

Joe looked up. It was Brandt who had spoken. His
face was as white as Shockey's.

Suddenly, he bolted for the door. Before Joe could say or do anything, Louis ran after him.

It was quiet. Except for a whimpering sound. Joe looked for the blond woman, but she was gone. Joe turned toward Shockey.

He was kneeling over the skull, crying.

Chapter Nineteen

Louis had been in Michigan State Police substations a few times before. Once in 1984, giving a statement on an incident that involved two dead teenagers, a dead suspect, and a dead chief of police. The bullet that had killed the chief had come from Louis's service revolver.

The most recent time had been just last year, about an hour south of here, in Adrian. Detained and stripped of his Glock, he had again made a series of statements regarding the murder of three women and a dead man he had left floating in an icy lake.

So it didn't surprise him when the same state investigator, Detective Warren Bloom, had shown up here in Howell, the county seat. Bloom probably had heard Louis's name mentioned when the news of the bones in the barn hit the station. Bloom had been the one busting his chops last time, so Louis was certain he had made it a special point to drive the seventy miles up from Adrian.

Louis was standing at the observation window of an interview room. Inside were Bloom, Owen Brandt, and the Livingston County sheriff, Travis Horne. Horne was close to seventy and had the look of an old dog—

slow-moving and in search of a soft place to lie down.

When they called Horne to the Brandt farm, he had come with a local doctor he introduced as the coroner. Horne seemed to know Brandt from before. Once in the barn, Horne stepped forward, looked into the grave, and quickly suggested that they call the state police.

That had been yesterday. The crime-scene techs had spent the night sifting dirt and extracting bones. Joe had taken Dr. Sher and Amy back to the hotel. Louis and Shockey had stayed until after midnight before grabbing a motel room in the nearby town of Pinckney. They went back this morning, but the techs were done. The hole was empty. It was obvious that the barn had been thoroughly searched for other evidence. But no one had told Louis or Shockey if anything else had been found.

Louis slipped off his jacket and set it on a desk. He looked back into the interview room.

Owen Brandt had been answering questions for more than an hour. He wasn't under arrest yet. Louis knew they would need to make a positive ID on the bones first, which wouldn't be too hard. They hadn't found anything in the grave to help confirm the ID. But Shockey had pulled Jean's dental records nine years ago and had already handed them over to the county medical examiner.

Once the dental records were matched to the skull, Brandt would be arrested and charged. With Amy's testimony of both prior abuse and what she recalled of the murder, it was a lock.

Brandt's initial shock at seeing the skull had disappeared. Now, as Bloom and Horne peppered him with questions, he showed nothing but arrogance. And he kept to the same story he had told the cops nine years ago.

She just left. She had a boyfriend. They found her car at the train station. Don't you fuckers know nothing?

Louis felt a nudge at his arm. Shockey was holding out a Styrofoam cup filled with muddy coffee. Louis took it and drank some.

"Your ass is in trouble, Jake," Louis said. "Brandt's going to sue you for everything you've got. You know that, right?"

"I don't give a shit," Shockey said. "As long as he goes down for this."

Louis shook his head.

Brandt finally said the magic words: *I want an attorney.* Bloom cut off the interview and left the room through a side door. He appeared in the hall with Louis and Shockey a few seconds later.

Bloom was a big man, his face ruddy from the Michigan winters, his golden hair cut square on his head. He wore a yellow dress shirt, sleeves rolled up, and a gold badge on his belt.

"I thought I smelled something out here," Bloom said.

"Cut the crap," Louis said. "What are you going to do with him?"

"I have to let him walk," Bloom said. "That should come as no surprise to either of you. Illegal search, police brutality, trespassing. Anything else happen out there you want to tell me about?"

"That's about it," Louis said.

Bloom eyed Shockey and shook his head. "I understand how Kincaid could pull this stunt, but you're a law-enforcement officer, Detective Shockey. Fifteen years in. How could you possibly think you'd get away with this?"

"Took a chance," Shockey said. "The way I read it,

that little girl had every right to be there. And all she did was invite us in that gate with her."

"You're an idiot."

"Maybe so," Shockey said, looking back at Brandt.

Brandt was staring at the window. Louis knew Brandt's side was mirrored and he couldn't see Shockey, but still his stare was unnerving.

"Can I ask you how that girl knew where to tell you two assholes to dig?" Bloom asked.

Louis and Shockey exchanged glances.

"Well?" Bloom asked.

"She had a dream or a memory or something," Shockey said. "Being in the barn must have brought it all back."

"And she was how old when her mother disappeared?" Bloom asked.

"Four," Louis said. "We can't find any records for her and—"

"She's smart," Shockey interrupted. "She's real smart, but she's also kind of strange sometimes."

Bloom raised an eyebrow.

"I think she might be a little psychic, too," Shockey added.

Louis looked at Shockey quickly. Psychic?

"And I think you're nuttier than a squirrel turd," Bloom said. "Stay here, both of you."

Bloom left them. Louis finished the coffee and tossed the cup into a nearby can. His thoughts, as they had done last night until about three A.M., started to drift again. Away from Amy and Jean Brandt and back to Lily. Eric Channing still hadn't called him. As much as he wanted to see Lily, he was afraid he was bringing Kyla more pain. He didn't want to break up her marriage. It seemed to be a pretty good one.

"Damn it," Shockey muttered.

"What?"

"My pager again," Shockey said, angling himself so he could see the display of the beeper on his belt. "My lieutenant's been paging all morning."

"You didn't call him last night?"

Shockey shook his head. "Nope. But I'm sure Bloom did. Bad part is, you know how I told you getting inside that barn was all my lieutenant's idea?"

"Yeah."

"It wasn't. He didn't even know we were going."

"Jesus, Jake," Louis said. "Why don't you just mail your badge in now?"

Shockey looked again to the interview room. Bloom was holding the door open for Brandt. Brandt gave a sneer and left the room. Less than a minute later, Brandt appeared down the hall, emerging through another door. He still wore the same dark T-shirt, denim jacket, and filthy jeans Louis had seen on him two days ago.

He came toward them, his eyes locked on Shockey. Brandt stopped in front of Shockey, hiked up his pants, and smiled. Louis braced himself for a confrontation.

"I know who you are now," Brandt said. "You're a cop. You live in Ann Arbor, and you were fucking my wife nine years ago."

Louis put a hand on Shockey's sleeve. The muscle was tight, but he didn't think Shockey was going to swing at him. Not here in the state police station.

Brandt shook his head, his eyes moving over Shockey's body disparagingly. "She had real lousy taste."

"Get out of my face before I rip your fucking tongue out," Shockey said.

Brandt was unfazed.

"Go, Brandt," Louis said. "Get out of here."

"I didn't kill my wife," Brandt said, "but if there was ever a bitch who needed to die, it was that slut."

Shockey started to lunge at him. Louis stepped between them and gave Brandt a shove.

"Get the hell out of here," Louis said.

Brandt walked away. Louis kept a hand on Shockey's chest until Brandt had turned a corner. Shockey pushed away from him.

"Sonofabitch," Shockey hissed.

Louis headed down the hall and through a door that led outside. Brandt was climbing into the green Gremlin. Margi Ames was behind the wheel, and when she leaned over to give Brandt a kiss, he pushed her away and made an irritated gesture toward the street.

"Hey, Kincaid," Bloom hollered.

Louis turned. Bloom was walking toward him. He had put on a brown jacket.

"The ME wants to see me," Bloom said. "You and dickhead want to come along?"

Louis almost shot back a smartass response, tired of Bloom's crap. But he suddenly realized that Bloom didn't have to offer the invitation at all. In fact, Bloom could have confiscated his gun and probably locked him up for a few hours on trespassing charges. In exchange, Louis knew Bloom probably wanted to save himself a few hours of reading by having them bring him up to speed on Jean Brandt's history.

"Yeah," Louis said. "We'd appreciate that."

"It's only a block, so we'll walk," Bloom said. "You up for that?"

"Let's go."

• • •

There were two hundred and six of them. That's what Joe had told him. Two hundred and six bones in the human body.

Louis looked down. The brownish-yellow bones were laid on a stainless-steel table, forming a disconnected but perfect skeleton. There was no quick way to count, but Louis guessed that all—or almost all—of Jean Brandt's bones were here.

They were waiting for the ME to join them, and Louis took the time to look for signs of a fracture on one arm bone. Shockey had told him Jean had endured two broken arms. He finally turned away and closed his eyes for a moment, trying to capture a minute of lost sleep.

The double doors bumped opened, and the ME came in. His name was P. Ward, according to the sign on the wall. He was fiftyish and slim, with shaggy salt-and-pepper hair matching a Van Dyke beard. He wore green scrub pants over an old T-shirt that said WET WILLIE '74 TOUR: "KEEP ON SMILIN' THROUGH THE RAIN, LAUGHIN' AT THE PAIN."

"Detective Bloom," Ward said. "Nice to see you again."

"Ditto, Phil."

"Phillip."

Bloom stared at him. "What?"

"Phillip. My name is Phillip."

Bloom tried hard not to roll his eyes. "Yeah, right. So what's the word here, Doc?"

Ward looked down at the bones. "Exquisite, aren't they?"

"They're bones," Bloom said.

"Yes, but it's not often we find every one. The techs did an exceptional excavation. Please give them my praises."

Louis heard something of the South in Ward's melodious voice. Maybe it was the cadence or the choice of words, but Louis's stay in Mississippi had been long enough and he had spent enough time at his old boss Sam Dodie's home for him to develop an ear for the Delta's special music.

"So, is it our victim or not?" Bloom asked.

Ward turned and flipped the switch on a wall-mounted light box. He shoved the copies of Jean Brandt's dental X-rays into the clip. Then, next to it, a larger X-ray of the skull.

Louis stepped closer.

They didn't match. It was so obvious even he could see it. The skull from the barn had a wider jaw and large teeth—a perfect full set. Jean's teeth were small and un-even, with several missing in the back.

"Talk to us, Doc," Bloom said.

"The victim is a woman, probably between the ages of eighteen and thirty-five. But these bones do not be-long to the owner of this dental X-ray," Ward said, point-ing to the screen.

Louis looked at Shockey. He had turned away and was staring at the bones on the steel table.

Ward carefully picked up a long, slender bone. "I was told the Brandt woman had two arm fractures," he said. "There are no breaks in this humerus or in any of the arm bones."

Shockey's eyes closed. "You must be wrong."

"I am never wrong, Detective," Ward said. "Not about things like this. Oh, and by the way, the woman you found in the barn was most certainly African-American."

Louis's gaze snapped back to the X-ray of the skull.

"A marked alveolar prognathism," Ward said, pointing to the X-ray. "Flat nasal region, broad nasal aperture, retreating zygoma, somewhat truncated nasal spine and a retreating forehead."

"All right," Bloom said. "We get the picture. This is not Jean Brandt."

"Precisely."

Louis heard footsteps, and he turned to see Shockey leaving through the double doors. He turned back to Ward. "Can you tell how she died?" he asked.

"As I said, there were no fractures in the arms," Ward said. "I found one old leg fracture that was well-healed. But I did find six other breaks in the legs and ribs that were all perimortem fractures, meaning they were inflicted minutes or hours before death."

Ward picked up a plastic container. "Plus there is this. Your techs brought back a dirt sample from the gravesite. It was saturated with blood."

"The woman was still bleeding when she was put in the grave?" Louis said. "Buried alive?"

"How alive, I can't be sure," Ward said. "But dead people don't bleed."

Louis closed his eyes.

"So I'm pretty certain this was a homicide," Ward said.

Bloom let out a grunt. "Well, ain't this a kick in the nuts," he said. "We got a missing woman and no body. Got bones and no victim. And on top of all that, she's a black woman in an area that don't have but a handful of black folks in it."

"Maybe it won't be too hard to find someone who's been missing, then," Louis said.

"It may be harder than you think," Ward said. "You

might be looking for a woman who's been missing for quite some time."

"What do you mean?" Bloom asked. "How long have these bones been in the ground?"

"Well, there's no way to know for sure without carbon dating," Ward said. He picked up the arm bone. "But see how brittle and chalky this is? As bones age, they lose the proteins that make up the matrix that holds the calcium."

Ward gently pressed a fingernail on the bone. Louis was surprised to see it leave an indentation. "If I were to try to break this humerus in two, instead of splitting like a green twig, it would break and crumble," Ward said. "So I'm guessing they are quite old."

Ward set the bone down and picked up a plastic bag, holding it out. "Then there's this, which—"

Bloom grabbed the bag. "What's this?"

"A piece of shoe leather with some buttons that the techs found with the bones. The style seems to date back to the mid-eighteen-hundreds."

Bloom stared at the black clump in the plastic.

"Do you want me to send the bones out for dating?" Ward asked.

Bloom tossed the plastic bag onto the table. "The state's not paying for that," he said. "This isn't a homicide case anymore, as far as I'm concerned."

"But the shoe doesn't prove anything for sure," Louis said. "Don't we want—"

Bloom cut him off with a raised palm. "I don't care about a hundred-year-old homicide. And if what Phil here says is true, she was probably just a servant anyway, maybe even a slave."

"What did you say?" Louis said.

Bloom's ruddy face colored a deeper red. "Sorry, Kincaid. Didn't mean it like that. I just meant there wouldn't even be any records for a woman like that. That's all."

"Right."

"And who the hell has the time to work a case like this, anyway?" Bloom asked. "Where you going to find any damn witnesses?"

Louis looked back at the X-ray, trying to imagine a woman's face on the skull.

"Well, I'm out of here," Bloom said. "Kincaid, you tell Sheriff Frye I'd like a word with her before she goes home. I got a bone to pick with her boss, too. If you'll pardon the pun."

Bloom left.

"Asshole," Ward said under his breath.

Louis rubbed his brow, looking down again at the bones. He was concerned about Joe's job, but he was even more worried about Shockey. He had put everything on the line to get into that barn, and it had been for nothing. Brandt was going to remain free, and they had only eight more days to find a way to keep him away from Amy.

"What kind of cop wouldn't be interested in something like this?" Ward said.

Louis looked up at him. Ward was holding a second plastic bag. Inside was something that looked like jewelry.

"What is that?" Louis asked.

Ward opened the bag and pulled out a necklace. "This was also found in the grave with her," Ward said.

"May I see it?"

Ward handed the necklace to Louis. It was a silver chain and what first looked to Louis like a cameo, until he

turned it over. It was a plain round silver locket, about the size of a man's pocket watch. There was no engraving.

He opened it.

Inside was a lock of black hair.

Chapter Twenty

Owen Brandt stood at the gate, staring at the farm-house. He never should have come back here. Should've just stayed in Ohio after he got out, or maybe should've headed down to Florida or somewhere where it was warm, at least.

He'd never liked this place, never wanted anything to do with farming, even though his old man, when he started to get sick and old, tried to get him to take over. Like he was going to spend his life getting up before dawn, driving a tractor in the freezing rain, standing in pig shit, and then dying before his time.

Then why did I come back?

Brandt turned up the collar of his denim jacket and started across the yard. He stopped, his eyes fixed on the bright orange foreclosure notice on the front door. He had tried to rip it off once already, but the damn thing was glued onto the glass.

He turned away. A couple of yards from the side porch, he stopped again. Through the window, he could see Margi in the kitchen, taking the groceries out of the bags. After she'd picked him up at the police station, they'd stopped at the Kroger in Howell, spending their

last eleven bucks on beer and stealing the rest of what they needed, the bread, baloney, and toilet paper.

The thought of the police made Brandt grind his jaw in anger. They wouldn't tell him anything about the bones in the barn, but since they'd let him go, he knew they must have somehow figured out they didn't belong to Jean.

Brandt turned and surveyed the barren, fog-shrouded fields beyond the barn. That meant the bitch was still out there somewhere.

He shoved his cold hands into his pockets, turned away from the house, and began to walk. There was no clear pattern to his path, and he didn't even know where he was heading. He just felt the sudden need to walk, like maybe it would clear all the shit out of his head somehow and help him think better. He wasn't thinking too good these days, and that bothered him.

He was back behind the barn now, and his eyes took in every warped board, every rusting piece of machinery lying dead in the weeds.

Why did I come back here?

This place had never brought him any luck. Never brought his old man, Jonah, any luck, either. Wore his bones down with arthritis before he was fifty, wrecked his heart before he was sixty and killed him when he was sixty-one.

And his mother, Verna . . .

That crazy bitch couldn't stand it here, either. A couple a times a year, usually in the fall, she used to wither up, get funny in the head and lock herself up in the attic. For weeks, she'd stay up there, crying and moaning and talking about things only she could see.

At first, his father didn't know what to do about these spells. Ashamed probably, he would let his kids tend to her. Leave it to his son to set the plates of food outside her locked door. Left it to his daughter to dump the shit pot and give Crazy Verna her bath, if she'd even let Geneva in.

His father would work the fields from "can see" to "can't see" and retreat upstairs with his whiskey to dull the constant thud of Verna's footsteps across the attic boards above his bed.

Sometimes, if he drank enough and was lonely enough, he'd get the extra attic key from the kitchen and head upstairs, bottle in one hand, undoing his pants with the other. His old man used to say he was just trying to shake her up enough to rattle some sense back into her, but Brandt knew now he was just taking from her what was rightfully his anyway. Not that his mother would have even noticed when she was like that.

Then, one morning, Crazy Verna didn't unlock the door to get her milk and toast. The plate was still there, eight hours later when Brandt brought up a bowl of rabbit stew. The next morning when he saw that the stew was untouched, he took the key from the kitchen and let himself in the attic.

Crazy Verna was hanging from the rafters in a piss-stained nightgown, her bare feet raw from all that running.

He had been just ten when he found her.

Brandt stopped and turned. The kitchen window of the farmhouse was a small smudge of yellow in the fog. He didn't realize he had walked so far. He started back.

He let himself in the kitchen door. There was no sign of Margi. He got a beer from the cooler, popped the top

and took a gulp, still thinking about that orange foreclosure paper on the front door.

Shit, he should have sold the place nine years ago when he had the chance. Just taken the money and run and hoped Jean's body didn't turn up. He wasn't sure what he was going to do now. Where the hell was he going to get twelve grand to pay the taxes on this place? Margi would give it to him, but who knew when her settlement was going to come in and how much would be left once the fucking lawyers got done?

Brandt wandered into the dining room, his eyes falling on the sealed cartons. He knew they held nothing but old pictures, dishes, and junk, nothing worth even carting down to the secondhand shop. Nothing worth selling. Except . . .

He walked to the parlor and stared at the piano. It had been Jean's, the only thing she'd brought from her folks' house when she married him.

Married me. That was a joke. I did her the god damn favor. And she shit on me.

"Fuck you, Jean," he said softly. He drained the last of his beer.

A waft of perfume drifted from behind him. Margi appeared at his side, holding a can of Budweiser. He crushed his empty can, tossed it to the floor, and took the fresh beer from Margi.

"Where'd you go?" she asked.

"Went for a walk," Brandt said.

"I got worried about you," Margi said. "I mean, when you didn't come in the house. I got worried you—"

"I just needed some air," Brandt muttered, going to the window. He pulled back the lace curtain, leaned his

forehead against the frame, and stared out at the empty road. He was vaguely aware of Margi moving in the background, and he hoped she'd just go away and leave him alone. Ever since the cops took him away earlier, she'd been acting weird, turning all clingy and quiet.

A tinkling noise drifted from behind him. He turned to see Margi sitting at the piano. She was poking at the keys.

"Get away from there," he said.

"Hey, this thing has pedals," she said. "I never seen a piano with pedals. What do you use these for?"

Margi's feet started pumping the worn old pedals. Inside the piano's window, the yellowed roll began to turn. The plinky, off-key music filled the small room.

It was like the screech of metal on metal in his ears. That song. That same damn song that Jean had played over and over and over for the kid.

"Look, Owen, there's words here. But they're like foreign or something."

Margi started to sing, trying to read the words. "Catch Don set a seal . . . you and me pearl. What do you think it means? Hey, Owen?"

He closed his eyes as Margi's voice faded. But their voices . . . he could hear them real clear, the two them, singing those words that only they could understand, like it was some big fucking secret between them, and he was left out.

He opened his eyes and turned. His eyes were fixed now on the dusty ivory keys, watching them move up and down, up and down, all by themselves, like some fucking ghost was playing the damn thing.

"Stop it!" he shouted.

The music stopped, and silence filled the room. He felt like he'd gone deaf.

"I'm just having some fun, Owen."

Margi's white face wavered in front of him.

"Why can't I have a little fun? There ain't nothing else to do in this crappy place."

"This is my *home*."

She turned back to the piano. "Ain't no wonder she left you if you made her live here," she whispered.

"*What?*"

Margi didn't move.

He was at her side in one step. He grabbed a fistful of her hair and slammed her face forward into the keyboard.

"She didn't leave me!" he shouted.

He yanked Margi off the stool and, still clutching her hair, dragged her toward the kitchen. Margi clawed at his hands and started to kick.

"Stop it!" she screamed.

He shoved through the kitchen door, holding her by the hair as he started searching drawers. Empty. Empty. Damn it. *Where are the fucking knives?*

"I'm sorry . . . I'm sorry," Margi whimpered.

"You're not leaving me!" Brandt shouted. "No one leaves me!"

"I won't!" Margi cried. "I won't ever!"

That was the same thing Jean had said. But Jean had lied.

He threw the last drawer across the room. It crashed and splintered against the wall. His fist smashed into her face so hard it would have sent her flying had he not had a grip on her hair. And Margi . . . now she was suddenly fighting back, ripping at his hands and kicking at his shins, fighting him. She never fought back before.

But she was fighting now, fighting like her life depended on it.

Just like Jean.

He shoved her down onto her hands and knees on the floor and held her there by the back of the neck. He heard coughs and screams, felt her bony body shuddering under his grip.

Just like Jean.

He pushed her flat to the floor, spread-eagle on the linoleum as he dropped down hard on her thighs. His blows came like a pendulum, swinging fists from both sides, slamming into her back and ribs and head. Over and over and over like that fucking song.

Suddenly, he stopped.

Deaf again and numb to anything but the feel of a warm stickiness on his face and hands. He drew a breath heavy with the stench of blood.

He opened his eyes and looked down at what was beneath him.

Red on blue. Slick black leather. Matted yellow hair.

He pushed off her and slumped back against the wall, legs spread out in front of him. His chest filled with something that made it hard to breathe.

He opened his eyes slowly, trying to get his bearings, trying to get things to stop spinning. He brought his hands up slowly and squeezed his head between them.

The cops thought he had killed Jean and buried her out here. But he hadn't buried her. Not in the barn or anywhere else.

He'd left Jean lying here on this very floor. He had left her to go to the barn to get the axe after he broke the knife. When he got back, the bitch was gone, nothing in

the kitchen but a bloody smear across the linoleum to the back porch.

It was raining like hell that night, and he couldn't follow the blood trail, so he waited until morning to walk the farm to find where she had finally fallen down and died.

Two weeks of walking, and he never found her.

For nine years, even after he had left the place, he had told himself she had to be dead. Carried away and eaten by animals. She was dead. Had to be. Chopped-up, bleeding women just didn't vanish into the corn.

Where is she?

A soft moan pulled him back.

He looked over at her, but still it took him a moment to understand it was Margi. Her skinny body was trembling like she was in shock or something. And she was trying to move her arms and legs, but all she could seem to do was slide around on the floor, kind of swimming in her own blood.

But she was alive.

Just like Jean.

Chapter Twenty-one

Louis stood by the bedroom door watching Amy's face. Joe was sitting next to her on the bed, and although he couldn't hear Joe's soft voice, he knew what she was saying: "It wasn't your mother in the barn, Amy."

Amy's expression registered surprise, then settled into

something he could read only as deep disappointment.

Louis had expected tears or even resignation, anything but the quiet look of blighted hope that colored Amy's face. But in the end, he understood it. He had seen the expression before in the faces of those who had lost loved ones. With loss came the relief of grief, but only if there was someone to grieve over. Amy still had not found her mother. The hole in her heart remained.

Still, he was surprised when Amy told Joe that she wanted to go back and see Dr. Sher again. "I need to keep looking for her, and Dr. Sher can help me do that," Amy said.

It was only after Joe finally agreed to take Amy back to Dr. Sher the next day that Amy went back to bed.

Now, two hours later, Joe was stretched out on the sofa, hand over her forehead, and Louis was sitting close by. There was a bucket of chicken and a bottle of cabernet on the coffee table between them. Louis reached over and poured the last of the wine into Joe's glass and held it out.

She shook her head, closing her eyes.

"Did you call your sheriff?" Louis asked.

"Detective Bloom called him," Joe said.

"Is Mike upset at you?"

Joe shook her head. "He'd like me to come home, but he told Bloom whatever I did, he'd back me a hundred percent."

"He sounds like a good guy."

Joe nodded slowly.

The room was quiet. It was nearly eleven, and Louis knew Joe was as tired as he was. Still, she had been quieter than usual all evening.

"So, I guess you haven't changed your mind about running for sheriff this fall," Louis said. "You're going to stay in Echo Bay?"

She opened her eyes. "You knew that when I left Florida," she said. "Nothing has changed."

He nodded. "Thank you for staying," he said. "I think Amy likes you a lot."

Joe didn't comment.

Louis glanced to the bedroom door, open just enough so they could hear if Amy had a nightmare. But she had been out for hours now. Her need to sleep seemed to have lessened some, and she had not had another episode.

"You want to talk any about Lily?" Joe asked.

"No," Louis said, not looking at her.

He heard her sigh. Maybe she felt the need to talk about it more than he did, but he couldn't right now. He didn't know what he was supposed to say. Not to Joe and certainly not to Lily. He wouldn't know until the day came when he met her.

Louis rose, gathered up the chicken bucket and empty wine bottle, and went to the kitchenette. He tossed the garbage and opened the fridge. There were six Heinekens and two sodas. He grabbed a soda.

"Oh . . . stop! Stop! God, help me, please! Stop it!"

Amy.

He ran to the bedroom, Joe at his heels. Amy was in the bed, sitting straight up, both hands rigid in front of her face. He grabbed her shoulders before he realized it might scare her even more.

"Amy! Wake up."

She started thrashing at him, twisting away from him so violently she tangled herself in the blankets. He

reached for her again but caught only the sleeve on her pajamas. It ripped as she scrambled from the bed.

"I have to get to the corn!" she said. "I can't lead them to John. I have to run. Oh, Lord, help me, please!"

Joe tried to catch her, but Amy pushed away from her, stumbling across the bedroom. She was heading right toward the window. It was thick glass, but Louis wasn't sure she couldn't put herself through it.

He lunged for her. They both tumbled to the carpet.

"No! No!" Amy cried.

He pinned her wrists and looked to Joe. Amy was crying, bucking against his hold. She wasn't very strong, and it was easy to hold her down.

Joe dropped to her knees next to them. When Amy felt Joe's hands on her back, she started to relax. Louis let go of Amy's wrists, and she drew her arms under her face, weeping.

"I'm going to die," she whimpered. "I'm going to die."

"You're not going to die, Amy," Joe said, rubbing her back. "I promise you. You're not going to die."

Amy was on her side, hands clasped against her chest, eyes closed. She had lapsed into a sudden, comalike sleep, just as she had done at the farmhouse.

Joe sat back on her heels. "Louis, we can't keep doing this," she said. "This girl belongs in a hospital."

"Dr. Sher doesn't think so," Louis said.

"Dr. Sher has only seen Amy a couple of times," Joe said. "And she hasn't seen one of these attacks. We could be doing her irreparable damage by not having her in a place where she can be watched twenty-fours a day."

"And medicated so she can't remember any of this stuff?" he said.

"Maybe she's not meant to remember," Joe said. "Maybe there's nothing to remember that has anything to do with her mother. It's probably memories of her own abuse. Why force her to relive it?"

"Not remembering makes it worse," he said. "And you heard her tonight. She wants to remember. She wants to go back and see Dr. Sher again."

Joe sat back against the wall, staring at Amy. "I don't know if we're doing the right thing here," she whispered. "She scares me. This whole thing scares me."

Amy was resting on the red settee, eyes closed. Louis and Joe were seated near the piano, far enough away not to be a distraction but close enough to hear. Amy had asked that Louis be allowed to sit in this time. It had surprised him, but ever since he had given her the locket, she didn't seem to mind him being around. In fact, this morning, on the way to the Bronco, she'd whispered to him that he shouldn't tell Joe about the necklace because she would take it away from her.

He hadn't told Joe about the locket. Nor had he given voice to the question that had been in his head since the trip to the medical examiner: Why had Amy put her own hair into the locket?

The *click* of the tape recorder drew his attention back to Dr. Sher. The room was quiet and warm. He and Joe waited in silence while the doctor again took Amy back to her nightmare, telling her there was nothing to be afraid of and that she was safe.

"Tell me where you are," Dr. Sher said.

"I don't know," Amy said.

"Look down at yourself," Dr. Sher said. "Look at your clothes and shoes. What do they look like?"

"I'm wearing a blue dress," Amy said. "And black leather lace-up shoes. They don't fit me right, and they're heavy and hard to run in."

"Are you running now?"

"No," Amy said. "But I'm afraid. I hear the horses coming. I see a white horse pulling a black carriage. I hear the men. The fire is in their hands."

Louis caught Joe's eye and mouthed the word *Carriage?* She just shook her head.

"Are there other people with you, Amy?" Dr. Sher said.

"He is there . . . and his wife."

"Who?"

"I don't know. They're watching."

"What do they look like?" Dr. Sher asked.

"He has eyeglasses and a long black coat, heavy to keep the cold away. She wearing a long yellow dress, and her hair is black and piled up on her head."

Louis glanced at Joe. She was leaning forward, elbows on her knees, mesmerized by Amy's narrative.

"I'm running," Amy said. "I'm running through the corn. It's cold, so cold. My chest hurts."

"Why are you running?"

"They're chasing me," Amy said. "I hear the horse's hooves on the dirt. They're close, very close. But I can't go to the cellar. John is there, and I can't let them find John. So I run to the corn."

Amy's breathing became labored.

"What is it, Amy?"

"They found me. They found me in the corn. They're dragging me back, back to the barn. No!"

"Calm down, Amy," Dr. Sher said. "You're safe. Just tell me what you see."

"He has a whip."

"Who? The man with the eyeglasses?"

"No, one of the others," she said. "The fire . . . I can feel it on my skin."

"Is the barn on fire?"

"No, no," Amy said impatiently. "Torches! They scare me, but I can't move. I can't move. I am naked now. They have taken my clothes. I'm so cold."

"Slow down," Dr. Sher said. "Relax."

Amy's voice suddenly deepened, became almost unrecognizable. "Stand back," she said. "You stand back, Amos. You let us do what we need to do."

"Who is speaking, Amy?"

Amy let out a low moan. "The ropes . . . they are pulling me up on the hook. The whip . . . it hurts. It rips and rips. I don't want to die. I don't want to die."

"Amy, pull yourself away from the pain, and get past the whipping," Dr. Sher said. "Look down now. Where are you?"

For the next few seconds, Amy was quiet. Dr. Sher glanced up, meeting Louis's eyes. She seemed as mystified as he was.

"I'm lying on the ground," Amy said softly. "I'm freezing but warm with my own blood."

Dr. Sher placed her hand gently over Amy's.

"I hear digging," Amy whispered. "They are digging a grave. It is my grave."

Louis heard Joe pull in a quick breath.

Then, suddenly, Amy went limp. She fell quiet again. It was the second or third time she had, but Louis got the feeling that her memory—or whatever this was—was over.

Dr. Sher awakened Amy and told her to rest. Then she motioned Louis and Joe from the room. Once in the foyer, she closed the French doors to the living room and took several deep breaths. She was watching Amy through the doors.

Louis glanced at Joe. Her face was white, and she was holding her arms over her chest like she was cold.

"All right," Louis said quietly. "What the hell was that all about?"

It was a while before Dr. Sher turned to face them. When she did, her pale blue eyes took a moment to focus. "I don't know," she said.

"Those weren't memories of her mother's death," Joe said.

"No, they weren't. At least, not all of them," Dr. Sher said.

"She had one of her episodes last night," Joe said. "It's like a nightmare, but she's awake. She mentioned the name John last night, too. And she said she was dying. Not her mother, Dr. Sher. She said *she* was dying."

Dr. Sher looked at Amy again. And this time, when she looked back, first to Louis and then to Joe, her clinical mask had slipped back into place.

"I think Amy believes she was the black woman whose bones were found in the barn," she said.

"Jesus," Joe whispered. She took a step away, walking in a small circle in the foyer.

"What, she's mentally ill?" Louis said.

"I—" Dr. Sher hesitated. "I don't believe she is."

Joe turned back. "Then what is causing this?"

Dr. Sher took a second to gather her thoughts. "Memory is a complicated process," she said. "But research tells

us that the qualities of a memory do not always provide a reliable way to determine accuracy. For example, a vivid and detailed memory may be based on inaccurate reconstruction of facts. Or even on self-created impressions that appear actually to have occurred."

Joe was listening intently.

"Also," Dr. Sher went on, "memory is a reconstructed phenomenon, and so it can often be strongly influenced by various biases such as social expectation, emotions, the implied beliefs of others, inappropriate—"

"Doctor," Louis interrupted, "help us out here."

Dr. Sher gave him a small smile. "Sorry." She glanced back at Amy before she went on. "I'll try to keep this simple," she said. "Some doctors believe that childhood abuse can cause repressed memories. Later, these memories can resurface on their own or with help."

"But why does Amy think she's a dead black woman?" Joe pressed.

"People think memory is just a matter of recall, but it is also about how the brain reconstructs that memory," Dr. Sher said.

Joe was shaking her head.

"Let me give you an example," Dr. Sher said. "A child might have a memory of standing on a street looking into a scary alley. As an adult, he might falsely remember the alley as containing a dead body, when in fact the child saw only a homeless man sleeping in an alley."

"So, you're saying Amy is mixing real memories of the farm with things from her imagination?" Louis asked.

Dr. Sher nodded. "It's called confabulation. Put simply, it is the mixing or confusion of true memories with irrelevant associations or bizarre ideas. And no matter

how strange or untrue, these ideas can be held with the firmest of convictions."

Louis had to ask the question again. "Is she mentally ill, Doctor?"

"Confabulation is a function of brain chemistry, and it is associated with patients who have suffered brain damage or lesions," Dr. Sher said. "We'd have to do some tests . . ." Her voice trailed off.

Louis was watching Joe, knowing she was seeing Owen Brandt backhand Margi and thinking about what horrors Amy might have suffered at the farmhouse. Things she couldn't, or wouldn't, remember, because maybe, unlike the made-up memories of some dead black woman, the real memories were too close to home.

"This still doesn't explain everything," Louis said.

"What do you mean?" Dr. Sher asked.

"Like why she can sing in French," Joe said.

"Or how she knew where those bones were buried," Louis said.

"No, I guess it doesn't," Dr. Sher said softly.

They fell quiet. Louis was looking at Amy. And Amy was just sitting there on the settee, looking back at them. Through the wavy old glass of the French doors, Amy was just a soft-focus pink blur.

"Okay," Dr. Sher said softly. "There's one other thing I need you to consider."

They both turned to her.

"Before I retired, I was head of research here at the university. I've written many papers on various disorders and conditions. I can't believe I am going to say what I am about to say."

"What?" Louis asked.

"If one believes in repressed memory—and that is a big *if,* as far as I am concerned . . ." Dr. Sher hesitated again. "Hell's bells, I might as well just say this and get it out in the open."

She blew out a hard breath that lifted the red curls from her forehead. "Have either of you ever heard of past-life regression?" she asked.

Louis looked at Joe, who shrugged. "Reincarnation?" Louis asked.

"Well, that would be part of it, yes."

"Good God," Louis said. "You're kidding, right?"

"Louis," Joe said softly.

"It's all right," Dr. Sher said, holding up a hand. "Look, I'm as skeptical as you. But there is some work being done in this field. There's a doctor in Miami who's written some remarkable papers—"

"A doctor?" Louis said.

"Yes, he's the head of psychiatry at Mount Sinai, a professor at the University of Miami Medical School. He was treating a patient with routine therapies, and during a hypnosis session, she—"

Louis held up his hands. "I don't mean to be rude, Dr. Sher, but you just said a minute ago that Amy could be mentally ill. If that is the case, we need to know, because time is running out, for her and for us on this case. If we don't have hard evidence, there's nothing we can really do."

Dr. Sher held Louis's eyes for a moment. "Hard evidence," she said softly. Then she looked to Joe. "I think I'll see how Amy is doing," she said.

She went back into the living room, closing the French doors behind her. Louis watched her go to the settee and sit down next to Amy.

He turned to Joe. "You're awfully quiet."

She looked at the floor.

"Don't tell me you're buying into this past-life crap, Joe."

"I don't know what to think anymore."

"I can't believe what I am hearing," Louis said.

"What do you mean?"

"You're a cop, Joe."

"I don't need you to remind me of that," Joe said quickly. "I just think we have to keep an open mind."

"Well, if you keep your mind too open, your brains fall out," Louis said.

Her eyes shot back to him. "And what the hell does that mean?"

"It means that this can be explained," he said. "There's a reason she knew where those bones were, and I'm going to find it."

Chapter Twenty-two

Louis had been sitting behind the Texaco station for two hours when he finally spotted the green Gremlin coming up Lethe Creek Road. Margi was driving, and Brandt was hunched down in the passenger seat. The car turned and headed north toward Hell.

Louis pushed the Bronco into drive and started toward the farm, one eye on the rearview mirror. He couldn't count on having much time once he got in. But at least this time he knew what he was looking for.

Anything that made sense out of Amy's memories.

This whole case had become too damn strange. So that morning, he had told Joe he was going back to the farm.

"What for?" she had asked.

"Some answers," he said.

"To what?"

When he didn't reply, Joe said, "You don't even know the questions."

The farmhouse came into view. Louis stopped, turned off the engine, and stared at the place through the muddy windshield. Oh, he had questions, all right. The same ones neither Joe nor Dr. Sher had any answers for.

Such as why Amy could sing in French when she didn't even know where she was born. Or how she knew where to dig for those buried bones. And the question he still hadn't told Joe about: Why had Amy put a lock of her hair into the locket he gave her, mimicking the one found in the barn?

All of the "memories" that had come out of Amy's latest hypnosis session—the screaming horses, the men with torches, the names John and Amos—all of that he could easily chalk up to Amy's vivid imagination fed on her reading of *Gone with the Wind*. Joe told him Amy had read the book so many times she could quote whole passages of it.

But the rest? There had to be logical explanations for all of it.

He went to the front door and tried the knob. Locked. Around at the kitchen, he found the same thing. Brandt had installed a new lock. He peered into the door's window. A light was on inside. Brandt had somehow got the power back on. He paused, thought of trying the windows, then remembered something Amy had said.

Joe had asked her recently how she got into the Brandt house the first time. Amy had said there was a cellar door in the back, covered with weeds.

Louis tramped through the weeds to the back. It took a while, but he finally uncovered the two faded blue doors. No lock. He pulled one door open, peered down into the blackness, and went in. Clicking on a flashlight, he found the narrow stairs leading up to the house.

Once in the kitchen, he took stock of the situation. There was a Coleman cooler shoved into one corner. An old table was piled with canned goods, toilet paper, bags of potato chips, and Styrofoam take-out containers. Empty beer cans littered the floor. There was also a red smear on the linoleum. He knelt, running a finger through it.

Blood . . . and he had a fleeting angry image of Brandt hitting Margi in the barn.

Louis went quickly to the front of the house. He started with the boxes in the dining room. But they were filled only with old dishes and glasses. In the hallway, he found boxes of old clothing, boots and shoes, musty books, and one carton brimming with moldering magazines.

There were no boxes in the parlor. But he stopped at the door, staring at the piano.

Amy had been playing it that first day. He went to the piano, noticing for the first time that it was a player piano. He squinted to read the titles on the slender old roller boxes: RAMONA, MY BLUE HEAVEN, TILL WE MEET AGAIN, MAPLE LEAF RAG. He scanned the titles, but there was nothing of note.

Still, there was something about the piano that was tugging at him. He sat down on the stool and put his feet on the pedals. He began to pump them, and a tinny

sound emerged. The piano was so out of tune, the thing so warped and damaged, that the notes barely sounded like music at all.

He stopped. The quiet quickly moved in. His eyes settled on the yellowed piano roll stretched in the window above the keyboard.

The words ran down in a narrow column to the right of the old paper's perforations. He leaned forward to read them:

> *Caches dans*
> *cet asile ou*
> *Dieu nous*
> *a conduits*
> *unis par*
> *le malheur*
> *durant les*
> *longues nuits*

He rewound the roll, eased it from the piano's rollers, and unfurled the top so the title was visible: "BERCEUSE," DE L'OPERA "JOCELYN" PAR BENJAMIN GODARD.

Berceuse. That meant "cradle," or maybe "lullaby." It didn't take much imagination to envision Jean Brandt sitting here playing this old roll and singing the words to her child. *Hidden in this sanctuary where God has led us, united by suffering through the long nights we rest together, rocked to sleep beneath their cover we pray beneath the gazes of the trembling stars.*

But how did Jean know French? And how did Amy retain it all these years? He didn't care. This, at least, explained something.

He stuck the roll under his arm and left the parlor. More boxes in a second back room offered up nothing of use. He paused at the stairs leading to the second story, then went up. He didn't have time to search every box, so he opened flaps, peered in, and closed them, working quickly through the two front bedrooms. At the bedroom in the back, he drew up short.

The pink wallpaper.

He hadn't noticed the pattern before, but then there had been no reason to. Now, all the details registered: a large white plantation-style home, a white horse pulling a black carriage, tall-masted sailing ships. A couple—the man in a long black waistcoat and the woman with her hair up in bun and wearing a long yellow gown straight out of the mid-nineteenth century.

This had been Amy's room. How many nights had she lain in here alone, staring at this wallpaper, absorbing its details?

Louis tore a piece of the peeling paper from the wall, folded it, and stuck it into his pocket. Back out in the narrow hallway, he paused. An open door caught his eye—another staircase.

The attic. He hadn't bothered with it on his first visit. He climbed the creaking narrow stairway. The dim, low-ceilinged attic was crammed with junk: furniture, countless old boxes, stacks of picture frames, an old violin case, rusting tools, and, near the door, piles of yellowed newspapers, some reaching to his chest. He glanced at the top newspaper: HAUSFREUND UND POST, ANN ARBOR MICH. 1891.

There was so much junk—and so little light coming through the one small circular window—he could barely move. And the place gave off a foul feeling. It was noth-

ing he could put a name to, but it was the same feeling he got being in the kitchen, like he had to get out and breathe fresh air. For a moment, he considered abandoning his search. But he knew if there was anything that could illuminate this house's past, it would be found here.

He spotted an old rope hanging from the rafters. He went to it and fingered the frayed end, thinking of Amy's memories of being tied up. But she always talked of being outside or in the barn.

He was about to give up when he spotted a large trunk. He opened it, but it appeared to be filled only with old clothes. Underneath the old lace and moth-eaten velvets, though, his hands closed around an old biscuit tin. It was filled with photographs, small, sepia-toned, and faded with age. There was no time to go through them now. He set the tin aside and dug further.

A Bible . . .

He pulled it out. It was a heavy old thing, its dark red leather scarred, its bindings eaten away by age and insects. He had seen one like it before, back in the Mississippi boarding house where he had briefly stayed while waiting for his mother to die. The woman who had rented him the room—Bessie, he could still see her face clearly—had brought the Bible out one night to show him her family tree because she had a notion that it would instill a sense of pride in his own roots. It hadn't worked—that was a different life, and he had been a different, younger man then. But he had been intrigued by Bessie's attachment to her past and her need to write it all down.

The Bible opened with a soft crack. And there it was,

whole lives laid out on the frontispiece in a listing of births, deaths, and marriages.

Louis took the Bible over to the small window for more light. The names at the top said FAMILY RECORD AMOS AND PHOEBE BRANDT. Patting his jacket, he found his glasses and slipped them on. The listings began in 1800, and a quick calculation told him he was looking at Owen Brandt's great-great-great-grandparents.

Family Record

Amos and Phoebe Brandt

Name	Place	Birth	Marriage	Death
Amos Brandt	Hell, Mich	1800	Phoebe Poole	1879
Phoebe Brandt	Hell, Mich	1802	Amos Brandt	1872
Ann Brandt	Hell, Mich	1829	Clay Stafford	1869
Lucinda Brandt	Hell, Mich	1830	Randolf Rawls	
Zachary Stafford	Kalamazoo, Mich	1849	Linda Wigginton	
Joseph Stafford	Kalamazoo, Mich	1853	Sharon Potts	
Thomas Rawls	Kalamazoo, Mich	1853	Joanne Sinchuk	
Caroline Rawls	Kalamazoo, Mich	1856	Jeremiah Healy	
Quince Stafford	Flint, Mich	1868	Catherine Carper	

This confirmed that the farm had been in the Brandt family for generations. And at least Louis had hard proof that the Amos of Amy's memories was a real man and that his name had been written down in a Bible that Amy could have seen.

As Louis studied the names, he found himself trying to imagine what kind of man Amos Brandt had been. And even stranger, he was trying to imagine what Amos Brandt would feel seeing his farm in ruin and worse,

knowing his family tree had produced such rotted stock as Owen.

He glanced at his watch. He had to get out of here before Brandt returned. He was about to close the Bible when a thought hit him.

He looked again at the names.

Damn. Amos and Phoebe had only two daughters, Ann and Lucinda. The daughters had married and taken their husbands' names. So, how had the Brandt name survived five generations without sons? Who the hell had Owen Brandt descended from? Something wasn't right.

There were two words scrawled under one of the death entries. The second word was CEMETERY; the other might have said BRANDT, but he couldn't make it out.

He closed the Bible, took it and the tin of photographs, and climbed down out of the attic and went back to the kitchen. He retraced his steps through the cellar and closed the blue doors, pulling weeds over them.

Back in the Bronco, he tore a muddy, gravel-spewing path back to the Texaco station. No sign of the Gremlin, so he chanced a quick stop at the gas station, parking out of sight just in case.

Inside, a pimply-faced kid was tipped back in a chair behind the register reading a comic book. He looked up at Louis with eyes that said he didn't get many black men in this part of his world.

"Hey, is there a cemetery around here?" Louis asked.

The kid frowned. "Well, there's a big county one up near Pinckney."

"No, I mean a small one, like just for one family."

The kid shook his head. "Ain't nothing buried around here."

Louis thanked him and left. Back in the Bronco, as he waited for the heater to chase away the chill, he looked again at the Bible's frontispiece.

Two things were gnawing at his brain. How had Owen Brandt come to inherit the farm and the Brandt name if Amos had no sons? And why had Amy screamed out Amos's name in terror?

He stared at the name AMOS BRANDT at the top of the register. This was the man who would give him answers.

All he had to do was find him.

Chapter Twenty-three

A phone call to the Livingston County records office had led Louis to a clerk who had patiently gone through the records but found nothing with the name Brandt in it. It didn't even appear on the countywide survey of family plots the Daughters of the American Revolution had done back in the forties.

But the clerk had told Louis that her grandfather often talked about an abandoned cemetery somewhere out by Lethe Creek. She directed him to Talladay Trail, a dirt road that ran along Lethe Creek. The creek, Louis knew, was the northern border of the Brandt land.

The Bronco bounced along the rutted road, overgrown branches scraping the windows. Louis slowed to avoid a hole, and that was when he saw the small break in the trees. He stopped and peered out of the side window.

He thought he caught a glimmer of water through

the brush. But no way could he get the Bronco down that road. He switched off the engine and got out.

Through the quiet, the trickle of water pricked his ears. He followed the sound through the brush and down a hill, emerging into a marshy slough.

Lethe Creek spilled out before him, its tea-colored water cutting a slow, broad swath through the cattails and sedge grasses before disappearing into a tunnel of black trees to the west.

There was a patch of high, cleared ground on the south bank and what looked like headstones. Or maybe they were just rocks jutting from the ground. He couldn't be sure.

Louis eyed the dark water. Upstream, it narrowed enough for him to venture a leap across. He made it—barely—almost leaving a shoe in the muck on the bank as he fell forward trying to break his momentum.

Wiping his muddy hands on his jeans, he went up the rise. He was standing on a hill, and he looked south. There, through the bare trees, he could just make out the faded red of the old Brandt barn a mile or so away.

He headed east toward the clearing where he thought he had seen the gray stones. They were, indeed, grave markers, mostly small square slabs of granite, some lying toppled in the weeds, others broken and listing.

He went to the front of the largest headstone. The inscription, mottled with moss, was so worn he could barely make it out:

AMOS BRANDT

BORN MAY 3, 1800

DIED JUNE 6, 1879

WHERE THERE IS MUCH LIGHT

THE SHADOWS ARE DEEPEST

The wind sent the trees sighing, and Louis shrugged off the shower of dead leaves. He surveyed the other headstones. There was one of equal size and shape but it was in two pieces, facedown in the weeds. He pried the edge from the dirt and flipped it over. The only word still visible through a swirl of ants was PHOEBE.

Amos's wife.

He went to the nearest stone, the one just to the right of Amos's large marker. He was expecting to see one of the daughters' names from the family Bible, Lucinda or Ann. The carved letters were completely covered in moss. He found a stick, squatted down, and dug out the moss until the letters emerged:

CHARLES BRANDT

BORN JANUARY 1832

DIED APRIL 1895

BELOVED SON OF AMOS

Louis rose slowly. Charles? There had been no record of this name in the family Bible. Louis moved on to the nearest headstone. Most of it was sunken in the ground, leaving only one name and part of a date visible;

CLEONA

1889

Near this one was a tiny marker with the inscription

INFANT DAUGHTER

Gone to the Angels 1856

Was this Charles Brandt's wife and daughter? There were three other headstones that were too old and decayed to make out the inscriptions. Louis noticed another, newer-style headstone in the far southern corner of the clearing and went to it. It was a simple gray marker:

JONAH BRANDT	VERNA BRANDT
D: 1967	D: 1957

This had to be Owen's parents. Louis looked across the grass, back at the first headstone. And Amos must have been the patriarch who had first settled here generations ago. So, why were Amos's "beloved son" Charles and his family buried here at Amos's right side, but their names were not recorded in the family Bible?

Louis felt something touch his leg, and he jumped. He looked down to see a large dog sniffing at his pants. Louis backed away slowly, and the dog gave out a low growl.

"Don't move."

Louis spun at the sound of the voice. An old man was standing at the edge of the trees. How had he not heard him or the dog coming? The dog was staring at him. It had one blue eye and one brown eye.

The old man came forward. He was wearing a red plaid jacket over mud-caked overalls, a John Deere cap pulled low over a thin face elongated by a full gray beard. He carried a stripped-down tree branch as a walking stick.

"Here, give him this, and he'll leave you be," the old man said, holding out a Milk Bone.

Louis, one eye still on the dog, took the biscuit and held it out. The big mutt snatched it and trotted away. Louis let out a breath.

"What's your business here?" the old man asked.

There was a challenge in the man's voice, and Louis was about to ask the same thing when the old man gave him a gap-toothed smile.

"You're one of them history nuts, right?" he asked. "Snooping around graveyards looking for your roots."

Louis nodded, deciding it was better not to be caught trespassing on the Brandt land.

"You got kin here?" the old man asked.

Louis searched the man's face for a smirk. But his expression was merely one of mild curiosity. Then it came to Louis in a cold, clear rush: Charles wasn't in the family Bible because he wasn't Phoebe's son. Charles had a different mother. And she was black.

"You part of the Brandt clan?" the man asked again.

"No, I'm just interested in old cemeteries," Louis said.

"Lots of folks are," the old man said, and went off to find his dog.

Louis walked back to Amos's headstone, an idea forming in his head. The mid-1800s . . . of course, there would have been black servants living on the farm. A young black servant woman, an older man who wielded power over her. An illegitimate son.

Beloved son of Amos.

The dog was back suddenly, sniffing at Louis's feet. Louis felt the old man at his side a moment later.

"Do you know much about the Brandt history?" Louis asked.

"Little bit," the old man said. "Been walking this earth

a long time, son. Now I just walk Henry here every day
this time."

"Do you know about the bones found on the farm
this week?"

"Yup, read about it in the paper. They say they
belonged to a black woman. Been there a long time,
they said."

"Charles Brandt," Louis said. "Was Phoebe his mother?"

"Well, there was always talk about the Brandts. Way
back, I mean," the old man said. "That there was . . .
well . . ."

"A black woman in the family," Louis said evenly.

The man nodded.

Louis went to Charles's headstone. The big yellow
dog trotted over and sat by Louis's feet.

"Is Charles's mother buried here?" Louis asked.

"Don't know. Hard to tell with these old stones being
as messed up as they are," the man said. "Nobody to care
for this place anymore. Things went to hell after Jonah
died. The daughter, Geneva, ran off, and the son, Owen,
got in trouble with the law, I heard."

Louis was thinking about the bones of the black
woman buried in the Brandt barn. It struck him odd that
Amos's "beloved" black son, Charles, was buried here but
that Charles's mother was not.

His eyes traveled over the other ruined and half-
buried headstones. Maybe her headstone had simply
been lost. Or was she the woman whose bones had been
found in the barn?

"Folks are saying she was probably a slave," the old
man said.

Louis looked over at him.

"That woman they found in the barn, I mean," the man said.

"Michigan was a free state," Louis said.

The man tugged at his beard. "Maybe she was runaway and the slave catchers found her at a station here."

"Station?" Louis said. "You mean the Underground Railroad?"

The man nodded. "Two of the lines ran right through these parts, they say."

Louis looked past the old man, southward through the bare trees, to the faded red of the Brandt barn. He was seeing the bones in the dirt, but he was hearing Amy's descriptions of men on horses with torches.

He shook his head slowly.

"What's the matter, son?" the old man asked.

"Nothing," Louis said.

The old man tugged the John Deere cap down on his head. "This is a haunted place," he said. "You can feel it, you can." He scratched the dog's head. "Let's go home, Henry."

Chapter Twenty-four

Joe was perched on the edge of the bed, the old tin of photographs, the Bible, the piano roll, and the scrap of pink wallpaper spread out on the blanket.

"You haven't said what you think about all this," Louis said.

"It certainly explains some things," Joe said.

"I think Dr. Sher is right," Louis said.

"About what?"

"Imagination, real memories, that Amy is just mixing all this up in her head," Louis said.

Joe gave him a warning with her eyes to lower his voice. He looked to the open door and went to it. Amy was sitting on the floor of the living room watching Phil Donahue. Joe had been slowly introducing the girl to television, and she was mesmerized by everything. She was sitting only a foot from the screen, and for a second, Louis thought about telling her to move back, but then he remembered how it annoyed him when his foster mother, Frances, bugged him about the same thing. He closed the door and turned back to Joe.

She was going through the photographs from the tin. She held one out. "Did you see this?"

Louis came forward and took it. It was a sepia-toned photograph of a white man and woman. And a second woman, dark-skinned, holding a baby.

He turned it over. No names or date. But the clothing looked as if it could be of the Civil War era. The man was bearded, with wire-rimmed glasses, wearing a suit. The woman was thin-faced, with severe dark hair, wearing a light printed gown and a dark shawl bound with a cameo brooch. The black woman was much younger, her ebony skin a sharp contrast to the white of her blouse, which seemed too large for her slender frame. Her hair was bound in a scarf. The face of the baby in her arms was as white as its long christening dress.

"Amos and Phoebe?" Joe asked.

"That's my guess," Louis said. He took his glasses from his pocket and slipped them on.

"Then who's the other woman?" Joe asked.

"Charles Brandt's mother?" Louis said.

"And maybe the woman we found in the barn?"

"There's no way to prove it."

Joe sat back against the headboard. "But you want to."

Louis took off his glasses, bringing Joe back into focus. He had known her for more than a year but had told her little about his past. Yet she seemed to know him so well at times. He came over to sit next to her on the bed.

"When I was on the force here in Ann Arbor, I had to take a leave to go to Mississippi," he said. "I didn't want to go. I hadn't been there since I was seven, but my mother was dying, so I went."

"I didn't know you were from Mississippi," Joe said.

"I was born there but went into foster care here in Michigan with the Lawrences when I was seven," Louis said. "While I was down there, I got involved in this old case. Some bones were found in the woods. They turned out to be a lynching victim. No one wanted to know who this man was. No one wanted to speak for him. So I had to."

"Did you ever find out who it was?" Joe asked.

Louis nodded. "His name was Eugene Graham."

Joe drew in a long breath. "Louis, we have other things to consider here. We can't get distracted by this."

"I know that, Joe."

"We have Jean's murder to think about," Joe said. "And we have another hearing coming up in less than a week, and if we don't find something, Owen Brandt will step in front of that judge and ask for his daughter back."

"I know that, too. Maybe the judge will give us more time."

Joe shook her head. "But I don't have more time. I have to get back to work."

Louis rose and walked away, waiting a moment before he turned back to face her. He held up the old photograph. "Things like this are important to me, Joe."

"Well, what happens to that girl out there is important to me, Louis," Joe said.

Louis was quiet. A sudden crazy thought had come to him: Phillip and Frances taking in Amy. But the Lawrences hadn't taken in a foster kid in more than a decade.

A squeak drew their eyes to the door. Amy poked her face in through the crack. "I'm sorry to bother you," she said.

"It's okay, Amy. What is it?" Joe asked.

"Mr. Shockey is here." She lowered her voice. "And I think he's been drinking beer."

Louis went out into the living room. Jake Shockey was standing just inside the door. His face was flushed, and his jacket looked as if he had slept in it. But it was his expression that made Louis go to him.

"Jake, what's the matter?"

Shockey managed a hard smile. "Hey, peeper. Just wanted to drop in and see how things are going." His red-rimmed eyes drifted past Louis and found Amy standing with Joe at the bedroom door. "How's the kid?"

Louis glanced back at Joe, then took Shockey's arm. "Come on, I think you need some coffee."

Shockey didn't seem to hear him. He was still looking at Amy.

"I'll be back in a while," Louis said to Joe. He took Shockey's arm and steered him out the door.

They were the only two people in the hotel lounge. It was a sports bar, strung with NASCAR banners, UM pen-

nants and Big Ten flags. A maize-and-blue football jersey was encased in plastic behind the bar: #48—GERALD FORD, 1932–34.

Shockey hefted himself onto a bar stool and leaned on his elbows. Louis took the stool next to him, looking around for a bartender. The place was quiet except for the *swish-swish* of the glass-washing machine.

"You don't have to babysit me, Kincaid."

"You look like you had a tough day."

"Tough doesn't begin to cover it," Shockey muttered.

A woman emerged from the back room. Her eyes brightened when she saw them, apparently surprised to discover she had customers.

"You want something to eat, Jake?" Louis asked.

"Beefeaters, straight."

"How about a coffee?"

"I said I didn't need babysitting, peeper."

Louis looked back at the bartender. "Club soda for me."

The bartender set down both drinks. Shockey swallowed his shot of gin before the bartender had picked up Louis's ten dollars. Shockey motioned for a second. Louis waited until Shockey downed it before speaking.

"So, what happened? Did you get your ass chewed at work?" Louis asked.

"I got my ass fired," Shockey said.

Louis was quiet as he picked up his change off the bar. Shockey should have been fired, but Louis wasn't about to offer that opinion. He was almost sorry now he'd asked the man down for a drink. He had been in this situation before—spending the evening with middle-aged cops who for one reason or another were washed up. Sometimes it was a screw-up and flat termination;

most times it was burnout. But Jake Shockey looked like a man hanging on to the last knot in the rope.

"You can find another job," Louis offered.

"At thirty-six?" Shockey asked. "Most departments only want guys under thirty. Or women. Or . . . hell, you know it better than me . . . minorities."

Shockey was right. Things were different from ten, fifteen years ago. The rookies were younger and stronger, better trained and better educated. Being white and male was no longer the huge advantage it had been in the seventies and early eighties.

"There's other kinds of jobs," Louis offered.

"I could never be a peeper," Shockey said.

"What about security?"

Shockey grunted and gestured for another shot of gin. He dug into his pants pocket for some money and came out with a twenty and a worn leather wallet. The kind a badge was kept in. He set the wallet next to his shot glass and pushed the twenty to the drink well.

"Look," Louis said. "Life throws you a curve now and then. I don't have to tell you that. I know a guy in Florida who tried to hang on to his job even though he was going blind. Almost killed a kid before he realized he couldn't be a cop anymore."

"How's he doing now?"

Louis took a long drink of his club soda. "He's fine," he lied. "Still adjusting, but he's getting there. But you're not going blind, Jake. You're not old, and you can do other things."

Shockey picked up the leather badge holder and opened it. Sure enough, the depression carved for his shield was empty.

"I've had this fifteen years," Shockey said. "Bought it with my first paycheck. It cost me nine dollars and eighty-six cents."

Louis leaned on the bar and stared absently at the rows of liquor bottles, tempted to order himself a drink and swim the afternoon away in a bottle with Shockey.

"Funny thing," Shockey said. "I didn't come here intending to be a cop."

Louis looked at him. "Here meaning Ann Arbor?" he asked. "Where you from, then?"

"Grew up in Howell," Shockey said. "Not far from the substation where we were the other day. My old man was on disability, and we never had much, but I made all-state my senior year and managed to snag myself a football scholarship to Eastern."

"What position?"

"Running back."

"Did you graduate?" Louis asked.

"Nah," Shockey said. "I blew out a knee my sophomore year and had to drop out. I'd always felt like I was some kind of hometown hero, getting the scholarship and all, and I was too embarrassed to go home, so I just stayed in Ypsi for a few months, working odd jobs. Then one day, I saw the Ann Arbor PD was hiring."

Louis was quiet. It had been the same for him. He'd seen a similar ad, the summer after his senior year. He'd scored well on the LSAT and had a place waiting for him at the UM Law School. But an itch had set in that year, the need to get out from under Phillip Lawrence's financial support, the need to see other places and meet interesting people. The need to make his own money, his own way in the world, and start living his life.

By his twenty-first birthday in November, he was in uniform, patrolling the same streets he used to walk to class on.

"You want another?" Shockey asked.

Louis shook his head as Shockey ordered two more shots for himself.

"Man," Shockey said. "What am I going to do? This is all I know. And Jean . . . what about her? Who's going to help her now?"

"I'm going to stay around for a while," Louis said. "You can still help me. Off the record, you know."

Shockey glanced at him and turned away. He finished one shot but suddenly seemed in no hurry to pick up the other one.

"Fuck, maybe I should just let that go, too," he said. "Maybe she isn't even dead. Maybe she just took off on me, too."

"You don't believe that," Louis said. "And you're making excuses."

Shockey toyed with the empty glass, turning it slowly between his thumb and finger.

"I lied to you," Shockey said softly. "And I lied to her."

Louis sighed and rubbed his brow, his gaze drifting again to the Remy Martin bottle behind the bar. There was only one thing worse than listening to a drunk cry in his beer: having to do it sober.

Shockey finally downed the second shot and slammed the glass down on the bar. "I'm nothing!" he said. "Fucking nothing."

"Calm down."

"Fuck you, peeper, and fuck Brandt, too. Fuck all of 'em, the god damn sonofabitches."

The bartender looked over. "Keep him quiet, would you?"

"Jake, come on," Louis said. "Let me take you home."

"Fuck you."

Louis leaned down to Shockey's ear. "The bartender's going to call the cops," he said. "Don't make things worse by getting your ass arrested. Come on."

Shockey pushed off the stool so hard it tipped. Louis caught it, and as he straightened it, he noticed the brown wallet still lying on the bar in a puddle of gin.

Louis picked it up, stuck it into his pocket, and followed Shockey out into the hotel lobby and to the front doors. Shockey stumbled as he pushed through them, digging again in his pockets to find his car keys.

Louis caught up with him outside. "I'll drive you if you can remember your damn address."

Shockey ignored him as he pulled his entire pocket inside out, dumping everything—keys, coins, bills, and slips of paper to the asphalt.

"Damn it," Shockey muttered.

"I told you, I'll drive you," Louis said, snatching up the keys. "You argue with me, and I'll deck you."

"Fuck you, peeper."

"Come on, let's go."

"Wait," Shockey said. "I need my money."

Shockey knelt to gather his bills and loose change off the ground. Louis thought about helping him but changed his mind and stepped out from under the portico and into the sun. For the first time since he'd arrived in Michigan, there was a spring warmth in the air. It felt good.

"Oh, shit," Shockey said, pushing clumsily to his feet. "I forgot about this."

"What?"

Shockey held out a small piece of paper. "This is a message for you. One of the sergeants gave it to me this morning."

Louis took the paper and unfolded it. It was a note, written on a piece of Ann Arbor PD stationery. The handwriting was bold and dark:

> *Lily wants to meet you.*
> *Tomorrow, 1:00 p.m.*
> *Halo Hat Shop,*
> *122 West Cross Street, Ypsi.*
> *Don't disappoint her, please.*
>   *Eric*

Shockey looked up at him with unfocused eyes. "Something important?"

"Yeah, very important," Louis said, sticking the note into his pocket. "C'mon, I'll drive you home."

Chapter Twenty-five

Louis sat at the window of the sub shop, staring out at the Halo Hats store across the street. He had been sitting here for a half-hour now, nursing a cold coffee and working up the guts to go over there.

He looked at his watch. Two minutes to one.

He tossed a couple of bucks on the counter, got up, and went outside. He paused, tugging on the collar of

his khaki jacket. It was in bad need of a dry cleaning, and a button was missing on one pocket. He wished he had packed his blue blazer. But how the hell could he have known when he left Florida that he was going to be meeting his daughter?

Daughter . . .

He ran his sweating palms down his thighs. At least his jeans were clean. And his loafers were shined. He had paid ten bucks last night at the hotel to send them out.

He stared at the shop across the street.

I can't do this.

He let out a long breath, trying to slow his heart, then walked across the street.

Halo Hats was wedged between a Domino's Pizza and a coin laundry. Louis peered through the front window, but it was so filled with hats he couldn't see anything inside.

A woman emerged suddenly from the door—a thin, imperious black woman in a red suit. She gave him a quick glance, then strutted off down West Cross Street, a pink and white HALO HATS box bouncing against her thigh.

Taking in a final deep breath, Louis pulled open the door and went in.

A bell announced his arrival. But there was no one in the shop to greet him. At least as far as he could see. All he *could* see were hats. An explosion of color—blues, purples, yellows, greens, reds—hats of all shapes and sizes mounted on wire displays like flowers turned to the sun. And there was a smell to the place, overwhelmingly sweet, like the magnolia gardens he had smelled in the South.

He heard a hiss and turned.

A black woman was standing there holding out a can of Glade. She stared at him like he was an insect, the air freshener suddenly brandished like a can of Raid.

"Yes?" she said.

"I'm Louis Kincaid," he said. "I'm here to see Lily."

She was a large woman, her ample body covered by a caftan printed with sunflowers, her broad face crossed with lines that put her age somewhere near sixty-five. But it was her eyes that held Louis—piercing and filled with judgment. The same eyes he had felt on him that day Eric Channing had pulled him over in Ann Arbor.

"I'm Alice Channing," the woman said. "Lily's my grandchild."

Eric Channing suddenly emerged from the back. Before he could say anything, the bell tinkled, and two women came in, stopping behind Louis because there was no room to move in the tiny shop.

"Momma, go take care of your customers," Channing said.

The woman held Louis's eyes for a moment longer, then, with a shake of the head, she came forward. Louis squeezed back into a rack of hats to let her pass.

Channing motioned Louis forward with a wave of his hand. Louis followed him behind the register and into the back room.

She was sitting on a bench in a corner, almost hidden behind a stack of boxes. She sat with her back straight, ankles crossed, her small hands gripping a pink drawstring bag. She was wearing a pink leotard and tights, a filmy little skirt, and pink ballet slippers. Her eyes went first to Channing, who had stopped at the door, arms

crossed over his chest. Channing gave a subtle nod of his bald head.

Lily looked at Louis from under spirals of golden-brown curls.

Kyla . . . she was there in the girl's high, broad forehead and full lips.

But he . . . oh, God, he could see himself there, too. He was there in her pale gray eyes.

He came further into the room, not knowing where to stand, exactly. There was no room for him on the bench, and he wasn't sure she would let him sit down there anyway.

"What should I call you?" she asked.

"How about Louis?" he said.

She nodded and brushed at something on her tights. Her face scrunched in thought when she looked back up at him.

"You're bigger than I thought you'd be," she said.

"Is that okay?"

"Yes," she said. "People can't help how tall they are."

Louis glanced at Channing. He wished he would leave them alone, but Louis understood his need to stay. Channing didn't know Louis, and he probably just wanted to make sure he said nothing inappropriate. In fact, he seemed mildly amused at Lily's last comment.

Louis took a step closer. The room was very small, and he had a thought that maybe she felt overwhelmed by him. He knelt down.

Her eyes found his again. He was the one who felt overwhelmed.

"Where do you live?" Lily asked.

"In Florida," Louis said. "Do you know where that is?"

"Yes," she said. "It's shaped like an upside-down

thumb at the bottom of the country. The capital is Tallahassee."

"That's right," he said. "It's also where Disney World is. Have you ever been there?"

"No," she said. "But I took the train to Chicago and saw the Degas ballerinas at the museum of art. I've seen the *Nutcracker,* and I saw *Cats,* too. At the Fisher Theater."

He shook his head. Here he was talking Disney World, and this little girl was telling him about museums and ballets. Kyla always had more class than he did.

"What is your job?" Lily asked.

"I'm a private investigator," Louis said.

"What's that?"

"Well," Louis said, "it's a little like being a police officer, but you work for yourself, not for a department."

"Are you married?" Lily asked.

"No."

"Why not?"

"Well, I just haven't made that decision yet," Louis said. "It's not something people should do until they're ready."

"Is that why you didn't marry my mother?" Lily asked. "You weren't ready?"

Here it was, the first of the tough questions.

Louis glanced back at Channing, but there was no answer there. He stared at the carpet for a few seconds, trying to find the right words to explain something like this to an eight-year-old. But then he realized she had said it more aptly than he ever could.

"I was immature," he said. "Do you know what that means?"

"Yes," Lily said. "It means you act like a child when you're old enough to know better."

"That's right."

She lowered her head, and for a moment, her face was lost behind the cascade of curls. Her voice was almost a whisper. "How old were you when you made me?" Lily asked.

Louis closed his eyes for a second. "Twenty."

"How old are you now?" she asked.

"Twenty-nine."

"So, you didn't get mature at all until now?"

If he could have vanished from the room, he would have. What the hell was he supposed to say? The truth was, he didn't know she existed. But if he said that, her next question would be *What did you think happened to me?* And he sure couldn't answer that one.

He couldn't even bring himself to meet those tender eyes until he heard Channing clear his throat.

"Lily," Channing said. "Mr. Kincaid didn't know where you were. When he and your mother broke up, they stayed mad at each a long time and didn't talk."

Thank you, sergeant.

Lily seemed to accept that explanation, and she looked back at Louis, her eyes deep with a new thought.

"Do I have more grandparents?"

"My mother has passed on," he said, "but you have . . ."

He paused. He was about to tell this girl she had a grandfather whom he not only knew nothing about, but whom he despised.

"You have a grandfather," he said. "But I haven't seen him for many years. Not since I was a baby."

She blinked, a strange shadow coloring her eyes. "So your father never got mature, either?"

She was breaking his heart.

"No, I guess not."

"My daddy's father isn't mature, either," she said, looking to Channing. "He lives in California and doesn't care about us."

Louis glanced at Channing. He shifted his weight, obviously uncomfortable that Lily had revealed this little slice of family history to Louis. But it explained Channing's motives in telling Louis about his daughter. Channing was a man with holes in his heart, too.

When Louis looked back at Lily, she was studying him, her gaze moving slowly over his face, then to his hair, and finally coming back to his eyes. It was an intriguing stare, and he wondered what her next question would be.

"Is your father white?" she asked.

"Yes."

Her face scrunched again. Louis wondered why Kyla had never shared at least this part of Lily's ancestry with her. Or maybe she had told her there was some white blood in her but not where it came from.

"So that makes me a quarter white?" she asked.

"Yes," Louis asked. "Does that bother you?"

"No," she said. "I like how I look. Momma says I'm like a bouquet of wildflowers put together by God and all the prettier for it."

Louis smiled.

Lily sighed and folded her hands in her lap, the little drawstring purse hanging from her wrist. She didn't seem to have any more questions. But Louis was wondering what she was thinking. Would she simply dismiss this as a necessary but uneventful meeting, or did she want something more? And again, he couldn't ask. He did not want

her to feel obligated to see him again. He looked again to Channing for help.

"Lily," Channing said, "if there's nothing else you want to say to Mr. Kincaid, it's time to go."

Lily hesitated, then pulled open the drawstring purse. She dug inside and pulled out a photograph. She held it out to Louis.

"This is a picture of me," she said. "You can have it. If you want it, I mean."

Louis took it. "Thank you very much, Lily."

She pushed off the bench and padded to the door in her pink slippers. She turned back to Louis, but before she spoke, she took Channing's hand. His large fingers closed tightly over hers.

"Can I see you again?" she asked Louis.

Louis glanced at Channing. He gave a tight nod.

"Any time you want," Louis said.

"Saturday?" she asked.

"Okay. Here?"

Lily looked up at Channing.

"How about you take Lily to lunch Saturday?" Channing said. "I have to work. You know, on patrol."

Channing was offering alone time but also letting Louis know he wouldn't be too far away, sitting in his cruiser.

"I'd like that," Louis said.

Lily wet her lips and for a moment seemed a little lost about what she was supposed to do now.

"Goodbye," she said softly. "It was nice meeting you, Louis."

Chapter Twenty-six

Thirty-six years old, and here he was, committing his first crime. Well, not his first, exactly. His first was planting his ex-wife's bra in the trunk of Jean's car and asking a decent man to file a false report. But since nothing had come of that, it wasn't really a crime in his mind.

This *would* be a crime, Shockey knew. The minute that green Gremlin pulled away and he went inside a house that was not his, he would be a criminal, a trespasser at the very least, a felon if he took anything.

Jake Shockey unwrapped a piece of Dentyne and stuck it in his mouth. He was sitting in his car, an '85 AMC Eagle partially covered in gray primer. It was one of the few things he'd walked away with after his divorce. He hadn't minded giving the rest to his ex-wife, Anita: the twenty-seven-inch TV, the new bedroom suite, the canoe he'd wanted so badly for those fishing trips on the Au Sable River he had never gotten around to taking.

And the two kids, Brian and Ellie.

None of it had really been his, anyway.

You had to love something or someone to make it yours, and all of those things had been only temporary replacements, things he tried to use to fill the emptiness of something else. And when they were gone, it hadn't mattered much to him.

But when Jean was gone . . .

When he'd made the decision to come out to the farm that morning, he told himself he had nothing to lose anymore. The final replacement "thing" he had—his job—was gone now, too. And it was funny what people thought

about and what they were capable of when there were no more rules and they had nothing to lose anymore.

He heard the rattle of a small car's engine, and he slipped quickly from the wagon and crept to the wall of brush that camouflaged it. Brandt and Margi were leaving the house. They were far away, and he couldn't see Margi's face, but he could tell she was limping. He wondered if—no, he didn't wonder, he knew—Brandt had hurt her.

He watched the Gremlin leave, climbed back into his wagon, and made the quarter-mile drive to the farm. Brandt had left the gate ajar, and Shockey drove around back to park, remembering that Kincaid had told him the only way into the house was through the cellar doors.

In less than a minute, he was in the kitchen.

Something bad happened here . . .

That's what the girl had said. And Shockey was sure he knew what it was. If Jean had been killed in this house, it was here in this god-awful kitchen.

But where to start?

He stood in the center of the kitchen and took a long look around. No appliances, scuffed blue linoleum, dark scarred wood paneling halfway up the walls, then faded yellow paper spotted with black mold. One wall of built-in cupboards in the same dark wood, the doors flung open to empty shelves.

The cupboard.

Kincaid had said the girl had been hiding in there when he found her. Maybe that's where she had been that night, too. Shockey knelt by the cupboard and opened it wider. He grabbed his flashlight from his rear pocket and shined it over the inside.

Nothing but cobwebs and scratches. Maybe made by the sliding of pots and pans or maybe by the kid. No blood he could see, but then again, if the door had been closed during the murder, there would be no blood inside.

He had seen plenty of domestic homicides, and it was his experience that when the abuser was someone like Brandt, the scene was almost always bloody and violent, the result of a beating or a stabbing. It would not have been what the cops called a clean murder, a smothering or a strangling done quietly in a bedroom.

Shockey closed the door and carefully examined the outside. When he could see nothing, he drew his pocket-knife from his pants and opened it. Slowly, he scraped at the stains and grime stuck in the grooves of the old wood cupboard.

Small dark bits fell to the linoleum. He wet his finger and pressed it to a flake, bringing it to his nose. It had no odor. But he pulled a small envelope from his shirt and put some of the scrapings inside. He labeled it CUPBOARD DOOR and sealed it.

Still on his knees, he crawled across the blue linoleum. There were many holes and tears, and he shined his flashlight at each one, hoping to see something that resembled blood, but all he saw was black grime. He scraped some up, filling three more envelopes.

It occurred to him that he no longer had access to a lab or the authority to request an analysis of anything. But hell, if he had to, he'd find an independent lab and pay for it himself. Or get the peeper's girlfriend to do it for him.

He sat back on his heels and looked around.

This place was so filthy that any of the stains and dirt

could contain blood and he'd never see it. He should have pilfered some Luminol and a lamp from station supply. But using Luminol to bring out bloodstains required total darkness, and there was probably no way he could get in here at night. It looked as if Brandt had set up permanent housekeeping.

Shockey eyed the blue linoleum.

There were enough gaps and holes in it that if Jean had bled much at all, there was a good chance some of it had soaked into the floorboards below.

He shut his eyes for a moment. It was a horrible image and he wondered how he could even conjure it up to sit in his head beside his memories of her face.

That lovely, innocent face that never asked him any questions and never demanded anything from him. Never made him feel like the heel he was for leaving her in that shitty motel on Washtenaw and going home to the three-bedroom ranch in time to kiss his wife good night.

Stop it, you asshole. Stop it. This is how you fix it. This is what you do now.

He wiped the blade of the pocketknife on his pants and started digging at one of the small holes. He worked the linoleum up until there was enough to grab. Then he started ripping it away from planks below.

"What the fuck are you doing?"

Shockey looked up. Owen Brandt stood in the kitchen doorway. Black T-shirt, dirty jeans, three days' growth of whiskers. He held a large knife in his hand.

Shockey reached for his gun and leveled it as he rose to his feet. "Put the knife down, Brandt."

"It's just a kitchen knife. It's legal for me to have a fucking kitchen knife."

"I said put it down."

Brandt reluctantly dropped it to the floor. He even did Shockey the favor of kicking it away before Shockey told him to.

"You got a warrant to be doing that?" Brandt asked, tipping his head toward the torn linoleum.

"You worried?"

Brandt smiled. "Not one damn bit. But I still know you need a damn warrant to be tearing up my kitchen."

"Get up against the counter," Shockey said.

Brandt turned slowly and put his hands on the counter. Shockey patted him down. The fact that Brandt had walked in with a knife meant he might have another weapon, and Shockey was praying to find one on him. For a second, he even thought of planting one, but he knew he'd never get away with it, and he did not want this bastard suing the city and getting any money. Another idea crossed his mind, too. Plant drugs or a weapon in the Gremlin, and then make an anonymous phone call. But that idea was interrupted by Margi's nasal voice.

"What's going on?" she asked.

Shockey looked up, keeping one hand on the back of Brandt's neck. Margi was backlit by the open door, but he could still see the splash of bruises on her thin face. A cut over her left eyebrow was so swollen it left her eye shut.

Shockey banged Brandt's head against the wall. "You do that?"

Brandt twisted to look at Margi. She quickly faded into the shadows. Shockey slammed Brandt's head a second time against the wall, then jerked him back by his T-shirt.

"Answer me. You do that?"

"What are you going to do about it?" Brandt asked.

Shockey spun Brandt around and slugged him. Brandt's body smashed into the wall behind him. He never got his hands up before Shockey hit him again.

"Did you do that?" Shockey yelled.

"Why do you care?" Brandt said, wiping his lip. "You wanna fuck her, too? You like my leftovers, cop? Then take her, take her like you did Jean."

Brandt's ugly face blurred in a flash of white rage. Shockey started swinging. His fist busted into Brandt's jaw, nose, eye—anywhere he could hit him.

"She wasn't nobody's leftovers!" Shockey shouted. "You hear me, you stupid sonofabitch? You hear me?"

Brandt crawled along the counter, ducking the blows. "Stop it!" Brandt yelled. "I can't hit you back. You're a fucking cop. Leave me alone!"

Shockey grabbed Brandt's T-shirt and flung him to the floor. He kicked him in the gut before he could get up. Brandt groaned and tried to slither away, but there was nowhere for him to go. "She wasn't nobody's leftovers!" Shockey said. "She was a good woman, and you killed her!"

"She was a fucking whore!" Brandt shouted.

Shockey kicked him again. Brandt threw out his hand, trying to protect himself, but Shockey smashed his knuckles with the toe of his shoe.

"Shut up!"

"She was a fucking whore when I married her," Brandt said, crouched now against the cupboard. "Seventeen years old and already fucking pregnant with some other bastard's kid. You didn't have nothing special with her nobody else didn't have."

Shockey stared at him. "What did you say?"

"What?"

"What did you say about her being pregnant?"

"I said she was already a whore when I married her. Her father paid me to marry her."

"So that kid isn't yours?" Shockey asked.

Brandt looked up slowly, hand at his mouth. Blood dripped from his nose. His eyes were swimming with a different kind of fear, something more powerful than the fear of getting kicked again.

Shockey dropped to one knee and put his gun to Brandt's temple. "Is Amy your kid or not?" Shockey demanded. "Answer me!"

"Please, mister, please don't kill him."

Shockey looked to the kitchen door. Margi was watching them, one hand on the wall, the other at her mouth. Black mascara tears cut through the bruises on her face.

"Please don't kill him," she said again. "Cops can't just shoot people, can they?"

Shockey drew away from Brandt and rose to his feet. He knew he could have done it. And a second ago, it might have been worth it. But not now.

"You wanna press charges for what he did to you, lady?"

Margi shook her head, her nervous gaze going to Brandt, then coming slowly back to Shockey. She was the most pitiful thing he'd ever seen. And he had a horrible feeling about leaving her with this monster.

He reached into his pocket for one of his Ann Arbor PD business cards, then realized he didn't have any. He had a pen, though, and he scribbled his home phone on the moldy yellow wall.

He looked at Margi. "When you get tired of being a

punching bag, you call me," he said, pointing to the wall.

Her eyes pleaded with him to leave.

Brandt was pulling himself to his feet. "Get out of my house, cop," Brandt said. "'Cause you're finished. I'll make sure of that."

Shockey gathered up his small evidence envelopes and pushed out the back door. The gate was ajar when he reached it with his wagon, and he drove right through it, busting it from the post.

He was a mile down the road before he finally slowed to a safe speed and took a breath.

Seventeen years old and already fucking pregnant with some other bastard's kid.

Louis opened the door of the hotel room. He was expecting the pizza delivery man, but it was Shockey.

"Look, Jake—"

"I'm sober," Shockey said. "Let me in. We have to talk."

Louis glanced behind him at Joe and Amy. They were at the coffee table, playing a game of Yahtzee.

"You want to go downstairs?" Louis asked.

Shockey was looking at something over Louis's shoulder and Louis turned again to see what was so interesting. Shockey seemed to be staring at Amy.

"Jake?"

"I need to talk to both you and Joe," he said. "It's about the custody hearing. Can we send the kid—Amy—to the bedroom for a minute?"

"Yeah, sure," Louis said. "Joe?"

Joe rose and took Amy to the bedroom. Louis heard her turn on the television. Joe returned a few minutes later and closed the door behind her.

Shockey dropped into a chair. "I went out to the farm today," he said.

"Are you kidding me?" Louis asked.

"Just listen," Shockey said. "I gathered up these scrapings from the kitchen."

He laid the envelopes on the coffee table. "I'll pay to find out if there's any blood in them," he said. "I knew when I did it I couldn't bring it into court, but I had to know, Kincaid. I just had to know."

Louis shook his head. "You're crazy."

"But that isn't all," Shockey said. "Brandt came back while I was there. I knocked him around when he started running at the mouth about Jean."

"Aw, man, Jake," Louis said. "You're lucky he didn't kill you."

"Nah, he didn't even fight back," Shockey said. "He's scared of going back to jail. And that woman, that Margi woman, she was all beat up."

"And she didn't want to press charges, right?" Joe asked.

"Right," Shockey said. "I have a bad feeling about her being out there all alone with him."

"And you think telling a judge that you were out there doing an illegal search and you saw a beat-up woman will help keep Amy away from Brandt, right?" Joe said.

"No," Shockey said. "But I think telling a judge she isn't Brandt's kid might."

Louis leaned forward. "What do you mean, not his kid? How do you know that?"

"He told me himself when I was using him for a punching bag," Shockey said. "He said Jean was already pregnant when he married her."

Joe started to the box in the corner where they kept their files and notes on the case.

"If you're going looking for the date Owen and Jean got married, don't bother," Shockey said. "I already know it. It was November 1972."

For a long moment, the room was quiet. Joe came back to the sofa and sat down next to Louis. Louis was looking at the closed bedroom door. He broke the silence.

"That makes Amy sixteen, not thirteen."

"Louis, do you really think someone that young could just lose three years of her life?" Joe asked. "Surely someone was able to keep better track than that."

"Maybe she was so underdeveloped the schools kept putting her back," he said. "Maybe Geneva just lied to her. I don't know."

Louis looked back at Shockey. "But how do we even begin to find Amy's real father?" he asked. "Do we even know where Jean grew up?"

"She grew up in Unadilla," Shockey said. "It's a little town near Hell."

"I didn't see that in the report," Louis said. "Did she tell you that?"

"No," Shockey said. He drew a deep breath. "I lied to you both: I knew Jean before she started showing up at the farmer's market in 1980. I knew her when she was seventeen."

The second silence was longer than the first. This time Shockey broke it.

"I think I'm Amy's father," he said.

Louis closed the bedroom door and went to the kitchenette. He got a beer, his first in five days, and dropped down onto the sofa.

"She had another of her asthma attacks and couldn't breathe," Louis said.

Joe started to get up, but Louis waved her back into her chair. "She's okay now. She's resting. We can talk now."

Shockey set down his coffee cup and looked at Louis and Joe. Louis had seen many men on the edge, criminals, cops, and sometimes just ordinary men with not so ordinary secrets. Shockey seemed to hold something of all three.

"I met Jean when I was in high school," he said. "Her family was real strict, and she didn't get to go out much. But she made it to a church party one night, and I found her just sitting in the corner."

"When was this?" Joe asked.

"My senior year," Shockey said. "It was right after the last football game of the year. Anyway, I liked her right off. I mean, I didn't have much, with my dad being on disability and all, but she had less."

"Was she a farm girl?" Louis asked.

"Yeah," Shockey said. "Her mother was this holy roller who put the fear of God in her about boys and sex and all that shit. I think her father might have beat her. She never said for sure, but Jean was always talking about wanting to get away from them."

Shockey drew a slow breath.

"We started seeing each other, meeting secretly when she could get out of the house. I couldn't help it, I loved her, and I wanted her so bad. We started . . ." His voice trailed off as he closed his eyes. "At the end of summer, I had to leave to go to football camp. We had plans. I mean, I wanted to come back and marry her, get us both somewhere better. But when I busted up my knee, I couldn't face anyone, and, well, I finally stopped writing to her."

Shockey shook his head. "When I finally worked up the guts to go to her place, her mother told me Jean had moved away. Wouldn't tell me where. Just slammed the door in my face."

"Jean never told you she was pregnant?" Joe asked.

Shockey shook his head. "She wouldn't have," he said. "We talked a lot about not being the kind of people our parents were, always having to scrape for every dollar. We talked a lot about me needing to make something of myself before we could get married. I was supposed to go to college. That's what Jean wanted for me—for us. That was our ticket out."

Louis was quiet, some of this sounding too familiar.

"Nine years," Shockey whispered. "I should have . . ." His voice trailed off as he rose and went to the window.

Louis watched Shockey's broad back, hoping the man wasn't going to break down right here. Not with Amy in the next room.

"So now what?" Joe asked.

Shockey turned to look at her.

"Are you thinking of trying to prove this to a judge and taking custody of Amy?"

Shockey ran a hand over his eyes. "Why not?"

"It's going to be hard to prove, Jake," Louis said. "You know a blood test can't prove you're her father. It can only prove you're not. And besides, you'd need Jean's blood type—"

"I have it," Shockey said. "We got blood tests to get married. And I have a few pictures, and maybe I can find someone who remembers we were together back then."

Joe suddenly stood up and walked a small circle around the living room. "Jake, listen," she said. "I appre-

ciate your good intentions here, but I don't think a judge is going to find you much more fit than Owen Brandt."

"If Amy is mine, she belongs with me," Shockey said.

"It doesn't work like that, Jake," Louis said.

"But what are our options?" Shockey asked. "Some foster home?"

"Do you hear yourself?" Joe asked. "My God, up until today, you still called her 'the girl.' You haven't established any kind of bond with her. And she doesn't feel anything special toward you."

"That will come," Shockey said. "It's a natural thing, and it'll come. She's Jean's daughter. She's my daughter. I can do this. I know I can."

"Sorry, Jake, I can't let you do it," Joe said.

"You can't stop me," he said.

"As her temporary guardian, I can," Joe said. "Unless you can prove you're her father, no judge is ever going to let you have her. And I won't just sit back and let you disrupt her life all over again. At least, not yet. Not until you clean up your act and find a decent place to live and get a new job."

Shockey rose slowly to his feet. "She's my daughter," he said. "You have no right to keep her from me."

"Don't try to fight me on this, Jake. You won't win."

Shockey stared her at disbelief.

Joe grabbed her jacket off the chair. "I need some air." She looked at Louis. "Keep an eye on Amy."

When the door closed behind her, Shockey sank slowly back into the chair. The room was quiet, and for a long time, they just sat there. Shockey stared at his folded hands. Louis finished his beer and set the bottle gently on the coffee table.

"You've got to talk to her for me, Kincaid," Shockey

said. "You've got to get her to understand that Amy belongs with family."

"No," Louis said.

"But I don't understand," Shockey said. "That woman doesn't have a maternal bone in her body. Why is she doing this to me?"

"You did it to yourself, Jake," Louis said. "You don't fix what you did sixteen years ago with a blood test now."

"Just heap some more shit on me, why don't you?" Shockey said. "You think I don't feel lousy enough?"

Louis sank back on the cushions, thinking about his lunch with Lily tomorrow.

"Feeling lousy is the easy part," he said.

Chapter Twenty-seven

The cops had left the barn a mess. Crime-scene tape hung from the stalls and across the door. Evidence markers littered the dirt. And no one had filled in the hole where the bones of that woman had been found.

Owen Brandt stared and grunted.

They could at least have done that. Filled in the damn hole. Who wanted to look into an open grave? Who wanted an open grave on their property, like death was just waiting for them?

"I'm cold," Margi said. "Why can't we go back to the house?"

"Shut up. I'm thinking," Brandt said without looking at her.

"What are you thinking about?"

"Me and that," he said, pointing to the hole.

"What do you care about some dead black woman?" Margi asked. "What does she have to do with you?"

Brandt moved away from her, closer to the hole.

What do *those nigger bones have to do with me?* The question was eating at him, and he wasn't sure he wanted even to think about this. He hadn't thought about it since he was thirteen, hadn't thought about it for one second since that day Geneva had said it.

You know, we got colored blood in us, Owen. Ma told me once our great-great-great-grandma was colored.

That ain't true.

Is too.

Is not. I'm no nigger.

He didn't believe her, didn't want to believe her, because Geneva was always making up stuff to get him mad. But it had stayed there in his head nevertheless.

"Come on," Brandt said. "We're taking a walk."

He went out the barn door and headed north, across the cornfield. Margi trailed along behind him.

He hadn't been out to the cemetery since he was a kid, but he could still remember where it was. His old man had always made a big deal about coming out here when the lilac bushes were in bloom so they could lay some flowers on the graves of his own father and mother, Calvin and Muriel.

No lilacs this year. It had been too damn cold.

Brandt stopped on a hill and looked behind him to the south. Through the bare trees, he could just make out the faded red of the old barn.

Margi trudged up behind him, breathless and shivering. "Why are we here?" she asked.

"Because I need to know where I come from," Brandt said.

He walked toward the creek, to the small clearing where the cluster of old headstones lay half buried in the earth. He remembered where his old man and his mother were, and he went there first. It was a simple gray marker:

JONAH BRANDT	VERNA BRANDT
D: 1967	D: 1957

"That your parents?" Margi asked.

He didn't turn to look at her, didn't bother to answer. He trudged to the first row of old headstones and knelt to clear away the weeds. He had to use a stick to scrape the dirt and moss from the etching. Calvin and Muriel. On the stone next to it, only the name of Samuel was visible.

He scraped away at the next headstone until it revealed a name he had never heard before: Lizbeth. He guessed she was Samuel's wife and moved on. The next headstone in the row belonged to Charles, followed by two people named Amos and Phoebe. They must've been the ones to start this farm, since the dates on their stones appeared to be the oldest.

He had vague memories of his grandfather Calvin, but he had never paid any attention to the rest of these people. Never cared before today. Was it those nigger bones in the barn that had driven him here or something else?

"Wow, your family has been here a long time," Margi said, staring at Amos Brandt's stone.

"Yeah," he said.

Brandt pushed to his feet and started walking, kicking

at the weeds to see if there were other headstones hidden. At the edge of the clearing, the toe of his shoe hit something hard, and he bent to see what it was. Just a broken piece of granite, inscribed with one name: ISABEL.

Who was this, and why was her stone so far away from the others?

Mama told me once our great-great-great-grandma was colored.

That ain't true.

Is too.

Brandt brought his heel down hard on the stone. Bits of the edge crumbled away. Three more tries, but he couldn't smash it. Finally, he picked it up and started to throw it into the trees. But then he looked toward Lethe Creek. He carried the piece of granite down to the bank and heaved it into the water.

"Why did you do that?" Margi asked.

"'Cause it don't belong here."

"Why not?"

"Come on," he said, grabbing Margi's arm. "Let's get out of here."

He didn't like going up to the attic, but today he had no choice. That's where the Bible was. He had seen it up there once, seen Crazy Verna holding it against her chest and praying on it. Like God could actually free her of her demons.

She had shown him the Bible once, shown him where all the names of the Brandt family were written. He hadn't paid any attention then, but he wanted to see it now, wanted to know if what Geneva had told him was true.

He pulled himself up onto the plywood that covered the beams and looked around. The place was a mess here, too. Boxes everywhere, old books and pictures strewn around like someone had been searching through them for something. Probably that stupid girl looking for a picture of her slut mother, but he had burned them all years ago.

He pushed at cobwebs as he walked to the far corner of the attic. He ducked under the same beam Crazy Verna had hung herself from and knelt next to an old chest. This is where she had kept it, he remembered. But there was nothing but old clothes in the chest now.

He tore through the boxes, throwing the contents aside. But there was no Bible. He stood, panting, his eyes traveling around the attic. There was an old wooden crate wedged under the eave in the corner. He pulled it out. It was nailed shut, and he had to hunt up a hammer to pry it open. He lifted the lid.

Fuck. No photos or books in here, but there was one thing, a thing he had forgotten about. He reached in and pulled out the knife.

It was the one he had used on Jean that night in the kitchen.

When had he put it in here?

That night?

Hell, he'd been so drunk it was possible. He barely remembered cleaning up the kitchen.

He held the knife up to the thin light. It had been his favorite knife, the one he used to skin deer. He had bought it special out of a catalogue, not minding that it cost forty dollars, because when a man was standing out in the freezing cold trying to gut a deer, he didn't need his hand slipping down the grip.

And that night, when the tip of the blade had broken off in Jean's belly, it was like she'd taken the one good thing he had left.

Brandt stared at the broken tip, still crusted with her blood.

"Owen? What are you doing up here?"

He turned. Only Margi's head was visible above the opening. The shadows played across her thin face, and for a second, she looked a little like his mother.

"Leave me alone," he said.

"What's wrong with you, anyway? You're acting crazy."

You're acting crazy.

That was one of the last things Jean had said to him. He looked at Margi again. She had crawled up onto the plywood. Verna was there in her lopsided mouth and bony features. Jean was there, too, in her wide, frightened eyes.

"You see this?" he asked, holding up the broken knife.

Margi crawled closer. "You ain't supposed to have no weapons, are you?" she asked.

"No, I ain't supposed to have no weapons," he said, mocking her tone.

"Owen, that has blood on it."

"It's her blood," he said, picking at the crust.

When Margi didn't reply, he looked up. She had moved away into the shadows and was watching him. Again, it was weird just how much like Jean she was. Weak and scared all the time but still willing to climb into his bed at night and do what she could to make him happy.

"You ever think about leaving me, baby?" he asked.

"No, Owen. Never."

"Never?"

"Never."

Brandt beckoned her closer. Margi hesitated, then crawled across the plywood to him. He grabbed the back of her neck and crushed her mouth with his. Margi's hands instinctively came up against his chest until she realized what he was doing.

He jerked her head back and placed the broken blade against her throat. Her hands flew to his wrists, gripping.

"Owen, don't."

"Tell me the truth. Do you ever think about leaving me?"

"No, I love you. *I love you.*"

He stared at her. Fear colored her eyes a navy blue. Funny, the same fear had turned Jean's brown eyes black.

"Owen, please," she whimpered. "I won't leave you. I'm not her. I'm Margi."

He shoved her away. Still, the stupid bitch did not make any attempt to leave the attic. She huddled in the corner, holding her throat. For a long time, he just sat there, staring at the knife.

"She was going to leave me," he whispered.

"Is that why you killed her?" Margi asked.

He looked to her, surprised that she would ask that— or even speak.

"It's okay if you did," Margi said. "I understand why you had to. I still love you."

He held the knife to the sunlight. Still loved him? He didn't care if she loved him. But he had never told anyone what had happened that night, never given it voice. Maybe that was why he couldn't find Jean. Maybe if he talked about it, it would make things more real, make her more real.

"I think I killed her," he said.

"You think?"

"I stabbed her with this," he said. "Must've been a hundred fucking times. In the kitchen."

Margi was quiet, but he could hear her fast, frightened breathing.

"When the knife busted, I went to the barn to get the axe," he said. "When I got back, Jean was gone. And there was this long smear of blood on the floor, like she had drug herself out the back door."

"She got away?"

Brandt rose and walked to the tiny window that overlooked the cornfield. There was no rain today and no mud, but he remembered how it looked that night. Everything a dark, wet blur, making it impossible to see a trail or to find someone who couldn't have been but a few feet away.

Where had she gone to that night? Where was she now?

"Owen?" Margi whispered.

He didn't look back at her. This place, these memories and everything else were loosening his mouth, but just as he couldn't stop thinking about her, he couldn't seem to stop talking about her either.

"The next day," he said, "I searched the whole fucking farm for her, but I never found her. For a long time, I figured she made it somewhere and got help."

He turned away from the window. "I can't help thinking that she might be alive and living somewhere with another man," he said, "fucking another man and laughing at me for what I tried to do to her."

"She's gotta be dead, Owen."

"Then where the fuck is she?" he shouted. "You tell me that, god damn it. *Where the fuck is she?*"

Margi lowered her head. "I don't know, Owen," she said. "But you can't let it eat at you like this. You don't need to be thinking about her, anyway. You got me now. Ain't I enough?"

He looked down at the knife blade. He could still see Jean's face as it was that night when she lay on the floor. Her eyes electrified with horror, the color draining from her cheeks as her heart pumped the blood from her chest.

He stuck the knife into his belt and walked across the plywood to the hole. As he started to climb down the ladder, Margi reached for his arm. He shrugged her off.

"Owen, where are you going?" she asked.

"To walk the farm again."

"To look for a dead woman?"

He started toward her, but Margi scrambled into the corner. He stopped, let his fist fall. His eyes moved away from Margi, away to the small window that looked out over the fields.

"She ain't dead," Brandt said. "She's out there some-where, and I'm going to find her."

Chapter Twenty-eight

Joe pulled the Bronco to a stop, and Louis looked out the window at the Kerrytown market. The place had once been the site of the old farmer's market, but now it was a bustling complex of shops and eateries, the fruit and vegetable vendors competing with cafés, hair salons, toy stores, and boutiques. On this sunny Saturday af-

ternoon, Kerrytown was crowded with families pushing strollers and carrying bags of gourmet cheeses, wines, and fresh-baked breads.

He tried to conjure up an image of Jean Brandt selling tomatoes out of the back of her truck to Shockey but couldn't see it. All he could see was that faded snapshot of Jean's wan face. All he could think about was Shockey's desperation to prove that Amy was his daughter.

"Is that her?"

Louis turned to look where Joe was pointing.

Lily was sitting alone on a park bench in front of Zingerman's deli, wrapped in a bright red sweater, a plaid skirt, red tights, and patent-leather shoes. A second later, Eric walked up with a wad of napkins. Louis watched as Eric gently held a napkin to Lily's face while she blew her nose.

"She's beautiful," Joe said.

"She looks like her mother," Louis said, regretting it immediately. He didn't have to look at Joe to know his words wounded her. She had been unnaturally quiet all morning and he knew that Lily—and, by extension, Kyla—was the reason.

"I'll pick you up in an hour," Joe said. "We need to be at Dr. Sher's at two."

Louis glanced at Amy sitting in the backseat. Then he leaned over and put his hand around Joe's neck. He pulled her to him and kissed her. He felt her respond, but when he let go, her eyes still held doubt.

"Thanks," he said.

He got out of the Bronco and started across the old brick street. Eric saw him before Lily did, and he rose, holding out a hand.

Louis shook it. "Sergeant."

Eric glanced down at Lily, then back up at Louis. He looked like he was about to hand over his most precious possession in the world. With a small kick to his heart, Louis realized that was exactly what he was doing.

"You be good now, baby," Eric said to Lily. "Remember what we said."

Lily rolled her eyes. "No chocolate."

Eric looked at Louis. "She's allergic."

Louis nodded.

"I'll be nearby," Eric said, nodding to the cruiser parked around the corner.

"Thanks," Louis said.

Eric hesitated. Then, with a stiff nod and a last glance at Lily, he walked away.

Louis waited until he had disappeared before he looked down at Lily. "I'm hungry," he said. "How about you?"

She smiled. "Do you like hot dogs?"

"Sure."

"They have really good ones here. Let's go."

Louis wondered for a second if he should take her hand. But before he could decide, Lily hopped off the bench and led him to the door. The deli was swirling with noise and mouthwatering smells. Lily seemed to know where to go, so Louis followed her up to the counter, getting a tray for each of them. Lily asked him for a Coke. He got two. When the man asked Louis what he wanted, Louis looked down at Lily.

"Two Icky dogs," she said. She looked up at Louis. "Do you like French fries?"

"Love them."

"And a large order of fries, please."

They took their trays of food to the picnic tables outside.

Lily settled in across from Louis, spreading a paper napkin carefully across her skirt.

"This is my daddy's favorite restaurant," she said. "Momma doesn't like it, so he brings me here."

"It's a nice place," Louis said. Lily was having trouble opening the tab on her Coke, so Louis reached over and popped it open for her.

"Thank you," she said.

"You're welcome."

There was a long, awkward silence. But then Louis realized that it was awkward only from his viewpoint. Lily was biting into her hot dog, sipping her Coke, and looking around at the other diners with interest.

"Momma says hot dogs are bad for you," she said.

"This one's really good," Louis said, wiping the mustard from his mouth.

"That's because it's a coach dog," Lily said.

"Coach dog?"

"You know, a Jewish hot dog."

Louis frowned, then smiled. "Oh, a *kosher* dog."

"Yes, kosher. That's what I meant to say. Momma says regular hot dogs are made out of pigs' lips. But pigs don't really have lips!" She laughed, throwing back her head, sending her ringlets dancing.

Louis's heart melted.

They ate in silence. Louis finished his hot dog and was trying desperately to think of what to say to this little person—no, his daughter—sitting across from him, when Lily spoke.

"Who was that lady in your car?"

"Her name is Joette," he said. "I call her Joe. She's a sheriff up north."

Lily looked up at him, the last bite of her hot dog poised at her lips. "But who is she to you?" she asked.

Louis hesitated. He did not want to go into this with Lily for several reasons, but he wasn't sure if Lily had seen him kiss Joe goodbye. If she had, to hedge around the truth now was dead wrong. He guessed that Lily hadn't seen Amy sitting in the backseat.

"She's my girlfriend," Louis said.

Lily lowered her hot dog and wiped her lips with the napkin. "Momma thinks black men ought to marry only black women," she said softly.

Louis crumpled the food wrappers and stuffed them inside his empty cup, then took a long look over at the market across the street, completely lost for anything to say. Who was he to pass along his philosophies on race and relationships to a child he had no part in raising?

He looked back at her. "I understand why your mother feels that way," he said gently. "But we can't always help who we fall in love with, Lily."

Lily began to wrap up her papers. Louis watched her, sure she was still bothered by the idea of Joe and maybe the idea of having to tell Kyla that there was a white woman in Louis's life. And he had the horrible feeling that maybe this would be their last meeting.

"Can I tell you a secret?" Lily asked.

"Sure."

"There's a boy at school," Lily said, glancing around to make sure no one was listening. "His name is Kurt Vanderloop. He's ten. He likes me, but I don't think I'm allowed to like him back."

"Why?"

"Because he's white."

Louis leaned over the picnic table and gently covered Lily's small hand with his. She didn't pull away.

"Liking people is about what you feel in your heart," he said. "Not about what you can see with your eyes. And I think if you explained it to your momma like that, she might understand it better."

"I don't know about that," she said.

Louis smiled. "Well, she let you make the decision to see me," he said. "I have a feeling she'll let you make some other decisions, too. You have to trust her to do that, okay?"

"Okay."

He sat back and looked again toward the street. He wanted to take a walk, but Channing's cruiser was gone, probably on a call. Louis wasn't sure they should leave.

"Can I ask you another question, Louis?"

"Sure."

"Do I have more family on your side?"

Her pale gray eyes were steady on his. In them, he could see the same look he had seen sometimes on Amy's face when she spoke of finding her mother. That odd little look of hunger, a hunger for connection to your past, a hunger to know where you had come from. A hunger he had never acknowledged in himself, despite the fact that he kept a picture of his father in his drawer. One he usually looked at only through the amber glow of a brandy bottle.

"Yes," he said. "I have a half-brother and sister."

"Where do they live?"

"Mississippi, I think," he said. "I . . ."

Hell, there was nothing to say here but the truth.

"I haven't seen them since I was seven," he said. "The three of us were split up and put in foster care. Do you know what that is?"

"Yes," she said. "Daddy told me about it. Why did that happen to you?"

"My mother got sick."

"And you had no grandma or anyone else who could take care of you?"

Louis rubbed his brow. "No."

Her face wrinkled with a mix of sympathy and pity. He didn't like the idea that an eight-year-old felt sorry for him.

"I had good foster parents," he added. "Right here in Michigan. I was fine."

"And even when your momma got sick, your father didn't come back for you?"

"No."

"Couldn't you have called him or something?"

Louis sighed. "Truth is, Lily, I wouldn't have known where to call," he said. "I've never even met him. He left my mother before I was born."

"Like you did me?" she asked.

Louis met those eyes. The questions were getting tougher again but somehow easier to answer.

"Yes."

"But you came back looking for me," she said.

"Yes."

"But your father never came back for you?"

"That's right."

"How come you never went looking for him?" she asked. "Didn't you want to ask him why he didn't care about you being born?"

Yes, a thousand times.

"No," he said. "I . . . I told myself, if he didn't care about me, then I didn't care about him."

Lily was staring at him, either not understanding him or not believing him. Could she hear the lie in his voice?

"Would you do it now?" she asked.

"Do what?"

"Would you find him now?"

He was quiet.

"You're a private investigator," she said. "You could do it easy."

"What would be the point?" he asked. "I'm a grown-up now. You need fathers when you're young, like you. Plus, I'm not sure I'd have much to say to him."

"But don't you want to know?"

"Know what?"

"Where you come from?"

Louis couldn't think of an answer for that one.

Luckily, Lily didn't demand an answer. Her eyes had wandered away from him, off in the direction of where the cruiser had been parked, as if she wanted to end the lunch right now and head back to Channing.

He wondered if he'd been too honest, maybe too sharp in his reply, or worse, if he had disappointed her somehow. He was reminding himself that she was only eight and trying to think of a way to soften what he said, when she looked back at him.

"I didn't know what I was going to say to you, either," she said, "but here we are talking."

Jesus.

"Would you find him for *me*?" she asked.

Louis sighed and shook his head. "I don't know, Lily.

That's not as easy for me to do as you might think. I might be a grown-up, but there's still a little hurt there."

"I understand."

Louis gathered up the wrappers and rose to throw them away. When he got back to the table, she was standing and trying to work the puffs from the knees of her red tights. Beyond her, Louis could see Kyla walking toward them. She was all in black, with a red shawl thrown over her shoulder. His heart quickened. He had not expected her to come anywhere near him, and he didn't want words shared in front of Lily.

Lily saw her coming and looked quickly to Louis. "Will you come back to Michigan for my birthday?" she asked.

"For your birthday?" he asked.

"I forgot," she said. "You don't know when that is, do you?"

"No."

"It's September 2," she said. "If Momma says it's okay, will you take me to Mackinac Island?"

"You've never been?"

"Momma says it's ticky-tacky, but I saw a movie about it in school and want to go. Will you take me?"

"Sure. If it's okay with your mother."

Kyla stopped next to Lily. Her hand closed over Lily's, but her gaze was pinned on Louis—not with anger, just coolness.

"I don't know what to say to you except thank you," Louis said. "She's beautiful, and it's obvious you've been a great mother."

Kyla ignored the comment. "When are you leaving?" she asked.

"I don't know," Louis said. "Maybe a week or so."

"We need to talk before you do," Kyla said.

"I know."

Kyla turned and led Lily away. Just before they reached the parking lot, Lily broke her mother's hold on her hand and said something to her. Kyla nodded. Lily ran back to him, out of breath by the time she reached him. He knelt down to meet her eyes.

"I just wanted to tell you," she said, "I'll help you find him and talk to him if you're scared to do it alone."

Louis stared at her.

"'Bye," she said as she ran off again.

He rose slowly and watched her until she was inside the car and Kyla had buckled her into the passenger seat. When the car left the parking lot, he turned and wandered the market until he found a café.

He needed to wait for Joe. He took a seat near the window, ordered a beer, and thought about Jordan Kincaid and the courage of eight-year-old girls.

Chapter Twenty-nine

They got to Dr. Sher's home early, and there was a note pinned to the front door from the doctor saying she would be a little late. So now, Louis, Joe, and Amy were waiting on her front porch.

Amy was sitting in a wicker chair, engrossed in a book. From his place sitting on the steps, Louis could see the cover. *A Tree Grows in Brooklyn*. Yesterday, it had

been *Gone with the Wind.* Tomorrow, it would likely be *Little Women.* She read the same three books over and over, rotating them in no particular order. Joe had offered to buy her something new, but Amy had politely declined, saying the people in the books were her friends, and she didn't want to lose them.

Francie, Ben Blake, Mammy, Aunt Sissy, Marmee, Big Sam, Cornelius . . . she could name them all.

Louis looked across the porch to where Joe sat, a hip propped on the porch railing. She was watching Amy, her expression one Louis could never remember seeing before, tenderness mixed with a sort of quiet terror. Was that the maternal instinct? An aching urge to protect even when you knew how impossible the job was?

Joe rose from the railing suddenly and went down to the yard, looking down the street for Dr. Sher's Volkswagen. Louis knew why Joe was so edgy. Dr. Sher was going to hypnotize Amy again. But this time, it was with the intent to retrieve Amy's memories of the black woman's death. Joe had been against it, but Dr. Sher had convinced her that the old memory, even if it was a fabrication, was so powerful that it was blocking everything else. And until Amy came to terms with this imaginary past life, they would never access her memory of her mother's death.

He still didn't buy it, this regression stuff, not for a second. But if making Amy believe she could go back a hundred years could somehow lead them to how Jean Brandt died, then he'd play along with this idea of a past life.

He reached into his jeans for his wallet. The snapshot of Lily was tucked behind his driver's license. He pulled it out and ran his finger over the surface.

"Who is that?"

Louis turned and looked up. He hadn't heard Amy come up behind him. She sat down next to him on the step, cradling her book to her chest.

"That's your daughter, isn't it?" Amy said before he could answer.

Louis nodded, surprised. He hadn't said anything to Amy about Lily. He was sure Joe hadn't, either.

Amy glanced at Joe, then back at the snapshot. "Miss Joe isn't her mother, is she?"

"No," Louis said.

"But you and Miss Joe—"

"She's here," Joe said, coming up onto the porch.

Louis slipped the snapshot back into his wallet, glad that Joe had not heard Amy. He went down to the sidewalk as Dr. Sher got out of her car.

"I'm so sorry," Dr. Sher said. "I had a meeting at the university and had no way to reach you."

"We found your note," Joe said.

"Good," Dr. Sher said, smoothing her hair. "Come in, please."

She led them into the living room, dropping her coat onto a chair, and turned to face them, giving Amy a smile.

"How are you feeling today, dear?"

"I'm okay, Dr. Sher," Amy said softly.

Dr. Sher looked up at Joe.

"She didn't sleep well last night," Joe said. "She had another asthma attack."

"The inhaler I prescribed isn't helping?" Dr. Sher asked.

Joe shook her head.

"Are you sure you feel up to this today?" Dr. Sher asked Amy.

Amy nodded. "I want to do it. It's the only way I can help my mother."

Dr. Sher put her arm around Amy's shoulders. "Then let's get started."

The drapes in the living room were closed against the bright sun. The room was quiet except for the ticking of an old alabaster clock on the mantel. Louis had removed his jacket twenty minutes ago in an effort to get comfortable in the too-warm room.

Amy was having trouble going under for some reason. From his vantage point sitting with Joe on the sofa, Louis could see the anxiety etched in Amy's face. But Dr. Sher was persistent, gently taking Amy through a series of breathing exercises.

Finally, Dr. Sher began slowly to count backward from ten. Louis watched as the tension melted from Amy's face and her breathing deepened.

"We're going back now, Amy," Dr. Sher said. "Back through your childhood, back to when you were a baby."

Amy's eyelids fluttered but remained closed. Dr. Sher tried to elicit memories from Amy's days on the farm as a child, but Amy did not seem to want to stay in that place.

"All right, I want you to go back even farther," Dr. Sher said. "Go back to as far back as you can remember."

The room was quiet except for Amy's breathing and the ticking of the clock.

"Amy, where are you?" Dr. Sher asked softly.

"I'm not sure," Amy whispered.

"Look down at your feet. Can you tell me what you are wearing?"

"Boots . . . black boots. Laced up around my ankles. They have mud on them, and one of the laces is broken. I had to tie it together."

"Can you see anything else?"

"My skirt. There is mud on the bottom of it, too." She frowned slightly before she went on. "It's spring. I see a big house and a barn. I am in a carriage. Someone is bringing me to the house. I feel . . . afraid."

"Are you at the farm?" Dr. Sher asked.

Amy nodded slowly. "Yes. I can see the oak tree in the front. But it's smaller. Everything else looks different. The house looks different, newer and pretty, with white trim. A man and a woman are standing in front of it. They are waiting for me."

"Do you know how old you are?"

"I . . . I am seventeen. I am very tired from the long journey. I miss my mother. She got sick from fever and died, and that is why I am here, because I have nowhere to go."

"Can you tell me your name?"

"Isabel. My name is Isabel."

"Do you know the man and the woman who are waiting for you?"

"No. I just know I am supposed to work for them now. The man is very tall and wears glasses. They reflect the sun like mirrors. He is smiling at me. The woman . . . doesn't smile."

"Can you tell me what year it is?" Dr. Sher asked.

"I . . . it is 1842."

Louis heard Joe's sharp intake of breath, but he didn't look at her.

"Amy," Dr. Sher said, "I want you to move ahead

now. Go ahead a couple of years. What do you see now?"

"Snow. I had never seen snow before I came here," Amy said. "It is very cold outside, but I am warm, because I am in the kitchen near the stove. I am holding a baby."

"Is it your baby?"

Amy slowly shook her head. "It is Miz Phoebe's daughter, Lucinda. I take care of her because Miz Phoebe stays in her room so much now. She is a very good baby and never cries. I love Lucinda."

Louis thought about the photograph he had found in the old tin. Had Joe shown it to Amy? Had Amy found the Brandt family Bible? Is that where she saw the name Lucinda? Or was she remembering all of this simply as part of Geneva's handed-down family "stories"?

"Oh . . ." Amy was grimacing.

"What's wrong?" Dr. Sher asked.

"I didn't do it! Don't beat me, don't beat me!"

"Who's beating you?"

"Miz Phoebe," Amy whispered. "She hates me so much. But I didn't take her comb! He gave it to me and said it was mine to keep! He told me to hide it, but Miz Phoebe found it. It's mine! Mr. Amos gave it to me!"

"Amy, move ahead," Dr. Sher said firmly. "Go to a time when you are happiest. Can you do that?"

Amy's breathing deepened again, and her expression became calm. For a long time, the room was quiet. Then Amy slowly brought up her arms, as if she were cradling something. She began to hum softly.

"Don't cry," she murmured. "Mama's here, Charles. We're safe now, Charles, we're safe in the corn."

Louis felt a trickle of sweat make its way slowly down his back.

"Charles is your son, Amy?" Dr. Sher asked.

She nodded.

"Who is Charles's father?" Dr. Sher prodded.

Amy took a long time to answer, and when she did, it was in the softest of whispers. "Amos." Her face creased into a frown that made her look suddenly much older. "Miz Phoebe tried to kill Charles. She took him one night and went to the creek to drown him. Amos stopped her. We . . . Amos has built us a house out in the cornfield. He is good to me."

The mantel clock chimed two times.

Dr. Sher's face had a sheen of sweat on it. She drew a handkerchief from her pocket, dabbed at her face, and looked down at Amy.

"I want you to go to the time when your breathing problems first started, Amy," she said.

Amy didn't respond.

"Can you do that? Can you tell me about the first time you felt like you couldn't breathe?"

"I don't . . ."

"I'm here with you, Amy," Dr. Sher said softly. "It will be all right, I promise."

The room fell quiet again.

"It's dark tonight, no drinking gourd to light the way," she said. "But the preacher says there's a parcel coming. So I light a candle and put it in the parlor window."

For a moment, Amy said nothing more.

"I am afraid," she whispered.

"Why are you afraid?" Dr. Sher asked.

"The wind blows from the south tonight," Amy said.

A loud *click* made Louis jump. Dr. Sher waved a hand toward him, then pointed at the small tape recorder on the table near Amy's head. She made a flipping motion with her hand. Louis realized she wanted him to turn over the tape. He did so, then returned to his place beside Joe.

Again, it was silent, except for the sound of Amy's breathing.

"He's here," Amy said suddenly.

"Who?" Dr. Sher pressed.

"He calls himself John." Amy whispered another word that, to Louis, sounded like "lapel." Then she was quiet again.

"He is so thin, and he is coughing," she said. "His clothes are ragged. I give him one of Amos's old coats and take him to the hiding place. It is so cold there, and I feel bad about leaving him, but he will be safe here until the shepherd comes."

A small smile came to Amy's face.

"He tells me about his wife, Fanny, back in New Orleans." The smile faded. "She was taken from him. His son, too. Leaves stripped from the trees . . .

"He misses them so much. He says someday, when he is a free man, he will go back and find them." Amy's eyes fluttered. "He shows me her locket."

Louis stiffened. Another long silence. He felt Joe shift on the cushions beside him. She had moved forward, her eyes intent on Amy's face.

Amy's face . . .

It had grown tight and contorted, and Louis had the crazy thought that she looked like someone who was staring down the barrel of a gun. He had seen that look be-

fore, because he had been the one holding the gun, and he had never forgotten that look on the other person's face. Like he had no skin, and every nerve was exposed.

"Amy? What's happening, Amy?" Dr. Sher said.

"Horses," she whispered. "I hear horses and now dogs. The soul catchers are coming."

"Who?" Dr. Sher pressed.

"I have to get back to the cellar. I see the horses by the barn and the men. The horses make clouds in the air."

"Amy, who is there with you?"

"I can't let them find John."

"Amy, where are you?"

"No, not the cellar. John is there. The corn . . . I have to get to the corn."

"Amy—"

"Run to the corn, make them chase me, so they won't find John." She began to pant, like she was out of breath. "Oh . . . oh! Oh, God!"

"What's happening?"

"They caught me . . . they are dragging me into the barn. Amos! Where are you? Amos, help me!"

"What is—?"

"They've tied me to the hook and are pulling me up. My blouse, they ripped off my clothes . . . oh, it's so cold. The horses are screaming."

"Amy—"

"They're whipping me . . . but I won't tell them. I won't tell them where John is. They want to find him and take him back. I won't tell, I won't tell . . ."

Suddenly, Amy began to cry. Dr. Sher leaned forward and put her hand over Amy's.

"What is it, dear? Tell me."

"Amos," she whispered. "He is here. I can see him. I loved him, and he did this to me."

Amy's hands came up to cover her face as she cried. Dr. Sher pulled back, her face pale.

Amy began to gag. Louis felt Joe tense, and he looked at her. She was holding a hand over her mouth, her eyes brimming.

"What's happening, Amy?" Dr. Sher said.

"I . . . can't . . . breathe."

Dr. Sher leaned forward. "Why? What's happening to you?"

Amy hands came up, as if she were warding off a blow. "They are burying me. *But I am not dead yet.*" She gagged and drew in a hard breath. "Charles!"

Amy went limp. It was quiet.

Dr. Sher picked up Amy's wrist to feel her pulse. She looked to Louis and Joe and nodded, mouthing, "She's okay."

"Amy?" Dr. Sher said softly after a few seconds.

It took a long time, but finally, a whisper. "Yes?"

"Where are you now?"

"Floating. They want me to rest now."

"They?"

Amy didn't answer.

The clock chimed again. Louis looked to the mantel. It was two-thirty. A soft sound made him look back at Amy. She was humming. Hugging herself, rocking gently back and forth as she lay on the settee. The humming became words.

> . . . *we poor souls will have our peace,*
> *there's a better day a-comin'—*

Will you go along with me?
There's a better day a-comin',
Go sound the jubilee . . .

Louis listened, not moving a muscle. He didn't know the words, yet something about the song was familiar. Then he realized where he had heard it, or a song very much like it, once before. At his mother's funeral back in Mississippi, the "going home," as they had called it. A cluster of women in black softly singing his mother home as he stood apart, listening.

It was time to bring Amy out of her trance. Louis watched as Dr. Sher began to count backward from ten. "You will remember all this when you wake up, Amy, but you won't be afraid," Dr. Sher said.

And with that, Amy opened her eyes. She sat up, self-consciously pulling the top of her blouse closed. Her cheeks were dotted with color. Louis thought she looked like someone who had just emerged from a nap.

But Dr. Sher? She was pale, her red bangs plastered to her forehead with sweat. And Joe? She was standing over by the piano, her back to them. When had she gotten up off the sofa? Louis hadn't even felt it.

"How do you feel, dear?" Dr. Sher asked.

It took a second or two for the doctor's question to register. "I'm fine," Amy said.

"Do you remember what just happened?"

Amy nodded. "I didn't help things, did I?"

"What do you mean?" Dr. Sher asked.

"I couldn't remember anything about Momma," Amy said.

Dr. Sher took Amy's hand. "That will come."

Amy shook her head. "But I need to help. Can we try again?"

"No, dear," Dr. Sher said. "You've done enough for today."

Louis looked to Joe. She was staring at Amy. Suddenly, Amy got up and went to her. She wrapped her arms around Joe's waist and rested her head on Joe's chest.

Joe hesitated, then put her arms around Amy.

For a moment, Louis couldn't decipher what he was seeing in Joe's face. Then, suddenly, he knew what it was. He had seen the look before, on the face of his foster mother, Frances, when she found out her husband had been in love with another woman for the last thirty years. Frances's world had shifted, because that one thing had forced her to question everything she believed to be real and solid.

Louis rose and went outside to the porch. He blinked in the bright sunlight and pulled in a breath of the crisp air. A breeze kicked up, sending the chimes tinkling. Louis focused on the spinning whirligig bird out on the lawn, thinking about Amy's story.

As moving as it was, he knew it wasn't real. Amy believed it was. And if he had read the look on Joe's face correctly, so did she.

He could almost understand that her growing attachment to Amy was clouding her judgment. He had warned Shockey that his obsession with Jean had made him useless as a cop. And now Joe's willingness to accept this past-life thing was becoming just as dangerous.

Louis turned to look in through the window. He could see Joe and Amy talking quietly. He had to find a way to prove to Joe that she was wrong.

Chapter Thirty

The hotel room suddenly had become too small. First, Joe had opened the sliding glass door, letting in the cool night air. When that didn't work, she sent Amy to the bedroom with her new sketchbook and colored markers. Finally, Joe had asked Louis to go out and find some take-out Chinese, knowing it would take him a while.

Still, the walls closed in.

Slipping on a sweatshirt, Joe took her glass of wine and her books out onto the balcony, leaving the sliding glass door open a bit so she could hear Amy.

But Amy didn't seem to need her watchful eye. Ever since they had returned from Dr. Sher's house that afternoon, Amy had been oddly calm. The need for long naps was gone. The asthma attacks had disappeared. The girl seemed to have suffered no ill effects from the latest session, despite the belief that she apparently had recalled her own brutal murder.

"I can only guess that by excising this confabulation, Amy is finding a place in her personality now to accommodate it," Dr. Sher had told Joe and Louis afterward. "If it has somehow brought her some peace, I suggest we don't question why."

Joe leaned her head back in the chaise, put up her feet, and closed her eyes, letting the cold night air wash over her.

Peace. She was the one who craved it now.

There had never been a time in her life when she felt more unsettled. Maybe when she was ten, when her father died. The hole he left had never completely

healed, but she had gone on, grown up, found her footing in life.

But now, this new unease, this felt like the ground was shifting beneath her. Part of it, she knew, was because she had compromised her integrity as a cop on this case. She had bent the rules once thirteen years ago and vowed she would never do it again. But now she had.

Still, it went deeper than that.

Watching Amy this afternoon, she realized that everything she believed in had been turned upside down.

Joe set the glass aside and pulled the zipper of her sweatshirt to her chin. Her hands moved over the three books in her lap. Dr. Sher had given them to her that afternoon. Louis had no interest in them, but Joe had spent most of the evening reading them.

There was a slender paperback about life-regression therapy written by the Miami psychiatrist Dr. Sher had mentioned. One of its ideas was stuck in her mind: everyone is reincarnated with the same "family" of souls over and over.

The second book was by a Canadian psychiatrist named Ian Stevenson, *Unlearned Language: New Studies in Xenoglossy.* Xenoglossy, Dr. Sher had told her, was a paranormal phenomenon in which a person is able to speak a language that he or she could not have acquired by natural means.

Joe picked up the third book, titled *Twenty Cases Suggestive of Reincarnation.* It was a scholarly compilation of cases documented by Stevenson, who had devoted his life to researching children in India who claimed to remember previous lives.

This book she hadn't been able to set aside as easily.

Stevenson himself admitted that the lack of physical evidence made it hard for people to accept his argument for reincarnation. But his cases of twenty children who could remember past lives was chilling in its authority.

Joe set the books aside.

She didn't need a fancy word like *xenoglossy* to tell her why Amy could sing in French. The fact that there was a piano roll in that farmhouse was concrete, real.

But the other things? After what she had seen today, she wasn't sure Amy's vivid memories of her "life" as Isabel could be explained away as easily.

And that, more than anything, was what was leaving her feeling so lost.

Joe looked out over the clear night sky, focusing finally on the waning white moon.

Tonight, she had thought about calling her mother. Florence Frye, with her astrology books and visits to psychics. Her father had cheerfully ignored his wife's "dipping her toes into the occult ocean," as he called it. But Joe, growing up, had been mildly embarrassed by her mother, hiding the tarot cards when her friends came over, wincing whenever her mother would ask her date what his sign was.

When she was fourteen, Joe had started going to the Presbyterian church down the block. Her mother teased her that she was going only to be with Troy, the boy she had a crush on. That was part of it, but it was also wanting to feel that she was part of a "normal" family, and going to church was what "normal" families did on Sunday. But sitting on the hard wooden pew, mouthing along with the hymns, listening to the deep voice of the minister warning about "the devil prowling around

like a roaring lion, seeking someone to devour," she felt strange, like she was putting on a dress that was two sizes too big to impress someone she didn't care about.

She never returned to church after that. Her work as a police officer—the single thing that most defined her—became her religion. And it depended on what was tangible, what was provable by evidence. Even that time in Miami, when the department had brought in a psychic to find a missing child, even when the psychic was able to describe the drainage ditch where the child's body was found, even then, Joe had remained a skeptic.

But now? After what she had witnessed that afternoon in Dr. Sher's home, after hearing the terror in Amy's voice? No matter what Louis said, that was "proof" enough for her.

Louis . . .

Joe pulled her sweatshirt tighter around her shoulders. The fissure she had felt between them before had widened. Tonight, he had picked up one of the reincarnation books, looked at it, and tossed it back onto the bed. He didn't say anything, but she read his thought in his face: *What is happening to you, Joe?*

"Miss Joe?"

Joe swiveled. Amy was standing at the open door.

"Something wrong?" Joe asked, immediately tense.

"I'm not sure," Amy said. She ventured out onto the balcony. "It's going to rain real bad," she said.

Joe was about to say it was the clearest night they had seen since she had come to Ann Arbor. But the seriousness of Amy's face kept her quiet.

"Can I come out and sit with you?" Amy asked.

Joe hesitated.

"Please?"

Amy was backlit by the living-room light, so Joe couldn't see her face, couldn't see what was bothering her. "Okay. But go put on a sweater first."

Amy disappeared, and when she came back, she was wearing one of Joe's sweatshirts and had brought a blanket from one of the beds.

There was only the one lounge chair on the balcony. Amy stood there, clutching the blanket, until Joe finally scooted over. Amy wedged herself into the small space left and carefully spread the blanket over them both.

Joe could feel the press of sharp hipbones against her own, could smell the strawberry of Amy's just-shampooed hair. She could feel the tension in her own body at this unfamiliar closeness. Even as she could feel the softening of Amy's muscles and skin.

For a long time, it was quiet, with just the occasional drifting up of car noises from five floors below.

"Something's wrong," Amy said softly.

"What is it?" Joe said.

Amy was silent.

"You can talk to me, Amy," Joe said. "Don't you know that now?"

"Yes."

"Okay. Then tell me what it is."

"I'm not sure. I feel like something bad is going to happen to me."

"Does this have anything to do with what you remembered today at Dr. Sher's?" Joe asked.

"No, that's past now," Amy said. "This is something that hasn't happened yet."

"You know we'll protect you, Mr. Kincaid and I," Joe said.

"I know. But you're going home soon."

Joe hesitated. "Not until I'm sure you're okay."

Amy was silent.

"Do you believe me?"

She felt Amy nodding slowly.

Again, they were quiet for a long time.

"Something else is wrong," Amy said. "With you and Mr. Kincaid."

The closeness kept Joe from turning to see Amy's face. "Why do you say that?" Joe asked.

"I can . . . sometimes I . . ." Amy let out a long breath. "Never mind."

"Go ahead and finish what you were saying."

Amy's head dipped. "I know things sometimes," she said softly. "Like I can hear people talking . . . but only to themselves. It feels weird, like . . ." Her head came up. "I was outside once when there was lightning. I could feel this tingling in my body when the lightning hit close. Do you know that feeling?"

"Yes, I do."

"That's how it feels when I can hear people talking to themselves. Like there is this lightning thing between us or something."

Joe was silent.

"You and Mr. Kincaid," Amy said. "You love each other."

Joe hesitated. "Yes, we do."

"And you feel like you and him . . . are . . . like you're in the same room, but like it's dark, and you can't find him?"

Joe cleared her throat. "Yes."

"He's there, Miss Joe."

Joe's eyes welled.

"People lose each other in the dark sometimes. That's what happened to me and Momma. Mr. Kincaid . . . he's right there by your side. You can't see him right now. But you have to just kind of believe. He's there. You'll find each other again."

Joe couldn't move. The night wind was cold on her face. But then, beneath the blanket, she felt the warmth of Amy's hand covering her own.

Chapter Thirty-one

It was still dark when Louis slid from under the sheets. He dressed quickly, looked back at Joe curled deep in the blankets, and crept from the bedroom. The cartons from last night's Chinese dinner still sat on the table. After glancing at Amy, fast asleep on the pullout sofa, Louis grabbed a leftover egg roll and slipped silently from the hotel room, locking the door behind him.

The campus was asleep as well, the wind kicking up the gutter litter of paper cups and cans from the night's revelry. A misty rain followed him as he drove deep into the countryside.

He ate the cold egg roll and chased it down with Dunkin' Donuts coffee as he drove. Just east of Hell, Louis flicked on the high beams, looking for the cutoff road to Talladay Trail. He spotted it at the last second and swung the Bronco hard onto the gravel road.

The sky was turning a muddy gray as he parked and

picked his way through the high, wet grass to Lethe Creek. The creek was running fast and deep, swollen by the recent rains, and for a second, he thought about going back to the hotel and slipping in next to Joe's warm body.

Instead, he turned up the collar of his jacket, found the same narrow part of the creek he had braved before, and waded across, grabbing on to low-hanging willow branches to stay upright.

With sodden shoes, he continued up the small incline to the cemetery. In the mist, the headstones seemed small, insubstantial things, like they were slowly being absorbed into the earth. Louis stood, looking down at Amos Brandt's grave.

What am I doing here?

Looking for answers.

You don't even know the questions, Louis.

He knew that a troubled sixteen-year-old girl had somehow come to believe she was a murdered black woman from long ago. And he knew he had to find an explanation for her memories. Yesterday, after the session at Dr. Sher's home, he had asked Amy if she could remember ever visiting a cemetery. Amy said she had a fuzzy memory of old gravestones in trees. Had Jean brought her here once? Or had Geneva just told her about a family plot far beyond the cornfields?

Had she seen the name Isabel here?

A sound behind him made him spin around. He half expected to see the strange old man with his dog. But there was no one.

You got kin here?

The old man had asked him that. Why had it stuck in his mind?

Don't you want to know where you come from?

Lily had asked him that.

And what had he answered? *What would be the point?*

It was a harsh thing to say to a child, let alone his own. He had realized it as soon as he said it. What made it worse, it was not something he even truly believed. He used to believe it, back when having no ties to anyone took the shape of freedom rather than loneliness.

What *would* be the point? He still wasn't sure. Maybe just to feel connected to something tangible and unbroken? His mother was dead, and he had no idea where his half-brother and sister were, or if they were even alive. He had no one he could claim as his blood—except Lily.

The sun had broken through the clouds. The letters on Amos Brandt's headstone took shape. Louis stared at them for a moment, then turned away.

He walked slowly through the clearing, examining every headstone he saw. Just the same names he had seen before.

There was one last piece of half-buried granite. He knelt in the damp grass, digging it out. His fingers stiff with cold, he scraped the dirt and moss out of the faded carved letters. It said: MURIEL BRANDT.

He hadn't seen this one on his first visit. He stood up, wiping his muddy hands on his jeans. In the quickening light, he could see there were no other headstones he hadn't examined.

No one named Isabel was buried here.

After one last look around the cemetery, he left.

Louis hung up the pay phone with a sigh. He had called Joe to tell her where he had gone. She hadn't chastised him, but he could almost imagine what she was thinking:

What are you doing chasing down ghosts in graveyards? She had, however, felt compelled to tell him they had only two days before they were scheduled to appear again in custody court.

He didn't need to be reminded. The thought of turning Amy over to Owen Brandt made his stomach turn.

"You want a fresh cup?"

Louis looked up at the kid holding the coffee pot and nodded, going back to his stool. The kid refilled Louis's mug and retreated to the far end of the counter to read his book.

Louis ate the last of his omelet, observing the kid. He was black and slender, with the red-rimmed eyes and chin stubble of a hard studier. It struck Louis that the kid had the same lone-wolf look he himself had at that age, when he had sat in this very seat at the Fleetwood Diner, lost in his prelaw books. Louis wondered what the kid was reading.

At that moment, the kid closed his book, giving Louis a look at the cover: *Pathologic Basis of Disease.* Louis smiled slightly. Premed.

"Excuse me," Louis called out.

"You want more coffee?"

"No, just some help," Louis said.

The kid came toward him, pushing his glasses up his nose. "With what?"

"Is there a historical society or something in Ann Arbor?"

The kid frowned. "Historical society? Probably, knowing this burg. What kind of history you interested in?"

"Black," Louis said. "Especially slave history, the Underground Railroad."

The kid rubbed his whiskers. "I saw a sign over on Main the other day in a store window. Something about African-American Cultural Society or something."

"That might do." Louis rose, leaving a twenty on the counter. "Thanks. Keep the change."

"Hey, thanks, man, I can use it." He pocketed the bill. "Can I ask what you're looking for?"

For some strange reason, Mel Landeta's line popped into Louis's head: *Cherchez la femme.*

"A woman," Louis said.

The sign in the storefront on Main was hand-lettered: ANN ARBOR AFRICAN-AMERICAN CULTURAL CENTER. An old neon martini glass above the door told of the place's previous life as a cocktail lounge.

Inside, the fifties-style blond-wood bar was still in place, cardboard boxes covering it and filling the liquor shelves behind. Turquoise vinyl booths lined one wall, with tables and chairs stacked in the back. The lights were off, giving the place an alleylike feel.

"Hello! Anyone here?"

He heard the *click* of heels on terrazzo. A woman emerged from the back, carrying yet another cardboard box. She was tall, about forty, with close-cropped black hair, wearing a black sweater and slacks and big gold hoop earrings.

"Can I help you?" she asked, setting the box down on the bar.

Louis came forward. "I'm looking for some information on the Underground Railroad."

"We're not officially open yet," the woman said. She

reached over the bar and hit a light switch. The fluorescents spit and hummed into life. "As you can see."

In the harsh light, the woman's odd beauty registered. She had smooth, dark skin and a long, solemn face that made Louis recall a Modigliani portrait he had seen in a book once. The book had sat on his foster mother Frances's coffee table, a big shiny thing that went untouched except for all those times as a kid when he furtively thumbed through it looking for naked women. The Modigliani face had stuck in his mind, because it looked just like an African mask he had seen in one of Phillip's *National Geographics*.

"The grants just came through last month," the woman said. "All we're doing now is bringing in the stuff from storage. We don't even have our computers yet." The woman saw his disappointment and offered a smile. "Maybe if you told me exactly what it is you're looking for?"

"I wish I knew," Louis said, shaking his head. "I'm trying to find out if a farm near here could have been a station on the Railroad."

"Well, Ann Arbor and Ypsilanti were right on the routes." She hesitated, then moved away, her long fingers tracing the writing on the boxes. She stopped, dug inside one box, pulled out a paper, and unfolded it on the bar in front of Louis.

It was a map of southern Michigan, with colored lines cutting up from Ohio and Indiana, across lower Michigan toward Detroit and over to Canada.

"There were seven main routes on the Underground Railroad, and three of them ran right through here," she said. "Where is the farm?"

"South of Hell," Louis said.

The woman pointed to a red line that ran up along Lake Michigan, veered east to Lansing, then south. "This is the old Grand River Trail," she said. "A slave using this route probably would have gone right through there."

Louis couldn't take his eyes off the red line.

"Do you know much about the Underground Railroad?"

Her soft voice drew his eyes up to hers. She wasn't patronizing him, but he had the sense that she had asked this question of many others before. She had the evangelistic energy that all good teachers had.

"I know it wasn't a real railroad."

She smiled.

"How did a place become a station?" he asked.

"There were always people—Quakers, abolitionists, and just regular folks—who hid runaways. We think there were as many as three thousand people involved when the system was running at its strongest."

"Where did people hide?" Louis asked.

"Churches, barns, attics, cellars, anywhere they could," she said. "The stations were about twenty miles apart, and there were secret ways to alert someone that it was a safe place, like a lighted candle in the window. Some say the patterns of quilts were codes, but no one has proven that."

"Michigan was a free state," Louis said. "I always thought once someone got this far, he was safe."

She shook her head. "They could still be captured and sent back. Especially after 1850."

"Why then?"

"Congress passed the Fugitive Slave Act. There were so many escapes that plantation owners in the South pressured the government to step in. The act gave slave

owners the right to come up here and hunt down their 'property.' There were posses of men called slave catchers who were paid bounties to capture runaways and take them back to the South."

Louis was thinking now of Amy's tortured account of Isabel's death. "What happened if someone got caught helping a runaway?"

"They could be fined and imprisoned," she said. "At the least, they were hassled by the law or others in the community. At the worst, they were killed."

Again, the images from Amy's dream came to Louis. Men on horses with torches and dogs. A woman hanged from a hook and buried alive, as a white man in eyeglasses—Amos Brandt?—stood by and watched.

"Is there any way to find names?" Louis asked.

The woman just stared at him.

"I mean, of runaways or people who might have helped them?"

She gestured toward the boxes. "Oh, Lord, we have thousands of records here, journals, photographs, ledgers, property records. People have heard about us and keep bringing things in." Her hand dropped. "But we are years away from getting it all organized."

"So, you would have no way of telling me if a man named Amos Brandt had a station somewhere on his farm?"

"No, I'm sorry."

"Or the name Isabel? She was a black woman who—"

The slow shake of her head cut him off. "Except for me, everyone is a volunteer here," she said. Again, she sensed Louis's disappointment, and her eyes softened. "But you're more than welcome to look yourself."

Louis let out a long breath, his eyes dropping to the map spread on the bar. When he glanced up, there was a mild look of pity on her face.

"Is this woman part of your family?" she asked.

"No," Louis said. He held out his hand. "Thank you for your time."

She shook his hand. "Can I give you my card? If you find any proof that your farm was a station, we'd really like to hear about it so we can document it."

Louis took the card. Daphne Mayer, Ph.D. He was about to give it back, telling her he wasn't going to be in Ann Arbor much longer, but then he paused. He dug in his jacket, found his wallet, and pulled out Eric Channing's business card. He spotted a pencil on the counter and used it to scribble his name on the back of the card.

He handed it to the woman. "On the small chance you do find something about the Brandt farm, could you call me?"

She looked up at him with mild surprise on her face. "I can do that, Sergeant Channing."

He pointed to the card and smiled. "I'm on the back. Louis Kincaid. And I'll be leaving town soon. But the sergeant will know where to find me."

She pocketed the card and give him a smile of her own. "I hope you find her," she said.

"Thanks."

Louis eyed the mountain of cardboard boxes. But as he said it, he knew that even if Isabel was buried in there, no one was ever going to unearth her.

Chapter Thirty-two

"So, how does this regression stuff work, exactly?" Shockey asked.

Louis turned to him. The detective was perched on the edge of the piano bench in the far corner of Dr. Sher's living room. Shockey's face was wan, lines cutting deep parentheses around his mouth, his eyes red-rimmed and puffy. Louis wondered for a second if the guy had been hitting the bottle hard again, but something told him it was a different demon chasing him this time.

Jean. Always Jean.

Shockey had been watching Amy all morning. And Louis had the feeling that it wasn't out of some new-found love for the girl. Shockey was still obsessed with finding Jean, and he now believed that Amy was his last chance of doing that.

That is why he had insisted on coming to see Dr. Sher with them this time. Dr. Sher was going to make a last attempt to access Amy's memories of her mother's murder. And Shockey wanted to be here to see it.

Louis watched as Shockey chewed at his ravaged cuticles. Amy was across the room, lying quietly on the settee as Dr. Sher prepared to put her under hypnosis. A part of him understood what Shockey was going through. To find out you suddenly had a kid, that was hard enough. But then, what did you do with all the emotions swirling inside you? Especially that one nagging feeling that maybe you didn't feel any close connection to this person, this little stranger, you were supposed to care about?

Louis sat down on the bench next to Shockey.

"What happens? Does she just, like, go to sleep or something?" Shockey whispered.

"Kind of," Louis said.

Shockey heaved a sigh and rubbed his face. Louis rose and went over to stand next to Joe near the French doors.

"What's the matter?" he whispered.

"I don't know," Joe said quietly, her eyes on Amy. "She's having trouble going under. She was nervous all morning about this. She is really afraid she's going to fail again." Joe hesitated. "This means everything to her, Louis, finding her mother."

"Joe, her mother is dead," Louis said.

Joe gave him a sharp look. Louis let it go, focusing his attention on Dr. Sher.

It looked as if Amy was finally going under, and now Dr. Sher was trying to get her to zero in on the night of Jean's murder. Amy's face was tight with concentration, which Louis knew by now was not a good thing.

"Let that go for now, Amy," Dr. Sher said gently. "We'll start with something easier. Tell me about your life on the farm. And I want you to see it not like when you were little. Try to remember it as you are now."

Still, Amy was silent.

"Where are you? Tell me what the room looks like," Dr. Sher prodded.

"I'm in my room upstairs at the end of the hall. There's pink wallpaper with the old-fashioned people, the big white house and the horse and carriage," Amy said softly. "I like the wallpaper, because the house looks so beautiful and the people look so happy."

"Did you feel happy there, in the farmhouse?" Dr. Sher asked.

Amy gave a slow, almost imperceptible shake of her head. "Only when Poppa went away," she said softly. "When Momma and I were alone, we were happy."

"Yes. Your mother played the piano for you."

Amy nodded. "She sang the French song for me over and over. She taught me all the words. She said it was about angels looking over us in our hiding place. She said I had to learn it in French so it could be our secret song."

Amy's brows knitted.

"What's wrong, Amy?"

"He hits her," she said. "He hates it when we sing, and he hits her."

Louis glanced at Shockey. The man was rigid, his face pale.

"What else can you remember, Amy? Tell me more about your father."

Louis looked back to Dr. Sher, and he knew she was trying to lead Amy slowly to the murder. Louis wondered if Shockey was going to be able to sit there and passively listen if the worst came out. He tensed, ready to lead Shockey out of the room if necessary.

But Amy didn't—or still couldn't—go to the night of her mother's murder. Instead, she began a slow and chillingly calm litany of abuse.

Winter nights with blankets withheld. A sweltering summer day spent locked in the dark attic because she had wet her pants. A terrified run down to the cellar and out through the cornfields, where she hid listening to her mother's screams coming from the house. No children to play with, no school allowed except what Jean could teach her at the dining-room table. And always the threat

that if she ever told anyone, she would be thrown in "the hole"—the outhouse.

Owen Brandt's treatment of his wife and her child had gone beyond cruelty. It had been a calculated plan to isolate them, tear them down physically and psychologically, until their wills were broken and their world had been narrowed down to that hellish house.

Louis listened to it all with clenched jaw, his hand finding Joe's and holding it tight. And Shockey? At some point, he had got up from the chair and gone to the window, where he stood, head bowed, quietly weeping.

Louis was watching Dr. Sher. The woman looked shaken to her core and didn't seem to know what to do next. Then, with a glance at Louis, she sat up straighter, stopped the tape to turn it over, and hit the play button again.

She knew she had to get Amy to the murder somehow.

"Amy," Dr. Sher said, "can you remember the last time you saw your mother?"

It took a long time, and finally Amy nodded.

"What happened that day?"

"Momma was gone all day," Amy said. "I think she went to sell vegetables, but maybe not, because I remember now it was very cold and raining hard. But she was gone a long time."

She fell silent. Oddly, she smiled slightly.

"Momma was always so happy after she got home from selling vegetables. I loved seeing her happy like that."

Louis heard a sound. Shockey had turned and was watching Amy again.

"We're in the parlor playing the piano and singing

our song," Amy said, still smiling. "Momma tells me a secret. She says we're going to run away soon."

Amy's smile vanished.

"Poppa is home. He sees us at the piano. He . . . he hits Momma. He . . . he starts to come for me, but she stops him, talks to him and takes him upstairs. I . . . can hear them up there. I can hear him making ugly noises and hear Momma crying. But she told me never to come upstairs, just wait for her to come back and get me. She told me to go to my hiding place and wait."

"Where was this hiding place?"

"The cupboard," Amy whispered. "Sometimes it took her a long time to come for me, but she always did."

"Did you have any other hiding places, Amy?" Dr. Sher asked. "Maybe a place you and your mother went together when things were bad?"

"Momma has a special hiding place," Amy said.

A floorboard creaked, and Shockey came forward. Louis put up a hand, motioning him to stay back, to stay still.

"Do you know where her hiding place is?" Dr. Sher asked.

Amy frowned.

"Do you know where your mother went, Amy?"

"I . . . can't . . ."

Dr. Sher let out a breath of frustration. "It's all right, Amy. Just stay with the memories. What happened the night your father came home and heard you singing? What happened after your mother went upstairs?"

"It started to rain again. It was raining really hard, and it was very cold. I was downstairs by myself, and I was scared. But Momma came down to get me. She looked . . . she looked scared, too."

"What did she do?"

"I . . . I knew something was different, something was wrong this time, because Momma was really scared."

"What did she do, Amy? What did your father do?"

"He was yelling at her. He was yelling, and she was trying to get away from him. She grabbed me and told me to go to my hiding place. I didn't want to, I didn't want to leave her . . ."

Amy's breathing had become labored.

"But she made me go, she made me go, and I didn't want to, but then Momma told me I had to go to my hiding place, and she would go to hers. She told me when it was all right again, she would come and get me."

Louis felt Joe's hand tighten on his.

"Then . . . then the lights went out, and I couldn't see her anymore. I lost her in the dark, so I did what she told me to do. I hid in the cupboard."

Amy drew in a sharp breath.

"You can do this, Amy. You're strong enough now to do this," Dr. Sher said gently.

"He is stabbing her with the knife, and she is screaming. It is right there in front of me, but I can't see all of her, just pieces of her through the gaps in the boards. And when the lightning comes, I see her shoes, and everything is red, everything is red and blue, the blue floor has turned red, and I can't see her face, just her shoes . . ."

Joe pulled her hand away from Louis.

"I can't look anymore. I can't look anymore, so I close my eyes and put my hands over my ears. I can't look anymore . . ."

Louis glanced at Shockey. There were tears on his face and rage in his eyes.

"Amy? Amy, can you remember what happened next?"

When she answered, her voice was small, as if she had become five again. "He's gone. The kitchen door is open, and the rain is coming in. I crawl out. Momma is gone. And I . . . am alone."

"Did your father take your mother somewhere?"

"I don't know. Momma is gone, and I am alone."

Dr. Sher looked up at Louis and gave a subtle shake of her head, her eyes seeming to ask him what to do next. But he knew it was over.

Whatever Amy had seen in that kitchen, this was all she could remember. If Brandt had dragged Jean out and buried her, Amy had not seen it.

Louis felt Joe pull her hand away and looked over at her. Her eyes were wet. She looked exhausted.

He heard a shuffling and then the soft *click* of a door closing. Shockey had left, closing the French doors behind him. Louis saw the blur of Shockey's brown jacket as he bolted through the front door. Louis rose and went to a window, afraid the man was going to do something stupid like go after Brandt. But he could see Shockey through the window. He had stopped and was just standing on the porch, staring up at the gray sky.

Dr. Sher's soft voice brought him back. The doctor was bringing Amy out of her sleep state. She ended by telling Amy she would be able to remember everything she had said. Louis wondered now if that was cruel.

Amy slowly swung her legs to the floor and looked at each of them before her eyes focused on Dr. Sher.

"I didn't find her," Amy said.

Dr. Sher hesitated, then shook her head.

Amy looked first to Joe, then to Louis. And in Amy's

eyes, Louis saw something he had never seen there before: despair. The same aching despair that filled Shockey's eyes.

Amy began to cry.

"Now I know," Shockey said.

They were standing out on the porch, Shockey staring out at the street, Louis at the window, watching Joe and Amy. They were sitting together on the settee, heads bent low, talking.

"Yeah, now we know," Louis said. He turned back to Shockey. "But given the fact that this all came out under hypnosis, there is no way they will let Amy testify against Brandt."

Shockey shook his head. "Then what was the point?"

"Of what?"

Shockey gestured back to the window. "Of that! What was the point of putting her through that?"

Louis had the thought that Shockey meant "putting *me* through that," but he kept quiet.

"The point is, Detective, that girl needed to remember it," he said. "And you needed to hear it. Even if you can't do a fucking thing about it."

"I want to kill him," Shockey whispered.

"Then what would happen to Amy?"

"I can't do anything for her, Kincaid."

"You can show up in court Monday and tell the judge you think you're her father."

"Father," Shockey said softly. He looked at Amy through the window. "I don't even know what that means. I look at her, and I . . ." He ran his hand over his face. "I look at her, and I don't feel anything for her, and it's like I'm not even

really seeing her. I look at her, and the only thing I can think about is Jean."

Louis was silent.

"Your girlfriend's right," Shockey said. "I have no business being that girl's father."

Shockey walked off the porch. Louis watched him get into his car and drive away.

Chapter Thirty-three

It was dark. And she was alone again.

The power had gone out forty minutes ago, and Margi had been sitting on the floor in the parlor, listening to the crack of thunder and the fierce rush of rain against the windows. Somewhere under the floorboards, she could hear the trickle of water.

Margi drew her knees closer and leaned her head back against the wall.

She had lived in lots of shitty places and had been in a slew of men's beds in her twenty-nine years, but nothing had been as bad as this place.

Had Jean Brandt sat here once in this same spot? In the dark? Heart in her throat as she waited for the door to open and Owen to come back?

Margi wiped her face and pulled in a breath that rattled her ribs.

How had this happened? How had she come to this? Owen hadn't been a monster when she met him. He'd been a friend of her cousin she visited sometimes in the

Ohio prison. Her cousin had told her Owen was in jail for throwing a woman from a car. She should've known then that he was mean. But he had been so nice to her, and she figured any man could change if he had a woman he loved enough to change for.

Plus, she was so tired of being alone. Willy had kicked her to the curb after he sobered up and decided he could do better than a skinny high-school dropout who couldn't have no babies.

Owen didn't care about babies. He told her that on one of the afternoons she spent talking to him through the Plexiglas. Told her he didn't want any kids, because once he got out, he was going to move to Florida and get a high-paying construction job and a condo on the beach.

She believed him.

Eventually, he'd told her the woman jumped from the car and that she was mental or something and later ended up in an institution.

She believed him.

He told her every woman he ever loved had left him because he was just a poor, hardworking farmer who couldn't provide luxuries for a woman, but deep down, he had a good heart.

She believed him.

He smiled a lot and told her she was pretty. And when he told her there must be a hundred other guys out there who would love on her and that he was damn lucky to have a woman like her, she believed that, too.

A laser of lightning lit up the parlor. Outside, a piece of glass fell from somewhere and crashed to the porch. The trickle of water under the floor was beginning to sound like a running faucet.

Owen never told her she was pretty anymore. Never kissed her on the mouth and never bought her gifts. Never even thanked her for a hot meal or for sex or for even being there outside the prison the day he got out.

And now he brought her to this hole in the middle of nowhere, took her car keys, twisted her arm so bad it was numb, and left her alone while he walked in the rain looking for a dead woman.

Margi pushed to her feet and felt her way along the walls to the kitchen. She knew there were some candles on the counter, and she found them, but she couldn't find the matches. Owen hid those, too. Probably afraid she'd set him on fire one night.

Cursing softly, she moved to the back door and stepped out onto the covered porch and into a spray of rain. She squinted into the storm, looking for the beam of Owen's flashlight. It took her eyes a minute to adjust, and when they did, she saw the sliver of white, jumping in the darkness out in the cornfield.

Margi watched him, more in morbid fascination than anything else. She grew wet from the rainy wind, and she felt a shiver snake up her spine, but she couldn't take her eyes off Owen. And she couldn't help but wonder if this particular ghost might just be real. She'd always believed in things like ghosts and ESP and UFOs. Heck, she'd had her fortune read more than once at fairs and by that psychic woman down on Burton Street in Akron.

Not one of them had ever told her she would win the lottery or marry a millionaire or find true love. But one time, a woman dressed like a gypsy told her she would die young and that she should purchase a set of special salvation candles for sixty dollars and light them daily to save herself.

Margi had been nineteen at the time and had brushed the prediction off as something the woman said just to suck her into buying the candles.

But now she was almost thirty and living with a lunatic, and she wondered if the gypsy woman had been right. Was this where it would all end for her? The same way it had ended for Jean and all those other poor people buried out there in that crappy graveyard?

"If you was going to leave him, Jean, I don't blame you one bit," Margi whispered to the air.

The jumpy beam of Owen's flashlight came closer. A few seconds later, she could hear the slush of water around his shoes and his guttural mumbling. Owen stopped at the bottom step and shined the light on her.

"Get in the house," he said.

She slipped inside and stood against the cupboards as he came inside behind her. He spotted the candles and dug in his pocket for the matches. He was still muttering, but all Margi could make out was Jean's name.

The candles bathed the kitchen in a yellow glow, with shifting black shadows that jumped with the windy slap of branches on the windows.

"You okay, Owen?" Margi asked.

He spun around. His skin was slick with water, his eyes glinting like some sick animal that knew it was going to die. He held the flashlight in one hand and the broken skinning knife in the other. His palm was dripping bloody water from where he had cut himself.

"No, I'm not okay." He set the knife on the counter.

Margi let out a breath, her eyes going from the knife to his face. "Owen, please," she said softly. "You can't keep doing this. We should leave here. We should go some-

place you won't have to think about her. Maybe Florida. You said you wanted to go to Florida. We could go there and—"

Brandt drew back to smack her. She twisted away from him and his blow caught her behind the ear. She dropped to her knees against the cupboard.

"Stop it!" she cried.

He kicked her in the thigh. With a cry, Margi tried to scramble into the open cupboard. She couldn't fit her whole body in, but the door gave her some protection.

Brandt reached down and grabbed her hair, jerking her head back out so he could see her face. His hand went up again, but suddenly he froze.

"Get out of there," he said.

"No!"

He jerked her from the cupboard by the hair and tossed her across the slippery kitchen floor. She huddled up, thinking he would come after her, but he was just standing there, staring at the cupboard. Then he bent and looked inside. When he stood up, his eyes were glazed with something new, something that looked like it scared the hell out of him.

He was clutching something in his hand. For a second, Margi thought it was a dead animal. Then she realized it was just a stuffed rabbit.

"She saw it," he said. "The damn kid saw everything."

"What are you talking about?" Margi asked.

"This fucking cupboard," Brandt said, pointing. "This is where that kid hid the night I killed her slut mother. She saw everything."

Margi kept silent.

Brandt threw the rabbit down. "Fuck!" he said, pac-

ing. "That's why she has a damn shrink around her now. They're trying to get in that screwy brain of hers and dig it out."

Brandt kicked the cupboard shut and snatched the bottle of Ten-High whiskey from the counter. He stood at the window and stared out as he drank it.

Margi pulled herself to her feet, grateful Brandt had found someone else to be mad at but still scared at the way he was talking.

"She was always weird," Brandt said, like he was talking to himself and she wasn't even in the room anymore.

Margi stood perfectly still, her eyes riveted on the knife, still on the counter by Brandt's elbow.

"She always had this way about her, like knowing people were going to die before they did," Brandt muttered. "Knowing a tornado was coming before the sky ever clouded up."

Margi pressed back against the wall, trying to think of something she could say to get him calmed down. "You mean like ESP, Owen?"

He spun to her. "Don't you understand nothing?" he shouted. "If she was in that cupboard that night, then she knows where Jean went!"

Brandt set the bottle down and grabbed the knife. His eyes scanned the kitchen, finally finding his denim jacket. He snatched it up and started for the door.

"What are you doing?" she asked.

"I'm going to get the girl."

Margi wet her lips. Her heart was thundering, and she could barely find her voice. First he was chasing a ghost, and now he was going to go after a little girl. What was it about this place that turned people nuts?

"Owen," she said softly. "Why do you have to go after her? In a few days, a judge might give her back to you, and then you can ask her where her mother went. You get caught with a knife, they'll send you back to jail."

He was shaking his head. "I told that fucking cop I wasn't her father. This is the only way."

"But she's got all those people around her," Margi said. "You'll never get close to her."

Brandt shoved the knife into his waistband, picked up the whiskey bottle, and took a long swallow that dripped down his chin. "So I'll kill that nigger cop and that bitch woman and that stupid old doctor if I have to," he said. "And when the girl tells me where her mother is, I'll kill her, too."

Margi brushed back her hair and looked around. The candles were getting low, and soon there would be no more light at all.

"And that motherfucker Shockey," Brandt said softly. "I'm going to take extra special care of him. He's going to pay for fucking my wife. He's going to pay real hard."

"You going tonight?" Margi asked.

"Yeah."

Brandt took another drink and turned back to the window. From behind, she could see his reflection. The watery glass gave a distorted shimmer to his face.

"Owen, please don't go tonight," she said. "You been drinking, and it's raining . . ."

Brandt mumbled something and took another drink, but he didn't move away from the window.

Margi drew a shallow breath and walked up behind him, never more scared in her life than she was right now. She reached around him and began stroking his zipper. He

wasn't responding real quick, and she knew it would be a grueling effort to get him off, since he'd already finished almost a whole bottle since dinner, but she wanted to try.

"I'm afraid of storms," she whispered in his ear. "Stay here with me, and I'll suck you off real good."

He took another drink, quiet as he thought about her offer. She continued to stroke him. When he started get hard, he turned and faced her, put a muddy hand on her shoulder, and pushed her down to her knees.

As she unzipped his pants, she wondered if Jean had ever knelt on this same floor and done this same thing.

And she wondered if she had enough courage tonight to do what she needed to do. She didn't want that little girl to die. And she didn't want to die herself in this horrible place.

She didn't want that gypsy woman to be right.

He didn't fall asleep until after one A.M. Snoring and sated and naked from the waist down, he passed out on the old mattress in the dining room.

It was easy to rifle his pockets for the keys to the Gremlin and easy to slip out the kitchen door and lose herself in the darkness. It wasn't so easy to keep driving through the swirl of rain, the tiny car slipping and sliding on the muddy road and her head filled with guilt and fear and just about everything else a woman could feel when she was about to betray the man she loved.

She couldn't use the pay phone outside the closed Texaco, because she only had dollar bills, so she had to drive all the way into town. A couple of lights glowed in the murkiness, but as she pulled into a parking lot, she saw the stores were closed. The only thing open was the tavern.

Two bearlike guys sat at the bar, hunched over their beers. They gave her a quick once-over, and seeing her battered face and dripping hair, they looked away. She wondered if either of them or the bartender knew who she was and what she was doing. Men like Owen had pals all over. Would one of these guys quietly slip away and drive out to the farm to tell Owen she was here?

She got four dollars' worth of quarters from the bartender and quickly left the tavern for the phone booth outside. The light was burned out, and she had to use five matches to get enough light to read the phone number she had written in ink on the back of her hand.

She dropped in the quarters and dialed. As the phone rang on the other end, Margi looked out at the darkness and shivered. A sick feeling filled her belly, and she shut her eyes.

A man's deep voice broke the monotonous ringing. "Hello?"

"Detective Shockey?" she asked.

"Yeah . . . who's this?"

"This is Margi," she said.

"Margi who?"

"Margi," she said, glancing around. "Owen's woman."

She heard a crash and a bump on the other end of the phone. Then the detective's voice came back, stronger and wide awake.

"Where are you?" he asked.

"I'm in Hell."

"What's going on?"

One of the bear-men came out of the tavern and hurried toward a semi parked under a floodlight. He stopped at the cab's door and squinted at her.

"Margi, what's going on?" Shockey asked.

"Owen's got a knife, and he's going to come there and kill you and take the girl," she whispered. "He said he'd kill everyone else, too. That woman and that black guy and anyone who tried to stop him."

"Where is he now?" Shockey asked.

"Passed out," Margi said. "He won't come there till morning."

"He said he wants Amy? Why?"

The bear-man was sitting in his truck, watching her. She turned her back to him and lowered her voice again. "He thinks the girl saw him kill Jean," Margi said. "He thinks that lady doctor is trying to get her to remember it all. I'm telling you, he's just crazy now, Detective, walking around all night looking for a dead woman and talking to himself."

"Take a breath, Margi."

She did, but it didn't help calm down her hammering heart.

"All right, look," Shockey said. "I want you to come here to me. If you're willing to say he beat you up and threatened people, we can put him back in jail. You understand that?"

"Put him back in jail?" she said. "Owen can't go back to jail. He'll kill himself if he has to go back."

"He'll kill you if he doesn't," Shockey said. "Can't you see that? You want to die out there like Jean did?"

Margi closed her eyes against the burn of tears. "No, but . . ."

"You've come this far," Shockey said. "You've taken the first step. You can't go back now."

She ran a hand under her nose and looked at the

parking lot. The man in the semi was gone, and the light on the tavern roof was out. There was nothing to see but darkness.

"Come to me now," Shockey said. "I'll give you directions to my apartment. You got a pen or something?"

"No, but I can remember," she said. "If I get lost, I'll call again."

"Okay. You know how to get to I-94?"

"I think so."

"Good." He gave her directions to his apartment in Ann Arbor and made her repeat them back three times. "South State Street. It's the blue apartment building just before the sports museum. You can't miss it. Building two, apartment two upstairs. I'll have the balcony light on."

Margi shut her eyes again. Her chest hurt, and it was hard to breathe.

"Repeat the directions back to me again," Shockey said.

She did, surprised that she remembered any of it.

"You're going to come, right?" he asked.

"Yes . . ."

"Promise me, Margi," he said. "Promise me right now you'll get in that car and start this way. Don't you go back to that farm for nothing. You hear me? Nothing."

"I promise, Detective."

"Okay," he said. "You're doing the right thing. I'm proud of you."

She was quiet. A police detective. Proud of her.

"Go," Shockey said. "I'll see you in about a half-hour. Okay?"

"Okay."

She hung up the phone and pushed open the door to the phone booth. She heard the rumble of another semi

pulling in, and a second later, its headlights washed over her. She froze in the glare.

The squeal of brakes, the hard thud of a door. She brought up a hand to shield her eyes as a fuzzy silhouette got out of the passenger side of the truck and advanced toward her. She recognized his walk immediately.

"Who did you call, bitch?"

Chapter Thirty-four

A release of air brakes and the growl of an engine. The semi's headlights moved away, and for a second, Margi couldn't see anything in the engulfing darkness. The truck rumbled down the highway, leaving them alone.

A bolt of lightning split the blackness, illuminating Brandt's face for a second.

"Who did you call?" he asked again.

"No one."

He was just standing there staring at her, water dripping down his face. She focused on his fists, clenching and unclenching. Why wasn't he screaming at her? Why wasn't he already hitting her?

"Give me the keys," he said calmly.

She dug the keys from her jacket and held them out to him. He took them and pointed to the Gremlin.

"Get in the car," he said.

The puddles were deep, the rain on her face like icy pin pricks. Brandt followed her around to the passenger side, pushed her inside, and slammed the door.

When he got in on his side, the car filled up with the stink of whiskey. She closed her eyes as shivers rattled through her bones.

"I'm going to ask you one more time. *Who the fuck did you call?*"

"No one," she whispered.

He grabbed her by the hair and jerked her head to his. His other hand pinched her cheeks. He leaned close. In a flash of lightning, his eyes were filmed with that same sick look he got when he talked about Jean.

"I . . . I called that cop," she said. "I wanted—"

"You did what?"

"I called him to warn him," she said. "I was trying to keep you from doing something stupid, Owen! I was trying to save you. Don't you understand that?"

He smacked her. Her head hit the window, and for a second, she couldn't see anything except a spin of darkness. Then he jerked her back to him.

"You're fucking him, aren't you?" Brandt asked.

"No! I didn't want you to go back to jail!"

She covered her face, expecting another punch, but none came. The engine roared to life, and the Gremlin jolted into gear, spinning gravel until the tires hit asphalt.

She wiped her face and looked up. Nothing ahead but a tunnel of white-washed trees and the splatter of rain on the windshield.

"You're too stupid to live," Brandt said.

"I'm sorry," she said. "I'm sorry. But I love you. You know I love you. I was trying to save you from yourself!"

"What did he say?"

"What?"

"What did the cop say to you?"

"He wanted me to come to his place and make some statement against you, but I told him no," she said. "I wouldn't do that. I would never say nothing bad against you."

"His place?" Brandt asked. "You mean his house? He told you to come to his house?"

"Yeah, but I told—"

"Shut up," he said. "Where does he live?"

Oh, my God. He would go there if she told him. And that detective would open the door thinking it was her, and Owen would kill him. What was she supposed to say now? How could she be so stupid?

Brandt tried to backhand her, but she pressed back against the door. The car skidded and hit gravel before Brandt managed to right it.

"Where the fuck does he live?" Brandt shouted.

"I don't know!" she cried. "He didn't get that far, because I told him—"

Brandt smashed her head against the side window. It stunned her with an explosion of white sparks behind her eyes.

"Answer me!" he said.

You're doing the right thing. I'm proud of you, Margi.

"I can't," she whimpered.

For a few seconds, it was quiet, except for the hard pounding of rain on the roof of the car. She kept her eyes closed, gripped by a rush of fear so strong it left her paralyzed. She clutched the door handle and started to cry.

Brandt pressed down on the gas pedal, the force of the sudden acceleration pushing her back into the seat. She made herself look. The car was tearing down the

road, the rain rushing toward them like a shower of silver pins.

"Where does he live?"

Don't tell him. He won't kill you. He loves you. He won't kill you . . .

She blinked and snuck a look at the dashboard. The little red needle on the speedometer jiggled at sixty. Something was thumping under her feet, like a loose piece of rubber.

"Where the fuck does he live?"

"I don't know!"

Brandt leaned over suddenly and pushed open the passenger door. A fierce wet wind swept in, whipping up the food wrappers and newspapers like a tornado. She grabbed at the door to close it, but he knocked her hands away and started to push at her shoulder. The car skidded but kept going.

"Oh, my God!" she screamed. "Stop it!"

"Get out!" he shouted.

"Please don't do this!"

The Gremlin fishtailed, throwing her against the dash and back again toward the open door. He shoved and slapped at her, forcing her farther across the seat and into the full spray of rain. The muddy splash of water filled her mouth and ripped at her face. The road—it was so close she could see rocks and weeds.

"Where does he live?" Brandt shouted.

"State Street! Next to the sports museum!" she screamed. "Blue apartment! Building two, apartment two, upstairs!"

The car went into a sudden skid, and she lost her grip. She saw nothing but the rush of gravel as it sprayed up toward her.

Chapter Thirty-five

Shockey looked at his watch. It was three-fifteen. Margi should be here by now. Damn it, where was she? Did she have an accident? Or had she gone back to the farm?

He stepped to the balcony and looked over the apartment complex's parking lot. It wasn't very big, and he could see both entrances. Through the rain, he could see the trickle of traffic along South State Street, too. No green Gremlin.

Damn it.

He went back inside and dropped to the sofa. The phone was sitting on the coffee table, silent. He checked his watch again. Only three minutes had passed. He should've gone to her instead of making her come all this way.

Where are you, Margi?

He pushed to his feet and wandered to the kitchen. The bottle of Beefeater was sitting on the counter. He stared at it for a long time.

He hadn't thought about it until after he'd hung up the phone, but what he had done was stupid. Giving his address to a woman who could have been playing him, pulling his strings as easily as Brandt was pulling hers. The pit in his stomach was telling him that this whole thing could be a setup, that Brandt was on his way here now to kill him.

It wasn't her fault, really. She was just weak, that was all. And he had let down every defensive shield he had because he himself was desperate.

He turned and walked back to the balcony.

Still no Gremlin.

He'd give her thirty more minutes, and if she didn't show, he'd have to go out there to that farm and at least make sure the bastard hadn't killed her.

But he couldn't go alone, because he knew if he did and found her dead, Brandt would end up dead, too. And he would spend the rest of his life in jail.

He went back to the phone and dialed the Ann Arbor Hilton. It rang eleven times, then went back to the front desk. He asked them to try the room again. This time, someone picked up.

"Peeper? It's me."

"It's three-thirty A.M.," Louis said. "What's going on?"

"I got a call from Margi," Shockey said. "She's ready to file charges against Brandt and said he threatened to kill me and you and take Amy."

"Jesus."

"I told her to come here," Shockey said. "It's been two hours, and she hasn't showed yet. I'm going to give her another half-hour, then head to the farm."

"Are you nuts?"

"What the hell else can I do?" Shockey asked. "It's like Jean all over again. Don't you see that? Her in trouble out there and me sitting on my ass doing fucking nothing!"

"Jake, calm down."

"She's dead, Kincaid. She's dead because of me."

"Shut up and calm down."

Shockey closed his eyes and pulled in a fiery breath. From the open door of the balcony, he heard the putter of a car engine.

"I think she's here," Shockey said.

"I'm coming over anyway," Louis said. "Stay there, and keep her there with you."

Shockey moved to the sliding glass door, but he couldn't see the parking lot below without putting the phone down and stepping outside.

"Promise me, Jake," Louis said. "Stay there until I get there."

"Okay, okay," Shockey said.

He hung up and went out onto the balcony. The Gremlin was parked under a street lamp. He didn't see Margi, and he called down to her, but no one answered. He went back inside.

He thought again about the possibility that Margi might bring Brandt with her. His revolver was on the coffee table, and he grabbed it before he went to the door. The chain was latched, and he opened the door two inches so he could see anyone coming up the stairs.

The door burst open, slamming into Shockey's forehead. He stumbled backward and groped for something to grab on to, but there was nothing to break his fall.

He hit the coffee table with a splintering of wood and glass. Brandt was suddenly over him. A muddy shoe came down hard on Shockey's wrist, pinning his gun hand to the floor.

Shockey started swinging at Brandt's body with his left hand, pummeling him with punches that hit only hard muscle. He could feel Brandt's hands close around his revolver. He tried to grip it tighter and get it turned toward Brandt, but Brandt was too close, too heavy, dripping water that was making everything slippery.

Brandt wrenched the gun from Shockey's hand.

The knife came down in a flash of silver.

Shockey grabbed at Brandt's hand, but the thrust was too powerful to stop. The blade plunged into Shockey's shoulder.

"Christ . . . fuck . . ." Shockey gasped.

Brandt stabbed him again, slicing blindly at Shockey's raised arms. The blade ripped through the sleeves of his shirt and sliced skin.

"You sonofa—"

Shockey groped for the knife, but Brandt's thrusts were wild, puncturing Shockey's hands and chest and spraying the air with a mist of blood. He could feel his strength fading with every furious beat of his heart.

"This is what I did to her!" Brandt screamed. "You hear me? This is how I killed the bitch! You hear me? You hear me?"

The next thrust of the knife plunged into his lower chest. In a flash fire of air, his lungs emptied, and he was paralyzed. Left with only the burn of the gaping hole and the feel of blood pouring from his body. His shirt grew warm and heavy. His head filled with the horrible image that he was sliced completely in half.

"Don't you die yet, motherfucker," Brandt said. "Look at me. Look at my fucking face!"

Shockey opened his eyes. Brandt loomed above him. His face was splattered with blood and mud.

"Where's the girl?"

"Fuck you, Brandt . . ."

Brandt hit him with the same hand that held the knife. It tore a fresh gash across Shockey's cheek.

"Where's the god damn girl?"

"I won't tell you . . . go ahead and kill me."

Brandt shifted his weight, and for a second, he was gone. Shockey's mind screamed at him to struggle, but he had no strength to raise his arms or even roll away. Brandt's screams grew dull and distant, absorbed into the darkness that was starting to strangle his mind.

"Where's the fucking girl?" Brandt shouted.

Shockey closed his eyes. An unexpected calm moved through him, something dull and hard and final.

He was going to die.

The bastard had gotten them both.

Louis climbed out of the Bronco and slammed the door. The Gremlin was sitting two spaces down. There was no one else in the parking lot and not a car on the street. A light burned on Shockey's balcony.

He hurried through the drizzle to the steps. He was halfway up the stairs when he heard a crash from above, like a door being back-slammed against the wall.

Louis froze, then spun back toward the Bronco.

Damn it. His Glock was in the glovebox.

A man appeared on the landing above him. Dark shirt, dirty jeans, a gun shoved into his belt. And holding a knife slick with so much blood it was dripping at his feet.

Brandt.

Jump the rail. Run.

Brandt barreled down the stairs, the knife raised. Louis pressed himself against the railing, hoping Brandt's momentum would propel him down the stairs. But Brandt wasn't off balance. He rushed into Louis, screaming something about Amy.

The knife came down into Louis's arm, slicing the sleeve of his sweatshirt.

Louis groped for Brandt's wrist, not wanting to give him time to go for the gun. But Brandt was strong and slippery and fighting him like an animal. The blade plunged into Louis's shoulder and hit bone.

Christ!

"You die, too!" Brandt screamed.

Louis was trapped, pinned against the railing. He ducked, throwing an arm against the flashes of metal. The blade sliced across his hand and his bicep as blood rained down in a warm spray.

Sonofabitch!

Suddenly, Brandt slipped off the step, and for a second, the struggle stopped. Louis lunged into a punch that slammed into Brandt's head and almost sent him over the railing.

Louis grabbed the back of Brandt's shirt and, with both hands, swung him sideways, trying to throw him down the stairs.

Brandt spun around, desperate for something to break his fall. The knife came around with him in a vicious arc.

Louis tried to jump away, but there was nowhere to go. No way to block the knife—both his hands were on Brandt's shirt.

The blade ripped through the hard muscle of Louis's chest. Fire razored through his torso.

"Jesus . . . Jesus," Louis gasped.

He dropped to the step, hand to his chest. God, he couldn't breathe, couldn't think, couldn't feel anything but a wet burning beneath his fingers.

Stay calm.

Stay calm, and breathe.

It can't be too deep.

Somewhere in the night, sirens swelled and died and swelled again. Were they coming here? Had someone heard something and called the police?

Look at something. Focus. Think.

Brandt . . . nowhere. He was gone. Louis dropped his

head against the iron railing and tried to see the parking lot. It shimmered, wet asphalt and gauzy white spots of light. Blue lights sparked beyond the trees.

He blinked to clear his tears.

The Gremlin was gone.

Shockey . . .

Louis pushed to his feet and used the rail to steady himself as he stumbled up the stairs. Shockey's door was ajar. Louis pushed it open and looked inside.

Shockey was lying on his back, a pool of blood soaking the gold carpet. His eyes were open and vacant, his face shredded.

Louis dropped to his knees next to him and tried to feel for a pulse, but the skin at Shockey's neck was too slick. The smell of blood filled his nose. He shut his eyes, fighting a wash of nausea.

Margi said Brandt threatened to kill me and take Amy.

Louis's head came up.

Brandt didn't know where Amy was. Had Shockey been tortured into telling him?

Louis crawled to the shattered coffee table and found the phone. He dialed the hotel.

"Room four-ten. Hurry, please."

The phone began to ring. Two, three times.

Answer the damn phone, Joe.

"Louis?"

"Joe, Shockey's dead, and Brandt's looking for Amy, and he might know where she is. Get out of the hotel, and meet me at the university hospital. Now!"

Chapter Thirty-six

The needle in his hand burned. The young nurse who had put it in had apologized over and over as she stuck him, over and over, trying to find his vein.

It had taken forever. Louis had almost fainted.

He fucking hated needles. He could stand almost anything except someone sticking needles in him.

He closed his eyes, letting his head drop back against the pillow. The IV was necessary, the doctor had told him. So was staying one night in the hospital, no matter how much Louis had tried to argue that point.

"I'm all right," Louis had told everyone who hovered over him.

"Your chest muscle is slashed," the doctor had told him. "We just want to watch you for twenty-four hours."

Twenty-four hours . . . Brandt could be in Canada by then.

Detective Bloom had left ten minutes ago. He had questioned Louis relentlessly, his undercurrent of irritation kept in check only by his need to get things under control. Bloom had pulled rank on the Ann Arbor cops and taken charge of the search for Brandt. Not that anyone needed motivating. Even though Shockey had been fired, Louis knew the bond between cops didn't end with a pink slip. Every available officer was out scouring the farmlands for Brandt.

Bloom had brought other news. A semi driver had found Margi by the side of a country road out near the Brandt farm. She had arrived at the hospital in Howell near death. They weren't sure she would live.

Louis lay there, listening to the noises out in the hall-way. Brandt wasn't going to get in; there was a cop sta-tioned outside the room. But Louis wasn't going to get out—not even to go check on Shockey.

No one would tell him anything. Finally, a nurse checked and came back to report that Shockey was not expected to make it through the night.

"Oh, God."

He opened his eyes. Joe was standing at the door.

"Oh, Jesus, Louis . . ."

Joe was there, suddenly, at his side, clutching his hand, her head on his chest.

"Easy, easy," he whispered.

"What?"

"My chest . . ."

She drew back, her eyes wet as she focused on the swath of gauze encasing his chest. "They wouldn't tell me any-thing," she said. "I didn't know if you—" Her eyes welled as they traveled over the other bandages on his arms.

"I'm okay, honest," Louis said.

She ran a hand under her nose. Her hair was pulled back in a messy ponytail, her face splotchy. She was wear-ing a Browns sweatshirt and a pair of shapeless pink pants imprinted with cats that Louis recognized as the bottoms of her favorite pajamas. He had a sudden vi-sion of her, slumped on the floor of his cottage that night a year ago when a madman had broken in while he was gone. Invaded his home, attacked Joe, and left her for dead. His heart softened. She had every right to that awful panicked look on her face now. He knew what she was feeling.

Joe bent down and gently kissed him. Her lips were

a balm on his dry mouth. She drew back and let out a ragged breath.

"I can't believe Shockey's dead," she whispered.

Louis had forgotten he had told her that over the phone. "No, he's in ICU," he said. "But they said he's not going to make it."

Joe shook her head slowly. "Brandt?"

"On the run," he said. "And they found Margi by the side of the road out near Hell. Looks like Brandt threw her from the car. She's in bad shape."

"God."

He was about to close his eyes when it hit him, and he struggled to sit up. "Where's Amy?"

"Out in the hall with the officer," Joe said. She hesitated. "Can I bring her in? She's worried sick."

Louis nodded and lay back against the pillow. He didn't want to admit to Joe that he felt weaker than he was letting on.

He heard a faint shuffling and looked toward the door. Amy was standing just inside the room, staring at him. Her eyes were dark and huge in her pale face.

He tried to smile, but it hurt, and he had the feeling a smile, given his beaten face, might make him look even more grotesque than he was. But as Amy came toward his bed, she didn't look frightened. She looked . . .

"He did this to you," she said softly. "Poppa did this to you."

He looked to Joe.

Amy's eyes teared. "I'm sorry," she said.

Joe was there. "Amy, it's not your—" But Joe didn't finish. She pulled Amy into her arms and held her close.

Louis thought suddenly of the small, blurred pic-

ture he had of Jean, the only photo that existed of the woman for all he knew. He thought of Shockey, lying in a bed somewhere in this huge, anonymous place without anyone to care whether he lived or died. He had a sudden, jarring vision of a cruel man named Moe, one of the countless blank faces whose blank homes Louis had passed through as the foster system funneled him downward. He thought of all of that and knew that Amy needed to know the truth.

She needed to know where she came from.

He met Joe's eyes. She was thinking the same thing.

Joe led Amy from the room, giving the officer stationed outside a nod as they went by. They walked a short ways down the hallway and finally, Joe stopped and took Amy's hand.

"Amy, come sit here with me for a second," Joe said, pointing to a bench.

Amy sat down, but her eyes went beyond Joe to a woman sitting at the end of the hallway, who was sobbing into the shoulder of an elderly man.

"I have to tell you something," Joe said, sitting down. "Amy, Owen Brandt isn't your father."

Joe held her breath, watching Amy's face as it passed through surprise and confusion before settling into a lost look that made Joe's heart ache. Then Amy's expression changed, and Joe could almost see the girl's mind racing, racing backward as it searched desperately for a sign or a clue to remember. For a second, Joe regretted telling Amy about Brandt. Her sense of identity was so fragile, and as despicable as Brandt was, he was the only real link to her past.

Except for Shockey. Even if there was no way to prove he was Amy's father, he had loved her mother. This was an awful place to tell her, this ugly, sterile hallway. But Amy needed to know this, too.

"There's something else I need to tell you," Joe said.

Amy had been staring at the crying woman down the hall and looked back at Joe.

"It's about Mr. Shockey," Joe said. "He might . . . Mr. Shockey and your mother knew each other before you were born. They loved each other."

Amy blinked in surprise but said nothing.

Joe drew in a breath. "Mr. Shockey thinks he might be your real father."

Amy's eyes widened, with surprise but also with an odd look of recognition.

Joe touched her arm. "Are you okay?"

Amy could only nod.

"This is a lot to take in, I know," Joe said.

Amy didn't seem to hear her. She was just sitting there, staring at nothing.

"Where is he?" she asked.

"Mr. Shockey?"

"Yes, where is he?"

When Joe didn't answer immediately, Amy searched her face. "Did he get hurt, too?" she asked.

Joe nodded. Then she linked her arm through Amy's. "Let's go find him," she said.

The nurse at the ICU stopped Joe and Amy at the door, telling Joe that children weren't allowed to visit. Joe took the nurse aside, discreetly showed her badge, and explained why she wanted Amy to see Shockey. The nurse told her Shockey was not going to regain consciousness.

"I don't think you should let her see him," the nurse said.

Joe glanced at Amy, who was waiting at the door. "She can handle it," Joe said.

The nurse led them into the small room. Joe watched Amy's face as she moved forward slowly, taking in the monitors and tubes, the bleats and blips of the machines that were forcing air into Shockey's ravaged lungs.

Shockey's head was wrapped in gauze. Only the left side of his upper face was visible, the skin mottled purple, the eye swollen shut.

None of it seemed to bother Amy. She went right to the bed and looked down at Shockey.

"Can he talk?" she asked softly.

"No," Joe said from the shadows.

"You said he loved Momma?"

"Yes. Very much."

"Is that why he was trying so hard to find her?"

"Yes. He tried for a very long time."

Amy looked like she was trying to figure something out. She turned back to Joe. "How old am I?" she asked.

The question surprised Joe, because there was no reason for Amy to wonder when exactly Jean and Shockey had been together.

"You're sixteen," Joe said.

In the dim light, Joe saw that the answer pleased Amy. At least there was that.

Amy turned back to Shockey again. She was quiet, just standing at the bedside, staring down at him. Even when a shrill beeping sound brought a nurse into the room, Amy didn't move. The nurse briskly adjusted a machine and left.

"Why didn't he come get us before?" Amy asked.

The words had been spoken in a whisper, and Joe wasn't sure she had even heard right.

"He didn't know about you until just a little while ago," she said finally.

Amy fell silent again. Joe let out a breath of relief that her answer seemed to satisfy her. For now, at least. There would be a million questions later.

And no one left to answer them, Joe thought, looking away.

"Does he want me now?"

Joe's eyes shot back to Amy. There was nothing to do but lie. Not for Shockey's sake but for Amy's.

"Yes," Joe said.

It had hit her only in that second. She was going to take Amy back to Echo Bay. The thought had come out of nowhere and left her heart beating so fast that Joe felt a sudden warmth flood her body. It was just the rush of adrenaline, she knew, the same rush that came when you were afraid or backed into a corner. But that was exactly where she felt like she was right now. There was no other choice. There was no one else.

The beeps of the machines moved in to fill the silence. Joe was watching Shockey's swollen eye, almost willing it to open. Finally, she focused on the jagged green line jerking slowly across the heart monitor.

"He's going to die," Amy whispered.

She picked up Shockey's hand and wove her fingers through his.

Chapter Thirty-seven

He wasn't going to die. Not like this, damn it.

Brandt stumbled on through the brush and mud. The icy rain stung his face, and his hands were so cold he couldn't feel them anymore.

He stopped, trying to get his bearings in the dark. Where the hell was he? Was he going south or north? He couldn't even figure that out anymore. There was no moon and no lights out here and if he didn't figure this out soon, he was going to freeze to death.

He pulled up the soaked collar of his denim jacket and trudged on through the mud and blackness.

A sudden memory hit him: his father walking ahead of him, the crackling of his boots on ice the only sound in the gray morning light. Trees bent and broken from the ice storm the night before, barbed-wire fences dripping ice daggers. And then, there in the field, the frozen carcass of a calf that had gone lost in the storm.

I'm not going to die out here!

Not cold and wet and hungry, like some pitiful animal someone was trying to hunt down.

But that's what he was now. A hunted animal.

Why hadn't he had the sense to take a warmer coat? Why hadn't he stopped to get some food? Why didn't he take a flashlight? Why hadn't he fucking *planned* this whole thing better, instead of just showing up at that cop's apartment?

The cop was dead. At least he had done that right.

But everything else was all so fucked up now, and he couldn't even think straight.

Margi . . .

He had even fucked that up.

He should have gone back right away. He should have gone back and made sure she was dead after he pushed her out of the car.

But he didn't. And when he finally did go back and look, she was gone. He had driven along that road five times looking for her body, stopping to stare down into the ditches thinking she had crawled into one to die. He had kicked the brushes, looked in drainage pipes, and even walked out into the fields. But she was gone.

Like a fucking ghost.

Like Jean.

And then he had seen the cop car, a cruiser tearing east on Territorial Road, and he knew they were coming after him.

The cop hadn't seen the Gremlin. But he knew they would soon. So he had headed north, driving clear up toward Unadilla, where he had found an abandoned old barn and left the Gremlin hidden inside.

Then he had started walking.

Keeping off the main roads, cutting across fields and muddy meadows in the dark. Hours of walking in the icy rain as the plan took shape in his head. He would get back to the farm. He'd come in from the north across the creek, because they'd never be looking for him like that. He would get back to the farm, find a way past the cops, pick up what food and clothes he could, and then find a place to hide until things calmed down.

They always did. Even cops got tired of looking. He had learned that in Ohio after he'd robbed the liquor store. A man just had to be smart.

He'd be even smarter this time. And when things were quiet, he'd get out. He'd get out of Hell forever. Forget about Florida. He'd run to Canada. That was a place where a man could be free. Free to do what he wanted. Free of his past and his ghosts.

Brandt stopped.

Water . . . he could hear rushing water somewhere in the darkness.

It had to be Lethe Creek. He pushed on, the brambles tearing at his hands. The rushing sound grew louder. He felt the ground give way, and he slipped, falling forward.

The cold water hit him like a slap. He sputtered to his feet, waist-high in the creek. It was rushing so fast he couldn't keep his balance, and he flailed in the dark, trying to grab anything to stop from being swept away.

His hand hit a branch, and he hung on.

Slowly, he pulled himself out of the water and staggered up the muddy bank. The ground leveled, and he dropped onto the wet grass, gasping.

He lay there shivering, too cold to move. Slowly, he became aware of something cold and hard under his left hand.

He jerked up to his knees.

Fuck. He was lying on somebody's grave.

The cemetery. He was in the cemetery. But that meant he was close now. He staggered to his feet and strained his eyes to see something, anything, in the blackness. And then he saw it in the east—the faintest gray light behind the bare black trees.

He turned to his right. South . . . that had to be south. And the farm was just a mile away. He was going to make it.

• • •

His feet . . . he couldn't feel them at all now. And his teeth were chattering so hard his jaw ached. But he could make out the black shape of the barn ahead and the house and—

He stopped.

Blue lights.

Fuck, no! No! No!

He ducked behind a tree. Two cop cars. He could see them on the road. But he couldn't see the cops. Where the hell were they?

His clothes were iced to his skin. The cold was affecting his brain.

Think! Think!

He had to get warm and dry. Then he could figure out what to do. He had the cop's gun. He could shoot the other cops if he had to. But he had to get warm and dry first. Maybe if he could get into the barn and hide . . .

He crept forward, his eyes on the blue lights. No other choice. He had to chance going into the barn.

Then he saw the bobbing beams of flashlights. And a second later, he heard the men's voices. They were searching the barn.

The beam was coming toward him now. Or was his brain playing tricks on him?

He began to back up slowly, hands outstretched, eyes on the flashlights, heart hammering.

He was almost to the edge of the cornfield when his foot caught, and he went down hard in a thicket of thorns. He lay there for a moment, panting and bleeding. Then he carefully reached out for something to pull himself

from the thorns. Hard, cold stone, then . . . rough wood.

Slowly, he eased from the thicket and tried to see what he had fallen against. He carefully pushed the briars away.

A door. An old wooden door, hanging by one rusted hinge in a crumbling stone-framed archway.

But there was no building attached that he could see. Just a low hill of wild weeds and overgrown trees.

What the fuck was this?

The wind brought the sound of the cop's voices to him again.

He had to find a place to hide.

He pulled on the door. It gave easily, and he stared into the black hole. Feeling his way, he went in. He stumbled again and caught himself. Steps . . . stone steps! It was like the cellar back at the house but smaller. What was this place?

Slowly, he went down. Four steps. He couldn't see a thing, but the air was cool and dry, smelling only of dirt. He reached out, and his fingers found cold, rough stone.

Suddenly, he remembered the lighter in his pocket. If it still worked . . .

With fumbling, cold fingers, he pulled it out. It took four strikes but then flared.

Stone walls. A cave of some kind. Maybe four feet across, but he couldn't tell how deep, and he sure as hell didn't want to venture back there.

What the hell is this place?

Then he saw the corn cobs hanging from the wood rafters. And on the dirt floor . . . clumps that looked like dried potatoes.

A memory flashed into his brain. Crazy Verna standing at the broken icebox bitching about what it was going to

cost to get a new one and how in the old days her grand-
mother just put fruits and vegetables in the root cellar
to keep from rotting. That's what this had to be, a damn
root cellar. No wonder he had never seen it before. It was
carved out of a small hill maybe a hundred feet from the
barn entrance and covered with sod, dirt, and weeds. No
one had used this place for maybe a hundred years.

He realized he was feeling warmer. It was still cold in
here but not as bad as outside, and at least it was dry.

Brandt stared at the shriveled potatoes. Maybe he
could even eat some of this shit if he had to.

The voices . . .

He pocketed the lighter and scrambled up the steps.
Through the tangle of thorn bushes, he could see the
faint beams of the cops' flashlights. But they were moving toward the house. Away from him.

Brandt carefully arranged the thorn bushes to block
the entrance, then pulled the broken door shut. If he
didn't know this place was here, then maybe no one else
would, either.

He backed down the stairs and stood in the pitch-
blackness, holding his breath.

No voices. And then the sound of a car pulling away.

Feeling his way to the wall, he slid down onto the
ground, his back against the stone. The gun was digging
into his waist, so he pulled it out.

This would be okay . . . at least, until he could get
warm and get his brain working right again.

Tomorrow, maybe he would get on the road.

He laid the gun down on the dirt near his foot,
brought up his hands, and blew on them for warmth. He
sat there, the darkness so black he couldn't see his hand
in front of his face.

No sounds now. Just the wind whistling through the old boards of the door.

He was alone.

Except . . .

He turned and peered into the blackness.

A shiver snaked up his wet neck.

He fumbled in his pocket for the lighter, flicked it with his thumb, but it jumped out of his trembling hand.

Frantic, he patted the dirt around him. His fingers touched plastic, and he snatched it up.

His other hand paused on the dirt, then closed around a clump. He brought it up to his nose.

This place. This farm . . .

This was the reason he had come back here.

It was his. He hated it. But it was all he had.

Could he leave this place?

Could he leave Jean?

She was here. She was close now. He could feel it.

He let the dirt fall through his fingers.

He couldn't go. He couldn't leave this place yet.

There was one more thing to do. Then he would be free.

Chapter Thirty-eight

Louis sat down on the wooden bench and let out a long sigh through gritted teeth. He had never thought breathing could be this painful. The muscles across his chest felt cauterized, and the tiny stitches itched like hell. Thirty-six of them.

"You look like you're going to pass out," Joe said.

He looked up. Joe and Amy stood nearby. Amy was glancing nervously around the courthouse lobby, as if she expected Brandt to come bursting through the front doors. Joe was holding her hand.

"What do you think the judge will do?" he asked.

Joe glanced at Amy, then whispered something to her. Amy nodded and moved away, taking a seat on the next bench. She wore jeans and the pale pink parka Louis had bought for her at Kmart. Her hair was pulled back and clipped with a barrette. Louis realized she was starting to look like a young woman, as if being told she was sixteen had forced her to grow three years overnight.

Joe sat down next to him. "I'm going to ask for permanent guardianship," she said, keeping her voice low.

"Permanent? Like adoption?"

Joe gave a half-smile. "I don't know," she said. "But for now, just something longer-term."

"Have you told her?" Louis asked.

"Not yet."

Louis looked back at Amy. She was fondling her locket. He tried to imagine Joe, *his Joe*—a thirty-six-year-old woman who wanted no chains and, as far as he knew, no children—taking on a strange girl like this one.

"Are you sure you know what you're doing?" he asked.

"She has no one else."

"She has Shockey."

"For how long?" Joe asked. "It's a miracle he's lived two days."

"And every hour brings more hope."

"Amy says he's going to die," she said.

"And you believe her?"

Joe's eyes moved away from him, to Amy first, then to nowhere. "I don't know," she said. "I'm just trying to put a Plan B in place. I want her to know, if he does die, that she still has someone."

Louis started to say something, but he stopped himself. His eyes caught a glimmer of white outside the glass doors. He watched as an Ann Arbor cruiser pulled to a stop. He checked his watch. It was ten to one. He hoped Margi was arriving.

They had learned yesterday that she had not only pulled through, but she wasn't as seriously injured as Bloom first thought. Apparently, her skull was pretty thick, and it wasn't the first broken arm she had ever endured.

When Margi heard Brandt was on the run and Shockey was clinging to life, she demanded to be brought to Ann Arbor to help. As part of that help, she wanted to make sure the family court judge knew exactly what kind of man Brandt was.

Louis knew they didn't need her testimony, but he also knew she needed to give it.

Margi let the cop open the door for her and limped through it. She wore a pair of black leggings that outlined her skinny thighs and bulged where the bandages wrapped her knees. She had her leather jacket over her shoulders, with one arm in a cast. On her head was a goofy-looking velvet hat that spiked her brittle yellow hair out over her ears. He knew it covered a massive bandage on her partially shaved head.

She saw him and came awkwardly across the lobby in heeled sandals. As she neared, her face sharpened in the brighter light. One eye was pooled with blood.

He rose to his feet.

"Am I here in time?" she asked.

"Yes," he said. "How are you doing?"

"I'm still alive," Margi said.

She shrugged as she said it, but there was something in her voice that told Louis she didn't quite believe it.

"Have you been to see Shockey?" Louis asked.

"No, but I'm going right over when I'm done here," she said. "How long do you think this is going to take?" She glanced at Amy and lowered her voice. "They said he might not make it, and I want to talk to him."

"He won't be able to talk to you," Joe said. "He's not conscious."

Margi's eyes welled. "I caused this. It's all my fault."

Louis was quiet. He knew from the police statement that Margi had told Brandt the address only when he tried to push her from the car. He couldn't imagine her terror, yet there was a part of him that wished she'd been a little smarter in trying to get away in the first place. Why had she stopped in Hell to make that call? Why not drive fifty miles farther?

"Does he know?" Margi said softly.

"Know what?" Louis said.

"Does he know that I didn't go back? Does he know that I tried to get away? Does he know that?"

"What does that matter?" Louis asked.

Margi glanced at Joe before answering. "He told me he was proud of me. I'd hate him dying and not knowing that."

There wasn't anything to do but lie. Not for Shockey's sake but for Margi's.

"Yes," Louis said. "He knows."

Margi ran a hand under her nose. Louis didn't have a

handkerchief, and he looked to Joe. She found a Kleenex in her purse and gave it to Margi. When she wiped her eyes, he noticed most of the bright orange fingernails were broken.

The door to the courtroom opened, and someone called Amy's name. Joe moved away to take her inside. Margi watched them go, sniffed again.

"I'm a little scared. I never been in court before, at least not for testifyin'."

"I'm not sure they'll need your testimony," Louis said. "Don't be too disappointed if they don't, okay?"

"I won't," Margi said. She reached under her velvet hat to scratch her head, winced slightly as she touched the bandage, then with a sigh just dropped her hand. "I mostly wanted to be here just in case that judge decided to give that girl back to Owen."

"Not a chance. He's wanted for the attempted murder of a police officer."

She looked down at the wadded Kleenex. "He's going to go back to jail, ain't he?"

"Yes."

She sighed.

It was the strangest thing Louis had ever seen. This sad woman feeling sorry for a loser like Brandt.

"I suppose he'd be going back to jail, anyway, so I guess I oughta tell you this part," Margi said.

"Tell me what?"

"Owen told me he killed his wife," she said.

"He confessed to you?" Louis asked.

Margi hesitated, then gave a tight little nod. "He said he cut her up and stabbed her like a hundred times, right there in that kitchen. But he broke the knife, and when

he left to go get an axe, she like just crawled away and disappeared."

Louis was stunned. But it did match Amy's strange account of what she'd seen. She saw her mother attacked and closed her eyes. When she opened them, Jean was gone.

"Did you tell this to Detective Bloom?" he asked.

"No, I . . . I guess I still wanted to protect him," she said. "But I'm done doing that. I just can't anymore."

"Well, if you still want to testify," Louis said, "they'll want to hear this. Will you do it?"

"Yeah," she said. "It's the least I can do for Mr. Shockey."

"He'd be proud of you for that, too."

Margi's eyes held his for a moment. Then she wiped her nose with the back of her hand and looked to the courtroom. He knew that even if they caught Brandt today, his trial was months away.

"What are you going to do now?" Louis asked. "You going back to Ohio?"

She tried a smile that came out a quiver. "Well, once you know the gypsy woman is wrong, you can do almost anything, can't ya?" she said softly.

She limped off toward the courtroom. He started to follow but stopped when he saw another familiar figure come through the glass doors. It was Sergeant Channing.

Channing walked straight to him. Before he spoke, he took a second to study the lacerations that crisscrossed Louis's face and hands.

"I heard about everything that happened. How you feeling, Kincaid?" he asked.

"I'm fine. Is everything okay with Lily? I'm sorry I haven't called or—"

Channing cut him off with a raised palm. "Don't worry about it, man, please."

He pulled a blue envelope from his shirt pocket, LOUIS printed across the front in block letters.

"Lily wanted me to give this to you," Channing said.

Louis opened the envelope and pulled out a card. It showed a cartoon of a bandaged teddy bear and the text, PUT YOUR RIGHT HAND ON YOUR LEFT SHOULDER AND YOUR LEFT HAND ON YOUR RIGHT SHOULDER.

Louis opened the card.

AND GIVE YOURSELF A HEALTHY HUG!

She had signed it, in purple pen, in big letters: LOVE LILY.

"You told her I was injured?" Louis asked.

"Yeah," Channing said. "Kyla and I talked about it and decided she might find out. She reads the papers, believe it or not. Plus, she's going to see you again, and your face looks like you crawled through barbed wire. Kyla and me . . . we made a decision a long time ago that we had to be honest with her about this stuff."

"Because of your job?"

Channing nodded. "A few years back, I ended up in the hospital for a week with a gunshot wound. We didn't want Lily to worry or be scared for me all the time, so Kyla told her I went out of town." He smiled. "Well, one morning, Lily didn't show up for school and set the whole damn city in a panic. Turned out she overheard someone talking and walked three miles to the hospital to find me."

"Three miles?"

"Yup," he said. "Afterward, we had a long talk with her about my job and what could happen to me. It's amazing what kids can digest sometimes."

Louis looked down at the card. "Yeah, it is," he said.

Channing was quiet for a moment. "You look beat, man."

"I'm all right," Louis said.

"We're going to catch this fucker," Channing said. "I know you'd like to be a part of it, but you need to get some rest."

Louis looked away and nodded.

"When things calm down, give me a call at the station, and let me know your plans," Channing said.

Louis nodded again. "I will, thanks."

Channing started to leave, then turned back. "I almost forgot. I got a message for you from Kyla. She says don't you dare go getting yourself killed now."

Channing walked away. Louis folded the card and slipped it into his back pocket.

By the time he slid into a back-row seat inside the courtroom, Joe was standing in front of the judge, asking him to allow her to take Amy home with her to Echo Bay.

He looked over at Amy. She was staring at Joe, her eyes filled with love. And he thought it was amazing that with everything Amy had been through, not only was she still able to feel love, but she was also willing to give it to a woman she barely knew.

He pulled Lily's card from his pocket and stared at the bandaged bear. He opened the card, read the two words printed in the loopy purple letters three times, then carefully tucked it away.

Later that afternoon, they changed hotels again, because Shockey hadn't regained consciousness, and there was no

way to know that he hadn't told Brandt where they were. Louis checked them into the only place that had two available adjoining rooms, an outdated Red Roof Inn out near the freeway. The first thing Joe did was call her boss, Mike. He told her the trial for a hit-and-run case she had been working on for months had been moved up to next week. She was the investigating officer and the one who obtained a confession from the driver. The case would be dismissed without her testimony.

She told him she would be home in forty-eight hours.

The three of them spent the evening eating pizza and playing Yahtzee until Amy finally went to bed.

Joe and Louis shared a bottle of wine, but they had barely talked. Then, finally, Louis took her hand and led her to the bed. They made love, for the first time since taking custody of Amy. It was quiet and quick, both of them afraid Amy might knock on the door at any time.

Joe knew Louis's body was still struggling for strength and that he felt guilty for what had happened to Shockey. But even with all that, she sensed that something was missing from his touch.

It was near four when she slipped quietly from the bed and pulled a robe over her goose-bumped skin. Through the darkness, she felt her way toward the bottle of wine she'd left on the small table. Her toe hit the edge of a suitcase.

"Damn," she hissed.

Louis stirred and rolled over, pulling the blanket up over his shoulder.

Joe shook the sting from her foot and fumbled for the remote to turn on the TV. She muted the sound as the room's white walls took on the glow of the television.

The bottle of wine was there on the table. As she poured herself some in a plastic cup, she noticed two things on the table.

One was the card Lily had sent Louis. The other was a map of Michigan that Joe had bought Amy after they left the courthouse.

So many questions. *Where do you live? What kind of house do you have? Is Lake Michigan big? Do they have bears up there?*

On the map, Amy had traced the route from Ann Arbor to Echo Bay in red marker. Printed across the outline of the Leelanau Peninsula were the words: MY NEW HOME.

Joe took a sip of wine and stared at the flickering lights of the television.

God, was she ready for this? Just the idea that someone else was going to be dependent on her was unsettling. Protection . . . she could manage that. That was her job, after all. But what about the rest? The nurturing and soul shaping and all those other things mothers were put on the earth for.

Her eyes went to the phone, and she thought for a moment about calling her mother. Florence Frye was often awake this early. But Joe was almost afraid of what her mother would say. She had a sudden memory of when she was seven, coming into the kitchen cradling yet another bedraggled stray cat. And her mother's words: *You can't save them all, Joe.*

She would call her mother when she and Amy got back to Echo Bay. She'd find a way to explain. Maybe her mother would come for a visit. Maybe when she met Amy . . .

Joe shut her eyes. Maybe this was a mistake. But it was one she was willing to make.

She opened her eyes, set her glass down, and went quietly to the door between the two rooms, opening it softly. The lights were off, and Joe slipped in. As she moved deeper into the room and her eyes adjusted, she slowed.

Amy's bed was empty.

Joe hurried to the far side of the bed to see if Amy was sleeping on the floor. When she didn't see her, she pushed open the bathroom door and flicked on the light. Nothing.

She hurried back to the bedroom and hit the light switch. The blanket was crumpled, but there was no sign of a struggle. She spun to the outside door. The chain was off.

In two steps, she was there. It was unlocked, and she threw it open. The narrow hall was deserted and quiet. In desperation, she rushed to the window at the end and frantically scanned the parking lot below. Nothing was moving.

She ran back through Amy's room into her own and hit the light switch. When Louis didn't move, she shook him.

"Louis! Wake up!"

He bolted upright, almost hitting her in the face with his elbow.

"What's the matter?" he asked, squinting.

"She's gone!" Joe said.

"What? Who?"

"Amy! She's gone. He took her, Louis. That bastard took her!"

Louis bolted from the bed and ran to the adjoining room. Joe followed him.

"He couldn't get in here without her unlocking the

door, and she wouldn't do that, Joe. She's probably hiding." He searched the closet, then got onto his knees to look under the bed.

"No, she wouldn't do that! I know—"

Joe froze as her eyes found the piece of paper wedged under the lamp on the desk. She snatched it up.

Dear Miss Joe,

I want to go to Echo Bay with you. But I am worried that when Mr. Shockey dies there will be no one left here to look for Momma. So I have to try one more time. I didn't ask you to help me because you need to stay here and take care of Mr. Kincaid. Please don't worry about me. I know where I am going and I am not afraid. I will be back sometime tomorrow.

Amy

Joe pushed her hair from her face, the flood of relief that Amy wasn't in Brandt's hands quickly giving way to dread. Her eyes went to the empty chair in the corner. Amy had taken her backpack.

Louis noticed Joe's pale face and the paper in her hand. "What is it?" he asked.

"She's gone to the farm," Joe said.

Chapter Thirty-nine

She wasn't afraid to ride in the big trucks now. At one in the morning, the freeway near Ann Arbor, the one

less than five hundred feet from the hotel door, rumbled with a caravan of them.

She stood in the cold darkness for less than five minutes before a big, muddy red semi squealed to a stop. The driver was dirty, and the cab smelled like cigarettes, but she climbed up into the seat anyway. Because she wasn't afraid of him, either.

Where you going, little girl?

I'm not a little girl. I'm sixteen. And I'm going to see my mother.

For the next hour, as they drove west, the man talked of his son and his fishing boat and the thousands of miles he'd spent behind the wheel of this old truck. She'd listened politely, fighting sleep and hoping Miss Joe wouldn't be mad at her in the morning.

The man must've felt sorry for her, because he offered to drive off the freeway and drop her closer to the farm. She was going to tell him no, but it was so cold and dark. So she changed her mind and told him she would appreciate that.

Where is this farm, Missy?

Just south of Hell. But if you miss the road leading in, you end up down in Bliss.

The semi was too big to make it down the rutted gravel and dirt of Lethe Creek Road. And when the man pulled to a stop in front of the closed Texaco station, he said he wasn't sure he should leave her out here alone.

You sure you're okay, Missy?

Yes, sir, I got kin here.

She slipped out of the truck and closed the door, clutching her backpack to her chest. With a rattle of gears and a churn of mud, the truck pulled away. She stood in

the darkness under the old Texaco sign, but she wasn't afraid. There were no strange voices in her head anymore, no flashing memories of green corn, no screaming horses.

There was just her.

As she hurried down the dark road, it started to drizzle. The dark outline of the barn came to her, then the house beyond. She went through the fence and stopped under the old oak tree in the front yard. It was so quiet the *pop-pop-pop* of the drops falling on the leaves overhead was the only sound she could hear.

She stood as still as possible and closed her eyes, waiting for that tingling she sometimes got when she felt her mother's presence near.

But there was nothing.

She crept up to the house. The kitchen door was ajar, the lock hanging on splintered wood.

She stood there and stared at it.

Had someone come here looking for her father? No, he was not her father anymore. Mr. Shockey was her father, and . . . that other man had hurt him.

She pushed inside the broken door, stopping again in the kitchen. There was just enough light to make out the gray shapes of the counters and a cooler on the floor. The air was heavy and spoiled, stale with the smell of him.

She set her backpack down and once again closed her eyes and stood very still.

Are you here, Momma?

Silence. She felt nothing but the cold swirl of air.

What was wrong? Why couldn't she feel anything? Why wasn't something coming to her like it did in Dr. Sher's office?

Amy moved to the cupboard and opened the door.

letting out the dank smell of rusted pipes. She brushed aside the cobwebs and climbed inside. It felt different, smaller, like she didn't fit anymore. But she huddled up, pulled the door closed, and stared out through the jagged cracks in the wood slats.

She saw nothing but the torn linoleum.

Amy closed her eyes and leaned her head on her knees. She didn't want to cry, but she couldn't help it. The tears just came, hot and hard.

Why couldn't she remember?

With a small cry, she crawled from the cupboard. She stood for a moment in the kitchen, wiping her face and taking small breaths to calm herself. She knew she needed to be calm for this to work. Dr. Sher always told her to stay calm.

That's when she saw it . . . there on the floor.

Toby.

She scrambled to the corner and snatched up the stuffed rabbit. She held it to her nose, inhaling its sweet-musty scent.

Her eyes snapped open.

The parlor. That is where she would be!

But when she got there, she felt nothing. And the roll of music was missing from the piano. She shut her eyes tight and tried to think of the song. If she sang it, her mother would hear it. But nothing came. Not one word. The song was gone, too.

Clutching the rabbit, Amy opened her eyes.

There was no one here anymore.

She slowly retraced her steps back to the kitchen, picked up her backpack, and stuffed Toby inside. She left the kitchen and stood on the porch for a moment, look-

ing out over the farm. The barn and the other buildings were just black outlines in gray mist, and beyond was nothing but the empty fields fading into the darkness.

No lights, no movement, no sounds. No signs that anyone had ever lived here. And for a moment, she had the weird thought that maybe even *she* hadn't really lived here.

She had to go back to Miss Joe. She'd be so worried.

But the rain was coming down harder now. And she was cold and tired.

She would wait until it was light, and then she would walk back to the Texaco station. It would be open in the morning, and someone would let her call the hotel, and Miss Joe would come and get her.

Amy glanced back at the kitchen. She didn't want to go back in there. She looked at the barn. She would wait there.

Hoisting the backpack over her shoulder, she jumped off the porch and ran across the yard to the barn. The heavy sliding doors on the bottom level stood open just enough for her to squeeze through.

It was warmer inside but dark.

She picked her way across the dirt floor, trying to make out the shape of the old stalls in the gloom. There was hay, she remembered, and she could sleep there until morning.

She was halfway across the barn when she felt it.

Like the brush of a warm breeze on her cheek. But she knew there was no wind in the barn. It came again, the gentlest of caresses.

"Momma?" she whispered.

No, child.

She stood very still and closed her eyes, her heart hammering, waiting for the feeling. But the only feeling that came was a small constricting of her throat.

There was just her.

And the voice she heard now was her own.

It's not safe here, John. Come with me.

Amy opened her eyes. The darkness pressed close around her, but she wasn't afraid. She walked slowly but surely across the barn, moving easily among the rusted tools and rotting bales, into the farthest corner of the barn.

An instinct told her to reach out, and when she did, her hand touched wood. A ladder. She had known it would be there!

The backpack secured on her back now, she began to climb. She couldn't see anything above, but still, there was no fear for herself now. Just for . . .

It's too late. We have to get out another way.

She emerged into a new darkness, but she could feel the boards of a floor, and she pulled herself up. The old hay was scratchy beneath her hands. She knew she was up on the old barn's second floor now, and a stab of recognition came to her. This was where she had found the kitten! But a different memory was crowding that one out with its urgency.

This way, John!

The old boards groaned as she made her way across the rotted planks, but she kept moving until . . .

She stopped, knelt down, and brushed the straw away. Her fingers found the cold metal ring of the trapdoor. She pulled, but it wouldn't move.

Horses . . . she could hear horses outside!

She pulled in a deep breath and yanked on the trap-

door. It cracked and gave way, falling back on the hay with a thud.

Hurry! Hurry!

Without a second thought, Amy launched herself into the black hole. She landed with a hard jolt in a pile of hay. She was stunned for a second, but then the feel of the rain on her face brought her back. Outside . . . she was outside.

She was on her feet at once and moving through the darkness, away from the barn, through a thicket of high weeds.

Faster, John, you have to walk faster! Just a little ways more, and you can rest. Here! Here! Let me help you . . . you can hide here—

Amy stopped suddenly.

The voice was gone.

In front of her was a high thicket of thorny brambles.

Chapter Forty

Dawn. Coming to him as a sliver of gray in the corner of his eye. He had survived another night. Two now . . . two nights and two days in this stinking hole.

Owen Brandt ran a dirty hand under his nose and pushed himself to his feet. He wiped his frozen hands on his pants and made his way through the darkness to the steps. Memory spurred him in the right direction. That's how it was now, depending only on his senses and what he could remember to survive when the darkness closed in.

His hands had told him this place had stone walls and wooden rafters. His feet had told him it was nine feet wide, because he had walked it back and forth in the dark. But he didn't know how deep it was, because he wouldn't go back any further than he could see. But sometimes, if the sun was bright enough to bleed around the edges of the old wood door and down the stone steps, then he could make out the dirt pile back there. He was sure the ceiling had caved in, but he wasn't about to go back there and risk getting himself buried alive.

He staggered to the steps, his head thick from lack of sleep. He'd been too cold and hungry to sleep.

The rotten corn and potatoes left in the cellar had been too hard to eat. Finally, driven by hunger, he had ventured out and crouched in the thorn bushes, watching for cops. He watched for hours, finally figuring out that they came by to check the farmhouse twice a day, in the morning and again toward dusk. The cop would get out and do only a quick walk around the farmhouse and leave, like he was too cold to bother to stay.

Last night, after the cop left, he had sprinted across the field to the house, where he had gathered up what was left of the food Margi had bought—half a package of baloney and some potato chips. And the whiskey. That was best of all, the hot sting of rye on his throat as he sat here, shivering.

But the whiskey was gone now. The food was gone now. It was a different hunger that had brought him out of the hole a second time.

He had emerged into the cold, moonless night and walked the farm. Thirteen times—he'd counted—thirteen times he had walked the fields in the syrupy dark-

ness. Listening for her voice, seeing shadows that drifted away from him as he grew close. Always conscious of the feel of the dirt under his boots, because he didn't want to step on her.

He hadn't found her.

Brandt stood, shivering at the bottom of the stone steps, looking up into the thin gray light leaking around the door.

He couldn't stand it any longer. He had to get out.

He staggered up the stone steps and pushed open the old wooden door. The creak of the hinge sounded like a shriek, and he held his breath. But he didn't hear anyone, no voices, no cop talk. He pushed aside the thorn bushes and climbed out.

A gray mist hovered over the straw-strewn cornfield. In the distance, the house seemed to float, and the barn seemed to shiver, like neither of them was real but just imaginary fixtures in an imaginary life.

Something moved. Or was his mind so gone now that he was seeing things? He started to withdraw into the hole, but then he froze.

There it was again.

Through the tangle of thorn bushes, he saw something waver, like it had just risen from the ground. A flutter of dark hair and slender build told him it was a woman.

Brandt squinted.

Jean.

And she was coming closer.

His hand went to the knife in his waistband. His throat tightened with the pounding of his pulse as her form took shape in the mist.

No . . . it wasn't Jean.

It was the damn girl.

But this didn't make sense. Why would the girl be here?

Then it came to him. She had come back to meet her whore mother. The girl coming back here now to this place—just like he had!—it had been like some weird gift, like it happened this way for a reason.

He had been right all along. Jean was here somewhere.

He retreated into the root cellar, not wanting the girl to see him. He had to think about this, had to figure out what to do. He crouched on the stone steps behind the half-open door, watching, waiting.

Pink. Something pink. The pink of her jacket moving across the gap in the boards.

Come closer, girl. A little closer.

He heard the snap of a twig as she walked along the edge of the cornfield. So close now he could almost smell her.

He held his breath.

Silence.

Had she stopped? Why wasn't she coming inside? She was just standing there, frozen. Her weird eyes were colored with the same look she used to get when she was little, like when the tornados were coming.

She knew he was in here.

And she was going to run.

Damn the cops and anyone else out there.

Brandt pushed open the door. At the sound, the girl's head snapped up, her eyes—those weird fucking eyes—pinned on him.

Suddenly, she bolted toward the cornfield.

He was slowed by the thorn bushes but he caught up with her at the edge of the field and threw an arm around her neck, knocking her to the dirt.

"No!" she cried.

He started to drag her back to the root cellar. She was light, no heavier than a bundle of sticks, but she was kicking hard, her hands clawing at his arms.

A pain seered through his hand.

Fuck!

She had bitten him. He dropped his hand and clenched his teeth to keep himself from yelping. Blood. The bitch had drawn blood.

"God damn you," he hissed.

He smacked her. She cried and covered her head, crumpling to the weeds in a whimpering heap. He dropped a knee into the girl's chest and pulled his knife from his waistband.

He wanted to slice her up right here but he couldn't do that—not yet. He leaned close, holding the knife inches from her face.

"Where is she?" he asked.

She didn't open her eyes, just held her cheek, crying.

"Where is she?" Brandt said. "Where's your momma?"

She opened her eyes. "Momma?" she whispered.

Brandt grabbed a fistful of her hair, pushing the broken blade into her cheek. "Tell me now, or you die," he said.

Tears streaked the girl's face, and she was gulping in air like she was drowning. She sounded like she was having one of those damn breathing attacks.

"Stop it!" he hissed.

Her eyes came up, staring right into his. It was the

same kind of look he'd seen in Jean's eyes just before he plunged the knife into her chest. And the same one he'd seen in Margi's before he pushed her from the car.

And the screaming. The same screams that Jean had made and—

But no one was screaming, he realized. It was a siren he was hearing now.

A thud. Voices.

Brandt's eyes shot to the road. Blue lights cut through the fog.

He looked down at the girl. She had heard it, too. He thrust a hand over her mouth, his knee digging harder into her stomach to keep her still. Ten feet away, a rusting tractor sat surrounded by a heavy curtain of brush. He dragged the girl behind it.

Brandt crouched behind the tractor's wheel, watching the cops. One of them was heading toward the farmhouse. The other was going toward the barn.

Brandt knew the second cop couldn't see him behind the tractor. But they'd start searching out here soon enough. And there was no way he could risk trying to drag the girl back to the root cellar now.

Think! Think!

The Gremlin. If he could make it to the creek, he could get back to the old barn where he had hidden the car and get away.

Brandt yanked the girl to her knees and held her by the neck. "Crawl," he said. "You make one sound, I'll slice you open and throw your body in the fucking hole where no one will ever find it."

Chapter Forty-one

Louis saw the blue pulse of the lights ahead. The fog had almost burned off, leaving the sun a pale smudge in the eastern sky, and as they rounded the bend on Lethe Creek Road, the farmhouse came into view.

Two Livingston County sheriff cruisers were parked at the gate. Joe had called them from the hotel in Ann Arbor, knowing they could get to the farm faster. A report of a runaway girl wasn't high priority, but when Joe told them that Amy could be a target of Owen Brandt, the response was swift.

There were three deputies standing in the yard. But they were alone.

"Where is she?" Joe said, leaning forward in the passenger seat.

"Take it easy, Joe. Let me get the car stopped," Louis said.

But Joe was out of the Bronco before he got it into park.

Louis followed as fast as he could, his chest aching and his brain still fogged with painkillers. He had insisted on driving, because for the first time since he'd known her, Joe was incapable of a single rational thought. By the time they had turned onto Lethe Creek Road, she had managed to calm down some, making the transition back into cop mode, as he called it, but she still was not herself.

He came up behind Joe, recognizing the shortest man in the group as Sheriff Travis Horne.

"Look, we've been here almost an hour already," Horne

was saying to Joe. "We've searched the house and the barn and every other damn building out here."

"Did you search the attic?" Joe asked.

The sheriff sighed. "Yes, ma'am, we did."

Joe spun and looked out at the fields. "Then we do a grid search," she said.

"With three men?" Horne asked. "Are you nuts?"

"There's five of us here," Joe said.

"And sixty-some acres out there, plus two or three miles of nothing beyond that," he said, gesturing toward the barn. "It'll take days."

"For God's sake," Joe said. "She's only a child."

The sheriff tipped back his hat. "A child who made her way out here twice now all by herself. She sounds a mite more capable of taking care of herself than you're giving her credit for."

Joe glared at him, then spun away from the group and walked away. Arms crossed, she stared out at the cornfields. Her shoulders jerked with a smothered sob.

Louis looked at Horne. "Sheriff," he said, "we're sure Amy will come back here, and we're going to stay. I would appreciate it if you'd leave us one of your deputies to help."

Horne cut his eyes to Joe, chewing at his lip as he considered the request. "I still have men on overtime patrolling the back roads for Owen Brandt," he said. "Who you *also* told us would come back here, and he hasn't showed, either. I'm sorry, I can't use what little manpower I have to keep looking for your ghosts."

"Would you at least call Detective Bloom and let him know Amy's missing and ask him if he can spare a few men?" Louis asked.

Horne nodded. "That I can do," he said.

Louis stuffed his hands into his pockets and looked to Joe. She was walking toward the barn, already anxious to start searching. He knew it would be hours before Bloom could dispatch anyone to help them. If he sent anyone at all.

"Kincaid?"

Louis looked back at the sheriff.

"I'll send Sam here back with some coffee and doughnuts in about an hour for you."

Horne started toward his cruiser. His deputies followed him, and in less than a minute, the two cruisers headed away, down Lethe Creek Road.

Joe had disappeared. Then Louis saw her coming around the north side of the barn. She was stopping to look under every piece of rusted machine, inside every metal drum, and through every bramble and bush.

Louis squinted into the pale sun, then did a slow turn in a circle, surveying the land.

He had never believed in ESP or telepathy, but he did believe in instincts. Especially his own. And he had the feeling Amy was here somewhere.

Maybe she had seen the cops and, thinking they would take her back before she found her mother, found a place to hide. Maybe she had simply curled up somewhere and fallen asleep.

He knew one thing for sure. Amy wouldn't hide from Joe.

He cupped his hands around his mouth and shouted as loudly as he could. "Amy!"

Joe's eyes shot to him from her position by a coil of barbed wire.

"Joe, call to her," he said.

Joe hesitated, then called Amy's name. She called again and again, her voice growing hoarse.

Louis strained to hear anything, any response. But there was nothing but the empty echo of Joe's voice floating on the wind.

Amy . . .

Brandt spun around, his ears perked at the sound of the voice. He raised a hand to shield his eyes from the sun, trying to see who was back there calling to the girl.

"It's Miss Joe," Amy whispered.

Brandt's hand shot out and clipped her by the ear. "Shut up."

He grabbed the sleeve of her parka and manhandled her the rest of the way up the slope and into the cemetery. She tripped on a headstone and fell to the grass.

Brandt yanked her by the collar to her feet. "Keep walking," he said. "We got a long way to the car."

"You're going the wrong way," Amy said.

"What?"

"She's back there." Amy pointed south.

"No one's coming to get you, girl."

"She's back there. If you leave now, you'll never find her."

Brandt stopped and stared at her.

"Momma's back there," Amy whispered.

Brandt twisted to look over his shoulder. But he saw nothing. What the hell had he expected to see? Jean standing there and looking back at him?

The bitch is lying to me. Like they all lie.

He jerked her arm so hard she cried out. "Don't you lie to me, girl," he said. "Don't you ever lie to me about your god damn momma, you hear me?"

The girl's eyes welled with tears, but for the first time, he didn't see any fear in them. Suddenly, she didn't seem to be afraid of him at all.

Damn it, he'd *make* her afraid.

He hit her in the side of the head. The blow knocked her to her knees. He yanked her back up and pressed the broken blade of the knife to her cheek. But still, he saw no fear.

He smacked her again. This time, the blade glanced off her chin, ripping skin and drawing blood. She started to cry, hands at her face.

"Where is she, then?" he asked, leaning into her. "Where is your momma?"

"In the hiding place."

"What fucking hiding place?"

"The root cellar."

The root cellar?

No. He'd been in the root cellar. Been there for two days. There had been no one else in there with him.

Suddenly, the girl twisted away from him. He groped for her sleeve, but she was gone, stumbling down the hill, arms flailing, trying to keep her balance.

He broke into a run after her, letting his momentum propel him down the slope. He caught her on the muddy bank of Lethe Creek, but she spun away from him and plunged into the water.

He trudged into the stream, clawing at her parka. But she was fast, flying through the water. He couldn't keep up, slowed by the icy rush against his thighs and the sucking of mud at his shoes.

"Stop, you little bitch!"

She stumbled onto the rocks on the other side, gasp-

ing and trying to get her balance. He lunged at her. All he could catch was her ankle. With a jerk, he pulled her backward. She slammed face-first to the bank, her screams smothered in the mud.

He flipped her over so he could see her face. Now he could see the terror burning in her eyes, feel the hot pulse of panicked air from her lips. This was the way it was supposed to be.

He plunged the knife into the soft flesh of her belly.

Her small hands flew up, groping for something to grab, but he ripped them off his shirt and shoved her away from him.

She fell back into the water.

He was going to go after her and cut her up good, but it didn't look like he had to. The bitch was motionless. One arm wedged between the muddy rocks, the other floating limply in the rippling water that rocked her thin body.

Her eyes were open, looking at him. But there was nothing in them now.

Brandt sucked in some cold air to steady himself. His knees felt like rubber.

She's back there.

He turned slowly to the south, toward the farm.

The bitch had been lying to him. They all lied.

But he couldn't stop himself.

He slogged back through the stream and up the rise on the other side. When he got to the cemetery, he paused. There to the south, through the bare black trees, he could see the barn.

He started toward it.

Chapter Forty-two

J oe, wait."

"I'm going to look in the barn again," she yelled back.

"We've been over it twice, Joe. She's not in there."

Joe stopped. She was about twenty feet from the barn door, hair whipping around her face, the tip of her nose raw from the wind.

Louis trotted over to her. She was just standing there, staring out at the cornfields. They had already been back through the house, searching it from attic to cellar. They had scoured the barn from the loft to the stalls. The only buildings left to search were a pump shed and the outhouse.

"I've never been this worried about anyone," Joe said softly.

"I know."

Joe pushed her hair from her face. "Maybe she didn't make it this far, Louis," she said. "I keep thinking maybe somebody picked her up on the highway, and we're wasting valuable time here, and . . ." Her voice trailed off as she shook her head slowly.

Louis reached out and zipped up her jacket. His hand lingered on her cold cheek. "She's here somewhere," he said.

She ran a shaky hand under her nose. "Okay," she said. "I'll take the shed. Will you . . . ?"

She motioned toward the outhouse. Louis nodded and headed off in that direction. He didn't think Amy would be in either building, but they had to look. He

was coming to believe there was another possibility that neither he nor certainly not Joe wanted to consider. Had Amy regressed to the same childlike state she'd been in when they first found her in the cupboard? That was the only logical explanation for the fact that she hadn't responded to their calls.

Because she *was* here. He hadn't said that to Joe just to calm her down. He believed it.

He stopped outside the outhouse to grab a breath, then pulled open the door. Hand to his nose, he fished the flashlight from his back pocket, stepped inside, and looked down into the dark hole. Nothing.

He let out a breath of relief and backed out into the cold air. Joe was coming out of the shed, and he walked toward her, taking time again to scan the horizon. His step slowed as his mind tripped with an idea. There was a place they hadn't thought of yet.

The cemetery.

But why would Amy go there? She had no reason to think Jean would be there, buried or unburied.

Joe suddenly disappeared behind a low, grassy hill out toward the cornfields. He didn't like the idea of her being out of view, and he hurried to her. He found her digging through a tangle of heavy brush on a west-facing slope of the hill. He could see a peeling white board behind the branches.

He stepped closer. "What did you find?"

"I don't know," Joe said. Her hands were bleeding from pulling at the thorn bushes, but she didn't stop. She yanked away the last of the bushes.

They stood silently, staring at a rotted old door hanging by one hinge, embedded in the side of the hill.

He hadn't seen this door on his other visits. But he realized now that it had been easy to overlook. The small hill was just one of several on the gently undulating ground surrounding the farmhouse and barn. All of the rises were dense with brush hidden by garbage and rusting machines. Maybe the deputies had found this door and already searched what was behind it. If there was nothing inside, there was no reason for the deputies to mention it.

But why was his gut telling him something was wrong about this place?

Joe reached to the door.

"Joe," Louis said, "draw your weapon."

She glanced back at him, then pulled her .45 from its holster. She stepped back to let Louis pull the door away.

Joe slipped inside, arms rigid, gun pointed. Louis stayed at the entrance, clicking on his flashlight and wishing like hell he'd thought to put his Glock on his belt. But they had not come here with the idea of finding Brandt.

The beam of his flashlight swept over the back of Joe's leather jacket, then picked up gray stone walls and sagging rafters.

What was this place? A tornado shelter?

"You can't go in there."

The man's voice was deep and familiar. And it was coming from above him.

Louis's head snapped up to the hill above the door.

"You can't be in there!" Brandt screamed.

A second later, Louis saw the broken knife in Brandt's hand.

"Joe!"

Brandt lunged at him, coming off the top of the hill with the force of a two-hundred-pound boulder. Louis stumbled backward and threw up both arms, trying to deflect the impact of Brandt's body.

But he was knocked off his feet and slammed to the ground onto his back. A splintering pain fired through his chest.

The knife. Get the knife.

He saw a flash of metal. His hands flew up, locking around Brandt's wrist to stop his downward thrust. Brandt started hitting him, desperate to free his knife.

"Joe!"

But he knew why she hadn't fired. She had no clear shot. He and Brandt were too close, too tangled up.

He gritted his teeth and steeled his arms, using all the strength he had to force Brandt's shoulders back and up, pushing until Brandt was on his haunches and erect.

The six gunshots came rapid-fire.

Brandt spasmed like he had been electrocuted, and with a gasp, he went limp, tipping forward. Louis pushed him aside and scrambled to his feet.

His chest was on fire. He couldn't pull in a good breath.

Joe was standing over Brandt, her gun pointed at the ground but still held with a white-knuckled grip. Her eyes were pinned on the knife near Brandt's fingers.

"Are you cut?" she asked Louis without looking at him.

"No."

She started to crumple.

Louis's eyes shot to the knife. It was covered in fresh blood.

And he knew what Joe knew. The blood had to be Amy's.

Louis stepped to her and gently worked the .45 from her hand. The move seemed to sap her remaining strength, and her knees buckled. He caught her and pulled her close.

"It's all right," he said.

"I let him get her. I let him . . ."

"No, you didn't."

Louis wrapped an arm around her neck and held her. She fell against him with a sob. And he realized that until this moment, he'd never seen her cry.

He pulled her tighter to his chest, his hand cradling the back of her head, holding her until her body stopped its terrible shaking.

It was a long time before she was able to pull back and look at him.

"We need to find her," Joe said, her voice cracking.

He knew she was right, but where should they start? Would it be quicker to drive into town and get the deputies back out here or to head off by themselves?

Louis looked down at Brandt.

His clothes were filthy, his jaw whiskered with a week's growth. Louis guessed he'd been hiding in this bunker since he attacked Shockey. But where had Brandt been just before he appeared at the top of the hill?

Louis eased away from Joe and knelt next to Brandt. His clothes were soaked from the waist down. And his shoes were caked with mud.

"Joe, you take the Bronco and go get help," he said, rising to his feet. "I'm going to look for Amy."

"No, I'm going with you," Joe said.

• • •

The Bronco bounced across the cornfields, getting mired in mud a few times but heading steadily north toward Lethe Creek. Finally, Louis was forced to bring the truck to a stop at the edge of the tree break. The copse of trees and brush was too thick to get through.

Joe pushed out her door quickly and started away from the truck. "Which way?" she asked.

"Straight through the trees and up the hill," he said.

She broke into a run and pushed through the brush. Louis quickened his step to keep up with her. He wanted to be next to her when they crested the hill in front of the cemetery. Because if he was right about how Brandt had gotten wet, Amy would be lying in or near the stream on the other side.

Joe stopped at the top of the hill.

"Oh, my God, Louis . . ."

He drew up next to her. At first, nothing registered. Then he saw the splash of pink bobbing in the water.

Amy was in the water on her back. Her pink parka was ballooned with air, keeping her shoulders afloat.

Joe raced across the cemetery and down the slope. Louis followed, his stomach knotting as other details registered.

Chalky white face, blue lips, hair streaming out behind her in the fast-moving brown water. He realized in that instant that if her body hadn't somehow gotten wedged in the rocks, it would have been swept downstream.

Joe was wading across the water. The stitches in Louis's chest forced him to move slowly down the muddy slope behind her, but his eyes were riveted on Amy's body.

A final thought hit him like a hard punch. Amy

wasn't all cut up as Shockey had been. At least Joe would be spared that.

With a splash, Joe dropped to her knees in the water and gathered Amy into her arms.

"Oh, my God! She's ice cold."

Louis reached her side and tried to pull Joe to her feet. "Joe, calm down. Let's get her out of the water," he said.

Joe grabbed Amy under the arms. Louis took her feet. He could see now the rip in her parka and the stain of blood that surrounded it.

They set her on the grass. He dropped down next to her, his fingers going first to her neck. Even under the collar of her jacket, her skin felt like frozen meat. He moved his fingers up and down, searching for the slightest pulse.

"Amy!" Joe said. "Can you hear me?"

"Joe, calm down."

Joe looked up at him as if he'd slapped her, then turned her attention back to Amy. Something changed in her, as if she'd suddenly found a way to shut down her emotions and unlock fourteen years of training. She roughly pushed Amy's hair off her face and bent over her, putting her cheek against Amy's mouth.

"Louis, she's breathing."

He finally found a feeble pulse. She was alive, but barely. And he knew they not only had to get her to a hospital, they had to get her warm—now.

He started to rip off his jacket, then realized it was not heavy enough to do Amy any good.

Joe saw him and frantically pulled at the zipper of her leather jacket. Louis eased the sodden parka off Amy. He was trying to remember his academy training, all the stuff about hypothermia, but nothing was coming.

He reached down to pick Amy up. Joe caught his arm.

"Your stitches. You can't carry her," she said.

"I'll do it. Just help me get her up."

He slipped his hands under her and, with a soft groan, pushed clumsily to his feet. Amy seemed to weigh twice as much as she did that day he first carried her from the house.

Joe draped her leather jacket over Amy's chest, then looked up at Louis.

"You okay?" she asked.

"I'm fine. Just help me stay steady crossing the water."

Joe wrapped an arm around his waist, and together they trudged back across the stream.

Breathless, Louis stopped in the cemetery, trying to cool the burning in his lungs with deep pulls of air. Through the branches of the black trees beyond, he could see the bright red paint of Joe's Bronco.

He felt Joe's arm around his waist. With a grimace, he hefted Amy up against his chest and started south.

Chapter Forty-three

He was alone now. It should have been Joe who stayed. She was the police officer and the shooter of a wanted man. It was her duty as a cop to stay on the scene and help secure it.

But he knew Joe wasn't thinking like a cop right now. So he had let her go.

He looked at his watch. She should be halfway to Howell by now with Amy. He remembered seeing a road sign for a hospital there, and he had rattled off directions to Joe before she pulled away.

He hoped she remembered them. And he hoped she kept herself sane enough on the drive to handle the rolling country roads. He'd never transported a dying person before, but he could imagine that every mile must feel like a hundred. What he could not imagine was hearing the person next to you gasp her last breath and being able to do nothing about it but keep driving.

Louis pushed through the gate and walked toward the cornfields behind the house. His jacket was still damp, leaving his skin cold and clammy underneath. He wondered where that deputy was with the coffee Travis Horne had promised two hours ago. It would taste damn good about now.

He stopped walking and looked down at Brandt's body.

They hadn't touched him. Except to make sure he was dead. The broken knife still lay near his hand. The blood was dry now, coating the blade with a red film. Brandt's denim jacket was peppered with bullet holes. Five of them in his right side. The sixth had ripped through his neck.

Louis looked down at his own khaki jacket. There was a speckling of dark red drops—Brandt's spatter probably—and a smudge of pink that belonged to Amy. He wondered if he had Brandt's blood on his face and he didn't really care, but he found himself wiping his cheeks anyway.

It wasn't something he liked to admit to himself be-

cause it seemed heartless and almost inhuman, but he was glad the bastard was dead. He was glad it had been Joe who had killed him.

Louis shivered and looked around.

The door to the storm shelter—or whatever it was— hung open on one rusty hinge. He stared at it for a moment, then looked up at the hill Brandt had leaped from.

You can't go in there.

Why did Brandt care who went in there? He had abducted Amy and dragged her through the cornfields, all the way to the creek. Most likely running from the deputies who had been there that morning. The Gremlin was probably hidden out there somewhere, too. An easy escape for him and Amy, at least for a few miles until the deputies saw them.

So why had he come back? What had he left that he was willing to die for?

Louis withdrew the flashlight from his back pocket and clicked it on. He stepped inside the bunker. The stone steps crumbled some under his weight, almost sending him to the dirt. He dropped the flashlight as he tried to catch himself. It was a cheap one, and the cap popped off, spilling the batteries and killing the light.

He inhaled slowly.

There was a small square of sunlight near the door, but still, he felt buried in a darkness that seemed to have no end. He didn't like being underground. It brought back all the terrifying moments of the time he had spent locked in the tunnels of an abandoned asylum while he listened to a madman murder a young woman.

He picked up the flashlight and slid the batteries back in. The weak beam offered only a thin gray wash

over the stone walls. The rafters were bowed under the press of the soil.

He turned the light toward the back and started walking.

Food wrappers, an empty bag of potato chips, a whiskey bottle. Nothing of value to Brandt or anyone else.

He stopped at a large pile of dirt topped with a broken rafter. Louis turned the light up to the ceiling. The roots of the weeds above had penetrated the dirt, sending down spindly, pale tendrils above his head.

The ceiling had caved in back here. But it didn't look recent. The dirt and splintered wood looked dry, and the roots were withered.

He started to turn away, but something glinted in the beam of the flashlight. He knelt next to the sloping dirt and moved the beam of the light slowly across edge of the dirt pile where it leveled into the ground.

Again, a glint. He brushed gently at the soil.

It was a small, narrow bone, the color of the ivory keys on the piano in the parlor.

He gently dusted away more dirt. Another bone emerged. Seconds later, he'd unearthed a third and a fourth. Then, finally, as his fingers grew numb, he stopped.

The small bones were embedded in the ground, still perfectly positioned to form a human hand. But it was the plain gold wedding band at the base of the fourth finger that held his eyes.

Louis pushed slowly to his feet.

This is what Owen Brandt had come back for.

Jean.

Chapter Forty-four

L ouis followed Detective Bloom back into the root cellar. Bloom was shining a powerful battery-operated lantern over the stone walls as they ventured toward the back. Louis felt something brush his neck and jumped, but it was just a withered corn cob hanging from the rafter.

When the bright beam of the lantern came to rest on the bones, they stood out against the black dirt as stark as an X-ray.

Louis's gaze traveled over the sagging wood rafters and the heap of dirt in the corner where the ceiling of the cellar had collapsed. If these bones did belong to Jean, what had her final minutes on earth been like? She had been brutally stabbed inside the kitchen, yet she had managed to crawl all the way out here, a good fifty yards from the house, before she died of her wounds.

And then to be buried and forgotten.

No, not forgotten, never forgotten. Just lost.

Did you have any other hiding places, Amy?

Momma has a hiding place.

"You think this is Jean Brandt?" Bloom asked.

Louis stuffed his cold hands into his pockets. "Who else could it be?" he asked.

"Hell, I don't know," Bloom said. "It could be another slave woman, for all I know. Or another old girlfriend of Brandt's we don't know he killed. This farm seems to get a hold on people in a way that makes them crazy. And dead or alive, they can't seem to find their way off it."

Bloom started back toward the door. Louis stayed for a moment, staring at the wedding ring, then turned and followed Bloom back into the dull wash of white sunlight.

The farm buzzed with cops, deputies from the county and troopers from the state. Blue cruisers and Livingston County patrol cars were wedged haphazardly on the grass. Two television vans were parked beyond the gate, reporters and cameramen craning to see over the cop who was blocking their access onto the property.

"Someone cover this asshole up with a tarp," Bloom hollered.

He was talking about Brandt, who still lay a few feet from the root-cellar door. Dead leaves had gathered along the length of his body.

Louis hurried to catch up with Bloom. He caught him near the barn as Bloom muttered something into his radio. Louis heard Amy's name and a crackle of static, but then Bloom veered away to finish the conversation in private. It irritated Louis, but he remained where he was, not sure he'd get any information if he pissed Bloom off.

Bloom came back to him. "The girl is okay," he said. "The docs said they lost her once when her heart stopped, but they brought her back."

Louis blew out a breath in relief.

"The wound itself wasn't too deep," Bloom said. "Her parka cushioned the thrust of the blade, and the cold water stifled the blood flow. But they also said if you and Frye had been ten minutes later, she would have died from exposure."

Louis looked out to the fields. He had almost given up looking for her.

He turned to Bloom. "Look, if you don't need me any more right now, I'd like to catch a ride into Howell," he said. "I'll bring Joe back to do her statement and answer questions."

"Yeah, you do that," Bloom said. "But let me tell you something first."

Louis waited, figuring Bloom was about to chew on his ass for allowing Joe to leave the scene and for letting Amy run off and probably a dozen other things.

"You remember a man named Mark Steele?" Bloom asked.

"Yeah," Louis said. "State police investigator. Stepped into a case I was working on up north in '84."

Bloom nodded. "He's still with the MSP, and he's a major with the professional standards section. You know what that is?"

"Internal affairs."

Bloom nodded again. "His job is to maintain the integrity of the entire agency in any way he can. I had a talk with him about you yesterday. You curious about what he said?"

"I think I know what he said."

"Well, then know this, too," Bloom said. "He keeps files on people like you. And yours has a big red flag on it."

"I haven't broken any laws. Not now and not then."

"You're still trouble," Bloom said. "You're like some poisonous gas that sneaks in, leaves a few people dead, and disappears again."

"What are you trying to tell me, Detective?"

"I'm telling you this," Bloom said. "If you've had even a passing thought of trying to come back here and get a PI license or wiggle your ass back into a uniform,

think again. That ain't going to happen for you in Michigan. Ever."

Bloom didn't give him time to respond. He walked away, heading back toward the root cellar to direct the excavation of the bones.

Louis turned up the collar of his jacket and wandered toward the road.

If you've had even a passing thought . . .

He hadn't. There had been a few lonesome nights since Joe left last January, but they weren't enough to compel him to pull up the roots he had worked so hard to put into the Florida sand. He had connections there now—to a blind ex-cop who needed his friendship and a boy perched precariously on the cusp of manhood who needed to be caught if he fell.

Under the old oak tree, he stopped walking and looked out over the barren land.

This wasn't his place in the world, and he knew that. Despite the fact that he'd spent most of his childhood here and went to school here. Despite the fact he had once dreamed of wearing a badge here. Despite the fact that the woman he loved now lived here. Despite the fact that he now had kin here.

"You're Kincaid, right?"

Louis turned. A state trooper was standing there. He had Amy's backpack in his hand.

"We found this out by an old tractor in the fields. My boss said you might want it back. We figured it belongs to the girl."

"Thanks." Louis took the bag and looked toward the TV vans and the clot of reporters.

The trooper started toward his cruiser.

"Hey," Louis called out. "Could you give me a lift?"

"Sure."

Inside the cruiser, Louis sat staring out the windshield at the old farmhouse. The fog had burned off, and the sun was now high in the sky, outlining the house's unforgiving angles in sharp relief.

"Which way you heading?" the trooper asked.

"Just get me out of here," Louis said.

Louis and Joe spent the next morning in Adrian filling out statements and giving taped testimony. Joe called Mike to tell him she had been involved in a fatal shooting that was probably going to get publicity. She promised him she would still be back in Echo Bay for the hit-and-run trial on Monday morning. She didn't tell him she was bringing a sixteen-year-old girl home with her.

Shockey had made through it another night. Louis had learned he was awake and talking, anxious to know what was going on with the case. They hadn't had time yet to go by and update him. Their first stop after Adrian was Saint Joseph Hospital in Howell to pick up Amy.

Louis stood at the door and watched as Joe helped her settle into the wheelchair. Amy was clutching the mud-stained backpack and the tattered stuffed rabbit. Louis thought she seemed a little subdued. Maybe it was just the painkillers, but he guessed it also had something to do with the fact that Joe had told her Owen Brandt was dead.

They hadn't told her about Jean yet.

Phillip Ward, the Livingston County ME, had compared the skull found in the root cellar with Jean's den-

tal records and confirmed that it was Jean. Joe and Louis decided they would tell Amy on the way back to Ann Arbor.

When they got down to the hospital lobby, the nurse held the wheelchair while Louis helped Amy from it. Joe reached into the Bronco and pulled out a new jacket. This one was denim and lighter than the parka. Amy looked at it and smiled.

"I don't need a jacket, Miss Joe," she said. "It's nice today."

Louis looked up. He hadn't noticed, but she was right. The sky was blue and cloudless, and the sun was generous.

Joe started to help Amy into the backseat, but Amy hesitated. "Wait," she said. "I haven't apologized to you for leaving. I won't do it again. I promise."

Joe looked at Louis. His subtle nod told her there was no reason to wait.

"Amy," Joe said. "We found your mother."

Amy's eyes widened. "Where?"

"In the root cellar on the farm," Joe said.

Amy sat back in the seat, hugging the rabbit to her chest. "She was in there the whole time?"

"It looks that way."

Amy was quiet. There were no tears, just a faint sadness and, to Louis's amazement, a quiet kind of joy.

"You know the hiding place you spoke of during your sessions?" Joe asked. "We think maybe the root cellar was it. Did you know it was out there?"

Amy pushed her hair from her face. "I must have," she said. "Because I told—I told him that's where she was."

Louis noticed Amy's hesitation when she said "him," and he wondered how long it would take before she

would stop thinking of Owen Brandt as her father.

"I told him she was there, but I don't know why I said that," Amy said.

Joe glanced at Louis.

"So, you don't remember ever being inside the cellar, maybe when you were little?" Louis asked.

Amy's sigh was heavy. "I don't know."

Louis thought it made sense that at some point, Jean Brandt had taken her daughter to the root cellar to escape one of Brandt's rages. Maybe Amy would remember it someday. But he saw no point in pressing it now.

"Where is Momma now?" Amy asked.

Joe had been about to close the door and hesitated, again glancing at Louis. "She's not far from here, at the medical examiner's office," she said.

"May I see her?"

"Amy, her remains are—"

"I know there will be only bones," Amy said. "Please, may I see her?"

Joe was silent.

"She can do it, Joe," Louis said.

"All right," Joe said softly.

The bones weren't laid out in a neat skeleton the way the black woman's bones had been. The ME had taken possession of the bones only that morning, and when he got the call that Jean Brandt's daughter was coming in, he had hastily tried to arrange them at least to hint at their once-human shape.

Louis didn't think Amy cared.

She was standing next to the stainless-steel table looking down at the bones. Joe was close by so she could step

in if Amy broke down. But from his vantage point on the other side of the table, Louis thought Amy seemed fine, her expression almost wistful.

Amy looked up at the ME. "May I touch her?" she asked.

Ward looked as if the question didn't surprise him at all. "Yes, but be very careful," he said. "I haven't had a chance to examine them . . . examine her yet."

"Why do you need to do that?" Amy asked.

Ward's eyes found Louis's before he spoke. "To determine cause of death," he said.

"She died because he stabbed her," Amy said.

Ward again looked to Louis. He was a man who dealt with death through the lens of a microscope. As with a cop, detachment was part of the job. But Louis suspected he had never encountered someone like Amy before, whose self-possession in the face of a loved one's death was almost unnerving.

Amy picked up a small bone, looked at it for a moment, and placed it carefully back in its place on the table. "When can we take her home?" she asked.

Ward looked at Joe.

Louis knew what she was thinking. Amy had no home, and other than Joe's court-mandated temporary custody, she had no clear future.

"Amy," Joe said evenly, "you're going to be up north with me for a little while. Why don't we leave her here until we can figure out where . . . where she'll be buried?"

Amy considered this for a moment, her face solemn, then nodded slowly. She looked around the large tiled room.

"Is Isabel here, too?" she asked.

Joe was too stunned to speak. Ward looked to Louis in confusion.

"The bones that were found in the barn," Louis said.

"Ah." Ward nodded. "Yes, they're still here."

"Can I see her?" Amy asked.

Joe started to object, but Amy didn't even look at her. Her eyes were fixed on Ward. Louis gave a tight nod, and Ward went to a closet in the corner. He came back with a large gray box and set it on a second steel table.

"I was just preparing to ship her to the university," he said as he took off the lid. "I'm hoping they can narrow down the time period of death so I can see how close I was."

Louis watched Amy. She was peering into the box with awe.

"It was 1850," she whispered.

Ward looked at Louis with a confused expression. Louis cleared his throat. "Amy, we probably should get going now."

"May I take her with me, too?" Amy asked Ward.

Ward blinked. "I'm sorry. We only release the remains to the next of kin."

"I think that's me," Amy said.

Ward put the lid back on the box. "We don't even know her name," he said. "And without that, there's no way to connect any family to her."

"Her name was Isabel," Amy said.

Ward let out a sigh and addressed Louis. "Look, I'm not sure what's going on here, but before these bones can be released to someone, I need some proof that someone is a descendant, and if—"

Joe stepped forward quickly, a hand on Amy's shoulder. "Amy, we have to get going."

Amy looked up at the medical examiner. "Will you take good care of my mother until I can come back and get her?" she asked.

"You have my word," Ward said.

"And Isabel, too?"

"I promise," Ward said.

"Thank you." With a last look at the gray box, Amy turned to Joe. "Okay, I'm ready."

Outside, they paused in the parking lot while Joe helped Amy put on the denim jacket. Louis noticed that Amy was moving gingerly and that she looked tired. Maybe this hadn't been a good idea. Physically, the girl had survived a knife attack, and emotionally, she had just endured a second bruising.

"Amy, are you okay?" Joe asked.

Amy was silent, looking back at the plain gray brick building.

"Are you upset, I mean, about leaving her here?"

Amy slowly shook her head. "Momma's not really there anymore," she said softly. "Those are just bones now."

Joe looked at Louis and gave a small confused shrug.

"I saw her, you know," Amy said softly.

"Saw who?" Joe asked.

"Momma," she said. "In the hospital. I saw her when I left."

Louis met Joe's eye over Amy's head. The doctor had told them that Amy had been clinically dead for three minutes before they had been able to restart her heart.

"She looked beautiful and happy, and I knew she was safe. I wanted to stay there with her," Amy said. "But she

told me I had to go back and take care of Mr. Shockey."

Amy looked at Louis.

"I think we should go see him," she said.

Chapter Forty-five

Joe put a hand on Amy's back and gently urged her into Shockey's hospital room. Despite Amy's anxiousness to see Shockey, her hesitation now was obvious.

In all ways but one, this was simply a visit with a man Amy had already met a dozen times, during lunches and in discussions about Jean, as an escort to Dr. Sher's office, and even that night he showed up drunk at the hotel room.

In all the times Joe had seen them together, she had never felt either of them had made a connection to the other. Shockey had called her "the girl." And Amy still called him "Mr. Shockey."

What was Amy feeling now? Joe wondered. What did it feel like to look into the eyes of a stranger and know that you were tied to him in a way you could never have imagined and a way that could never be completely severed?

Joe stopped Amy just inside the door. There wasn't much time left. She and Amy were leaving for Echo Bay right from the hospital, and there were many things Joe still needed to discuss with Shockey.

"Amy, would you stay here for a minute?" Joe said, nodding to a chair by the door.

Amy slid into the chair.

Joe went to the bed. Shockey was lying flat on his back. His size was minimized by the cluster of machines and the patchwork of bandages on his body. Most of the gauze had been removed from his face, leaving spidery stitches of knotted black thread. The pull of death had left a chalky gray pallor on his skin.

The nurse had told Joe that Shockey was conscious, but his eyes were closed, and it didn't appear as if he had heard the door open.

"Jake?" she said.

His eyes opened with a drugged flutter.

"Jake, it's me, Joe."

"Joe . . ."

"How you feeling?" she asked.

"Like shit," he said.

Joe glanced back at Amy. She had a small smile on her face.

"Did you get the bastard?" Shockey whispered through cracked lips.

"Yes," she said. "He's dead. I had to shoot him."

Shockey closed his eyes, his lips forming a small grimace of a smile. "Wish I could've been there."

"There's something else," Joe said. "We found Jean's remains."

Shockey's smile vanished. His eyes were still closed, and he was very still, but Joe knew he hadn't gone back to sleep. The moment was for the grieving, a kind he had not allowed himself for almost ten years.

"She was on the farm," Joe said softly. "Just like you thought."

Still, nothing. Then he opened his eyes and lifted

a finger to motion that he wanted the bed raised. Joe picked up the cord, and the whir of the bed motor filled the next few seconds.

Angled upright, Shockey's glazed eyes went beyond her. "Hey, peeper . . ."

Joe looked to the door. She hadn't heard Louis come in. He had gone to rent a car so he could drive to Ypsilanti later and say goodbye to Lily. His flight back to Florida left at six tonight.

"Hey, Jake," Louis said.

Then Shockey saw Amy sitting in the chair. Amy looked to Joe for permission to come forward, and Joe gave her a nod. Amy clutched her backpack a little tighter and came to Shockey's left side.

"Miss Joe told me you are my father," she said.

Shockey's eyes cut to Joe with questions.

"We thought you were going to die," Joe said. "We wanted her to know."

Shockey looked back at Amy. His red-rimmed eyes studied her face, as if he were desperate to see some indication of how she felt about being his daughter.

Joe decided to help him. He was pitiful.

"Amy, why don't you tell Mr. Shockey what happened to you when you were in the hospital?"

Amy began her story with her abduction by Brandt in the cornfield. Joe wondered if that part would upset Shockey, but Amy recited it with such quiet poise that Joe decided not to interrupt.

Amy told Shockey that the doctors at the hospital in Howell said she had been dead for three minutes. Shockey's eyes never left her face.

Her hand came down to the bed to cover his. "I went

and saw Momma," she said. "I wanted to stay with her, but she sent me back to take care of you."

Shockey turned away from her and focused on the blanket that draped his legs. But Joe could see his eyes well with tears.

"Don't cry, Mr. Shockey," Amy said. "She wouldn't want you to keep being sad."

Shockey went to wipe his face, but the IV tube taped to his hand caught on the bed rail. He moved to use his other hand, but it was completely wrapped in gauze.

Amy picked a few tissues from a nearby box and dabbed at Shockey's face. He closed his eyes in embarrassment.

Joe motioned discreetly for Amy to stop. She seemed to understand and wadded the Kleenex in her fist.

"I can leave you my books," she said. "To give you something to read while you're in here. Would you like that?"

Shockey seemed grateful for a more mundane subject. "Yeah, sure," he said. "I like to read."

Amy removed two books—*Little Women* and *A Tree Grows in Brooklyn*—from her backpack and set them on the table.

"Thanks . . . Amy," Shockey whispered.

Hearing her name, she smiled shyly. "I don't know what to call you," she said.

Shockey looked dumbfounded. "I don't know, either," he said. "How about Jake?"

Amy was clearly disappointed in Shockey's suggestion.

"Can we try Dad?" she asked.

Shockey hesitated, then nodded slowly. "Yeah, we can try that."

• • •

Joe asked Louis to take Amy down to the cafeteria. When they had left, Joe came back to Shockey's bedside.

His eyes were closed.

"Jake?"

It took him a moment to open his eyes. He was sniffling. "I can't even blow my own fucking nose," he said.

She gently maneuvered the IV line to free his one good hand. She gave him a Kleenex, and he wiped his nose with a shaking hand.

Joe wondered how much to tell him. So much had happened in the last twenty-four hours. Legally, Amy was a Brandt, and the sixty acres belonged to her to do with as she chose. When Joe had asked her what she wanted to do with the farm, Amy hadn't hesitated.

"Can we sell it? Except the cemetery, I mean. I have kin there."

Louis contacted the real estate agency in Hell to start the process before the place could be repossessed for taxes. The agent told him a commercial food corporation was buying up the farmland around Hell and that a quick sale was likely. The money from any sale would have to be put in a trust for Amy until she was eighteen. Joe had already contacted a lawyer in Echo Bay to sort that part out. As much as everyone wanted to believe Shockey was Amy's father, there was still no way to prove it.

"So, you're bringing Amy back?" Shockey asked.

Joe nodded. "In a month, maybe, when you're out of here. Your doctors say you've got a long road ahead of you with physical therapy."

Shockey was quiet.

"When you bring her back, is it for a visit or for good?" he asked finally.

"Are you ready for 'for good'?" Joe asked.

Shockey looked down the length of his body, as if he were surveying the damage.

"I want to be a father to her, but . . . I've screwed up everything I've ever done. She deserves someone who will love her, not a selfish asshole like me."

"You're all she's got, Jake."

He closed his eyes.

"I think you can do this, Jake. Why don't we take it one step at a time, okay?"

Shockey nodded slowly.

Joe found Louis and Amy in the cafeteria. They were sitting in a booth near a window. Louis had a coffee cup in front of him. Amy had a Coke and Hostess Sno Balls, another new delicacy in her rapidly expanding list of approved food.

Joe slid in next to Louis. To her surprise, he took her hand. The beginning of the goodbye, she knew. She had told him she had to be on the road by eleven in order to make it home before dinner. She needed time to pick up a few things for Amy: extra sheets, pillows, and something else to eat besides yogurt and coffee.

Joe's eyes drifted to the window. She wished they had said their goodbyes last night back at the hotel, when they were alone. But Amy had been excited about her trip and hadn't retreated to her adjoining room until well after one A.M. By the time she dozed off, Louis was asleep, too.

It was Joe's first real sense of what it must be like when a child was a regular part of your life. Everything— from what kind of groceries you bought to when you

made love—was rearranged around the needs of some-one else.

She turned back to see Louis watching her over the rim of his coffee cup. They had never really talked about him and Lily, either, and she suspected he had much the same thoughts and doubts. But now there was no time to talk about any of it.

"You sure you won't come with us?" she asked.

As he lowered the cup, his eyes left hers. "I need to get home, Joe. Maybe . . ."

"What's a few more days?" she asked. "I'll be done with the case by Friday, and we can take a day trip somewhere."

He was quiet. Amy was peeling the rubbery pink frosting from her Sno Ball, discreetly eavesdropping. Joe wondered if she recalled the strange conversation they'd had on the terrace at the hotel.

You can't see him right now. But you have to just kind of believe. He's there.

Joe reached across the table to touch his hand. "When *can* you come?" she asked. "I'd love for you to meet Mike and the others. And see where I live."

"We'll see," he said. "Maybe this summer."

Joe withdrew her hand and sat back in the booth. She had learned a long time ago that this wasn't a man who responded to pressure or nagging. And she wasn't a woman who begged.

She glanced up at the clock over the cash register. "We have to get going," she said. "Are you ready, Amy?"

She nodded. "I don't want the rest of this, anyway. It's too gooey. Can we get a Big Mac on the way?"

"Maybe," Joe said.

They stood up. Amy grabbed her backpack but in-

stead of cuddling it against her chest, she strapped it over her shoulders the way other teenagers did.

Amy hesitated, then stuck out her hand to Louis.

"Goodbye, Mr. Kincaid," she said. "Thank you for finding Momma. And thank you for making me come out of the cupboard."

"You're welcome, Amy. Very welcome."

Amy looked at Joe and, with a dip of her head, walked away to leave her and Louis alone. Joe pushed her hair back and faced him.

"I'll call you tomorrow," she said. "I guess I'll see you . . . whenever."

"Drive carefully," he said.

He wrapped a strong arm around her neck and pulled her close and kissed her. There was need in his embrace. And she thought for a moment, he might . . .

Then he let her go.

Chapter Forty-six

Louis ducked through the door of Halo Hats. The same sweet smell and tinkle of the bell greeted him. Grandma Alice was behind the counter. The caftan had been replaced by a purple suit and a matching felt hat adorned with a taffeta bow and a clump of lavender netting.

It was Sunday. He realized they were all on their way to church. But Grandma Alice's eyes held no benevolence.

"Hello, Louis."

He turned.

Lily had stepped out from behind a rack of hats.

His first thought was of a baby chick, a ball of precious yellow fluff. She wore a dress of some kind of filmy material, the stiff flounce of a skirt topped off by a little white fur jacket. A yellow straw bonnet held her curls back from her face.

Her face . . .

Already he was trying to memorize it, because no photograph would ever do it justice.

The solemn gray eyes met his, and there was a single thought in his head. It was a very forgiving world that allowed a guy like him to play any part in the creation of something so perfect.

Kyla suddenly appeared from the back room, and a step behind came Channing. Kyla wore a peach-colored suit with a matching hat. Channing's suit was dark blue over a starched white shirt topped off with a perfectly knotted turquoise tie. Grandma Alice moved to them, completing the family portrait.

"Don't we all look pretty?" Lily asked.

His heart gave. "Yes, you do."

"We're going to church," she said.

"I kind of figured that."

She brightened suddenly. "Do you want to come with us?" she asked.

"Well, I—"

"You can come like you are. God doesn't care if you don't have a tie."

Louis smiled. Then he caught Kyla's eye over Lily's head. She wasn't smiling.

"I can't come with you, Lily," Louis said. "I just came by to tell you goodbye."

Lily blinked. "You're going back to Florida?"

"Yes, I have to get home."

Questions, all those questions there in those gray eyes. But before Lily could say anything, Kyla stepped forward and put a hand on Lily's shoulder.

"We'll wait for you outside. Don't be too long, okay?"

"Okay," Lily said softly. Then, head down, she went to a bench by a full-length mirror in the corner. She sat down, taking off her hat and holding it in her lap.

Kyla watched her, then pulled Louis away. "Please don't make any promises to her that you won't keep," she whispered.

He nodded. Kyla started to say something more, then just shook her head. She linked her arm through Grandma Channing's, and the two women left without looking back.

Channing had been watching Lily and turned to face Louis. He pulled a folded paper from his breast pocket.

"Before I forget, a woman named Daphne Mayer called me yesterday looking for you. She wants you to call her." Channing held out the paper, one eyebrow cocked. "The African-American Cultural Center?"

Louis took the paper. "It's a long story," he said. He hesitated, searching for just the right words. "There's no way I can ever thank you for doing what you did, Sergeant."

"Yes, there is," Channing said. He tilted his head toward Lily. "Just do like Kyla said."

They shook hands, and Channing left. The bell tin-

kled, and the store was quiet. Louis went to the corner.

"Lily?"

Her face came up. Tears glistened on her cheeks. "I don't want you to go," she whispered. "I don't even know you yet."

She lowered her head again, picking at the yellow ribbon on her hat. He knelt in front of her.

"We have lots of time to get to know each other," he said. "And I won't be far away."

"Florida's a long ways away. I looked on the map. And I'm afraid you'll forget about me again."

"I have the picture you gave me, remember? How can I forget somebody so pretty?"

She suddenly came off the chair and threw her arms around his neck, smothering him in rabbit fur and soft curls. It surprised him, and for a second, he froze. Then his arms closed around her, crushing her to him.

Lily broke away first. He was grateful she made the move, because he had no idea how she would have read it if he had. Her eyes were brighter, the tears dry.

"So, are you going to do it?" she asked.

He knew what she meant. Was he going to look for his father? He had no answer for her that didn't sound wrong. Maybe he had no answer at all. Because, suddenly, that familiar and resounding no was not the first word that popped into his head.

"I can't promise you that yet," he said gently. "Can I give you a maybe?"

Disappointment colored her eyes, and she dropped her head. He touched her chin to bring her head back up.

"How about I let you know September second?" he asked.

"On my birthday?"

"Yeah," he said. "On the ferry on the way over to Mackinac Island. If your momma says it's okay. Is it a deal?"

She stuck out a white-gloved hand. "Deal."

They shook on it. Then she looked to the door.

"I need to go," she said. "If we get there late, I won't get any of the M&M cookies before service."

He pushed to his feet. "You go ahead," he said. "Tell your momma I'll call her when I get home."

Lily grabbed her bonnet from the floor and hurried out of the store. He walked out behind her. Channing and Kyla were in the front of a silver Lincoln idling at the curb. Grandma Alice was waiting for him to leave so she could lock the door.

She gave him a final stern look and grunted a good-bye. She ushered Lily into the backseat and got in beside her.

The Lincoln pulled away. Lily waved from the back window. He stood on the sidewalk watching until the car disappeared.

Chapter Forty-seven

The air smelled of lilacs. The smell was so strong he stopped to look for the source, but the bushes beneath the windows of the Law Quad were still brown and bare. He walked on, the sun warm on his back.

You sure you won't come with us?

I need to get home, Joe. Maybe . . .

Maybe. That seemed to be the word they said to each other most often lately.

Maybe. That's what he had said to Lily, too.

Maybe. Suddenly, it seemed like the most pathetic word in the world.

Daphne Mayer was coming up the street carrying a cardboard tray of four coffee containers as Louis rounded the corner onto Main Street.

She saw him and smiled. "You got my message."

"Almost didn't," Louis said. "I'm flying back to Florida tonight, so I thought I'd stop by." He lunged for the door. "Sorry! Let me get that for you."

He followed her inside. The place had been transformed since his last visit, most of the boxes restacked against a wall and the bar cleared. Some of the old cocktail lounge's booths had been turned into desks, topped with computers. Three young black women greeted Daphne, gave Louis a glance of curiosity, and went back to their work.

Daphne delivered a coffee to each of them and came back to Louis, holding the fourth cup. "Want to split it?" she asked.

Louis shook his head. "No, thanks."

"Mr. Coffee died this morning, may he rest in peace," she said. "And nothing gets done around here without a lot of caffeine."

Louis tried not to let his impatience show.

She sensed it and set her coffee down on the bar. "I guess you want to know why I called."

"Your note didn't say what this was about," Louis said.

"I know. Because when we first found this, we weren't sure it would be helpful to you," she said. "Wait here."

She went over to speak to one of the students, who handed her something. She came back to Louis and held out a slender book. The red leather was faded to brown, the edges rounded with wear. There was no title.

"Go ahead, open it," Daphne said. "But be careful. It's very fragile."

Louis took it. The spine gave a gentle crack as he opened to the first yellowed page.

THE NARRATIVE
OF
JOHN LEPELLE
A True Account of the Brandt Station Episode
Written by Himself

"Brandt is the name you were looking for, right?" Daphne asked.

Louis nodded. "Where did you get this?"

"I'm not sure," Daphne said with a sigh. "I'm ashamed to say we didn't even know we had it until yesterday. Brenda was logging some titles into the computer, and this was just stuck in a box of textbooks. She was the one who realized it was a slave journal."

Louis was looking at the name. John was the name Amy had spoken under hypnosis. Then it struck him: she had also said "lapel." Could he have heard her wrong?

He looked up at Daphne. "I know I can't take this with me—"

"You're welcome to read it here," she said. "You can use one of the desks in the back."

She led Louis to a corner booth. He was about to open the journal when Daphne tapped him on the shoulder.

She held out a pair of thin white cotton gloves. "You'll have to wear these, I'm afraid."

"No problem." Louis smiled slightly as he slipped on the gloves. He put on his glasses, opened the journal to the first page, and began to read.

THE NARRATIVE OF JOHN LEPELLE
A TRUE ACCOUNT OF THE BRANDT STATION
EPISODE
WRITTEN BY HIMSELF
IN THIS YEAR OF OUR LORD 1894

There are many things that are best left buried. The hurts men inflict upon each other, the evils that are witnessed and endured, these things can erode the heart until a human being can no longer go on. To keep silent about the past is sometimes the only way to survive. And survive is what all God's creatures must do. But there comes a time when the silence becomes an acid that eats away at the soul. There comes a time when a man must face his past and be silent no more.

I have never told this story before. But it is a true story that needs telling for those who came after me, for those who came before me, for those who, unlike me, were not able to fly away. I tell this story only now because I am far nearer to the end of my life than the beginning and this has weighed heavy on my heart. I tell this story only now because I have been blessed with a long life lived in freedom,

safe and loved in the bosom of my family. I tell this
story now because my life was possible only because
another life was sacrificed.

The journal was handwritten in faded blue ink in a large
cursive style that looked as if the author lacked a steady
hand. Louis wondered how old John LePelle had been
when he wrote it.

He turned the page. The next ten pages were devoted
to John LePelle's early life as a slave in Louisiana. At thirteen, he was taken with his mother and sister to New Orleans to be auctioned off at the slave market. Given clean
clothes and advised to "look lively and smart," they were
paraded before customers in a yard. Separated from his
family, he worked as a field hand in Natchez. It was a life
of brutality, terror, and small graces. Twice he tried to escape, and twice he was captured, the second time paying by having his right foot crushed in a vise to prevent
him from running again. He was nursed back to health
by a house girl named Fanny, whom he took as his wife.
When John was twenty-two, they had a son whom they
called Abram.

> My back was striped with scars, my foot so
> damaged that when the cold came I could barely
> walk. But I saw myself a blessed man. I stood by the
> bed of my beloved wife as heaven placed in her arms
> a pure soul, in an infantile form, a new being, never
> having breathed earth's air before, never having felt
> the earth's goodness or its pain. Yes, they had robbed
> me of myself, and freedom would never be mine.
> But there was new life from me and from that, new
> hope.

Louis took off his glasses and rubbed his eyes. The shadows in the old cocktail lounge had lengthened. How long had he been reading? He put his glasses on and opened the journal again.

In the winter of 1849, John's wife and son were sold to a tobacco farmer in Virginia. On January 3, in the dark of the moon, John slipped from his bed and began to run. Scared, starving, and crippled, he eventually crossed into Michigan, where he found shelter in stations on the Underground Railroad.

Louis began to skim the journal now, impatient to see a mention of the Brandt farm. Then, suddenly, there it was.

> After dark, I emerged onto a road but I did not know which way to go. I knew only that my destination was to be a farm owned by a man named Amos Brandt. I looked in vain for the North Star but the cloud cover left nothing to light my way. Presently, I encountered a creek and had no choice but to ford its icy water. I saw in the distance a faint light, which I prayed was the safe haven I sought. I was cold and ragged, transformed into a mere ghost of a man by my long journey. And I had nothing but faith to guide me now—and the single name of my next savior, Isabel.

Louis sat back in the booth, stunned. He turned to the next page. John remained hidden in the Brandt barn for the next two days as he regained his strength for the last leg of his journey before he crossed into freedom in Canada. There were rumors of slave catchers in the area, and John knew his owner had put a bounty on his

head. Isabel told John he had to leave the next night. On his last night spent in the Brandt barn, John told her about his wife and son. Isabel told him about her son, Charles, and how she worried about him growing up half black.

> It is common for white men to be fathers of children by their slaves, but I had never heard a colored woman speak of a white man with love. Yet this Isabel did when she spoke of Amos Brandt. Her love, her forgiveness, this was a balm to my soul which had been so ravaged by hatred. I had no way to thank her. So I gave her the only thing of value I had—a locket that had belonged to my Fanny. It held a lock of my beloved wife's hair and it had been warmed by its nearness to my heart.

Louis noticed that the writing in the journal had become shakier, as if the dreadfulness of what was to come next had been too much for John LePelle to record.

> That last night at the Brandt farm, I awoke to a horrible noise. I heard howling dogs and horses and then the sharp voices of men. Isabel came and told me someone had betrayed her and set the slave catchers on my heels. She led me through a trapdoor and we fell down the hay chute and were quickly outside in the cold. We crept away from the barn and to the edge of the cornfields where Isabel hid me in a root cellar. There I stayed, unable to see but, God help me, I could hear. I heard a woman screaming and when I could not stand it any longer, I crept from the cellar and hid outside the barn. I saw four white men holding Isabel. Another man with eyeglasses stood

apart with an expression of smothered horror and I wanted to believe this man was Amos, who could do nothing to help his beloved Isabel.

The men dragged Isabel into the barn, tied her to a hook and raised it until her bare feet just touched the dirt. I saw them whip her until her skin ran red. They wanted me and tortured her for my whereabouts. But Isabel did not betray me. I witnessed this, crouched in the weeds, my eye pressed to a gap in the boards, my body trembling with fear, my heart a dying animal in my chest.

But then I watched in dumb shock as a white woman came into the barn. As she gazed at Isabel's hanging body I was horrified to see the barest smile tip her lips, and I realized it was she who had betrayed Isabel. The man with the eyeglasses stood at her side as if made from stone. If this was Amos, I cannot ever know. Nor can I know if his heart was as guilty as my own. But the look on that woman's face I will carry to my grave with certainty.

What else I carry to my grave is of no concern to the readers of this journal. It is an issue between myself and the Lord. That I did nothing to help Isabel that dreadful night was to be my burden for all these years. That I turned away out of fear and ran is my shame.

Isabel died and I went on to live. I lived to become a free man in Canada. I lived to marry again, father four sons and three daughters and many grandchildren, whose abundant love has overridden my old hatreds and taught me to love in kind. I have lived sixty-eight years as a free man, except for the

chains around my heart, placed there that horrible night.

The chains will be cast off only when I forgive myself. So I write this journal as the final step toward my freedom. I can only hope that the good Lord will let me make my final amends in Heaven and not in Hell.

Louis closed the journal. He peeled off the thin white cotton gloves, took off his glasses, and leaned back in the booth. The room was dark. The three students had left; their computer screens were blank. He glanced at his watch. It was almost four. His flight back to Tampa left in two hours.

He rose slowly, picking up the journal. There was one light on toward the front, and he walked toward it.

Daphne was sitting at a desk, sorting through some papers, and she looked up as he approached.

He set the journal in front of her. "There's a long list of names in the back," he said. "I think they might be John LePelle's descendants."

She picked up the journal. "Good. We'll try to track them down. I'm sure they'd want to know where they came from."

Louis nodded. "I've got to go," he said. "Thank you again for your help."

"Any time."

He started toward the door.

"Mr. Kincaid?"

He turned back.

"You didn't tell me. Did you find what you're looking for?" she asked.

Louis hesitated, then nodded.

Back outside, he paused to turn up his collar and hurried back across campus to retrieve the rental car. He drove with the window down, the brisk April air still bringing the smell of phantom lilacs. The Burton Tower bell was striking four as he pulled up to the red light on State Street.

A left turn led him south toward the airport. A right turn would take him across the river and up north.

He looked at his watch. It was late, but there was still time.

The light turned green. The car behind him honked once, twice.

Louis swung the wheel to the right and headed north. She was four hours ahead of him, but if he drove fast, he'd be there before dark.

ACKNOWLEDGMENTS

We need to mention several people whose help was essential to this story's creation.

First, a huge thank-you to Holly Van Sickle, who allowed us to wander the grounds and prowl through the rooms of her splendid old family farm in Michigan. The real farm is a lovely place, as far from hell as one can get.

Second, the usual thank-you to Dr. Doug Lyle for his medical advice.

Third, our gratitude to Daniel, our editor of first-resort; to our talented editor at Pocket, Mitchell Ivers, who lets us sing in our own voice; and to our friend and agent Maria Carvainis.

Finally, we owe a debt in our research to Dr. Brian Weiss, M.D., whose books on past-life regression gave this story its grounding. And for futher reading on the Underground Railroad and slave journals, we highly recommend *The Great Escapes: Four Slave Journals*, introduction and notes by Daphne A. Brooks.

Edge-of-your-seat reads from Pocket Books!

ROBERT K. TANENBAUM / *Malice*
Manhattan DA Butch Karp discovers the depth
of true evil in men's hearts—and how far he'll
go to stop them.

JOAN BRADY / *Bleedout*
What can you believe when your own eyes
betray you?

BRIAN MCGRORY / *Strangled*
Boston reporter Jack Flynn is about to discover
that his biggest scoop may be his own demise.

CHRIS MOONEY / *The Missing*
Sometimes, going missing is the only
way to survive...

Get your pulse pounding with an unforgettable read from Pocket Books!

Joy Fielding
Heartstopper
Being beautiful has a deadly price.

John Connolly
The Unquiet
Detective Charlie Parker unravels a twisted story
of betrayal, unclean desires, and murder.

Thomas Greanias
The Atlantis Prophecy
In a hidden world beneath the nation's capital,
a centuries-old warning holds explosive
implications for today....

Mitch Silver
In Secret Service
The pages of master story-teller Ian Fleming's
long-lost manuscript is uncovered—and reveals
one of history's best-kept secrets.

Edna Buchanan
Love Kills
'Til death do you part.